with the
Flames
catching
Midnight

Flames catching Midnight
with the / Flames / catching / Midnight

NELLY ALIKYAN

To my future husband.
May I always need a reminder to behave.

ALSO BY NELLY ALIKYAN

Catchers Series

With the Flames Catching Midnight

With the Rains Catching Dawn

With the Ice Catching Twilight

With the Storms Catching Dusk

With the Winds Catching Sunlight

With the Ashes Catching Daybreak

Whittle Magic Series

Alluring Darkness

Beholding Darkness

Claiming Darkness

Desiring Darkness

ALSO BY N. ALIKYAN

Buttercup Baby

Promise of A Lifetime

SOUNDTRACK

1. My Side of the Story by Hodge

2. War of Hearts by Ruelle

3. Everything Falls by Fee

4. In My Veins by Andrew Belle

5. Flames by Donzell Taggart

6. Sad Song by We the Kings ft Elena Coats

7. If You Love Her by Forest Blakk

8. Armor by Landon Austin

9. What Love Is by Uku Suviste

10. She by Jake Scott

11. Hold On by Extreme Music

12. House of Cards by Tyler Shaw

13. My Heart I Surrender by I Prevail

PROLOGUE

QUEEN'S LADY'S MAID

The Queen cried out with another contraction, and Vitti had to pause because these did not sound like the ones that came with pushing out the placenta. That was worrisome. And Vitti was the only one left in the chambers, the four other nurses having already run off with the newborn Princess to greet the King. He'd have the babe's wet nurse by his side, ready and waiting.

The Queen screamed again as her head fell back onto the pillow, and Vitti's heart sped up. This wasn't supposed to be happening. All she could think was there must be something wrong with the Queen, and she alone could not stop it if the Queen was losing too much blood and close to death's door.

Vitti moved between her Queen's legs, hoping to stop whatever it was causing such distress. She was especially hoping it wasn't the placenta giving the Queen more trouble than normal.

Vitti paused between the Queen's legs, her eyes widening incredibly large.

"What?" Queen Rowena gasped out in pain as she fell back

with another cry. How others hadn't heard and come running was a shock all on its own. "What is it?" she gritted out when she could finally catch her breath again.

"Another babe. Twins." Vitti snapped herself out of her shock and prepared for the birth of the second heir to the Northern Lands.

It took two pushes after that before the room was once again filled with the wailing cries of a babe born. Vitti quickly cleaned the girl and placed her on her mother's chest and felt another shock hit her just as Queen Rowena looked down at the child. She met Vitti's eyes, and it was obvious that there was concern there that didn't need to be voiced.

Because this child may have been a twin, but the difference between the sisters was glaring.

The area around this babe's eyes was coated in black and deep blue veins. And as Vitti met her Queen's eyes, she knew that if she were to rush the child off to present to the King as was required, there would be no second heir. Because it was well known and understood that the King would not stand for such defects and would have her killed immediately.

Because the second heir to the Northern Lands was a magician.

✝

Hiding the child was difficult, but somehow they made it work. As the Queen's personal maid, Vitti was put in charge of mothering the child, the Queen only coming in when it was time to feed her.

It was in moments like these that they both found relief that it was customary for the royal heirs to be nursed by wet nurses and not their own mothers. Queen Rowena would have an ample amount of milk for the second heir.

And because Queen Rowena had her own wing in the palace, Vitti had plenty of space with the little girl, confined as they were to only a few rooms. In times when her presence was expected and required, she'd place the babe to sleep and hope with all her might she would not wake.

It was a temporary arrangement. They only needed to wait until the babe was off breastmilk, then Vitti could take her away from the palace and raise her in the Southern Lands, where magicians would not be killed for existing.

The babe was completely cut off from nursing from her mother's breast at just shy of two years of age. And they were a week away from leaving the palace grounds and starting a new —unhidden—life in a whole new nation. One Vitti would need to acclimate to quickly to make sure not to draw too much attention to herself.

Princess Rosaelia was off with her father in the King's Quarters, where she remained as the heir and most favored person to the nation's patriarch. And on the other side of the palace sat Vitti and Queen Rowena, watching the hidden heir run from one end of the room to the other. She looked just like her sister with the black locks and beautiful smile. But it was the eyes that differentiated them. Not only did this one have the veins— which had wavered in the years though were still very telling— but she had deep blue eyes. Opposite to her twin's shining green.

She ran toward Vitti and crashed into her legs, her giggles muffled by Vitti's skirts. In the years of hiding the child, Vitti had truly grown to love her and was glad she'd be the one to raise the girl, though it saddened her that her Queen would be parted from her daughter for at least the foreseeable future.

It was in that pleasant moment when Vitti heard a bang

outside of their suite and quickly reached for the hidden Princess, holding her tightly and stepping away from the door.

It burst open not a minute later to reveal four men dressed in black trousers and vests, weapons poorly hidden about their bodies.

Vitti's heart dropped.

The Queen rushed Vitti into the second room of the suite, barricading the door behind her and pushing Vitti back until she hit the wall. Rowena opened a hidden passage Vitti had used a multitude of times in the past couple of years to take the hidden babe outside and pushed Vitti within.

She pushed a torch into Vitti's hand. "Take her and run, Vitti." And before any arguments could be made, she started closing the door. "Go. Now, Vitti. Go!"

As much as she did not want to, Vitti turned from the closed passage door and ran away from her Queen. The light from the torch lit the way as she raced through the halls. The child clenched tightly to her chest as she attempted to calm her heart at the imaginings of what was happening to her Queen at that very moment.

✝

SHE'D MADE it to the edge of the Northern and Southern Lands.

They'd made it. The hidden Princess was almost safe.

Safe within their inn for the night, Vitti watched the child sleep in the middle of the bed for long moments before turning to the candlelight on the desk and pulling out long sheets of paper. There was no saying whether she would make it out of this alive, and Vitti needed to make sure whoever found the child would know everything. Would know who she was and keep her safe.

So she wrote it all out. Everything that had happened since the moment the second heir of the Northern Lands was born.

In the three days since their departure, Vitti still felt the pang of fear every time she heard a sound near her room. And every time anyone got too close when she was traveling with the child in arms, Vitti's blood rushed with the fear of being caught with a magician in the Northern Lands. They'd be imprisoned and killed and this entire trip—these last two years—would've been for naught.

When she finished writing it all, taking pages and pages to explain everything, Vitti allowed the pages to dry as she turned to watch the little girl in the middle of the bed.

Vitti truly loved that little girl and feared that anything may happen to her. She couldn't allow that. Come dawn, they'd be off again and Vitti would make it into the Southern Lands where she would not have to worry every moment any longer. Even recognized as a Northerner, she would not be bothered.

They were gone another two days, having passed into the Southern Lands early after departing from the inn, when Vitti's heart raced in fear again. Because now, as they edged the forests of the Southern Lands, she heard the loud chorus of men coming from behind. And something deep inside told her it was the same men from the palace. They'd found her.

They'd found the second heir.

Vitti crushed the babe to her chest, holding her tight and breathing into her ear how much she loved her, then lowered to a crouch.

She released the girl and held her by the shoulders, the letter tucked deep into the child's vest. "You must run now. Run into the forest and do not look back. No matter what you hear, child, do not look back." *Do not watch them kill me.*

When the deep blue eyes nodded their understanding, Vitti

brushed the child's cheek softly, holding on to this last moment before pushing her away. "Run, Evony. Run!"

Vitti turned as the child lost herself in the forest. She would not show the men which direction the Princess had run off to. All she could hope for now was that someone would find her and she would be safe.

CHAPTER 1
SPARROW

It was the second day of the week, and already they were in their fourth discussion about the rebellion that was brewing within the kingdom.

It was a common occurrence—rebellions.

Every few years, a group of no more than twenty people would round together in order to overthrow the King. And every few years, they were quickly quelled.

It was simple because the rebels normally meant no harm. They just wanted something to change within their towns and thought it a perfect way to get Sparrow's attention. And sometimes, they were right and Sparrow would help them in their quest for change. But usually, he would tell them their change would not be happening and scare them enough to stop them from attempting to cause any more trouble.

This time was not the same.

The rebels were far more organized and Sparrow hadn't been able to get any requests from them. From what he could tell, they didn't want anything to change anywhere specific. They wanted a whole change. A whole new ruler for the

Northern Lands. And it was ridiculously frustrating not knowing why.

But even more frustrating was not knowing who was leading this group. Because they were bloody well organized.

"The word sounds to all be turning back to the Islanders," Tristan said from across the table.

"How can you be sure that isn't what they want you to hear?" Edmund argued from the head of their small table, his deep russet hair falling over tired eyes.

Miels smirked from beside Sparrow, throwing himself back in his usual theatrics. "Oh, the travesty. To think the King believes us poorly trained spies. I cannot take this disappointment."

The King rolled his eyes and bit back on his smile. Princess Rosaelia on his right didn't even try to suppress the giggle as her eyes shined.

Tristan rolled his eyes and pushed back his dirty blonde hair. The hair was the one big difference between the two. Tristan had dirty blonde, Miels had blonde. Not too big a difference, but one, nonetheless.

They weren't twins, not even related, but they looked almost identical. And they called one another brother so often, most forgot that it wasn't true. It worked perfectly for when Sparrow needed them to play certain roles.

"The spying we've done wouldn't exactly be considered ethical," Tristan answered the King's original question. "They're teamed up with the Islanders."

Edmund's brows quirked as his gaze shot to Sparrow. "My assassin too?"

Miels barked out with laughter. "Of course not. High and mighty Sparrow would *never* stoop so low."

Sparrow rolled his eyes, making sure the annoyance was

clear on his features. He'd heard these bouts of jokes a million times over.

Miels threw a hand over Sparrow's shoulder, holding him with purpose. "Sparrow, mate, sleeping with a couple of women would get you your information much faster. You simply make the job more difficult on yourself."

Sparrow shoved his hand off, not allowing any emotion onto his features other than the irritation his brothers' whoring brought him. "I prefer the more difficult jobs."

Miels laughed and lounged back in his chair. "I cannot say I agree, brother. Tristan and I definitely have more fun."

Sparrow did not miss the blush that deepened Princess Rosaelia's cheeks as she looked down to her sketchbook. Tristan didn't speak as crudely as his brother, not with the Princess at the table, but the way his eyes shined told Sparrow he agreed with every word coming out of Miels's mouth.

"And what makes you think that it is in any way accurate information, Miels?" Edmund was playing with the man, they were all aware that Miels and Tristan were some of the best spies, making sure to check their information before ever considering it a viable truth.

Miels's smirk grew almost sensual in manner as he spoke. "Sometimes we're lucky and the sex itself gets them revealing everything. And I mean *everything*. But it's almost inevitably the aftermath that gets us what we want, dear King."

"Through the bliss afterward, it's normally easy to get a bit out of them," Tristan continued more properly. "But then we leave, and they think they're alone, and that's when we catch them. Sometimes we stick around a couple of days, have them thinking they're sly, and listen to their conversations, follow them to their meetings, all of it."

"We are good spies, Ed," Miels said as if they didn't all already know it. "It helps that our faces aren't recognized. I've even been offered recruitment in the past. And for some of those women, becoming a double agent so I could continue coming on them almost made me consider it."

Sparrow wanted to punch the ever-living shit out of the man for speaking so rashly in front of Rosaelia, especially when her face turned an even darker shade of crimson. They were Northerners, for heaven's sake. But to Miels, Rosaelia was like a sister, so he didn't feel the need to be proper.

"And most importantly," Sparrow finally voiced. "I just found elixirs in the house of a local."

Edmund turned to him, all teasing gone. "Which elixirs?"

"Nothing serious. Ailment and pain potions. They are still with the families. No need in them knowing I was there," Sparrow assured the King.

Miels and Tristan knew of this little discovery and were already looking into any other families that may have had a deal with the Islanders.

Rosaelia sat across from Sparrow at her father's opposite side and looked to be in thought at the new information. Her kind heart would want to allow the elixirs to continue to flow within their lands, but political understanding told her why that would be a problem. Her emerald-green eyes shined with concern through her black lashes, but she did not voice them. Knew not to. As much as she cared for her people, she knew they could not allow sorcerers to be giving the common folk of the Northern Lands elixirs.

When Sparrow turned to his King, he found the deep brown eyes of hesitation rather than concern. "What is it?"

Edmund's gaze narrowed on him. "I hate that you do that."

"You're an open book, my King. Cover up a little."

He rolled his eyes. "Only to you."

Sparrow merely smirked at the compliment. It was the

truth. Edmund was normally exceedingly good at hiding his thoughts and emotions.

Edmund took a hesitant breath, then met Sparrow's stare once more. "I think it is time we call for the Master Magician."

There was an echo of deep inhalations in the silence that followed. Sparrow narrowed his eyes at his King, the man that had raised him as a son. "Edmund."

"Sparrow, I know you do not like the idea," he interrupted. "I do not either. But we are out of options. If they are working with the Island Nation then they have sorcerers on their side. We need a magician. What better than the Master?"

"Edmund, believe me, I am well aware." He tried to remain calm. "But I know nothing of the Master Magician apart from her age. We will be completely blind to her."

"I know. But no other magician will have half the magic necessary to fight off the elixirs sorcerers are capable of brewing," Edmund pushed back. "We all know the pain-relieving potions are only a way to gain trust with our people. They will be given more deadly concoctions, Sparrow."

Sparrow didn't break eye contact with his King, his father figure. He saw exactly how the man felt about the possibility of having the Master Magician in their home. And it wasn't for his opposition to magicians either. It was for the same reason Sparrow fought against the idea—they knew nothing of her.

But he was also right. They would need the Master Magician if they were to expect elixirs *and* infiltrations from this rebellion.

Afraid he would come to regret inviting the magician he knew nothing of into the lives of the only people he cared for, Sparrow sighed in defeat. "Okay. I'll write to her immediately."

Edmund's brows shot up. "That was far simpler than I'd expected."

Sparrow smirked though there was an obvious edge to it. "I'm full of surprises."

"Consider this—with her here, you'll be able to learn everything about her," the King tried comforting through the silence that followed.

Sparrow looked to him and finally felt a bit of amusement fill his features. "You should've started with that, I wouldn't even have fought."

Miels laughed, and Tristan and Rosaelia followed immediately behind. Edmund smiled to him, and Sparrow felt the lightness that only his little family could bring him.

When they quieted, Tristan asked, "What will we offer her?"

"You do not think she'd agree?" Rosaelia rebutted in her soft voice.

Sparrow hid his scoff. He may not know anything of the Master Magician, but he knew she wasn't free. Or cheap.

"Something tells me she won't help out of the goodness of her heart," Miels joked, though there was a seriousness that pulled at his words.

Rosaelia met his gaze, then quickly looked back down. Sparrow sighed. He'd have to teach the girl how to better conceal her emotions.

"Is there a price she normally hires for?" she asked, the obvious distaste for having to pay the Magician to do something that would protect an entire people shining through her words.

Sparrow tsked. "She does not take coin. We need to have something we can offer that she would find appealing."

"What could she possibly want that she cannot get on her own using magic?" Tristan asked.

"She must get lonely." The smirk on Miels's face was wicked once more. "Maybe some companionship."

Miels *had* always assumed the Master Magician would be alluring.

Tristan mirrored his smirk and added a challenge. "And if we were to offer companionship, what makes you so high and mighty that she'd like yours?"

Miels's grin grew as his brow quirked. "You believe she'd choose *you*?"

"We do look alike, mate. How could that not even be considered?" Tristan was teasing the man. He loved riling Miels up about looks, knowing well and damned that they were both whores in their own right.

"We may look alike, but there is an obvious difference in our aires." Miels was back with his theatrics. "I always win the ladies."

Tristan smirked even wider, a spark growing in his eyes that almost worried Sparrow. "And if she wants Sparrow?"

Rosaelia choked on the water she'd brought to her lips, Miels joining Tristan in their laughs as Tristan smacked Rosaelia on the back.

"Will you two stop," she admonished. "What makes you think she cannot use magic to conjure companionship?"

"Or that she already has it?" Sparrow added.

Edmund looked to him, amusement at the wonder twins' argument still evident in his eyes. "Does she?"

Sparrow shrugged. "She has two companions she travels with. Whether they are romantic or sexual or familial, I do not know." And it really bothered him that he didn't know.

"But you still know the most about her in this room." Edmund turned his full attention on Sparrow. "What does she not have?"

Sparrow paused, staring off through the large windows past Rosaelia's shoulder and out to the greens and forest that would lead back to his childhood home. What did the Master Magician not possess?

A home.

Atop the fact that her identity was known by no one but her companions, she was known to travel from location to location. No one ever knew where she was at any given time since no one knew what she looked like. But everyone—at least those like Sparrow who kept tabs on the Master Magician—was aware that she did not own a residence.

"A home." He felt the words leave his lips almost like a whisper as he stared out the window, flashes of his childhood home racing before his eyes.

Miels leaned back into his chair. "She can use her magic to guard a location we give her. She will have a residence of her own and we will be the only ones to know it's the residence of the Master Magician."

Tristan leaned back in his chair. "Keeping us ahead of her. Leverage for the future."

"We will offer her nothing to begin." Sparrow brought himself back to the conversation at hand. "I have no doubts she will require payment, but let's not jump ahead."

There was a bout of understanding that followed in his final decision as they all leaned into their plush chairs. His family.

He, Miels, and Tristan had been adopted into the family at different times. None of them were actually considered anything but the King's lackeys to the rest of the world, but they all knew exactly how important they were to the King. They helped Edmund as they'd grown older and stronger and were considered just as much a part of his family as Rosaelia was. They would not inherit anything, but that didn't matter to them.

Sparrow looked to Edmund, the King, and he knew the man deserved every loyalty he harbored.

His gaze then naturally fell before him to the Princess of the Northern Lands. The girl stood six years younger and was the closest thing to a sibling Sparrow could imagine. His heart ached for her unrequited affections for Miels and hoped it was obvious only to him.

And hoped even more that she grew out of this little crush soon.

He stared past her shoulder once more to the large windows and considered the letter he would be sending to the Master Magician. A woman he knew only to be twenty years old—the same as Rosaelia—and craved to learn more about.

He ground his teeth as he stared out at the blue skies and considered the fact that he would be bringing danger to his family. Because not knowing anything about her meant she held all the cards in their game and he hated that he had to risk those cards being dangerous ones.

But he would send the letter, and like the King said, he would learn everything about her in the process.

✝

SPARROW WAS TRIMMING his hair in front of the hanging wall mirror in their private training room that opened up to the greens beyond when Rosaelia walked in. He'd snipped only bits from the ends so it stopped by his ears.

"Grooming for meeting the missus?" She swayed over to the stacked foams that acted as seats beside the mirror and threw herself onto them.

"Do I have a missus I'm unaware of?" There was a light

quirk to his lips as he pulled out his blade, figuring he could shave the shadow on his jaw while he was there.

"Were you not present at the meeting? The Magician may fancy your companionship." She leaned back and watched him, her hand falling into her hair as she analyzed the way he scraped the hair from his face.

"Jealous, sister?"

She grimaced. "Of what? I'm your sister. And trust me, I would not be interested even if I weren't."

"No." Sparrow smirked at her through the mirror. "You'd prefer a cocky blonde."

She did as she always did and ignored him. "You did not answer my question."

He turned his attention back to his work. "Which one?"

"What would I have to be jealous of?"

He pulled a small towel into the wash basin and cleaned his face before turning to face the Princess. "That another female may take your spot as the most important person in my life."

She smirked. "Impossible."

A chuckle drew out of him, and he threw the towel in her direction as he left the training room.

She matched his pace instantly. "But seriously, Spar, you *should* consider it."

He quirked a brow in her direction. "Bedding the Magician?"

She smacked his arm. "No! Finding a missus."

He looked at her indignantly. "For what?"

"Bedding, for instance."

There was a shine in his eyes as he smirked down at her telling her exactly what Miels would have put into words. "Try again."

"A family."

"I have you lot."

"Children."

He rolled his eyes.

She ran up before him, turning to walk backward so she could face him as he continued toward the palace. "Love."

"Ro, spare me." Everyone in their group knew he had no intentions to marry and especially no intentions to fall in love. Just the thought roiled his stomach.

"You deserve it, Spar. You deserve to find someone who will…"

"Who will what, Ro? Make me happy? Please." He scoffed as he walked around her.

"Who will fill your life with contentment, Sparrow. Who will be the reason you smile when you're alone with your thoughts and the center of every enraged and frightening moment you experience." She was so passionate when she spoke of this *particular* topic, Sparrow knew she wanted this for him desperately. And he also knew it was only because she cared for him so much that she truly believed a woman would make him content.

"Ro, do not allow your dreams to warp my reality. You will be scarily disappointed with the outcome."

She didn't argue with him as she turned to walk beside him until they reached the doors that would lead them inside the palace. When he opened it and stepped aside to allow her through first, she shook her head. "I'm going to walk a little." Before he could get inside, she called out behind him, "But please don't throw the idea aside. I know you'll make me an aunt."

Sparrow didn't turn to look her in the eyes so he wouldn't see the hurt when he said his next words. "Don't hold your breath on it, sister."

CHAPTER 2
EVONY

The village was in full bloom, the beauty of color surrounding Evony as she walked under the beat of the sun. Her hand slipped through the ends of flowers that almost reached her waist. She was in the middle of the Southern Lands, which was possibly the most difficult in the heat given there were no coastal winds, but Evony was enjoying her stay. Gemma had insisted she and James honeymoon here, and Evony had no intentions to disappoint her best friends.

Given Gemma and James were on their *honeymoon*, Evony made it her mission to remain out of their little cottage for as long as possible. And it was easy in the village of Kincardine, where she could take long and diverse walks and enjoy the scenery around her.

"Stalking me, are ya?" The elderly gentleman she'd met on her walks a week prior was sitting out before his cottage on the outskirts of Evony's favorite path along the forests. This village was especially beautiful because it had the forests on one side and a field of flowers on the other.

"Iskan, love, I cannot help it. You are a beauty to behold," she teased as she moved to the empty seat beside him.

He gave her a knowing smile, wrinkles crinkling around his dark skin. "Another walk away from those cousins of yours?"

Evony shook her head as she laughed. "They're animals, Papa Iskan."

Ever since she and Gemma had met James, and the two had fallen for one another, Evony had passed off Gemma as her cousin so that they could remain together as 'family' without bringing up any suspicions. Even with their differing skin tones, they easily made people believe it was just the marriage of a Southerner and Northerner that caused the difference.

Iskan laughed at her. "Dear Evony, you'll understand one day. When you find a man that runs your blood the way that James does your cousin, the way I do my love Beni, you'll understand."

She smirked over at him. "Papa Iskan, you old man, do you still make Mama Beni's blood boil?"

"Every day." The cocky grin and twinkle in his eyes were bright.

"But not in the way you desire, I presume?" She'd learned from him not even a week ago that a large part of a loving relationship was driving your companion crazy yet needing to be with them at all times.

He merely winked at her, the crinkled edges of his face showing the delight of decades with his wife and family. Evony's heart ached with the desire for the life that Papa Iskan and Mama Beni had made together.

Evony sat back beneath the umbrella that blocked the sun from beating down on them. She completely understood why Papa Iskan enjoyed sitting out there almost daily. It was unbelievably beautiful. The flowers in full bloom cascaded over miles and miles and painted an enchanting scene. Papa Iskan had told her on one of her visits a few days prior that he liked to go out into the fields every so often and pick out *the* most enticing flowers for his Beni. And Evony's heart panged again for the future she would not have.

Other than the beauty of this village, Papa Iskan—and at times Mama Beni, when she chose to also come out—had made Kincardine Evony's most favorite place in the lands. Every time she came for a visit—which had been every day since she'd met him the week before—she sat back and listened to another one of his stories.

Sometimes they were about his time growing up and seeing the love his parents had for one another. Sometimes it was about his love for Beni, and other times it was about the family they'd created. Evony would have loved to meet Papa Iskan and Mama Beni's children and grandchildren. They sounded exciting and loving.

Every time he told one of these stories, there was a love behind his eyes that made Evony's smile even warmer. It was the same look that came upon James's face when he spoke of Gemma or vice versa. It was the number one thing Evony craved more than anything in the world and the one thing she would never manipulate into happening with her magic. She wanted it to be real or didn't want it at all.

Evony sat back and listened to Papa Iskan tell her the story of the time he found out Beni was pregnant with their first. The anticipation of wanting it, needing to create a life that came from both of them. The thrill of finding out it had happened. The fear that something might happen to her or the child. Mama Beni came out at the tail end of the story, her hands falling over her husband's shoulders as she sat on the arm of his chair, looking sweetly on.

"He tells the story so sweetly. He forgets to mention how

protective he became. I wasn't allowed to do anything," she made sure to throw in.

Papa Iskan rolled his eyes as his smile widened. "And she doesn't let me forget it. But I could not help it any more than she hated it. This was my wife and child, my whole family. I couldn't allow anything to happen to them."

He looked up at his wife as she stroked his cheek. "And he did it again for all four of our children. Insufferable, incredible man."

Evony's heart would most definitely break with wanting *this* so desperately.

She wanted to sit out there with them for long hours, but all too soon, she felt the tingle of her magic telling her there was a letter waiting for her in the box. She'd carried the box with her everywhere for seven years now so that any requests to the Master Magician could land within. She usually ignored most of the letters' demands, writing back she wasn't interested in any offers, but she always checked them.

"I think it is time for me to return home," she said softly as she rose from her seat.

Papa Iskan rose with her, allowing his wife to reach for Evony first. Beni gave her a tight hug and light kiss on the cheek that made Evony feel warm inside.

When she moved back, Papa Iskan stepped up to Evony, a knowing look in his eyes. "You are sad, little bird."

Evony tried to force the lightness back into her eyes but knew he wouldn't be fooled. "No. Not sad. I love seeing your love, you insufferable, incredible man."

He gave a hearty chuckle and brought her into his embrace. It was exactly what Evony would have expected a grandfatherly hug to be if she'd ever had family. "You will find it, little bird."

Evony closed her eyes tight to stop the tears she felt

coming up and held him a little bit tighter. "No, Papa Iskan. I won't." She spoke so softly, she wasn't sure if he'd hear her.

His embrace strengthened, and he kissed her temple softly. "You will, little bird. He'll be insufferable and incredible, and you will love him dearly." He pulled away enough to look her in the eyes. "I know it, little bird. You will have what Beni and I have. What your Gemma and James have."

Evony didn't argue with him. She told herself it was because there was no point to it, but a larger part of her knew it was because she wanted what he said to be true so badly that she'd allow it to fill the air around her.

"Thank you, Papa Iskan. For being the remarkable man you are." Because he was remarkable to Evony. And had fast become one of her favorite people.

She kissed his cheek and finally pulled away, turning to walk back to the little cottage she shared with her best friends.

The box was hidden within the architecture of the back porch, a spot she'd chosen for instances like these where her friends were loudly *occupying* the cottage.

It was a box recognized as one a magician would be needed to open, and given they were in the Southern Lands, Evony did not have to hide it. She did, though. Mostly because she couldn't have anyone accidentally coming across letters to the Master Magician and learning her identity.

She pulled the letter out with her magic, watching it slide through the box like an apparition and land in her hand. It was nothing like the letters she'd received in the past. She was used to the demanding requests from power-hungry leaders who expected her to agree, the ones who ran small areas and desired more control. This letter was on fine, delicate paper, and when Evony turned it over, she found the seal of the King of the Northern Lands pressed into it.

Her breath caught as her heart stopped.

The King of the Northern Lands had sent *her* a letter.

Never in her existence had the King asked for anything to do with her. The only acquaintance she could booster up was the Master Assassin's attempts to learn more about her on a handful of instances. And never anything of consequence.

Evony slowly peeled the seal and opened the letter.

MASTER MAGICIAN,

I will not waste either of our time with the tedious workings of your life and well wishes for your health. We both know it is a deplorable waste of societal customs.

It is of high consequence that I write to you now. With the rebellion rising in the Northern Lands, I am in hopes to quell it before any true outcomes of casualties come of it. It is with sadness that I write that any of my attempts to stop the rebellion have come to naught. The rebellions association with the Islanders has made it increasingly dangerous with the concoctions of their making within the possession of Northern citizens.

We would not ask it if we had any other options, but we wish to keep our people safe and away from the machinations of the Island Nation, so we ask you this, Master Magician—aid us in handling this rebellion.

Yours,

Master Assassin.

MASTER ASSASSIN.

Evony wasn't surprised to see it was from him rather than the King as he led the safety of the nation, but she still couldn't believe what she was reading. She fell to the steps of the porch and reread it thrice more before the setting sun.

✝

Evony waited until the sun had set entirely before heading inside. It gave her plenty of time to think about the letter, about the possibilities it brought with it.

She found Gemma at the small hearth cooking a meal of potato soup as her husband cut fresh vegetables for their sides. "There you are!" she exclaimed. "I was beginning to believe you'd ditched us."

Evony sighed, unable to join them in their humor as she sat at the table beside James and let the letter fall to the middle of the table. When neither one of them moved for the paper, Evony nodded to it.

Gemma, who narrowed her beautiful hazel eyes at her, wiped her hands on the cloth around her waist and picked it up, moving to stand beside her husband so they could read it together.

It was obvious by their stiffening backs that they were reacting in the same way Evony had. And the fact that their eyes remained glued to the letter for long moments told her that they too were rereading it.

"The King wants *your* help?" James finally broke the silence ringing in Evony's ears. "A magician?"

"It appears so." Evony's heart still hadn't gone back to its normal pace.

Gemma dropped the letter to the table and moved to take the seat at Evony's side. "What are you feeling, babes?"

James too turned his full attention on her, and all Evony could do was stare at the rings they now wore on their fingers indicating to the world they were married. Evony could still remember the day James had walked into the cottage they had been staying at in the coastal village at the time and declared he wished to forever see the ring that evidenced she was taken. Wholly unromantic to society, wholly romantic to Evony and Gemma who had laughed and jumped for joy. After the two had been together for half a decade, it was an exciting time.

Evony shrugged in response and looked up to the man she looked to as a brother, the 'head' of their family. "What do you think?"

James took her hand in his. "Nice try, Eve. You know this is your call. That we'd follow you no matter what you choose." His thumb ran soothingly along the top of her hand. "But I think we all know what you want."

Evony stared at the flames cooking the soup. "I don't want to want it."

Gemma moved her chair until it was pressed against Evony's side and wrapped an arm around her. "I know, babes."

James followed his wife and cradled Evony's other side, all of their gazes falling back to the letter that still sat on the middle of the table. "What could the King of the *Northern Lands* want with the Master Magician?"

Evony couldn't even get herself to shrug as she dropped her head onto James's shoulder. "I'll write back to expect us in a week's time."

✝

Their small belongings were packed that night, and they were gone by morning. Evony stopped by Papa Iskan's cottage to drop a bag of coin and a letter of goodbye. She wanted to give him so much more for the small amount of kindness he'd given her in their short acquaintance, but coin was all she had at the moment. She would miss him dearly.

Evony knew her letter had reached the Master Assassin the moment she sent it and as the three of them rode toward the Northern Lands, he would be preparing his inner circle, the King's Posse, they were called, for her arrival.

They reached the border in a day and a half, and with Evony's magic, crossed it without a problem. Another day's travel would take them to the tavern she had informed the Master Magician they would be arriving to.

They arrived far earlier than they were expected, choosing to get there before the Master Assassin had the chance to be waiting for them. Though he didn't know what they looked like, he was well aware the Master Magician traveled with a female and male, so their group would be too telling.

After handing the horses in for caretaking, Gemma and James played their card and took rooms under false names as a newlywed couple traveling for their honeymoon. It was a common Northern occurrence—instead of choosing one spot to vacation like the South, the North chose to travel to different locations and get a taste of the lands. Evony couldn't argue that it sounded like the better option, though for the *honey-mooning* Gemma and James were up to, the Southern way definitely worked better.

Evony met them in the hall to their room, and the three walked in together. The room had a large bed in the middle and a couch off to the side. Being the Master Magician, it didn't take much thought to turn the couch into a small bed.

Only a few more days before they'd meet with the Master Assassin.

CHAPTER 3
EVONY

They spent their wait learning the land and getting a better idea of their surroundings. With two days until the allotted date for the arrival of the Master Magician, Evony still hadn't seen anyone show up to greet them.

It was the day before they were expected that the doors to the inn opened as they were eating breakfast and Princess Rosaelia and her 'guard' walked in. The Master Assassin wasn't recognized by most, but he could not fool her into believing he was merely a guard. Because unlike his cluelessness about her looks, she had memorized his long ago.

The Princess was instantly given the best rooms and though they would not know her, Evony kept her face hidden as they passed to get to their rooms. It was something Evony did often in the Northern Lands. She could not have people seeing her and mistaking her for another particularly adored face in the lands.

As she watched their backs walk up the stairs leading to

their rooms, Evony couldn't help but remember the first time she'd seen them.

Evony had been two years old when she'd been left in the woods on her own. Her magic had manifested itself entirely in those moments of solitude and kept her alive in the forests as she grew. It had kept the letter written by her nursemaid Vitti in a locket with a portrait of her mother and sister safe for her to open when she was older.

The letter had told Evony everything about her life up until the moment she was left for the forests, and her magic had kept it safe for her until she was old enough to read and understand it. Somehow she'd still been very young when her magic decided she was ready for it. By then, Gemma was already the only family she had and the two had decided against going forward with their findings. Especially to the Northern Lands where magicians weren't favored.

When Evony was fourteen, James had just reached his eighteenth year and had been sent to the Northern Lands for a week's worth of training. Gemma and Evony went with him—the three never even considering separating, even for the short duration of a week—and found themselves on the palace grounds. It hadn't been Evony's first time seeing Sparrow, but the first time she'd hardly paid attention so overwhelmed as she was at the Masters meeting.

She and Gemma had sat at the edge of the forest that surrounded the palace grounds, only about ten feet from Rosaelia and her companions, Tristan and Miels. Evony had lifted a shield around them so they would go unnoticed by the three, and they had simply watched. Surprisingly, Gemma had been just as desperate to see Evony's twin sister as Evony had been. They hadn't told James about their plans until after, and by then Gemma's flirtations were ready to calm his rage.

They'd watched Princess Rosaelia watch Tristan and Miels train from her perch on a stack of hay, laughing at the mess the two brothers *made. It was obvious the two were putting on a show for the Princess, Miels especially amping up his theatrics, and Evony and Gemma hadn't been able to deny it was quite amusing.*

It had been a lovely moment that had quickly ended when Sparrow had come running from the palace with palace guards rushing behind him. His form of twenty years bulked against Evony's fourteen at the time.

Sparrow had yelled at Miels and Tristan that the two of them were right beside the Princess. By then, she and Gemma had put their masks on and pulled their cloaks up. They'd smiled to one another as Evony dropped the magical shield and watched everyone's eyes widen at just how close they were standing. Unfortunately, Evony hadn't been able to enjoy their shocked horror since Sparrow's form was getting closer, and the two before the Princess were almost as fast and lethal. So they'd turned and run into the trees.

Having been raised in the forests, they were as talented as the tree animals, flying from one branch to another and keeping off the ground. They weren't delusional enough to believe themselves capable of outrunning men double their size.

They'd swung for about a mile, Evony enjoying the few times she caught a glimpse of Sparrow's fury-filled features as he followed them, far ahead of his companions, though she'd seen Miels and Tristan in the distance.

And finally, she'd garnered the energy needed to teleport them —something she tried to never do because of the amount of energy it took—and cawed to her sister to confirm before they swung at one another. Evony's magic caught them in the air and swung them through time and space, the air leaving the space around them before dropping them in the grassy lands about a mile out of the village James was stationed at. They'd laughed about the way things had gone the entire walk back to the small cottage James had been given for his family. But she'd gotten a glimpse of her blood sister for the first time that day.

Their backs disappeared up the stairs and Evony expected they would play this visit off as a normal outing for the Princess so as not to draw attention to any problems.

That night, Evony and her friends dressed in their regal Master's attire and headed out to the stables at an inn on the opposite side of the village. They took three horses and rode them out to the edge of town in order to wait until morning. There was a high probability that Sparrow had seen these horses in the second inn's stables, but it was their best bet at finding transportation since it was a guarantee that he'd seen the horses at their inn.

At the rising of the sun, they'd waited for the grounds to fill with life before making their entrance. Masked and cloaked, they would not be recognized as the small family that had ridden in a few days prior, but as the Master Magician and her companions.

Sparrow and Rosaelia were standing outside the tavern by the edge of the building, acting as if they were merely enjoying the day's breeze. Sparrow was dressed in full guard's uniform again and it truly baffled Evony how the entire village could be fooled by a simple outfit. Even having never seen his face before, she'd know there was something about him. She often wondered if that was the Master in her calling to the Master in him.

It would be a shock to no one when they rode up that Princess Rosaelia and her guard be the ones to approach them. In fact, it would be expected that Rosaelia called for the Master Assassin as soon as possible after an interaction with the Master Magician.

The three remained atop their horses as James led them into the village, the entirety of the gathered villagers quieting to an echoing silence as they recognized the masks as those the Master Magician was known to wear.

Rosaelia's back visibly stiffened in her nervousness whereas Sparrow's looked more irritated. He likely just wanted to know who she was. It amused Evony heavily that she could continue to dangle this little fact before him still.

The two stepped out of the groups of people, walking up to them and looking as regal as ever as they looked up to the three on horseback. Somehow Rosaelia still made herself look superior. A lifetime's worth of training, no doubt. "Master Magician. May we invite you into our meeting room?"

And get you away from our people. That is all the public would understand. Their Princess was trying to protect them.

Though his face couldn't be seen, Evony could *hear* the smirk as James spoke. "Why would we do that when there is all this space to meet?" His arms spread wide to show the expanse of the lands around them.

Rosaelia didn't look pleased to be playing this role, but she merely nodded and allowed for James to lead them away.

Away from the village, that's all the public would see.

The murmuring of the village folk was slow to rise, but by the time they stopped at the edge of the forest, she could see the gossip mills already running to the next village over.

"You asked for the audience of the Master Magician," James stated as they waited from atop their horses.

Sparrow remained the quiet guard, but his deep brown eyes took everything in. Evony knew he was trying to pick apart something that would tell him more. She wondered if he got anything, wanted to stare into those orbs and learn everything he was picking up.

Or not picking up. Her lips quirked up behind the mask. Oh, how it would frustrate him to not learn anything.

"The King asks for the Master Magician's assistance in

quelling the Island Nation's interference in this rebellion," Rosaelia told them exactly as the letter had.

Evony hated the politics of royalty, and was glad she didn't have to suffer the upbringing in it.

"And what do you offer in return?" James asked. He was always the one used for communication purposes when they wanted to consider a proposal from one of the letters.

"Would you not do it to protect our nations?" Rosaelia asked almost indignantly.

James scoffed. "Did you truly ask for the Master Magician's audience for a charity case, *Princess*?"

Evony felt Sparrow's eyes jump from Gemma to her. They'd all worn gloves—as usual—but had found it even more important now since neither Gemma nor James wanted to remove the rings that would give away another small fact about their group.

"We are ready to give up the small castle by the cliff off the coast of the border for the Master Magician. All ties with the Northern crown will be removed." Rosaelia didn't sound happy about the deal but hid it well.

James tilted his head. "We'll think on it." And as they turned to leave, James paused and turned back to the Princess. "Oh, and Princess, do not hide the Master Assassin as your guard the next time. No use in belittling our intelligence by attempting such an act."

Rosaelia's jaw ground tighter as her eyes grew darker, but she gave a simple, respectful nod. Sparrow's eyes simply narrowed on them.

†

A MISSIVE WAS SENT in the morning for a meeting with the King in two days' time, just enough time for the missive to get to him and for him to ride out to their village. The answer would obviously be yes, but there was no need to be too willing in their decision-making process.

When they returned to the village the next time as the Master Magician's group, they were horseless and walking without a care in the world as their masks covered their faces and cloaks flowed in the spring breeze. They were given the private dining area to use as a meeting room with the King's Posse. Evony even cloaked the room to make sure eavesdroppers wouldn't hear a thing.

The Posse arrived exactly on time. Not a minute before or after. Nifty.

James was standing between the two of them when the group walked in, and Miels and Tristan took guard at the closed door.

Gemma opened their conversation. "There's no need to stand guard, friends. I've cloaked the room for our privacy."

There was a silence that followed Gemma's revelation as the Master Magician before the boys pushed away from the door and stood on either side of the Princess.

The King turned to Gemma. "Master Magician. I received your letter. I would be happy to discuss further with you our offering."

Gemma waited, allowing Evony the final chance to back down before she spoke to her through their minds. *Take it.*

Sparrow's chocolate browns traveled from Gemma to James and then back again. Then his eyes flickered to Evony and remained there. She could feel his attention on her eyes as she focused on the King, but all of her periphery was focused on the Master Assassin, wanting to look into those deep browns and learn everything they discovered.

Gemma's face lifted ever so slightly as she said, "There's no need, King Edmund. We find your offer intriguing and would love a proper residence for our personal use. The castle, no guards or spies."

Fat chance.

The King smiled. "Of course, Master Magician."

Sparrow's gaze blazed into her skin through the layers that covered her every bit. They narrowed into slits and Evony had to bite back on her smile even behind the mask. Though a veiled cloth covered any visible skin tone, there was no need to show the crinkle of amusement that would line her eyes if she smiled.

"Clarify, Father." Rosaelia's tone had some authority to it. Again, a lifetime's worth of training likely holding her so high.

The King grinned, a wickedness in his eyes telling her he believed them on the losing end of the deal. "Master Magician" —he met Gemma's eyes—"do we have a deal?"

Before Gemma could respond, Sparrow started the real fun. "It is no use to us what she says."

There was an obvious hesitation from the others in his group as they looked to him. They almost looked worried that he'd just messed up their chances of learning more about the Master Magician.

"Sparrow," the King's tone warned. "What..."

Evony's gaze met the Assassin's, and she was caught in the scrutiny behind them. "That's not the Master Magician."

Evony could feel the pressure of everyone's gaze on her, but she couldn't look away from the Assassin's brown orbs. They were hypnotizing.

Sparrow stepped forward, so he stood before the rest of his group, still several feet from Evony, as his tone turned cocky and dangerous. "Tell us, *Magician*, do we have a deal?"

Evony felt a twinkle in her eyes that she had no doubt he

saw. She didn't break eye contact with him as she spoke to her friends through their minds. *Uncloak.*

Masks? James's voice came back.

Everything.

James was the first to move, slowly peeling the glove off of one hand, then the other. Showing the group the ring that sat on his finger and his Southern skin. Then he pulled his cloak down, his leisurely speed causing an irritation in the group that gave Evony just that much more amusement. As he finally pulled the strings off the back of his mask and revealed his face, all but Sparrow watched with held breaths.

Sparrow's eyes remained on Evony's and she couldn't help but love the attention.

Gemma moved next, following at her husband's speed as she started with the gloves, then moved for the hood of her cloak showing the room the spiraled russet curls that sat beautifully on her head. And finally, she let the strings holding her mask up fall and made the King's Posse privy to her stunning face.

Evony knew the Assassin was taking them in through his periphery, but his gaze remained unwavering. He was waiting for her, and the knowledge of that sent a thrill through her she'd never experienced before.

Evony moved slower than her friends, her removal of the gloves revealing the difference in her skin tone to her companions. And though she was darker than the Posse since she'd grown in the Southern Land's beaming sun, she was much lighter than her friends.

The drop of the hood to her cloak revealed the black locks that were the exact replica of the Princess's.

She took her time with the mask, knowing Sparrow's patience was running thin and delighting in every moment of watching his jaw tic as he controlled himself. It was almost erotic.

She internally scoffed as she untied the mask and agonizingly slowly pulled it down, never averting her gaze from the Assassin's. The gasps in the room echoed as Sparrow's eyes widened and his breath caught.

Evony smirked at him. "Deal."

Sparrow stumbled back a step as Miels and Tristan moved to cover Rosaelia and the King stood taller. Then Sparrow's jaw tightened to a point Evony was sure would crack his teeth.

"What kind of game is this?" The King's tone was no longer friendly. "I was under the impression you are unable to change appearances."

Evony allowed her gaze to flicker to the King. "That remains accurate."

"What the hell is going on here?" Tristan seethed.

Brave of him. No one, no matter how angry they were, spoke to the Master Magician like that. It would be a dangerous game to assume the Magician would not retaliate for the attitude.

Evony respected him for standing up for his friend though.

Sparrow pushed his shoulders back as he stood taller, like he was ready to pounce on her if needed—and a part of Evony she'd never known liked the idea of that. It was an odd feeling.

"It's quite simple, really." Evony smiled to the others. "I am Rosaelia's twin sister. Younger by six minutes."

The King's control was visibly running thin. "I do not have another daughter."

Evony pushed her brows into a furrow as a crooked grin rose on her lips. "Don't you?"

"Magician," Sparrow threatened.

Again, some distant part of Evony enjoyed that tone.

Evony looked to the King. "The Queen merely hid me from

you. I was born with some...oddities that would have given me away as a magician immediately. And from historical lessons, King Edmund of twenty years ago was not a fan of magicians."

There was a flicker of joy that rushed through her as the entire Posse flinched at the last retort.

"You're lying." Rosaelia spoke with force, but there was no conviction behind her words.

Evony sighed, though she was having a pleasant time. "The Queen had a portrait done of her with both daughters when we were a year old. Find it in her quarters, and you'll know I am not."

Sparrow's fists turned white, and she knew he was trying to control the need to rush back to the palace immediately.

"We will remain here a few more days. That should be enough time for you to find the portrait. If you would still like to work with us, send word, and I will ride into the palace grounds as the cousin of Princess Rosaelia. There is no need for anyone to know I am also an heir."

The King flinched at the final word.

Then James was by her side, his arm out for her to take as Gemma held on to the other side. Evony hooked her hand into his elbow, ready to throw up a shield to cover them as they left the tavern. They began to leave, but before they made it far, Evony paused beside the Assassin, so close they shared breath. "I'll see you soon, my assassin." Because she knew they would call for her.

His jaw grit harder as his eyes grew lethal and Evony's heart skipped with the knowledge she was causing this reaction from the Master Assassin.

CHAPTER 4

SPARROW

Sparrow wasn't able to sleep. Every time he closed his eyes, he saw her deep sapphire ones staring back at him, the twinkle of mischief pulsing. So instead he'd spent the entire night searching the Queen's wing.

They'd left the inn moments after the Master Magician and her friends, and were back at the palace in record time, all moving for the Queen's wing with purpose. They hadn't allowed any other member of the palace to follow them, but Sparrow knew gossip would be flying that they were going into the wing again for the first time since the Queen had been killed.

Edmund had closed the quarters off eighteen years ago and had never allowed another member of the palace to enter after placing the sheets to cover all the furniture. Because though it had been a loveless marriage, he had respected his wife greatly. Mourned her loss dearly.

Eighteen years of dust now coated the wing.

They'd searched for hours before calling it a night and heading to bed. And Sparrow had quickly risen and begun without his companions. Those eyes were haunting him, and he needed to know if what she'd said was true.

It angered him even more that he'd thought himself wise for having figured it out when the rest of his group had thought the friend the Magician. They'd always had their eyes covered when they'd been seen, so it really was skill that had picked her out. Or maybe it was the look in her eyes. It had called to him like a siren, and he'd known, without hesitation, that she was it. An eerie part of him knew he would have been able to figure it out without his lifetime of training, and he didn't know whether he liked that or not.

But it was never about hiding her identity.

She'd known. From the moment she'd agreed to meet them, she'd known they would be finding out her identity, and in turn, that the possible second heir to the Northern Lands was the Master Magician. And she had used it to play with them. It was exactly what Sparrow had been nervous about. She wasn't even there yet, and she was already playing games with them.

Sparrow grit his teeth to push aside his frustration as he pulled yet another small box of knickknacks out and began to search. Because the Magician had neglected to give them any specifics, like size or coloring, he had to check *everything*. And the Queen had had so many of these inane boxes lying about her wing. So much *crap*.

By morning, when the rest of their group joined him, he was still at a loss to where this painting could be. He truly hoped this wasn't just another one of the Master Magician's games. He wouldn't be able to hold in his frustrations then, possible Princess or not.

They were about thirteen or fourteen rooms into the wing when dinner rolled around and Sparrow finally found it. Sitting in the back of the closet of what he assumed was a random nursemaid's suite was a large painting. Edmund later mentioned it as the Queen's personal maid, Vitti's, rooms.

When he'd called the entire group into the room and leaned the painting against the wall so they could all get a good look at it, Edmund was motionless.

Standing at about half of Sparrow's height of six foot, three inches was the enormous evidence of the second heir's existence. It was so big that it was ridiculous no one had come across it eighteen years ago when they were closing off the wing.

But it was exactly what the Master Magician had said it would be—a painting of the Queen with a daughter on each leg.

Rosaelia sat on her left leg and her emerald eyes shined as she smiled at the painter. The sight of her chubby little arms reaching for the petals littering the air around them made Sparrow smile.

And on the other leg sat the Master Magician. Her eyes, like Rosaelia's, hadn't changed since the portrait was done. Staring back at Sparrow were the beautiful and striking sapphire blues. Like a crash of the ocean waves.

She was smiling and playing with the petals like her twin, but the difference was drastic, and it wasn't just the eye color. It was the part, like the Magician had said, that would've given her away. Veins of purple and black scaled around each of her eyes.

Yet somehow, they didn't take away from her cuteness.

As Sparrow stared between the portrait and the King, he knew the Magician had been right about another matter—the King Edmund of twenty years ago would've done something about this evidence of a magician.

It was about ten minutes before anyone spoke, Edmund being the first to break the silence. "I have another daughter."

Rosaelia followed close behind him with a breathless, "I have a sister."

Sparrow met Miels and Tristan's eyes and knew there was nothing any of them could do to help the two of them through this moment. They may be considered family now, but this didn't affect their lives the way it did Edmund and Rosaelia's.

Edmund's gaze didn't waver from the portrait. "I will call for her immediately. She will be introduced as the lost second heir. I will not hide my daughter."

"No." Sparrow didn't leave room for any argument.

But Edmund did so anyway. "*She is my daughter.*" There was pain behind his eyes. Both because of the lost years with a child he hadn't known he'd had and the knowledge that had he known, she may be dead now.

"And she is safer as a distant relative than an heir. As the heir, more eyes will be on her, the secret of the Master Magician will come out and that is something she's worked her whole life to keep hidden." Why was he worried about *her*? "Then the repercussions will fall to you from every magician and common folk who wanted a magician around. You would have to deal with the brunt that you'd banned magicians from your land, but your daughter is one."

It was obvious he wanted to argue because his emotions were so shot out in disarray, but finally, King Edmund relented.

"She will ride in as Rosaelia's cousin," Sparrow finalized. "And I'll watch her. Just because she's your daughter doesn't mean we can trust her."

Now it was more imperative that they come to the palace. Not for the help of the Master Magician, but because this was her family and she still deserved to be a part of it. It wasn't fair to her that her mother had taken away the chance before she'd been given one.

He controlled his breaths as he looked back at the painting

and the eyes took him back to that private meeting where her gaze had teased him. "I'll ready their rooms and send word to expect them immediately."

At a leisurely pace, it was a day's ride, so not the next morning, but the one after.

Edmund's sad eyes met his and he looked so lost as he nodded. Then he looked to Miels and Tristan. "Do you two mind taking that to my room?"

They didn't make a sound as they nodded and covered the painting with a sheet as they followed the King out of the room.

Sparrow looked to Rosaelia and walked to her slowly. "Ro?"

Her eyes met his, and he instantly threw his arm around her shoulders, bringing her in for a hug as she mumbled, "I have a twin."

✝

Two nights and one day. That was all the time he had to prepare for their arrival and every moment of it he was haunted by those blue crashing eyes.

They arrived precisely at eight in the morning on horse-back, a wagon following them with the little belongings they had brought. The Master Magician was known to travel light, but this was *very* light.

Sparrow awaited them at the front of the palace. He had Miels and Tristan running trainings that morning and the King was in meeting after meeting as he attempted to very slowly raise the bans of magicians, then in following years, sorcerers. Rosaelia sat in the library, wanting to be alone. She couldn't handle coming out to greet her sister and it hurt Sparrow that she felt guilty that she'd grown up with the privileges of royalty when her sister had grown up in the forests.

He felt the stares coming from every servant that ran around the palace, knowing the few that had been chosen to take the luggage and follow them to their rooms were reeling with firsthand knowledge. He also knew just about every available servant was finding a way to sneak a peek.

He didn't have to look around to see the shocks of finding Rosaelia's replica before them.

When the three emerged from their horses and stopped in front of Sparrow in her usual rankings—James in the middle— Sparrow bent forward as a show of respect. Had the servants not been around, he wouldn't have, and the look in their eyes said they knew it.

"I hope your journey went well." He hated niceties.

The Master Magician knew it too. "Quite."

He gave a single nod of acknowledgment, then turned. He couldn't pretend to be nice and proper with those ocean blues staring at him. He hated how much they affected him.

The servants carried their things and followed as Sparrow led them to the King's wing. Only the King's Posse had rooms in this wing and Sparrow would be stupid to not put the Magician and her friends there too. First, because they would be considered Rosaelia's family, and in turn, deserving of the best. But also because he needed them around at all times. He needed to be able to keep his eyes on them as much as possible.

He walked them into a small suite and turned to the three as the servants dropped the bags within. "This will be your rooms." He looked between the two companions. From what he guessed, they were married, so they probably wouldn't need the two bedrooms the suite had, but they could worry about that.

"And mine?" the Magician asked innocently.

He ground his teeth to calm himself so the servants wouldn't notice anything out of place. He left the room without a word and walked across the hall. When they were inside, he pointed to the door on the far-right wall. "That will be your room."

The servants quietly placed her bags within the room, but their widened eyes gave away that the gossip mills would be running extra fast that day as they left.

"What's wrong with your servants?" Apparently the Magician had noticed as well.

"What's your name?" He needed to know. It was gnawing at him that he still didn't know that small, simple fact.

But when she didn't answer, he relented, "They've never been here before."

Her brow quirked. "Oh?"

"I do not allow the servants into my suite. Only two older ones come in to clean, and they never speak of the matter."

Her gaze dropped and slowly took in his form, moving up his body until they landed on his eyes once more. "Are you trying to seduce me, Assassin?"

"Not at all, Magician."

Her lips quirked up and she moved to the door he had indicated as hers. She turned just before the door closed behind her. "Evony."

She closed the door and left him standing in the common area alone.

Evony.

The Master Magician's name was Evony and she was the second heir to his nation. She was the twin to the girl he considered a sister.

Evony.

CHAPTER 5

SPARROW

Sparrow was sitting at the small round table across from the front door when Evony walked out and across the hall an hour later. He opened the door behind her so he could see if they walked out, hoping her magic would not allow them the chance to travel about without his knowledge.

So he sat there until dinner, reading missives from his spies around the lands.

He stood at their door right before the start of dinner, telling himself he needed to act his part. He knocked and stepped back, holding his hands behind his back as he waited.

The man opened the door and upon seeing Sparrow, widened it to allow him in. That almost made Sparrow more suspicious of him.

"Dinner will be starting soon. I simply wanted to show you to the dining hall."

Evony popped up behind her friend. "Don't lie, Assassin. You want to keep your eyes on us at all times. Tell me, my assassin, did it kill you to not know what was going on behind these closed doors?"

She was teasing him and he hated that she could so easily play with him.

When Sparrow didn't answer, she laughed and stepped out, closely followed by her friends. Her hand clasped his elbow as they walked the halls, the servants staring. Sparrow tried to ignore them.

"Their names are Gemma and James."

"Did I ask?"

He didn't look at her, but she was pressed so closely into his bicep that he felt her smile. "You want to know. You're accustomed to knowing everything. I simply wanted to appease your curiosity."

He didn't entertain her with any comments.

The rest of the Posse was already in the dining hall, Miels's face breaking into a grin when he noticed Evony's hold on him. "What a gentleman you are, Spar."

Sparrow's jaw ticked, but he simply turned to the three. "You may choose your seats."

He peeled away from Evony's hold and felt the tingle of not touching her travel up his spine. Almost like his body missed the touch.

He breathed away the insanity of that and took his seat on the King's left. He didn't notice Evony had followed to the seat beside him—the one normally left empty between him and Miels—until he'd taken his seat. The chair was closer than he remembered it being.

She was playing another game, and Sparrow refused to fall victim to it.

Her friends sat at the other end of their small table with each of the wonder twins on their sides. Oddly enough, the table looked complete with the three new additions.

His gaze fell to their hands as the servants brought their plates in. Married.

He looked to Evony's bare hands. So she was not spoken for.

She was openly staring at him when his eyes glanced up and he shot his gaze away instantly. He normally didn't care if he was caught, but something about her stare caught him off guard.

Their plates were settled in the silence before the servants left the room and closed the large doors behind them. Edmund was the first to break the silence after everyone dug into their meals. "May I know your name? All of you?"

He could've just waited and asked Sparrow, but it was probably killing him not to know the way it had killed Sparrow. Except they had different reasons behind it. Edmund wanted to know because this was his daughter, Sparrow needed to know for his own sanity.

"I'm Gemma," the girl at the other end spoke. "This is my husband James, and that rascal is Evony."

Evony winked to her friends and it was obvious they were as close to one another as the King's Posse was.

Edmund watched her with a small smile. "Evony." A laugh passed through his nostrils. "Rowena gave me a daughter with her initial and gave herself one with mine."

"I wouldn't say she gave me to herself. I was offed to the lady's maid to raise and send away." Evony didn't sound bitter, just matter-of-fact.

"How do you know that?" Everything about the girl intrigued Sparrow, and he hated himself for it.

Her gaze drank in his features like she was enjoying elongating the wait. "Vitti, the maid, wrote a letter before she was killed. I got the whole backstory."

His gaze narrowed at her. He needed to see that letter.

She smirked, reading him too clearly. "I'll show you the letter later if you're a good assassin."

His jaw ticked again and he turned his attention to his food.

After a few bites, Evony turned to the King. "So what is this problem you needed the Master Magician's help with?"

"Rebellions have never been this organized," Tristan answered her from across the table.

"And never have they worked with sorcerers that may give them potions with any degree of power," Miels added.

"And you want Evony to do what exactly?" James asked.

"Quell the Islander's interference," Edmund said with conviction.

Evony laughed softly, like she thought them foolish. "That isn't how magic works. I can only do something with what I have. I cannot conjure up those in the rebellion or those giving out potions and put an end to it." Her tone softened. "But I'll look into it."

Edmund gave a single, almost thankful, nod and raised his glass to her. "For family."

That wicked smirk told Sparrow she was going to say something to irritate him. "Au contraire, King. I am only doing this so that I remain in Sparrow's rooms for as long as I can."

She and her friends were the only ones to drink to that though Miels's smirk said that he was close to joining. Then the blonde met his brother's gaze and rolled his eyes. "Oh fuck off."

"What?" Rosaelia spoke for the first time.

"Nothing," Miels grumbled.

Tristan's smirk said he was really enjoying his brother's reaction. "She chose Sparrow."

Sparrow rolled his eyes heavenward as Rosaelia's lips quirked up. At least they'd gotten her to smile.

Evony watched them skeptically but didn't question what they were talking about.

Then Rosaelia was talking. Good, she was getting out of her little funk. "How long have you two been married?"

"Two weeks," Gemma smiled proudly.

"We've been together six years," James clarified.

"And making my life miserable for three." Evony gave them a cheeky smile.

Rosaelia's brows furrowed. "How so?"

Sparrow cleared his throat at the innocent comment at the same moment Miels and Tristan almost spit their drinks out, but it was Evony who commented, "Innocent, aren't we?"

Rosaelia blushed and Gemma admonished her friend before Sparrow had the chance to. "Evony, you're just as innocent."

Now Sparrow's eyes were jumping to the Magician. Innocent? He didn't know why it shocked him. As the hidden Master Magician, she likely didn't allow anyone close enough.

"Though her mind is as dirty as the Rivorbant Waters," James added.

The Rivorbant Waters, the very northern edge of the Island Nation where every disgusting remnant ended up. Filthy.

Evony turned that wicked glance to her twin. "James knows exactly how to make Gemma feel good and she's not shy about letting him—and the rest of the village—know it." She caught her friend's eyes. "He's not so quiet either, but Gem is a whole other story."

Gemma flipped her friend off, but there wasn't an ounce of shame in her features. Southerners truly didn't care. "Just you wait, Eve. Once you find yourself a James, you'll be screaming so loud, your magic will carry it across lands."

Evony's hands wrapped around Sparrow's bicep again as she leaned into his shoulder, her lashes fluttering up at him. "I already have."

Gemma and James broke out in laughter, Miels joining them and Tristan trying—poorly—to suppress his.

Miels looked to Evony. "I like you."

She smiled back but didn't move from Sparrow's shoulder. "Of course you do." When conversation turned around and the room filled with Tristan and Miels's voices, Evony's breath tickled his ear. "Tell me, my assassin, learn anything about me yet?"

Only a few inches separated their faces when Sparrow turned to her and he could feel the King and Princess watching them intently but tried to ignore it. "You hold secrets behind those dark eyes."

Those dark, beautiful, haunting eyes.

Her answering smile held no amusement. "Not all secrets are dangerous. Some, in fact, are better left sealed."

Sparrow didn't know what to think about that as she finally pulled away and turned to her friends at the other end of the table.

†

Edmund stared at the painting he'd put up in his dark office when Sparrow walked in after dinner. He'd dropped Evony off at his suite, though he knew she'd gone to her friends' room, and came immediately here.

"You think sharing a room will tell you what you wish to learn from the girl?"

Sparrow fell into the chair across from his King. "More than not sharing the rooms."

His gaze flickered to Sparrow. "You think she's playing a game with us? With you?"

"Don't you?"

"I didn't," he said, then turned back to the painting sitting above the fireplace of the small room off of his common area—a space only those two older servants were allowed into. "Then I saw the way she acted around you. I cannot help but wonder if she does it because she knows you will not fall for her games or because she truly believes she can get you to fall."

"You're wondering what her end goal is." It wasn't a question. Sparrow was wondering the same thing.

"I cannot help but think it is revenge. That she is angry with me for the life she lived because I wouldn't have allowed her life had I known of her existence. Because I gave Rosaelia everything she missed out on because of something she could not control."

"Possible." Sparrow didn't see that in her eyes, but she could easily be fooling him.

His gaze was on Sparrow again and there was a lift to his lips. "You're not fooling me, Sparrow. You want her in your room because you need to learn everything about her. Be the only person in the lands that knows everything about the Master Magician. It's killed you all these years not to know it."

Sparrow smirked at him. "I won't be the *only* person. There's still Gemma and James."

"Something tells me you're trying to learn more about her than even those two know."

Now Sparrow felt the wickedness enter his eyes. Edmund was right. Apart from the Posse's safety, he needed her near so he could learn as much about her as possible. It was prickling his skin even in those moments to know she was in his suite and he was not there learning everything starting from the moment that letter had been written.

He stood after a bout of silence and headed for the door.

"You want that letter, don't you?" He didn't turn around, didn't need to, to know there was a smirk on the King's face.

"As much as you do," Sparrow replied and left the room.

CHAPTER 6
EVONY

There was an incessant need she felt to always be touching him.

It had started the moment she'd stood before him in that inn's private dining hall and known he would figure out she was the Master Magician. It was those cocky, knowing eyes that had started a tingle within her she wasn't used to. By the time they'd left that first meeting, Evony hadn't been able to help it, she'd needed to be close to him. She'd settled on whispering to him over touching him and her body had annoyed her about the incorrect decision the entire time they'd waited to come to the palace.

But seeing him waiting out there for them—even knowing he only did it because he didn't trust them—had made her happy. It was weird because she didn't trust him either, but an annoying and unfamiliar part of her told her that she could. That he wouldn't take advantage of her like anyone else.

It was a very annoying part of her and the only way to truly shut it up was when she was touching him. That played a role behind her clasping his arm on the way to dinner. But she wouldn't lie to herself, it was mostly just because she wanted to. She'd also allowed herself the chance because she'd never experienced this before and wasn't sure what it meant.

And in holding him, her face almost pressed into his arm as she took in his scent, she'd made a decision she wasn't entirely sure of until they'd reached the dining hall and Miels had smirked at them. She would continue this...whatever it was with the Assassin. Why not? She was obviously attracted to him and it would be a fun game.

And it humorously angered him so what more could she ask for?

"You're very quiet this evening, Eve," James pushed her out of her thoughts as they took their seats around the common area of their suite.

Good. Those thoughts were beginning to plague with Sparrow and she didn't need this. After all, after the palace was done with the Master Magician, she would be booted from their lives again.

"I think I like him." She stared off into space, then turned to her brother. "My body, at least, is very fond of him."

He smirked. "You've always been attracted to the man. I remember you gushing about how rugged and handsome he was chasing you two through the forest."

Evony laughed. "He was."

"He was," Gemma sighed dreamily and James growled her way.

James didn't look too pleased with the conversation any longer, but he turned back to Evony. "So you're attracted to him. Good. You two are sharing a suite, maybe you could get more out of it." He wiggled his eyebrows.

"James," Evony reprimanded. "As my older brother, you're supposed to *not* want me doing *more* with anyone. Least of all a dangerous assassin."

"Or a protective fighter. Perspective, Evie."

He took Gemma's hand possessively. Then his smile dropped as he took Evony in. "Just...I'm joking, Eve. Don't sleep with him."

"Oh? Now we're the older brother?"

"No. Now we're the best friend who knows you need to be in love with the man that takes all your firsts. We both know you're attracted to the Assassin and it'll be real fucking entertaining watching you annoy him, but you need trust and loyalty and love. The way Gemma did. The way I did."

He was right, of course. Annoyingly so.

"Yeah, yeah, yeah." She rolled her eyes and leaned back into the couch. "I won't ride him. Big shocker."

Gemma laughed and James grimaced at Evony's choice of words. They were Southern so not being formal was customary, but he was still her brother.

"How are you taking the father and sister part?" Gemma asked.

Evony didn't know how to react. "They both seem guilty and it's making them standoffish. So...I don't know yet. I guess we'll find out."

"Plus, we're all the family she really needs," James bolstered proudly.

Evony smiled. "Exactly."

✝

OTHER THAN THE vials of healing potion the boys had found, Evony had nothing to go off of for her end of the bargain. And even then, she didn't have anything to go off of because the vials hadn't been confiscated.

So she'd spent the majority of her first few days at the

palace learning the area with her friends and flirting with Sparrow. His narrowed eyes told her how much he didn't trust her and somehow made the entire experience more entertaining.

The first brush of true aid Evony could provide came almost a week later when an explosion in a small village under an hour's ride away plagued the winds with smoke. She'd been sitting with Sparrow in their suite, watching the brooding man read another one of his missives, when Miels barged through the door. Apparently, it was the first real act of rebellion that had taken place.

Sparrow had been adamant that Evony not join them as he'd rushed to the stables for his horse. She'd ignored him entirely, of course, and rode beside him the entire way, keeping perfect pace and biting back on the smile at his annoyance.

They were off of their horses at the edge of the forests in no time, looking down to the village. From what Evony could tell, the fountain in the center of town had blown up and the main shops remained mostly untouched, though some damage was done.

Sparrow held her back, his arm wrapping around her waist, as she tried to follow two of his men down their large hill and into town.

"Love," she said it with acidic sweetness. "As much as I'm enjoying being pressed against you, let go."

"We will not interfere. The rebels would want to see the King's men interfering. They don't know my men."

"They don't know me either." She struggled.

His arm tightened around her as he held her back to his chest and leaned in so his breath tickled her ear. "I think you forget, *Evony*, that you are the Princess's twin and this town borders the palace. Everyone here knows what the Princess looks like." Unlike most other towns, she'd be noticed immediately.

It was odd. She'd gone her entire life as one of the most notable figures of their age without a single recognition—though she'd always been extra careful around places of power knowing that they would have met the Princess at some point.

And now, as a 'nobody,' she had to hide back.

Finally, she relaxed into his arms, her hands falling onto the one that held her against him. "Keep holding me like this and I won't ever go against you."

She could *hear* his jaw clenching as he released her. Tristan and Miels stood by their horses, but 'ignored' them. They were trying not to laugh and Evony liked them even more for it.

Sparrow moved to the edge of the mountainside and stared out at the village, his arms crossed before his chest and his face devoid of anything but fury.

Evony placed a hand to his lower back because that unfamiliar, annoying part of her urged her to, and felt him stiffen against her. "Does my touch make you uncomfortable?"

He didn't turn to her as he said, "No."

Evony would've questioned his response if she hadn't felt him relax against her hand. Again, that little part of her that apparently controlled her actions around him made her step up closer to him, made her hand fall to the edge of his trousers and rest there as her head fell to his bicep. But still, he felt calm against her. Maybe he wasn't lying.

Or maybe he was just really good at faking it. Evony vexingly hoped for the former.

It was a long wait for the men to come back, but not a single one of them moved as they watched the town. To Evony's surprise, even when his men *did* return, Sparrow didn't move out from under her touch.

The first man, a tall blonde, held up a vial. "Definitely

Islanders. Collected three empty ones, two cracked, and four unused."

"What is it?" Evony asked.

The other man, with long black hair tied back and wide intimidating shoulders, answered, "It's what's used for fireworks in the sky. When added with pebbles mixed with baking powder, an explosion occurs. The powder is normally added in the air though, in order to avoid moments like these."

"You guys have fireworks?" She'd only ever heard of fireworks.

"No." Sparrow didn't look at her. "But those in the north of the lands see the remnants of the Islander's fireworks."

That made much more sense.

"Anyone hurt?" Miels asked the important question.

"No," the broader one said. "It takes a few seconds for the potion to react with the pebbles and powder. Enough to get others out of the way."

"The village folk say there were shouts to get away from the fountain moments before it erupted," the other added.

"Now we have to figure out if this has to do with the rebellion or if they were just playing their chances at fireworks," Sparrow sounded annoyed. "Though someone should let them know it's meant to be done in the dark."

†

THEY HAD MISSED lunch by the time they arrived back to the palace, but dinner was hot and ready for them at the table as they took their seats. Evony sat beside Sparrow, her friends opposite the King. Their self-assigned seats.

With their dinner of potatoes, goose, and vegetables sitting before them, the servants exited the room and shut the doors behind them as Sparrow began filling in the others about what they'd found.

Evony just listened to the boys recount everything, choosing not to throw in innuendos and flirtations with Sparrow this frustrated. Her bout of kindness toward him.

Tristan was telling them about his plans to go into the village the next day and find out what the firework potions were doing in the Northern Lands—apparently as the mediator, he was the best for missions like these—when Evony felt her stomach constrict. There was far more food on the plates they were served than she was used to.

She leaned into Sparrow so she wouldn't draw attention from Tristan's plans. "Have the rest of mine too. It's too muc..." As she was saying it, she realized he may not do it in fears that she had magically done something to the meal. He was already so suspicious of her, there was no way he would trust her with this.

She was going to cut herself off when he shocked her by switching their plates on the table so her half eaten one sat before him.

He didn't give her an ounce of attention as he did so, but he'd trusted her enough to take her food. He wasn't so disgusted with her to consume pieces that her fork had touched. It was annoyingly satisfying.

Evony didn't pay too much attention to the talk around the table as the men discussed back and forth what they were thinking and focused her attention on her twin. Rosaelia Lenoir, Princess of the Northern Lands.

She was quiet, but she had a perceptive gaze.

And she was staring at Evony. At both of them. Her and Sparrow.

Then she was out of her seat, the slightest blush of being caught staring lighting her cheeks, as she moved to the windows at the end of the room. Sparrow was so caught up in his conversation that he didn't pay attention to it, but Evony rose from her seat and followed the Princess. That, no doubt, caught the Assassin's attention.

"Are you all right?" she asked when she reached Rosaelia's side.

The Princess jumped and turned to meet her gaze. "I do not know how to act around you. You are more sister to Gemma and James than me, but we're blood. Twins. Exact replicas."

Evony smiled reassuringly. "Just treat me as a friend. Do not pressure yourself to treat me as blood. I won't be pressuring myself to do the same with you."

Rosaelia's cheeks remained pink as she nodded. She looked over to the table and her eyes landed on Sparrow.

"Do you fancy him?" Evony's flirtations would be of no use if she was getting in the way of their romance.

Rosaelia blanched, almost looking like the thought was nauseating. "Absolutely not. He is a brother to me like James is to you."

Evony knew her eyes glinted. "Good."

"You must hate him."

Hate him? He wasn't the one she would hate if she felt the need to hate anyone. "Why's that?"

"The way you tease him knowing he doesn't appreciate it. It's quite apparent he hates you."

Evony chuckled. "I don't hate him. And he doesn't hate me. He just doesn't know me and that bothers him. He's used to spying on everyone and knowing everything. The moment he figures me out, he'll be head over heels." She watched Sparrow glance up at them with a bit of suspicion and smiled. "And it's not that he doesn't appreciate my flirtations, he just doesn't like that I affect him when he'd rather I didn't."

Rosaelia's brow quirked. "You seem to have him perfectly read."

Evony shrugged and met her twin's stare. "No, but I know I'm right about this."

She turned back to watch the table and was shocked to find Sparrow's stare on her. And not suspicious or narrowed, but... curious. In a good way.

Her nerves skittered at his attention, but she just smiled at him.

CHAPTER 7
EVONY

The servants simply pointed when asked about the Master Assassin's whereabouts. Evony was really curious what they thought was going on. There had to be rumors and suspicions all around the palace about the Assassin's new suite mate. And the way Northerner's acted, they'd surely think them far more involved than just sleeping together.

Or they'd think Evony a Southerner and Sparrow the busy assassin looking for an easy fuck and assume that's all she was good for. Either way, Evony was curious.

But she wouldn't be learning today. Instead, she, Gemma, and James were going to find their little group. She had her arms hooked into both of her friends' when they found the space only the King's Posse used. Everyone but the King was in the private training room when they walked in, dripping sweat as their muscles bulged from overuse. Evony sighed. "Wow."

"Tell me about it," Gemma added.

James paused his laugh. "That's it,"—he turned for his wife —"we're leaving."

Gemma laughed and pushed against him. "I'm kidding. Baby, I'm kidding. Stop!"

He grumbled but stopped and turned back to the group.

Evony approached the men who had paused on the mats. "My love, you look well."

"What do you want, Evony?"

"First name basis? I don't like that. Call me something else," she purred and heard Miels joining her friends in laughter. Tristan, as always, tried to hide his. Rosaelia just watched from her perch on the stacked foam.

"What do you want, Magician?"

"Oh, c'mon, baby, you can do better than that."

Rosaelia cut in as Sparrow growled. "Is there something you needed, Evony?"

"Yes." She stared into Sparrow's dark browns. "To watch my assassin drip sweat. Preferably over me."

Rosaelia's eyes widened and every visible inch of her turned pink.

Sparrow didn't look amused. "What do you want?"

"My love, are you not listening? I want you to sweat over…"

"Evony." Her name on his tongue did wonderful things to her body. "Behave."

No.

Her name and that command on his tongue did wonderful, incredible things to her.

Evony bit the inside of her cheek as she felt her eyes shining. But before she could say anything, Sparrow interrupted, "Behave."

As she stared into his eyes, she knew she'd imagine this exact moment thirty times over tonight. And for the first time in her life, she might experience the wonders of release. Because she had a feeling this would finally push her over the edge. Sparrow's gorgeous face, his sweaty body, that brooding tone, and those sharp eyes.

She had to control her body's reaction before she could respond. "As you wish, my love."

"We didn't want to bother you," James broke the tension. "We just figured a bit of training would be nice. Evony does need to keep fit."

"Why just me?"

"Gemma and I have other ways of going about it."

Evony smirked at her friend. "Oh, I know."

Sparrow looked unconvinced as he watched her. "You can fight?"

"Of course." That was an odd question. Why wouldn't she be able to fight? "I must know how to protect myself in times my magic is depleted. Even you should figure that much, Assassin."

His expression didn't change, but Evony swore she saw a spark enter his eyes. "How well can you protect yourself, Magician?"

She enjoyed this side of him. It wasn't necessarily playful, but it was probably all she was going to get from him. "Try me."

His eyes darkened at the insinuation, but he simply spread his arms out. "Let's go."

Miels and Tristan moved off the mats and stood on the sides to watch. They looked almost excited as Evony took her stance.

Given Sparrow was double her size, it was an unfair challenge, but life was full of unfair challenges. Always had been.

They danced around each other before Sparrow attacked and the fight began. They both knew Sparrow would win. He *was* the Master Assassin after all, fighting was only second to killing in his book. But this would still be fun.

Since she was smaller, Evony took advantage of dancing out of his grasp before he could make contact, mostly dodging his attempts rather than truly fighting.

"Scared, Magician?"

"Growing tired, my love?"

He pounced on her, but she was out of the way in moments. He gave a light growl with a suggestive look as he said, "C'mon, *love*."

He'd played his card. And it had most certainly worked.

That moment's lost concentration at hearing him call her that word was all he needed. She knocked her elbow into his gut and tried to pull away, but he caught on too quickly.

He spun her legs out from under her, but she was able to catch herself and roll out from under him quickly. She was on her way back to standing when he hit her a final time, dropping them both to the ground. She knew he was going easy on her, trying not to hurt her, and she knew that new part of her was reacting to it.

He dropped her to her back hard enough to knock the air out of her lungs for a few seconds as he straddled her hips, his feet curling around her thighs to hold her down as his hands caught her arms. She watched his sweat glisten down his tanned skin and really wanted to taste it.

"Too slow." He pinned her arms above her head as they shared breath.

She saw it then, a vision of reaching up and pressing her lips against his. Of stripping out of the few pieces that separated their skin and feeling his flesh press against hers. Of spreading her legs for the feeling of being filled completely. Of all the sweat that would rack up both of their bodies as he pushed into her again and again and again before they were both moaning and screaming and...

Evony forced herself out of the fantasy and smirked up at

him. "Maybe I wanted you to win. To be *on top of me. Dripping. Sweat.*"

His jaw ticked. "What's your end goal, Magician?"

She didn't even think about it before saying, "You."

Her brows furrowed at her own response. Why had that been such an immediate answer? That was dangerous. She couldn't let herself get attached, then have to deal with being pushed out of his life. Or worse, used as the Master Magician and nothing more.

She was glad when he growled at her and pushed off the mat, moving to the swords table against the far wall. Evony let the air cool her a moment before Miels's hand was hovering over her and she was using it to pull herself up.

He didn't release her hand when she was up, but he also wasn't looking at her when he whispered, "I've never seen Spar so affected. I *really* like you."

When Evony turned to follow Miels's line of sight, she saw Sparrow staring at them with a darkness in his eyes that was what she expected happened when he turned Master Assassin. Odd.

Tristan pushed Miels so he released her and smiled down at Evony. "We both like you. But neither of us have a death wish and I have a feeling fighting your magic would warrant one?"

Evony smirked. "My magic makes me basically indestructible. But not entirely."

He glanced between Evony and Sparrow. "I want to see you two actually fight. Master against Master."

"No," Evony said softly the same moment Sparrow's harsh tone did. Her heart stopped at the suggestion. She'd never do that to him and she hated that she felt that way. She was liking him more than she wanted to.

But meeting his gaze at least told her that he had no intentions of hurting her either.

Miels's arm fell over her shoulders. "Shame." He smirked at Sparrow. "Let's train."

†

Sparrow ignored her right up until the point Gemma hurt herself falling against the weapons table and Evony rushed to her side. Then he at least he allowed his gaze to hover on her. But she couldn't enjoy it because her best friend was hurt.

James insisted he take her to the infirmary, but he was having so much fun with the boys that Gemma demanded he remain with them. And when Gemma demanded something of James, it happened, even if he didn't like it.

Evony gave her best friend a cheeky smile on the way to the infirmary. "You know he's just going to be worried about you the whole time and not be able to focus, right?"

She smirked. "He'll get over it."

At the infirmary doors, they met Old Lady Arba, the head nurse of the palace. She looked over the injury, found it to be a minor one, and sent them to the back office to meet with Ashtyn. Apparently even as the Princess's cousins, they weren't worth her time.

The back office was really just a block of space enclosed by hanging curtains rather than a real room. At the edge of one side was a sickbed and on the other a desk and a blonde woman about their age standing behind it.

"Do you know where Medic Ashtyn is?" Gemma asked nicely.

She made a mock of a bow before them. "At your service, *Your Highness*."

Evony's brow quirked, but her lips twitched up as Gemma moved to sit on the bed. "Feisty." The girl was definitely not inviting. "If you're the nurse, where's your uniform?"

"Wasn't given one."

"Why not?" Gem asked.

Ashtyn looked at her with a scrutinizing glare. "What do you want?"

Evony tried to stifle her chuckle. Palace personnel really needed to learn some social etiquette.

Gemma stuck out her hand, unbothered. "Fell on the weapons table. Cut my hand." She gave Ashtyn a seductive smile and lowered her voice. "Would the good nurse please fix it for me?"

Ashtyn snarled at her and got to work, moving for a rag and a vial. Evony could've tried to fix the gash with her magic but healing jobs usually drained her too much and she only did them when there were no other options.

"So, Ashtyn," Evony sat beside her friend on the bed, "why don't you have a coat?"

She was applying whatever was in that vial onto Gemma's hand and sounded bitter as she responded, "Didn't study medicine. Apparently that makes me unworthy."

"Why would you be offered the position if you're unworthy?" Gemma asked the question Evony was about to.

Ashtyn wrapped Gemma's hand, the goo she'd placed on it trapped and ready to soak into Gemma's wound. It was things like this—easy fixes—that didn't make Evony's magical fix worth it.

Ashtyn looked to Gemma. "Wait until nightfall and take it off. Should be good then. If it isn't, come back in the morning for a second round, then it'll definitely be okay."

"Great," Gemma exclaimed, but didn't move from the bed.

"What?" the medic bit out when neither one of them moved to leave or even get off the bed.

"We can wait you know," Gemma teased.

"All day." Evony elongated the words.

Ashtyn rolled her eyes and moved to her seat behind her desk. "The Master Assassin gave me the position. Said he thinks I can move up to head nurse swiftly with my talents. The others think it irresponsible to hire someone with no education. The Master Assassin disagrees and no one would ever argue against him."

Evony sent a hand fluttering to her heart as she feigned a swoon. "That's my Sparrow."

Ashtyn's gaze narrowed on her, but instead of commenting on what Evony had just said, she continued her story, "Old Lady Arba does the hiring for the infirmary and she isn't pleased that I got a spot without her approval and that I'm moving so high. She refuses to give me a coat."

"Shall I have Sparrow get you one? I'm very convincing."

Ashtyn's eyes deepened even more and jumped between the two of them when Gemma scoffed. "No need. The Master Assassin has done enough for me."

"I like you, Ashtyn." Evony tilted her head in consideration. "I think we'll be great friends."

She didn't look impressed. "You may leave."

They laughed as they jumped off the bed and wrapped their arms together. Evony turned before they left Ashtyn's 'office.' "Oh, and Ashtyn. Call him Sparrow. He won't mind."

Again, she didn't say anything as she evaluated Evony.

When they were out of the infirmary, Gemma laughed softly. "Making decisions for the Assassin now, are we?"

"No." Evony stood tall. "*I'm* making decisions for him. You can remain ruling over James."

Gemma shook her head. "You're right though. I don't think

he'd mind it coming from," her brows furrowed in feigned seriousness, "Nurse Ashtyn."

"I know he won't." Like she knew he didn't hate her. Instinctual. "And it'll royally piss of Old Lady Arba."

✝

Sparrow ignored her through dinner. Though this time, he took the left-over remnants—only a couple of pieces—off her plate and finished them without her having to say anything.

She was sitting on the couch in the common area of their suite when he walked in and strolled with purpose to his room. The way he'd walked, with the letter in hand, Evony had a feeling he didn't mean to stay long and she intended to be with him wherever he spent his night, so she was changed from her sleeping gown to a leather trouser and vest set and cloak when he walked out.

She could've easily misconstrued his presence and walked out to find him ready for bed, but she didn't care. If that were the case, she'd merely change back.

But she'd been right.

Not thirty seconds after she exited her room, he walked out in his leathers. Nothing too tight, but all accentuating his body perfectly. His body called to her so ceaselessly, she was glad she'd never been attracted to anyone in the past. It was very distracting.

He was still ignoring her when he left the suite and she followed after him, not giving her any semblance that he was aware of her presence—which she knew he was. As the spy, he was always aware of the things around him.

"Where are you going?" he finally asked.

"Wherever you go."

He scoffed. "Absolutely not."

"Whyever not? I was asked here to help with your rebellion. I intend to see whatever it is that's gotten you wound up. Then we can come back to our rooms and I can loosen you up." Her flirting always enraged him and always entertained her.

He stopped at the door that opened to the fields from the King's wing so they wouldn't need to make their departure known to the entire palace, and finally turned to look at her. He grumbled under his breath and held the door wide enough for her to pass through first.

As they moved for the stables, Evony asked, "So are you going to tell me where we're going?"

"Tavern an hour's ride from here. There's meant to be a meeting and I intend to listen."

"I thought we don't get too close because we're recognizable to the closer villages."

"I can blend it."

Evony shook her head with a smile at his use of 'I' rather than 'we.' "Fine. We'll blend in."

He didn't argue with her and Evony knew it was because he was very aware of the fact that she could go unseen. She'd done it her entire life after all. And *he'd* never caught her.

They stopped about a half mile from the tavern and tied the horses to a tree to walk the rest of the way. It was only about two minutes into their walk that they began to fill in with the village's population. Evony enveloped them in her invisibility shield immediately, the shimmer catching the Assassin's attention instantly.

His head snapped to her and Evony shrugged before he could say anything. "You said you wanted to blend in. What better way than not being seen at all?"

He analyzed her, then said with no real fight, "I noticed your shield the last time."

Last time had been six years ago. But he remembered. Of course he remembered. The Master Magician had gotten close to his Princess and he hadn't been able to catch her. It probably still ate away at him.

"The shield doesn't work outside a few hundred yards and you were at the top of the palace with a perfect vantage point. These people do not have that."

He didn't argue and that left Evony with the perfect opportunity to watch him. His jaw was set, his ear-length black hair, like always, was pushed perfectly back and out of his face, and his lips were in an eerily straight line. He looked domineering and all too enticing. His brown eyes harbored on black as he stared ahead.

Eventually, an annoyed grumble left him, "What?"

She wrapped a hand around his bicep and snuggled in close, bringing the shield closer to them so no one stumbled into it. "I'm merely staring at your beauty. It's hypnotizing."

He didn't respond and she loved that he never pulled away from her.

"Tell me, my assassin, do you find me hypnotizing?"

"No," he barked.

Evony laughed into his arm. "Beautiful then?"

His jaw twitched. "No."

"Liar."

His gaze hovered to her a moment before flying back to the path before them. They remained on the edges of the group walking into the village center and the shield kept them hidden. "You look like Rosaelia, so yes, I find you beautiful."

Evony tsked her disapproval. "You find her beautiful as a sister. I want more than that. Do not lie to me, Sparrow, do you find me *beautiful?*" His jaw ticked and Evony knew she had him. "Do you find me *enticing? Hypnotizing?*"

"Evony," he growled and her body felt the immediate effects. "Behave."

They were at the back of the tavern and away from prying eyes. Evony dropped the shield and answered his questioning gaze. "No use in wasting my energy if no one is around."

They drew their cloaks to cover their faces and reached for the back window that gave them a perfect view of the inside of the tavern. It had a stage on the opposite end and a plethora of small tables and chairs littering the space.

Sparrow pressed behind her, his large body covering hers as one of his hands gripped her waist to keep her close and the other leaned into the wall beside the window. Her breath hitched at the contact and though she looked into the tavern, she couldn't see anything. All she could concentrate on was his presence against her.

She stepped back just an inch so their bodies meshed together and felt the immediate effect it had on every nerve-ending in her body. He took in a large breath, but that was all the evidence she had that it affected him too. That, and the little bit more pressure his hand applied to her waist. It was too distracting, she wouldn't be able to focus on anything like this.

As they waited for this meeting to take place, Evony spent every millisecond memorizing the feel of Sparrow against her backside—his hand on her, his breath at her neck. She would play this scene on repeat when she fell into bed. Now that she'd had her first orgasm—ever—to thoughts of the Assassin, she knew she'd be soaking to thoughts of this moments. Coming over and over again as she imagined his fingers in place of her own.

She closed her eyes and swallowed back to push the thought away. She needed to focus.

Then a man walked to the stage with a guitar. And another

man followed with a small drum. And another with three even smaller drums.

Evony deflated. "This?"

Sparrow didn't move. "Just because this was not it, does not mean the meeting isn't happening. We just need to find it."

Evony turned in the tight space between the tavern and his body and found his eyes searching over every aspect through the window. He was so handsome. Masculine and frightening and deliciously handsome.

It was because of this distraction that Evony didn't notice until it was too late to throw up a shield that they were no longer alone in the back of the tavern. Coming toward them were five men and one of them had caught Evony's stare from over Sparrow's shoulder.

She froze and did the only thing she could think to stop the men from getting any closer to the two of them. She reached behind Sparrow's neck and pulled him down so their lips pressed together. For her first kiss.

Ever.

CHAPTER 8
SPARROW

He only stood frozen a moment before pulling himself out of the shock and...kissing her back.

The hand that he'd had resting on the wall moved to cradle her face as the other gripped her waist tighter, and he groaned a little at the feel of her lips against his. It was a soft, gentle kiss, but it affected every inch of his form.

And it didn't take long for him to change the pace.

Evony pressed herself closer to him, her fingers digging into the back of his neck in an inviting sting as her other hand reached around for the back of his shirt, gripping on for dear life.

He deepened the kiss, licking her lips to get them to open and allow his tongue the chance to roam. And with a haughty moan, she complied without hesitation.

She was inexperienced, he could tell that much, but she kissed him back with a fervor he'd never experienced before. Their tongues fought, though he won every time, and he could easily find himself addicted to the taste of her if he let this continue.

He had to let it continue. Was too weak to push away from it.

His fingers scraped into her hair, nails raking her scalp as he bent her head back to give himself better access. She moaned with the move and Sparrow felt himself harden at the sound.

He finally pulled away when her fingers pulled at his hair and realized that though he was ready to give up breath for that kiss, she wasn't accustomed to this. Inexperienced. Innocent.

He leaned his forehead against hers as they caught their breath, his eyes still closed as voices began filling the air around him.

"...said she knows this will work on..."

He opened his eyes and watched Evony's breathing as her eyes remained closed. Her lips were swollen and he felt himself harden even more remembering how they'd gotten that way.

"...they keep telling us to wait for..."

She opened her eyes and met his gaze, whispering against his lips, "I'm sorry."

"For what?" If she was apologizing for that kiss, she definitely didn't need to. He hated himself for thinking that, but all he wanted was to do it again.

"Distracting you," she said and Sparrow immediately felt like a bucket of ice water had been thrown over him.

He froze but remained pressed against her. He realized now that those sounds he was hearing was...the meeting? The one he'd traveled here to listen to.

And he'd missed half of it already.

"...are getting antsy. I don't know how to hold them off any..."

"Sparrow..." Evony began, but Sparrow pressed his lips to hers to silence her.

"...just need to listen. We can't get out of line. Every time that's happened before, the Master Assassin has caught on and stopped it."

"That's because it's never been this organized. The Master Assassin won't know what's coming for him." There were at least two of them.

Three. "The Master Assassin? He's just a tool. It's the King that doesn't know what's coming for him."

The first again. "Yeah, well, that'll only work if we keep organized. We cannot go breaking the plans. You need to keep your division in check."

"What are the plans?" A fourth man asked. "They won't tell us anything."

"That's for our own good. If we want the rebellion to come out victorious, we cannot have information leaking out. If anyone is caught, they cannot know the entire plan. For now we must trust them that they know what they're doing," the first answered and he sounded very confident in these leaders of theirs.

The second again. "But most important—keep your men in check. No going out and trying to attack outright. The Master Assassin will get you before you accomplish anything."

"And if not him, his lackeys." The first. "He's got the entire palace trained and we cannot fight them ourselves. We need the help of the Islanders and the best way to get that is to do as we're told. Aye?"

Sparrow turned his head slowly to get a peek of the men. He couldn't get a good look at the entire group and didn't know which was the first man—the leader of this smaller division—and which was a follower. None of it entirely mattered though. Even this little leader seemed not to know a thing.

But Sparrow got a look at two of the men. Neither very

discernible, but both ingrained into Sparrow's memory to research later.

"Aye," the rest answered.

They dispersed, but Sparrow didn't pull away from Evony's heat. He turned back to look at her and got lost staring down at her a few moments. Had it been a mistake to kiss her? Absolutely, that didn't need thought.

Had she truly meant to distract him or had it been bad timing? Was she playing another one of her games? What was it she was trying to gain from them?

When Sparrow finally peeled his body off of hers, she threw the shield up around them again and neither one of them spoke as they walked to the horses.

Before they got atop their horses for the ride back, she said, unable to reach his gaze for the first time since they'd met, "They were coming toward us. I panicked because I knew they'd recognize us if they got too close and I couldn't throw up a shield because they'd already seen two bodies."

So she let the rebels think they were just a couple hot for each other. "I understand." And maybe it was the way she shied away from his gaze knowing that 'quick thinking' was the reason they missed the meeting that he believed her.

†

LIKE IT WASN'T ENOUGH he had that incessant alarm go off in him every time anyone touched her, now he knew what she tasted like.

They were riding in the dark forests, Evony's magic lighting a route for them, when Sparrow's mind raced back to the first time he'd seen the Master Magician.

It was nine years prior and he had just turned seventeen when word was sent throughout the lands that there was another possible Master among them. Becoming a Master was not something one could train for. It was something you simply were and it didn't come easily.

He'd been titled Master Assassin when he was nine years old and all but King Edmund had been afraid of him. But he hadn't become The Assassin for fun, it was simply in him. The same way becoming a Master was in this girl.

It was reported she was a magician and a Master Magician sounded far worse than a Master Assassin ever could. And she was only eleven.

The moment the rumors had hit the palace grounds in the Northern Lands, Sparrow had gone down to the Southern Lands to find out if they were true. There was to be a meeting in two days' time in which the girl would come to them and answer questions about herself, as there was quite literally nothing known of her at the moment.

He'd arrived to the council rooms the day before the interview was to take place and had easily thrown his cloak over himself so no one recognized him. As a Master, he'd be allowed in, but he preferred to gain his information without others being the wiser.

The council room had filled prior to the girl's arrival and Sparrow had snagged a spot for himself on the back wall, off to the left of where the girl would be seated. Those seated around the tables were the Southern Lands most respected council men and women and any Masters that had shown themselves. The standing was anyone else given access to the meeting.

The room had gone silent when the girl had arrived. She wore a long black velvet cloak that covered her from head to toe, the hood even shadowing most of her face. What may have been seen of her face was covered by a mask, a light veil covering her eyes over that. Gloves covered her hands so not a single aspect of her was visible. Not her hair, not her eyes, not her skin tone. Nothing giving.

And she hadn't come alone.

Her companion was dressed exactly as she was so no one would be able to tell them apart. Given how well hidden she was in her choice of wear, Sparrow hadn't seen the point. But she'd been young and likely just wanted someone by her side. He remembered how it felt to have everyone staring at and interrogating him at such a young age.

They'd asked her three questions with no response before she'd finally given them what they wanted. But not through speech. She'd been smart not to give away the sound of her voice too.

Instead, she'd shown them. Shown them her thoughts so they didn't give away her identity and given them a glimpse into her life. It was remarkable how she was able to make them understand without narration. It was like living those memories.

Growing up in the forests. Nature, the animals, and her magic, raising her and helping her survive and thrive within the greens and danger the forests harbored. When she'd grown old enough to fend for herself—debatable five was old enough—the aids had stopped and she'd controlled her own magic to make her way through life.

It was in those memories that the council had learned that she could do anything but manipulate her appearance. Telling as to why she'd covered up so abundantly for this meeting. And it was only moments later that, without the need for deliberation, she was named the Master Magician.

She'd refused to give her name, so the world knew her only as her title.

But Sparrow couldn't be like the world. He had to know her. Had to learn everything about her. So when she'd left the rooms, he'd followed.

And lost her almost immediately.

By the time he'd figured that there was a shimmer in the air and she'd thrown up a shield to cloak where they'd gone, she'd been too far out to track. That was all he'd learned of her.

He pulled himself from his memories as they neared the palace and glanced her way. He didn't know whether she met his stare because she felt his attention on her or if she was merely turning to look at him, but she didn't shy away.

He watched her, forcing his gaze not to dip down to her lips, though he fell victim twice, and tried to figure her out. It irritated him immensely that he could not do so.

Neither one of them spoke as they returned their horses to the stables and walked through the door that led straight into the King's wing for their suite. But as Sparrow watched Evony turn to meet his eyes a final time before closing her bedroom door behind her, he felt the need to kiss her tingle back up his form.

Sparrow sighed out the frustration filling his large form when her door opened once more and she stepped out to him. She stopped a foot away and held up a large locket.

The thing was almost the size of her palm and far too big to truly wear around a neck. Something still told him that she'd done it though. At least for a few years.

She opened it to show the image within. "I don't know how they got it so small to fit into this locket, but this is how I knew of the painting."

Sparrow took the locket and stared into it at the image of Queen Rowena with a daughter on either leg. His sister's beautiful green eyes and his magician's enticing blue ones.

When Sparrow met her eyes once more, she held up a folded set of papers. "The letter," she said. "My magic hid it within the locket until I was old enough to read it. It's continued to hold it there all this time." She handed the letter over. "You may keep both."

Sparrow's brows furrowed as his gaze jumped between the two things in his hands. He was glad to have the letter, surely, but he had no intentions of keeping these things from her.

They were truly all she had from the life that was ripped away from her, and even Sparrow's savagery would not take that from her.

She didn't allow him time to say another word before she turned back to her room and closed the door without looking back.

CHAPTER 9

SPARROW

The walk to breakfast surprisingly wasn't awkward, just silent.

Evony normally took this opportunity to get in a couple of innuendos, but she withheld that morning. Sparrow wasn't sure how long her little bout would last, but was thankful for the reprieve. He couldn't afford time to waste revisiting the kiss, he'd done that enough times the night before.

After all the time he'd spent on the letter that is.

He'd reread it at least three times to learn all of the beginning of Evony's history as she knows it. Vitti's love for her, the hardships of keeping her from the King, the fear that anything may happen to her. It had been difficult to stop thinking of the guilt that went into running the Northern Lands after reading said letter.

That's when the kiss had plagued him and he'd tried desperately to sleep.

Miels and Edmund were the only ones in the room when they arrived at the dining hall. Miels had his legs thrown over the chair that Evony normally took and dropped them with a smirk as he watched them enter. "We're quiet this morning."

Sparrow pulled out his chair and ignored his friend as Evony gracefully took the spot beside him.

She smiled at him teasingly. "Yes, well, I just found out I'm with child. Your assassin sure works fast."

Miels snickered and fell back into his seat as Edmund laughed. "Fine. Don't tell me."

Evony smirked, a glint in her ocean blues that made Sparrow feel like he was crashing, and leaned back into her chair as they awaited the others.

Gemma and James were the next to enter, moving to their seats on the opposite end to Edmund and taking them quietly. They were closely followed by Tristan and Rosaelia who completed their table.

After their breakfast of grits, fruit, and ham with toast was placed before them and the doors closed, Edmund turned to Sparrow, his gaze jumping to Evony. "Did something happen last night?"

Did something happen? Just about the most intoxicating kiss he could imagine. He'd never jacked off to thoughts of a *kiss*, but he hadn't been able to help himself the night before. The memory had him so hard, there was no other way to catch sleep than to give himself the release.

He sounded like he meant it in the same way Miels had, but Sparrow ignored it. "We went to Wallacement. I was sent a missive that there was to be a meeting by the rebellion. One of my spies heard of it from the east and couldn't leave his spot so I went instead. And the Magician followed."

"Of course she did." Tristan gave Evony a teasing grin and a tingle of something he wasn't accustomed to shot up Sparrow's spine at the sight of it.

He ignored it. He had to. "There was no meeting in the

tavern, but we got the tail end of one outside. At least five men, I got a look at two of them. Seemed to be the leaders of their own divisions and one of them in charge of the whole. But they played it cool, didn't even give each other information. I highly doubt they know anything. Even the one leading the other four. He was coy, made it sound like he was protecting the others, but I reckon he didn't know a thing. But it was made clear—no playing this out on their own."

"It's more than one leader too. At least that those men thought so," Evony added.

"What?" Miels turned to her.

"They kept saying '*they* don't tell us anything.' It's more than one person calling the shots. At least to the masses."

"So what do we do with this?" Rosaelia asked. "It is important to have learned there might be multiple leaders, but this didn't give us much."

A flash of Evony's tongue dancing with his flashed across Sparrow's mind.

"If I had to guess," Gemma stated, "I'd say one was coming for the throne and the other was a sorcerer. At least this way we know you can fight one and Eve can fight the sorcerer. You know that you did not call us in vain."

"We already know we didn't call you in vain. Evony is my daughter and has every right to be here," Edmund argued and Sparrow knew that although he didn't trust the girl, he felt guilty.

He looked to Evony and caught a small smirk beginning to bloom. "As long as I remain in Sparrow's suite, maybe even in his rooms, I know it is not in vain."

Sparrow rolled his eyes and turned to his meal, but all he could imagine was getting the Magician beneath him like he had during their sparring match. Except this time he'd be tasting her.

He had to stop this.

✝

MIELS AND TRISTAN found him in the private training room after breakfast. They were meant to be leading training for the palace guards for an hour before he showed up, but sometimes they gave the job to the next best guys. It was a leadership experiment and the best way to make sure his men weren't just guards, but that they could be in charge too.

He was in the middle of push ups when Tristan sat on the mat before him, not even attempting to pretend like he was going to train. Miels at least grabbed for a roller and fell to the ground beside them, rolling out his back as he looked expectantly to Sparrow.

Sparrow pushed past the burn of doing so many push-ups and ignored them. He had a feeling he knew what this was about.

"C'mon, Spar, you can't ignore us forever." Tristan's tone was teasing.

Sparrow didn't say anything in return.

"Sparrow." There was a chuckle behind his words. "I saw the way you looked at me when I smiled at her this morning. The way you glared at Miels when he had an arm around her yesterday."

Sparrow grit his teeth and pushed through the burn in his arms. The more he did this, the more he could push away whatever they said *and* the memory of the Magician's mouth.

"Give it up, mate," Miels said as he rolled over the foam. "Spar is the least likely to admit his attraction to the girl." He turned a teasing grin on Sparrow. "Why is that, Spar? Because she's a magician?"

He'd keep doing push-ups until there was no way to respond to them, until speech wasn't viable to him.

"Or is it because she looks like Ro?" Tristan asked.

He froze at the top of his push up, grit his teeth, and continued. In Sparrow's mind, she looked nothing like Rosaelia. Those desires he felt had never happened with Rosaelia.

Miels tsked. "No, it's not that. Their personalities are too different. Eyes too. Both striking and beautiful, but too different. Is it because she's a weakness for you, Spar? Not used to those?"

She *wasn't* a weakness to him. She was just...distracting.

Tristan dropped to his back so his face was close to Sparrow as he smiled up at him. "You're going to tell us eventually, Spar."

No. He wasn't. Because it wasn't going to happen again and he wouldn't have anything to say.

He pushed against the shake of his arms. Pushed against the burn in his abs. Pushed against it all because none of it was working.

CHAPTER 10
EVONY

"So what truly happened?" Gemma asked as she crossed her legs beneath herself on the couch in her suite. James pulled a chair from the table in the corner and turned it around so he straddled it and his arms rested on the back support.

Evony had a friend on either side of her position at the edge of the couch and knew she would not be allowed to leave without telling them everything. She would do it anyway, she never hid anything from the two.

"I kissed him last night."

"*You* kissed *him*?" James asked.

"*I* kissed *him*. And he kissed me back. Like really kissed me back."

James's grin was turning wicked when Gemma's mouth opened in the shape of an o and she pointed to Evony. "That's why you missed half the conversation."

Evony bit the inside of her cheek but knew her eyes would be giving it all away.

James shook his head, but there was a proud smile on his features. "Evie, you tease, you were on a mission."

"And I was trying to keep us hidden!"

"Oh, I'm sure," James drawled.

Evony laughed, her head falling back as her grin widened. "We were leaning against a window outside looking in. He was standing directly behind me and I turned because we weren't finding anything. I saw them walking toward us over his shoulder, so I did the only thing that popped into my mind."

"Mhm," James hummed as his wife sang, "Excuses, excuses."

"No," Evony insisted. "I was making sure we weren't caught."

"Evony, please." James leaned into the back of the chair. "I'm sure you could've taken his hand and walked away."

"Sorry, not possible."

"Oh? And if it were you and I, you would have kissed me?" He watched Evony's face turn into a grimace. "Exactly."

Evony rolled her eyes but could no longer hold in the shit-eating grin. She'd kissed him and he'd kissed her back and it was all she could think about.

Gemma bumped her shoulder into Evony's. "So it was a good kiss?"

"A *very* good kiss," James stated.

Evony threw a pillow at him. "Shut up."

James caught the pillow with wide eyes. "A fucking incredible kiss. Look at how he's got her acting."

She brought her legs up to hide her smile behind as she muttered through her laugh, "I hate you. Both of you."

┼

SPARROW WAS LEADING trainings and it was something Evony could not interrupt as a vital part of the safety of the palace, so she spent the day walking the palace grounds. Sometimes she wished she could sit indoors and relax, but it was out in nature that she felt the most at peace.

Edmund found her at the outskirts of the gardens. "Evony."

She bent her head cordially. "Edmund." He hadn't insisted on being called father—which she assumed only partly had to do with everyone believing her a cousin and not a daughter—and she was glad for it. She wouldn't have done it either way, but at least this way it was less awkward.

"Alone this early afternoon?"

"James is training with the boys and Gemma is watching."

"You didn't want to watch?"

And get heated at the sight of Sparrow sweaty and emanating pure masculinity? If she'd had the opportunity to release her desires at the end of the trainings the way Gemma did with James, she'd be there. But knowing Sparrow wouldn't touch her afterward just made the whole thing torture.

"Not today."

Edmund's smile was warm as he extended an arm out. "Take a walk with me?"

Evony took his elbow and followed him as he led her into the garden maze. It wasn't necessarily awkward. Just odd. She didn't know how to act with *her father*.

"It is strange, is it not, to know we are father and daughter and yet not know how to act with one another. You are my daughter, you look exactly like your sister, but I feel that I cannot *father* you like I do Rosaelia."

"It is. But I am glad for it. I do not mind the speed our relationship is progressing. I don't *need* a father."

"No, I suppose you do not." He sounded lost in thought. "I suppose none of the three of you do."

Evony didn't respond, there was nothing to say to that. It was true. She, Gemma, and James had all grown up parentless, and they were adults now with no need for them any longer.

"May I hear about it? Your time in the forests?" he asked as they strolled through the blooming flowers. Gardens were so extraordinary in springtime.

It was not an unreasonable request. And being her father, he likely wanted to know what had happened when her chance at royalty had been ripped from her. "I enjoyed it. I don't think I would have changed growing up in the wildness of it all. But then again, I know no different."

"And as you grew, you moved into homes?"

"Yes." Her fingers danced across the flowers they passed reminding her of the fields before Papa Iskan's home. "Gemma and I mostly grew up in the forests. I was alone for the first few years, though I had the animals as companions and somehow still learned to speak the languages. I learned from the animals and I survived, and honestly, I had a great time. I truly enjoyed flying from tree to tree. Then I met Gemma. She was walking alone one day and she was so hungry, so I offered her food and found out she was only a year older and an orphan. We've basically been stuck at the hip ever since. I taught her to live in the forests and we had a great time. But that is also when we began to go into villages and towns and truly acquaint ourselves with people. It's when we began learning to read and write. I'd somehow been able to read the letter at a young age, but it wasn't from knowing how to read, it was my magic basically reading it to me."

"But you remained in the forests?"

She nodded. "We met James a few years later. He was an orphaned boy training for militia work because that's really all there is for orphaned boys. He was learned though so he's really the reason we can read and write so well now. And he linked with us, began to learn the forests with us when he wasn't training, and took us to the rooms he was staying in. They were small, but he'd stolen a cot to hide under his bed so he could give us the bed at nights and he could sleep on the cot. Eventually, we moved to another town so we could be introduced as family without anyone knowing James had previously been alone. That's how we began living in civilization."

"And you stayed in civilization from then on?" They were coming to the end of the gardens.

"Mostly, yes." Evony loved her past, every moment she spent with her friends. "James would move around with wherever he was sent and we'd go with him. We went from being introduced as his cousins to Gemma being introduced as his woman and me her cousin."

"And it was a happy life?" He analyzed her.

"The best." She smiled up at him.

He searched her face like he was looking for dishonesty. But he wouldn't find it because it was the truth. She'd loved the life they'd lived and wouldn't change a moment of it.

"That's good to know. All I've been able to think is that you are my daughter and you've lived a retched life so far, and how could I have allowed it to happen."

"Well, then your mind can rest easy. I have lived the best of lives."

They were out of the garden maze and walking along the palace when Evony turned to her father. She didn't know what she wanted to ask him, but she was scared he was looking for a way to boot her out of his life and maybe that was the reason she still felt weird around him. Because he would only want to use her like everyone else.

But before she could say anything, screams came from the middle of the fields that had them running in that direction without another thought. Her choice of trousers—a big tell on whether it was Rosaelia or her when looking from a distance—were a heaven send when she was sprinting like this.

The boys came running from the training yards at the other end of the field just as Evony stopped before a servant—an older man she recognized from the stables—bleeding out as two others laid atop another man with a bloodied knife in hand.

Sparrow called for Ashtyn immediately as he dropped to his knees before the stable hand and tried to stop the bleeding.

Evony crouched beside him, placing a gentle hand over his. "I can stop the bleeding until Ashtyn gets here."

It wouldn't be like healing. It would still wipe out her magic, but she wouldn't be as exhausted as trying to heal him. It was still weird to her, even after an entire lifetime with her powers, that as the Master she could do just about anything and not get tired, but healing was the last straw for her.

Sparrow stared at her a couple seconds before relenting and pulling his hands away, now soaked to the elbows with blood.

The Posse gathered around them to hide her magic as Evony's fingers hovered over the injuries. It looked like three stab wounds around the lungs. She closed her eyes and looked for the points of injury where the blood oozed out and pulled the pieces together, barricading the blood from draining any longer. She opened her eyes and looked down to the man who was half unconscious as it was.

Sparrow turned to two guards that had taken the attacker from the servants and told them to take the man to the dungeons as Ashtyn arrived. She pushed everyone out of the way and was beside the stable hand in seconds, already working the figurative magic that were her hands.

Old Lady Arba was right behind her with two more medics.

"Master Assassin, I can assure you we can handle this without her."

Sparrow grabbed Evony by the elbow and pulled her up and out of the way, holding her against his front as he turned his head to the head nurse. "I am aware of everyone's abilities, Arba. I called for Ashtyn to keep your lot in the infirmary. Because, as you so like to remind me, you've got a handle on the infirmary."

The old woman looked like she'd taken a strike but didn't argue.

Sparrow narrowed his eyes at them. "Well? What are you still doing out here? Back to the infirmary."

The displeasure was evident on all of their faces as they left, not hesitating to follow the Assassin's orders.

Evony leaned into him, his body comforting in a way she hadn't known possible. "They won't be too happy with you."

He still held her elbow, his thumb now grazing up and down a patch of skin. "They already aren't too happy with me."

Evony knew there were other things to focus on—the dying man before her for instance—but her body was hyper-aware of the hand that still clutched her arm and grazed her skin. Of his body still pressed into her backside, bringing back memories of the last time they'd stood like this not too long ago.

Their group's silence at watching Ashtyn work was broken when a boy probably James's age came running at them. "Papa Ignatius! Papa Ignatius!"

Tristan and Miels caught him before he could get too close, but he fought against them as his eyes watered on the brink of tears. "What happened?"

Sparrow sighed into her hair. "I don't know, but we have the best nurse handling it. You may remain here and walk with us to the infirmary if you settle down, Gabriel."

It still astounded Evony that Sparrow learned every servant's name even though it was in his nature to know everything always. That was a lot of names. A lot of information.

Gabriel relaxed in the boys' arms and was finally released to watch as Ashtyn worked. She'd already closed one wound and was halfway through another. They weren't healed, but the important part at the moment was getting them to stop bleeding, and she truly was the best nurse.

Evony relaxed into Sparrow, feeling his hand drop from her elbow and play with her fingers instead as they watched the medic. Evony would have assumed her a Master if she didn't know better. Even as a Master herself, she still didn't fully understand what made a person one. But if Ashtyn hadn't been declared one by now, then she couldn't be.

But Evony swore she had it in her. Had the medic in her the way she had the Magician and Sparrow had the Assassin. Ashtyn, the Master Medic. It fit.

It was another ten, maybe fifteen, minutes before Ashtyn completed the preliminary job and Gabriel was finally given the chance to drop down to Papa Ignatius's side.

Sparrow's lips touched the back of her head, but he didn't kiss her. His breath tickled her hair as his fingers played with hers until, finally, he pulled away. And Evony didn't know if she just wanted it to be true so much that she'd convinced herself it was, but she swore he had to peel himself away. Like he wanted to stay with her.

Impossible. She was definitely projecting her feelings.

Evony met Gemma and Ashtyn off to the side as the men stood about discussing how to take Ignatius inside. But they were giving Gabriel a few moments with the man, and Gabriel was so sweet the way he pushed the older man's hair back and whispered to him.

Gemma shoved Ashtyn softly. "He's cute." When Ashtyn didn't respond, Gemma laughed. "Nothing serious of course. Just a tussle in the hay could do you some good."

Ashtyn rolled her eyes. "It's not so great."

Evony quirked a brow. "I'd beg to differ."

Ashtyn looked her over. "You're a virgin."

"How did you know that?"

She smirked. "You'd beg to differ."

Gemma shoved her again. "I'm most certainly *not* a virgin and *I'd* beg to differ."

"Exactly," Evony argued indignantly. "You cannot base your theories on a bad time."

Ashtyn looked like she didn't want to be part of the conversation. "*You're* a virgin."

Evony wore a salacious grin as she looked over to her assassin. "And yet when I think of Sparrow every night, I come so hard the bed shakes."

Gemma's hand shot to her mouth to stifle the laughs—definitely not an appropriate moment.

Sparrow was before them, looking murderous, in moments. "If you lot cannot keep your attention on the situation, you can leave."

Evony feigned seriousness as her hand landed on his chest. "Why don't you tell me what else I can do."

Sparrow growled. "Behave."

"Yes, sir." His heart pumped beneath her hand and she felt it escalate as his pupils dilated with pure desire.

Then he was gone, back to the men.

Ashtyn wore a smile now and Gemma wasn't trying to hide hers either as Evony leaned into her. "Oh, I'm definitely thinking of this tonight."

CHAPTER 11
SPARROW

And yet, when I think of Sparrow every night, I come so hard the bed shakes.

Well there was a scene that would live in his fantasies for the rest of his days. And every masculine, predatory part of him demanded that he take her over his shoulder and run them to his suite so they could make that bed shake together.

At least he knew one thing for certain now—he hadn't been imagining the sounds of his name in a moan during the nights. She'd been doing it, calling out for him. Fuck, he did not need to know that.

He didn't know what had possessed him to hold her before. All he'd known was it was as much a comfort to him as it had been for her. Because he knew she took comfort in it, knew it by the way she leaned into him, pressing herself into him in a manner that she didn't sexualize. And holding her, feeling her skin beneath his fingertips, her hair against his lips, and her scent intoxicating his senses, somehow that had been all Sparrow had needed.

Papa Ignatius, the stables master, was breathing slowly as Miels and Tristan took his arms and legs and Gabriel held on to his torso so he didn't bed over and hurt his injuries. They carried him with the girls following behind, and Sparrow watched them go, needing to turn around and head to the dungeons.

When he turned, Edmund was waiting for him. "This screams unorganized rebellion."

"Maybe," he considered. "Or maybe that's what they want us to think. Or maybe they had a rogue rebel."

They moved to the dungeons, an entirely different building to the palace across from the outdoor training yard Sparrow had been at when the screams had reached him. It was a small building that had stairs leading down to an expanse of a hundred cells and six interrogation rooms.

Edmund walked with him as Sparrow remembered seeing Evony run out behind her father from the gardens. "What were you and Evony doing in the gardens?"

"She's my daughter," he responded. Then one side of his lips tipped up at Sparrow's disbelieving look. "And I wanted to talk with her. See if I detect anything...amiss. Anything to look out for."

Now Sparrow was smirking. He'd done that and hadn't found anything. But he also didn't know if his desires for her were beginning to cloud his judgment. "And?"

"I don't know. Yet."

Yes, Miss. Magician was a tricky one to read.

He heard the voices coming from one of the halls and moved in that direction, finding his men had chosen one of the interrogation rooms to chain the man into. He was the only prisoner they had.

A lowly farmhand.

If Sparrow had to guess, that's what he'd say this man was.

He had nothing against farmhands, but dimwits like this one thinking they could act with no consequence really annoyed Sparrow.

The farmhand was on his knees, the chains his men used too short to allow him to stand, and he was ready with his words when they entered. "I hope you rot."

"Aw, that's not very nice," Sparrow said as he moved before the farmhand. "Do you know who I am?"

The man's gaze finally moved from the King and met Sparrows. Then flinched away.

"I'd answer if I were you, boy." Edmund leaned back against the wall, crossing his arms before him like he was bored. The man was likely only a few years Edmund's junior, but the way the King said *boy* made him sound younger, worthless, inferior.

"The Master Assassin." Most didn't bother learning Sparrow's real name.

He crouched before the man with a cocky grin. "I consider myself a fair man...name?" His tone indicated he didn't intend on asking twice.

"Lind."

"Lind. I consider myself a fair man so I will give you the chance to explain."

"There's nothing to explain," he spit, and the man looked deranged enough for Sparrow to believe he wasn't with the rebellion, at least not in any way that mattered. "The old man was in my way so I got rid of him. I was coming for you." He turned on Edmund. "For *you*."

"Except you didn't, now, did you? He's perfectly fine." Sparrow tilted his head in that way he knew would infuriate the man even more. "Now, if you can't even kill a stable hand, what makes you think you can kill the trained King? Or me?"

Lind's face contorted with a deathly rage as his wrists

fought the chains. "You're easier, Assassin. Next time I'll just get your girl."

Sparrow was accustomed to the threats against those in his life. Especially against Rosaelia. He'd never paid them much mind and it wasn't about to start now. Even Edmund didn't care when threats were thrown the Posse's way. It was useless, those threatening never got a chance either because they ended up dead or too terrified to walk alone, better yet do anything.

"I saw you holding her out there. Pretty thing in those tight little trousers. I'll *gut* her, but I'll make sure to take my time with her first. You think she'd scream for you, *Assassin?*" The question ended in a gleeful hiss.

Sparrow froze as he realized he was getting threatened with Evony.

And for the first time in his life, the threat was getting the reaction it was intended for. His jaw ground together so hard he was liable to break his teeth.

Lind smiled cruelly with the happiness of getting a reaction out of the Master Assassin. "Yes. I'm sure she tastes amazing."

That tingling that Sparrow had begun to feel when others were touching Evony shot up his spine at the look in Lind's eyes. He schooled his reaction and smirked at the man, making sure it was vile and haunting. "It's entertaining. Believing you'll live long enough to even finish that fantasy."

The rage was back. "So kill me, Assassin! You're just the King's bitch."

Sparrow rose to his full height and looked down at the kneeled man. "I will. But I have a friend who'd like some time with you first. You've heard of Nuhmed, I presume."

Nuhmed was a prisoner they'd taken years back who lived in one of the interrogation rooms. Since the deal he'd made with the crown, he wasn't a prisoner technically. He was given proper lodgings and nourishment, and in exchange, he would be used whenever needed.

He'd been caught on charges of raping his way through a legion of men and Sparrow wasn't known as the Master Assassin simply for his skills. It was also for the methods he was prepared to use.

And though he only used Nuhmed on the worst of the worst—those who had similarly hurt women and children and deserved to feel the same things done to them—Sparrow was making an exception. He normally allowed Nuhmed to have his way with prisoners for weeks before finishing the job. Nuhmed didn't like to kill, which worked out for Sparrow because he was born to kill.

He'd never used Nuhmed for something so minuscule. But he'd also never felt a rage like this one before. All-consuming and everlasting. Lind had threatened Evony's safety, her autonomy, and Sparrow couldn't let that go.

Lind's eyes bulged out of their sockets as Edmund stood up straighter. He knew the protocol didn't call for a visit with Nuhmed. But he wouldn't argue Sparrow's decisions.

Sparrow walked out of the room while the sounds of Lind's cries and apologies followed after him. Everyone knew death was far better than any time with Nuhmed. He stopped at the base of the stairs and turned to the two guards who had brought the man in. "Take your rest. Allow him the fear of the unknown. Take him to Nuhmed around midnight. I'll finish him off tomorrow."

They nodded silently and took the stairs two at a time.

Sparrow followed them with Edmund at his back and was stopped from leaving the small building when Edmund's hand landed on his shoulder. Sparrow stared out the open door and into the beautiful spring afternoon before turning to meet his face.

Edmund looked suspicious. "Is there something I should know?"

"About?" He knew exactly what about.

"You," he answered softly. "And Evony."

Sparrow didn't answer. He didn't like lying to Edmund and he wasn't sure he could honestly answer at the moment. Because he wanted to say no. But then the fury of keeping her safe, the annoyance at anyone else's touches, the *kiss*. All of it plagued him and he knew there was something.

Edmund must have read the indecision in his eyes because he gave two small nods, squeezed Sparrow's shoulder though his eyes looked confused, and left the building.

Sparrow watched him leave with the picture of pushing Evony into the window flashing before his eyes.

✝

EVONY WAS TWIRLING around the room when he walked into the suite.

In only a large white shirt.

His large white shirt.

Her skin shined against the flickering light from the fireplace as his gaze raked her naked legs while she twirled in circles on the tips of her toes with a wide grin across her face.

He slammed the door to get her attention and she jumped in her spot, turning to face him and swaying a bit in the dizziness from the spins. Her eyes shined with the smile like she was enjoying herself immensely.

"What are you doing, Magician?"

She shrugged. "Nothing."

Then she was back to spinning, the bottoms of the large shirt flowing up with each cycle and catching his attention. "You're going to make yourself sick."

Her laugh was immense. "Worth it."

Sparrow sprawled onto the couch beneath the window and felt the light breeze from the slightly opened window on his naked torso. He'd only put on his sleeping trousers after his bath since he felt no need to dress properly with the bathing rooms so close to his suite.

He leaned back to watch her, the light silhouetting her perfectly, and if he really paid attention, he could see the browns of her nipples through the white shirt.

So he had to really not pay attention. Which was made simple with her ludicrous spins around the room. She looked ridiculous.

There was a light sheen of sweat that was mostly noticeable because of the way the firelight hit her skin, and her hair was mussed wild with her spins. Ridiculous.

He felt the firelight slowly drying the droplets of water he hadn't bothered to dry after his bath and finally witnessed the expected. She crashed.

Right into the table at the end of the room where he did his work. His gut reaction had him moving before he'd processed his actions, lunging to Evony's side as she rose to her forearms on the ground, giggles beginning to blossom.

He tried to suppress his vexed growl but didn't do too well a job. "Are you all right?"

She rose to her knees before his bent form, taking his face between her hands. "As ever, my assassin."

Her smile looked lucid, carefree, breathtaking. And he wanted a taste.

Then she was standing and before he could stop her, she'd

toppled over a stack of papers he'd had at the end of the table. "Oops."

"Evony," he growled around her giggles as a knock came at the door.

And Evony went to answer it. Great.

Sparrow was replacing the letters into a stack when he heard a servant's voice asking for him behind the door. Evony leaned into the door like it was just any other casual night and this were a normal scene.

Sparrow moved to the door, stopping just behind Evony and seeing Etel standing by the door. Her gaze flickered between his and Evony's barely dressed states—and Evony in *his* shirt—the light sheen of sweat on her and the droplets that could easily pass off as sweat on him, the muss of her hair from spinning and his from drying.

Great.

Etel's cheeks blazed red as she handed over a note. "From Sir Tristan, Master."

Sparrow tried for a small smile to lighten the mood. "Thank you, Etel."

She made a small bow and hurried on her way.

Evony pushed the door closed and leaned back into it, the smile still on her features and her eyes shining a brilliant blue.

"Rumors will spread like wildfire." He turned away from her as he found himself too distracted by the way she looked against that door.

He was back on the couch, opening the note when his gaze flickered to the soft chuckle by the door. "Rumors?"

"Do not play ignorant, Magician." He had to peel his eyes away.

He looked down to the note that told him the farmhand, Lind, hadn't known anything as had been expected. And that Tristan had taken him to await his execution in a cell after only half an hour with Nuhmed. Sparrow could easily send a note back to tell him to put *Lind* back—he wanted to, for what he'd said about Evony, he wanted to—but he'd control his urges. It wasn't normal protocol.

Evony was by his side, her hand falling to rest on his shoulder as she leaned over him. "What news have we received?"

"*I* received news of our little prisoner." He threw the paper onto the small table. If she wanted to read it, she could.

"Nothing useful, I suppose?"

"No." He leaned back into the couch again and her body followed along. Pliant, submissive to him.

"Oh well." She pushed herself up and moved to sit before the fire.

He wanted to move to her, put his hands on her, make her body submit to him the way he knew it would. He grit his teeth and strained his neck back to snap himself out of this new feeling.

CHAPTER 12
EVONY

Rosaelia was quiet, reserved, innocent.

She had a crush on Miels that was so obvious, everyone ignored it in hopes it would go away. But she was also observant, intelligent, resilient. A lot of her quietude had to do with analyzing those around her and Evony was convinced Rosaelia knew everyone else knew of her crush on Miels.

She was the Princess, born with the weight of a land on her shoulders and the politics of ruling at the forefront of her teachings. Unfortunately, she was also born naive to the world—though Evony couldn't realistically blame her for that.

It was damn near midnight and she was leaving the King's wing.

Evony was seated beneath her window in the common area of her suite waiting for Sparrow to return for the night when she noticed her twin passing by her window. If the girl was going to be sneaking round, Evony would need to teach her how to actually *sneak*.

Evony cracked her window open and jumped out to follow

her. It was in moments like these that Evony was glad the King's wing was on the ground floor—though it had been a shock when she'd first arrived at the palace.

There was a slight chill in the air as she followed the Princess into town.

If Rosaelia's innocent thoughts were anything to go off of, Evony could not fathom what the girl was doing heading into town without a cover. Had her crush on Miels and the deep blush when speaking of sex not been so blatant, Evony would've assumed she was leaving for a rendezvous.

Evony had her shield up to cover herself and felt the urge to send it toward Rosaelia as well, but that may hinder the reason behind the Princess's outing and Evony needed to know what she was up to.

When they reached the local village, as expected, Rosaelia got everyone's attention, but she didn't seem bothered by it. Her aloof expression also told Evony that the idiot thought everyone was watching her in awe rather than vile intrigue. Instead of guarding herself, she smiled as she passed every person. Smiled to every male whose gaze raked her form barely hidden behind her cloak.

What the bloody hell was she doing?

Evony followed a slightly different path so no one accidentally fell into her shield and realized that there was a magician among them, especially one that looked like the Princess. That would be too much trouble.

They were about five minutes into walking the village when Evony lost her concentration for a moment after bumping into a wagon she hadn't seen strewn haphazardly about. That slight interruption lost Rosaelia. Almost like the Princess knew she was being followed and she was waiting for the opportunity.

Impossible. It was more likely an awful coincidence, but all

Evony knew was that she had to find the Princess. That naive smile told her enough about what the Princess thought would be going on that night.

Evony pulled her shield as close to her body as she could, then stepped out into town. As much as she didn't want others to bump into her, she had a sick feeling she'd seen a group of men standing about that were no longer around either.

The path was dwindling down to a less boisterous and darker area. Fucking great.

A bout of laughter from an alley at the end of the darkened path sent Evony racing. She turned the corner to find the Princess of the Northern Lands surrounded in an alleyway by four men.

And the goofy smile was finally off of Rosaelia's face.

Evony let the shield drop from around her and immediately noticed Rosaelia's gaze shoot to her from behind the men. The fear in her green eyes was so deep that Evony thought the Princess may actually shit herself.

"Boys, boys." She toyed with the words. "What is it we have here?"

The men turned with cocky grins, then had to make a double take between her and the Princess.

"There, there're two of you?" one of them stuttered. Not in fear, but astonishment.

Evony's brows furrowed. "I don't know what you mean."

Another man, a short fat one with a slightly balding head, smiled in disgusting delight as he looked between the two of them. "Get her." He pushed the tall lanky one toward Evony. "And we can have double the fun."

Evony allowed the man to grab her arm and bring her closer. "Fun?"

"A fuck, darling." His grubby fingers began for his trousers.

"Don't worry, you'll enjoy it." His greedy eyes flicked to Rosaelia. "Won't you, you little whores?"

Evony's smile turned wicked. "Oh, I'm sure going to enjoy what happens next."

There was a spark behind the greed as he turned on Evony. "Thatta girl."

Evony tilted her head a centimeter as she smiled and kicked her leg out, getting the man in the balls as he was unbuttoning his trousers. She snapped her arm over the lanky one still holding her and heard the delightful snap of his elbow before turning on the other two. She could use her magic, but what fun would that be?

She backed up until she was before Fatty and waited for the men to rush her. She grabbed for the knives out of her boots—thankfully she hadn't changed since she didn't know if Sparrow would be headed out again—and jammed them into the two morons. And like idiots, they pulled the knives right out and dropped to their knees, blood already flowing out in a fury.

Evony righted herself and smiled wickedly as she watched their shock.

Then Fatty was on her again.

And Lanky moved for Rosaelia's shell-shocked form.

She could use her magic now. Or let events play out. Playing out definitely sounded more fun.

Fatty had one of the knives that had been pulled out of his friend in hand and was running at her. He was bigger, but she was much faster. And swifter. And trained.

She was behind him and controlling his use of his arm in moments, turning the hand with the knife so the pointed blade was aimed at his own chest. He fought her as she forced him to plunge it deep into his own chest, but to no avail.

She pushed out of the way before he fell back.

Now, she only had Lanky to worry about.

And he had a knife to the Princess's throat and a fear so feral in his eyes, it looked crazed. "Monster." He lightly tripped as he tried moving back. "You're a monster."

He held Rosaelia close to his form, but the idiot was moving in the wrong direction. He was trapping himself deeper into the alley rather than moving for the opening.

And he was taller than the Princess.

"And may I haunt you in the afterlife." Evony moved with the speed of light, pulling the knife from Fatty's chest and flinging it in Lanky's direction, watching as the point spun and landed directly between his eyelids. He went limp immediately.

And Rosaelia rushed out of his hold as he fell to the ground.

Evony evaluated her handy work. Beautiful. And surely to look like a brawl with no connection to the crown.

Now to deal with *the crown.*

"Why aren't you covered?" she bit out angrily.

Rosaelia's bewildered eyes jumped between all four men before turning and vomiting up her stomach. She heaved for a few minutes before turning back to Evony, though she was obviously trying to keep the men out of view. "I wanted to experience life outside the palace, without guards. I didn't think...I am the Princess. These are my people."

"You are a moron. This is real life," Evony translated. She scoffed. "Do not make the misfortune of believing they care for you the way you do them. Do not ever make the mistake of coming out unprotected again. If you're by yourself, cover yourself, *sister.*"

A few tears slipped from Rosaelia's eyes. "I'm sorry. I didn't know. I've never been out alone."

"That much is clear." Evony turned her sister so they could

leave the alley. "When we get home, I'm killing the men you call family."

"No! Please. Don't tell them."

Evony turned incredulous eyes on the Princess. "Are you insane? I thought I hadn't seen you train because you prefer to do so in private. I hadn't realized you were completely incapable. How irresponsible and stupid they must be to believe you didn't need it."

"Evony, please. I won't come out alone ever again."

Evony scoffed again. "Don't be ridiculous. You will not be a damsel. I won't allow you to continue on without knowing how to protect yourself. You cannot always depend on someone else's help."

Rosaelia's tears were silent as they continued to fall. But she didn't argue.

Evony stopped for only a moment into one of the taverns to get water for Rosaelia. In order to rinse her mouth of the vomit, but also to calm her racing heart. This night had undoubtedly gone different than she'd expected.

Her tears stopped about halfway to the palace, but her eyes were puffy and telling. Evony walked her to her door and sighed when the door closed before her.

Then she was walking to her door and slamming it behind her. Sparrow was sitting at one of the chairs from the table by the open window. "Where were you?"

Evony turned vicious eyes on him. "Nowhere."

His inhuman swiftness had him in front of her before she could make so much as two steps, his form drowning over her. His dark eyes demanding. "Where. Were. You?"

She looked up at him defiantly. "Why don't you tell me where you think I was, Assassin?"

"The rebellion does need a leader."

She gasped, hating that she felt the hurt enter her. "Fuck. Off."

She tried pushing past him, but he was stronger and faster. He had her slammed into the wall, a hand around her throat as he leaned down so their breaths mixed. "I can do this all night, Magician."

He wasn't hurting her, but it was evident he intended to get answers. And as the Master Assassin and therefore a master fighter, he'd be able to fight against her magic better than the average person. They'd both be drained if she didn't just give him what he wanted.

And she was so angry, she wanted to give it to him, just to hurt him too.

She growled and uselessly pushed against him. "I was following Rosaelia!"

His eyes widened, grip lightly loosening. "What?"

She stopped fighting his hold and met those chocolate browns that melted her. "I was waiting up for you when I noticed her passing the window. I followed her."

His grip was so loose, it was more resting around her throat than holding her anymore, but neither one of them moved it. "What are you talking about? Where was she going?"

Evony's earlier anger redoubled. "To the local tavern." She pushed his chest, but he didn't budge. "You ass, you never taught her to defend herself. You let her think the world was filled with *good* people."

His breath hitched and those browns filled with fear. "What happened?"

She pushed him again and this time he stumbled back. "She went out to the tavern. Completely uncloaked." Push. "A group of men noticed her." Push. "They took her into an alley-way. Have their way with *the Princess*." She spit the last words because she hated that title, hated that she was one too. And she pushed him again. "She could not protect herself." Push. "You four raised her with no training, no way to protect herself." Push. "You lot allowed her to grow up naive to the world!"

She was fuming and she could see the effect each statement was having on him. He looked broken as he searched her eyes, a shattered hope in him looking for the outcome of the night. "What happened?"

Evony still had a savage desire to knock him senseless, but she knew the terror of what could have happened was eating away at him. "Nothing." She sighed. "I took care of them."

His eyes jumped from her to the door twice before he was moving.

She grabbed his arm and used her magic to push him into the wall. Without her magic, she would've had no power over him. Even if he weren't the Master Assassin, he would've easily been able to move past her, and for that reason specifically, she was glad to have her magic's aid.

"Let go of me," he spit out as he struggled against her magic.

She softened her voice. "She's upset enough as it is, no need to add to it. I've already yelled at her enough for the both of us." There was a painful softening of his gaze as his body relaxed against the wall. "She just wants to be alone right now."

His gaze searched hers for long moments as they stood there. "Thank you."

Evony nodded and turned for bed, she needed to sleep this entire night away.

His grip was tight on her arm before she could make it a step and he had her turned to him, pulling her body into his as his free hand circled her waist. "Are *you* okay?"

Her heart fluttered at the question. She didn't want to, but she'd wanted him to worry about her too. Wanted him to want her for more than because she was the Master Magician. Wanted him to want her the way she wanted him. And it was all dangerous because hope had a funny way of always taking away everything she most desired. "I'm okay."

He didn't release her like she'd expected. Instead, his arm pulled her closer so she could feel every inch of his body against hers as his face fell to the crook of her neck and he gave her a million small nods. "Good."

✝

EVONY WASN'T sure what Sparrow would do the next morning, but she hadn't expected him to be outside her door waiting for her to walk to breakfast. He normally waited, but it was never right outside her door, almost like he'd wanted to come in there with her.

Or maybe that was the stupid hopeful heart of hers.

She hadn't promised Rosaelia she wouldn't tell, and she still wanted to kill the entire Posse, but after telling Sparrow, she wasn't sure she wanted to speak with the others anymore. Plus, a very large part of her was sure he would tell them, at least Miels and Tristan.

He still looked angry, but for once, it wasn't aimed at her.

She took his arm as usual and they walked in silence. He looked ready to murder Rosaelia, because now that he'd slept away the fear that something could've happened to her, he was enraged that she'd left on her own.

As they walked, Evony skimmed her thumb along his bicep to calm him and she could feel it working, if infinitesimally, before she dropped her hand to take his. She interlocked her fingers with his as they neared the dining hall, and he squeezed it as he took a large breath and they entered.

They were the last to arrive.

Hand in hand.

Everyone noticed, but before they could make a jab, they took in the fumes coming out of Sparrow and thought better of it.

Rosaelia visibly gulped as they moved to take their seats. Sparrow kept his hold on Evony's hand, leaving it sitting in his lap, as he stared at his 'sister.' For her part, Rosaelia stood her ground and stared back.

The servants were faster than Evony had ever seen them before, bringing in their breakfast and rushing out like they could feel the tension boiling off the Assassin and didn't want to be anywhere near him when it blew up.

No one touched their food for long moments and Evony tried brushing her thumb along the hand that still clasped hers to calm him, but he was so obviously of one mind that she doubted it was helping.

When she tried to take her hand back, he squeezed tighter and she realized it was working. Working in keeping him from raging out. Her heart jumped. That hopeful *fucking* heart of hers.

Evony finally leaned into him, realizing this could probably last forever, and whispered into his ear so only he could hear, "Drop it, love. Either tell them or drop it." She could hear his teeth gritting as he fought from telling the others. She knew he wouldn't want Edmund to hold that fear in him too. "Drop it, baby. She knows and we know." *And the others, apart from Edmund, will know soon enough.* "We'll deal with this, but for now, drop it. She cannot change what happened and you won't help by scaring her like this."

It was another long minute in which Evony remained

leaned into him, her breath tickling his ear, before he took in a large breath and turned to meet her gaze. Their faces were so close, Evony could taste his breath. He took another large breath, like he was breathing *her* in, and gave an imperceptible nod before turning to his food.

The others sighed out at the broken tension, but no one moved to break the silence.

Sparrow's hand never dropped hers, but she didn't care. She could eat with one hand.

Evony felt a nod into her mind—Gemma and James trying to get through. She opened her mind, making a three way 'call' between them.

What's going on, Eve?

Evony didn't look at them as she responded. *Rosaelia went out last night. Alone. Uncloaked.*

And? They both thought.

No training.

The sounds of their choking and utensils dropping came from the other side of the table and the room glanced over, but they recovered quickly.

None? James sounded as angry as she'd been, his face beginning to contort in his fury. *How could they raise her with no training?*

I had that argument with Sparrow last night.

And the others? Gemma asked.

Don't know. I don't intend on telling them. Sparrow will probably tell the brothers later, but there's no need for Edmund to fear what could've happened.

This is ridiculous. She needs to be trained! James sounded angrier than she had been, likely remembering what would have happened to her and Gemma had they not been trained in their years together.

And she will be. Evony was certain of that much.

✝

ROSAELIA WALKED with Evony after breakfast as they followed the men to the outdoor training grounds. Sparrow had peeled his hand away, but it had visibly been a struggle, and now he moved with Miels and Tristan on either side of him. And Evony had a feeling he was informing the two of last night's events.

"You told him," she said.

"Did you truly expect me not to?"

"No." They walked in silence and Evony noticed the way the boys stiffened and had to force themselves not to turn on Rosaelia. Then the Princess was speaking again. "Thank you. For calming him earlier." She eyed Sparrow like she wanted to stay far, far away from him. And Evony knew she could tell the others knew now too, so she'd probably want to stay away from them all.

"They're more angry with themselves for allowing this to happen." Evony didn't know why, but she felt the need to comfort her twin. "They'll calm down."

Rosaelia didn't speak but nodded her thanks.

At the training grounds, the group dispersed, but Rosaelia remained by Evony's side though she looked like she wanted to run when Sparrow stalked toward them. "You start training today."

Rosaelia swallowed but kept her head high as she looked to Evony. "Will you train me?"

Evony didn't hesitate to nod. "We'll start tomorrow. Today go to the tailors and get at least five training sets."

"Why five?"

"Why not?"

"Okay," she said softly and left the fields.

Sparrow remained by Evony's side, but his breathing was coming out harsh. He wanted to lash out and the calmness he had been able to hold during breakfast was fast breaking.

Evony placed a hand to his chest and his gaze dropped to her immediately. "I'll take care of her."

"I know." He didn't hesitate to respond.

Her lips quirked up, but it was a humorless smile. "Are you okay?"

His fists clenched at his sides. "I want to fight."

She looked to the men past his shoulder who were sparring, then back to Sparrow. As she searched the blackness of his eyes, understanding dawned on her—he didn't want to spare, he wanted to fight. And as the Master Assassin, he couldn't do so without hurting everyone, likely killing them all.

Her free hand reached for his jaw, her thumb playing with the stubble there. "Fight." Before he could argue, she added, "I'll make sure no one is hurt."

His hard-edged eyes softened infinitesimally as he understood her and she wanted to kiss him so badly in that moment.

He stepped away from her and toward his men and she took a seat on a stack of hay off to the side and watched, her magic ready to protect the men against the Master Assassin's power.

Sparrow took no mercy as he took on five at once. Round after round after round. And if Evony hadn't been there, they'd all be lying dead, she knew that much by the brunt of his power her magic took on.

CHAPTER 13
EVONY

As promised, Rosaelia's training began the next day.

Evony started the training simply by testing Rosaelia's stamina and strength. Both were surprisingly strong—though it shouldn't have been a shocker. As the Princess, Rosaelia had been taught a great many skills, just never how to defend herself.

They were just over an hour into Evony giving her twin exercise after exercise, and still, she hadn't gotten a complaint. She had a feeling the fresh memory of the other night kept her quiet.

Rosaelia shook as she attempted another sit up, and her body finally gave up and she fell back. Claps came from the entrance of the private training room and both twins gazes shot over to find Miels walking toward them. Rosaelia's already red face deepened.

And the rest of the group apart from the Assassin and the King followed behind him as he said, "Why were we not invited to the training, sister?"

Both he and Tristan had begun calling Evony sister not long ago and every time they did, a small piece of her sang with joy. Like she was fully accepted to the group and it was something she wanted so badly. She was afraid it would be pulled away from her like the fear of losing Sparrow.

"You're unwanted." Evony didn't allow the amusement to show on her face, but his smile told her he saw it in her eyes.

Both boys were better at keeping their composure around Rosaelia's night out than Sparrow had been. But even Sparrow looked calmer after his fight the day before. He'd gone so many rounds, it had been Evony's eventual interference that had stopped him. She could see that his men, though given a break as they waited for their turn again, were tired. And she'd been tired. There was only so much magic that she had and she hadn't had the same adrenaline pumping her that he'd had.

But the second she'd called out to him, knowing the exhaustion showed in her eyes, he'd stopped and moved to her. He'd rested his forehead against hers in a gesture Evony now had ingrained to memory, thanked her for the chance to let his anger out, and insisted on taking her to the infirmary to make sure she was fine. He'd settled with her allowance of walking her to their suite to head to bed early.

Miels's hand flew to his heart. "You wound us."

Her lips were losing the battle to remain stoic. "Entirely my intentions."

"Come on, Magician." Tristan stretched out his arms as he looked down at her on the mat with a seductive smile. "Let's train."

Evony laughed as she rose to stand, reaching to remove her sweater. The fabric would make it impossible to properly fight.

Dropping it to the ground, she looked up to find Tristan, Miels, and Rosaelia's horror-filled expressions. "What?"

Their eyes were stuck on her stomach.

She looked down to find that her undershirt had risen when she'd removed the top layer and her new friends were staring at the scar that raced diagonally across her torso. She pulled the shirt down and met their stares again.

"Evony?" Miels's tone was begging. It was so different from his usual manner that the hopeful part of Evony's heart ached for him.

She understood their reactions though. The scar was large and stretched from the bottom of her right breast to her left hip bone, the raised white skin ugly and contorted.

She met Gemma and James's stares and knew this was a story they could share with the Posse. "Sparrow killed a group called the Romanchi seven years ago. Two years after that, a smaller copycat group came out."

Romanchi was a rather large group of men who had taken regular girls and played with them. Tortured them. Girls who didn't have militia or guards to come to their rescue. Finding out Sparrow had killed them slowly had garnered Evony's respect for the Master Assassin instantaneously.

Gemma continued the story, "Evony's always hidden her identity so to the world, we were regular girls." Miels and Tristan stood taller, like the ramrod positions would help them keep their composure as they listened to this. "We were knocked out so Evony couldn't fight them off with magic."

"We woke up in a dungeon, the only light coming from the door in the hall that led outside. We were hung by our arms, the only reprieve was that they'd placed us across from each other so we could see one another." The chains had marred their wrists for months after they'd been found.

James scoffed. "They just wanted you to witness what they did to the other."

Evony didn't argue with him. It was exactly why they'd done it, but she was still thankful for it every day. "We were weak and they'd found us just rising from consciousness. We were beat, but most of my energy went to making sure they didn't do anything *more*—and there were so many thoughts to manipulate—so I couldn't get us out."

Gemma threw her a dirty look. She was still angry after all this time. "She also used that power to make sure more of the attack went to her. I had to *watch* them pierce her and watch her bleed out, unable to heal herself."

Evony didn't regret it. Given the options, she'd do so again.

James broke the echoing silence that followed. "It took me eight days to find them. I had others with me and we were able to make our way through the group. I hung those bastards, didn't allow my men to kill them so I could play with them for eight weeks. One week for each day they had my girls."

Evony caught Rosaelia's eyes and the distress there told her she hadn't been expecting this. A past like this from a Master. Especially as a magician, they likely assumed she lived a cozy life—which she had for the most part—and Evony knew they were coming to understand a deeper part of the life she'd lived. And a bit more guilt filled her twin's eyes that Evony had had such a different life than she had.

The moment was killed when a servant ran to the edge of the open wall to tell them dinner had been moved up so they should get cleaned up now. But Evony couldn't see the servant because her eyes locked onto Sparrow's and they weren't going anywhere else. She hadn't noticed him standing at the edge and didn't know how long he'd been there.

He was staring at her with a hard edge he hadn't even had the day before.

It was this look that made everyone fear the Master Assassin, that made him the Master Assassin. And it was this look that made Evony fall just that little bit more.

His arms were crossed over his chest and his form rigid. But he looked calm. Deathly.

From the look alone she could garner he'd heard the entire story.

Miels broke her from the stare as he grabbed her shoulders softly and brought her forehead in for a kiss. It was the kind James gave her. Brotherly and loving. And it told her he would kill the men if he could, that he wanted to in that moment.

She gave him a warm smile before he turned to Gemma, and Tristan reached for her and gave her the same brotherly embrace and kiss. Then he too was over to Gemma and the entire lot were walking out of the room.

Rosaelia watched her a moment but didn't step up. Funnily enough, as the only true sibling in the room, Evony felt the connection the least with her twin. But she acknowledged the nod of empathy Rosaelia threw her way before turning to leave.

The Princess stopped at Sparrow's shoulder, a hand there to whisper something in his ear, but his stare never left Evony. The entire time, they were on her. And they were deathly and inviting Evony to spend the rest of her days before him.

When the room was clear of anyone but them, Evony walked up to him. She stopped a foot away and placed her hands to his rigid arms and allowed her thumbs to soothe him. "Sparrow."

It was clear his strength was in controlling his breathing as he barely rasped out, "Let me see it."

So he hadn't been around long enough to see the scar, just hear the story.

"Sparrow," she tried to argue, but the argument was

landing on deaf ears. His gaze was locked on her stomach and the demanding black filled every edge of it.

"Let me see it," he said through clenched teeth.

Evony sighed as her hands dropped from his arms to lift her shirt. She let the material settle over her breasts as she left her stomach open to him.

He drank in the ragged line across the rest of her pristine skin, and it was like all the strength evaporated from his body as his arms fell limp. He dropped to his knees before her. His expression told her it was worse than he'd been expecting.

She watched as he reached a tentative, shaking hand to it and lightly grazed it. His hand shook harder, like touching it made it more real, and it broke Evony to see him so lost. She held his hand to her stomach and heard the little groan escape him before he looked up to her.

Those eyes were everything she wanted. "I wouldn't have killed them. I would've kept them alive to play with for the rest of my life."

Her heart jumped. What a declaration. What a hopeful beat of her heart.

She grazed her free hand over his stubbled face before cradling his jaw, her thumb brushing his lips. "I'm okay."

✝

His grip had been so tight on the walk to the baths that Evony almost worried circulation would stop to her hand.

They'd separated at the washrooms and Evony had found a private stall in the women's rooms to fall back into a stream bath. The taps worked quickly to heat up and she'd lain beneath it to feel the beat of the water on her skin as it filled the bath.

Her mind was filled with Sparrow, but unlike her normal thoughts about him, this time it was filled with their last few moments together. Given his nature, she may have expected some protectiveness, but never in her years would she have thought it would affect him so. Not only the memory of him dropping to his knees, but the helpless look in his eyes. It was all more than just protective. It was possession and affection and breathless need and everything that Evony forbade herself to feel around him. Forbade herself to see in him because there was no way he cared for her like that.

Evony tipped her head back to the still falling water and allowed the water to stammer against her face as her thoughts clung to the memory of Sparrow on his knees, then sprang to the memory of him pushing her against the window and his tongue fighting hers.

She didn't know what she'd been expecting—hadn't really thought about it—but she hadn't expected to find him outside the washrooms, waiting for her. His eyes snapped to hers as she walked out in a dress left in the washrooms for anyone that needed it. Given this was the King's wing, she, Gemma, and Rosaelia were the only ones that did.

She placed a hand over his heart and felt it stutter under her touch. "Sparrow, you cannot torture yourself like this. If was five years ago. It's over."

His jaw twitched like he was fighting himself as he studied her. His voice was soft and hoarse when he spoke, "I can't get the image out of my mind."

She let her hands move up his chest a couple of times before wrapping around him. His hands didn't hesitate to embrace her, his face falling into the crook of her shoulder as he squeezed her into him.

They missed dinner standing there and Evony couldn't find an ounce of herself that cared.

It scared her, this feeling. Knowing the joke she'd started when she'd arrived at the palace was turning serious and she was truly falling. And the fear of knowing she'd be kicked out of the family after she was done being used.

†

Sparrow had the servants deliver dinner to their suite. She watched as he rolled the carts holding their food to the corner table as the familiar nod nudged into her mind.

She opened the communication between her friends. *Yes?*

Where were you two? Gemma asked more serious than teasing. Given the conversation they had ended things on before dinner, it was a reasonable tone.

Evony breathed out watching Sparrow set their small table. *It affected him more than I could have imagined.* She'd never hide the truth from them, but she could tell them the whole story later.

Are you hungry? Should I get you something? James asked, always the older brother.

Evony's lips twitched upward. *Sparrow ordered dinner. It's here now.*

Okay. Then eat. Gemma finished the conversation and they were out of her mind.

She rose to meet him and took her seat as she watched him sit with his back to the wall. "Is this a date, Assassin?"

He instantly picked up the tease in her tone and he looked almost grateful for it. "Do not inflate your ego, Magician."

Dinner was a large steak—that she definitely wasn't going to finish—mashed potatoes, and steamed vegetables. She cut the steak that Sparrow would no doubt finish for her and brought it to her mouth. She knew the little moan she made would bring a bit more normalcy to their relationship.

His dark brown orbs were stuck on her mouth and her lips quirked up as she leaned over the table with a finger reaching for his lips. "Is that drool, Assassin?"

He pushed back, throwing her a death glare that was far too teasing for Evony's sanity, and started on his dinner.

CHAPTER 14
SPARROW

He still thought about it, almost on an hourly basis. The scar was ingrained in his memory, and the picture of her hanging by her arms as they pierced her plagued his nightmares. He'd find a way to overcome this, but he doubted he would ever be rid of the nauseated feeling that rushed him at the thought. He wanted to kiss every inch of that scar, praise it for the strength it signified.

"You know if we didn't look alike, I'd think it were her beauty that piqued the three of your interests. But that's impossible since she's my twin." Rosaelia twirled into his line of sight.

Sparrow quirked a brow at her from over the stack he had laid out on the small circular table on the top floor of the palace. It was the exact room he'd been in the first time he'd caught the Magician on their grounds.

"Is it because she's a magician and it intrigues you lot? She's got the three of you hooked around her little finger."

The three of them. Meaning Miels and Tristan too.

Sparrow didn't like the sound of that. Even though they

called her sister and likely saw her in the same way they saw Rosaelia, Sparrow didn't like that she'd garnered their attention as well.

"Oh?" He tried not to sound too bitter.

She laughed because she could easily read his annoyed tones. Always had been able to. "Except they kissed her and walked away. You dropped to your knees for her."

His eyes widened imperceptibly. He'd thought they'd all been long gone by the time Evony stepped before him. Though, to be fair, he hadn't exactly been paying attention to them. He'd been too focused on his magician.

"I've never seen you react like that, Spar." The teasing was gone.

Sparrow leaned back in his chair and stared into space. Evony's eyes were always at the forefront of his mind and as he thought back to what she'd said—the story of what she and Gemma had gone through—he knew it was more than that. "I stopped them. Romanchi. But I didn't think to check in for copycat groups. I've only ever had to deal with a copycat group once before and that was two years ago. I hadn't thought of it before and I think that's what kills me the most—how many women they'd gone through before James found them. Every time I stop one of those *fucking* groups, I just try to think of the future, that the women and children are living their lives now. But I'd never considered the scars that would forever remind them of that time. I'd never thought too much of it past torturing and killing the fuckers that did it."

Rosaelia sat beside him and took his hand softly into hers. She waited until his eyes met hers. "Sparrow, you've done so much good for this world, it's impossible for you to have done any more. Even as a Master."

"It feels impossible."

"I know. I cannot understand it as I am not the hero you

are,"—he scoffed at the remark, but she ignored it—"but I know that you always wish to have done more. You just need to remember that you cannot hold on to your every experience. *Because* you have many more people to save and protect."

"It's like now that it's in my head, I keep thinking they should be broken from what they've experienced. Their smiles not as wide; the spark in their eyes not as bright; their aura heavy with fear."

"Because that's reasonable, Spar."

"But they're stronger than that. I know they are. Now, I know. Because now I have someone in my life that wears that scar every day and still, she has a lightness to her that shouldn't be possible. I don't know how any of that fits together."

"She is an anomaly." Rosaelia smiled lovingly.

Sparrow looked out the window over his shoulder to the spot she'd been crouched that first time she'd visited the palace six years prior. "I can't get over what's happened to those women."

A beat of silence passed before Rosaelia asked, "Those women or that woman?"

When Sparrow met her emerald greens, he couldn't fathom how anyone thought they looked alike. This face staring back at him was one of a sister. That other one, the one that was currently no doubt fiddling through his shirts to borrow, was entirely different. "Her presence is a constant reminder that I should've checked for more."

Her smile was warm and her eyes shined with a spark. "Or it's a constant reminder that you have a working heart, brother."

His lips twisted down. "I've always had one. My heart has always pumped to shield and protect. Especially women."

"But you've never wanted one for yourself."

"Ro." He looked incredulously at her. "Please."

Her lips quirked up. "Deny it all you want, brother, but you dropped to your knees! And it wasn't because of the nastiness of the scar. It was because it was done to *her*." She brought his hand up to her lips for a kiss. "You've never dropped to your knees before, Master Assassin."

He sighed, unwilling to argue further, and looked out the window again. "I know."

✝

LIKE HE DIDN'T HAVE enough horrors plaguing his thoughts with the image of Evony hanging, he now had to deal with a visiting lord. He hated when they wanted to visit.

Sometimes it was for a specific reason. Other times it was because they were passing through. And the most annoying— and thankfully least common of the lot—it was just because. And usually those "because" reasons were that they wanted some tie to the palace, and with Rosaelia the only available contestant, they would try to woo her. It was those times that Sparrow loved that his little sister had a crush on his best friend. Though Rosaelia was smart enough not to fall for their ludicrous suggestions, even if she hadn't been infatuated with Miels. Always had been.

But this time, there would be two new members of the family to present. Gemma and Evony were passing off as sisters and cousins to Rosaelia, so they'd both be considered blood to the throne. And since Gemma was already married, it was Evony's hand that would be favored.

Especially since she looked exactly like the Princess, it was the more favorable of the hands.

It was for that reason specifically that Sparrow was especially not looking forward to Lord Alexei's visit. He was a cocky son of a bitch from the northernmost part of the lands, and though he was attractive, he was a meager little bitch. Sparrow hated him.

He had no doubts the fucker would try to win Evony's hand.

Though lords were not always accepted by their entire group, with the new members—and Evony's obvious likeness—Sparrow found it paramount to get the introductions out of the way immediately.

He stood out at the base of the stairs that lead up to the palace, Evony a mere three steps behind him and Rosaelia on his other side. The sooner the comparison was acknowledged, the quicker this would go.

The others stood about the stairs, with Miels and Tristan taking either end in case a need to protect the twins was in order, and Gemma and James a few steps before the King at the very top. It wasn't a large stairway, but it still showed his superiority.

The carriage carrying the lord stopped before them with a rattle of another carrying only luggage behind it. Another reason he hated these fucking lords. They believed themselves so mighty, they'd pack an entire town's worth of clothing for a week's visit. It was like the fucker already believed himself moved in.

Alexei stepped out with a superiority he didn't deserve, even in the town he lorded over. And his gaze instantly latched on Rosaelia, then Evony. And jumped with delighted intrigue and surprise.

When he finally pushed himself out of the shock, Alexei forced his eyes up to Edmund and stepped up a few paces, then bowed to the King. "King Edmund."

Then his gaze dropped to the twins, and he didn't look like

he knew which side to bow to—though it should've been immensely obvious by the way they dressed. It brought Sparrow immense pleasure that Rosaelia waited a few seconds before clearing her throat to indicate which she was. "Princess Rosaelia."

And finally, his gaze met Sparrow's before him. "Master Assassin."

Half the lords—really most of them—didn't acknowledge Miels and Tristan the way they ought to, and although it bothered Sparrow, it ended up working in their favor that the two were hardly acknowledged or recognized.

Then Alexei's gaze was on Evony, the intrigue so deep in his light brown orbs that he looked to be stripping her right where she stood. Like the likeness to the Princess already gave her away as blood, therefore a viable option as his missus. That cocky smirk he wore told Sparrow he believed this would be an easy win and that's why the twinkle in his eyes was already undressing her.

Sparrow was going to kill him. If he kept looking at her like that, he would live up to his Master Assassin reputation and kill the lord. He growled to garner the fucker's attention.

Mischievous eyes met with his brown ones. "And who do we have here?"

Sparrow didn't know where the next words came from, but they felt right. "My betrothed."

Mine.

The twinkle was immediately replaced with fear in Alexei's eyes. Good.

But the silence behind him was deafening too. He couldn't have the Posse ruin this for him. He needed Evony claimed, because there was no way he would allow this moron to lay a hand on her.

Alexei looked as if he were about to speak—his interpretation of the reactions around them obviously quelling a bit of the fear—when Evony stepped down the steps and stopped at Sparrow's side. Her hand moved to rest in the crook of his arm like it had a million times before. "I am Princess Rosaelia's cousin. I took my mother's genes while my sister, Gemma"— she pointed behind her—"took our father's genes. But yes, I am also Sparrow's betrothed."

He'd never experienced a firework show, but Sparrow had a feeling the same effect was taking place in his chest as she claimed him as hers. Claimed herself as his.

Alexei's eyes shot between the two of them before stopping on Evony. "It seems your family was quite surprised by the announcement."

"It is new." Evony easily smiled. "I was given leave to announce it, but I must say I truly enjoyed the possessive nature of Sparrow's words." The teasing was back in her tone, and Sparrow knew he'd be getting an earful of it later.

"I see." Alexei was analyzing the words like there was a work around on them.

Tristan interrupted just as another growl was forming deep in Sparrow's throat. "Your rooms are ready, Lord Alexei. The servants are aware of your stay and will escort you. We will see you for dinner."

Alexei's gaze didn't leave Evony as he took the hint that he was dismissed and followed the servants into the palace and out of sight.

Sparrow inhaled, needing the fresh air to wipe out the fury that was filling him before he turned around and killed Alexei for the way he still looked at Evony. She was *his*.

Evony's lips were on his bicep as her arms circled it, and she looked up at him through her lashes. "Are you well, my love?"

He took in a large inhale before meeting her ocean blues.

They crashed into him like a tsunami ready to break down every barrier. "Are you not angry with me?" *For claiming you without your permission?*

Her smile was light, but sinister. She kissed his bicep and left one hand holding his arm as the other dropped into his hand before they turned to follow the others.

He still wanted to hear her answer to his question. But apparently, that would have to wait until after their meeting with the Posse in the King's suite common area.

The doors were barely closed when Edmund turned on him. "Your betrothed?"

Sparrow forced a neutral expression but found it difficult with Evony still on his arm, still holding his hand. "He would have heard we're sharing quarters. Better he believes us involved than question it any further. Especially with Evony's constant antics. It would be telling of a Southerner in a committed relationship."

Sparrow doubted he believed him. Edmund had already been suspicious of anything going on between the two of them, and this declaration definitely wouldn't have helped.

Rosaelia turned to her twin. "And you? You did not look surprised at all to hear the news. Did you two plan this?"

He could feel the imprint of Evony's wide smile against his arm and had to muster his lifetime of training to school his reaction to it, when in reality he wanted to push her against the wall and kiss that grin raw.

She hugged his arm just a little bit tighter as she said, "Absolutely not. I don't think he even knew he would say it before it left his mouth. But if it's the Assassin's betrothed I must be, it's the Assassin's betrothed I shall be."

James fell onto the couch with a shining grin as he looked to Sparrow. "Lords help you."

Edmund's sharp eyes were still on him when he finally

caved. "I guess the positive here is that word will spread like wildfire that the Master Assassin is engaged, and all the lords will know you are not free to ask for. They've already been barred from asking for Rosaelia any longer so we won't have idiotic visits from those morons."

"They are morons, yet they run these towns of yours?" Gemma teased.

Edmund rolled his eyes. "Lordship runs in the family. It is passed down and continues to be so because they are taught from birth how to run their estates and villages. They are cocky morons, but they do their jobs. Which reminds me, I have one to do. I have three meetings before dinner and will be in the council rooms if I'm needed."

"Yes, sir," James joked as he reached for his wife's hand and pulled her out. "We have a meeting we must discuss as well. We will be in our suite."

Those two were animals the amount they fucked. Sparrow couldn't imagine Evony dealing with it their entire lives. Well, since the two had begun sleeping together.

Rosaelia tugged on both Tristan and Miels's arms. "We have a meeting too."

"No, we don't." Miels looked down to her confused.

She pinched his arm. "Yes, we do." And pulled them both out of the room.

Evony giggled into his arm and he finally looked down to her. "My twin is obviously on my side. I didn't expect her to give us some much needed alone time."

"Magician," he bit out to control his urge to throw her against that wall. "Behave."

She finally released him and took a couple steps back. "I don't want to behave."

"No. You never do." He squeezed his eyes shut to give

himself strength, then turned to meet hers. "What do you want, Magician?"

"I want to kiss you again," she spoke plainly, not an ounce of shyness in her tone.

His heart sped up. Those were the exact words he hadn't known he'd needed. And they were controlling him entirely from the moment they filled the air.

"Thank the heavens," he whispered as he rushed her and did as he'd been yearning to do all day. He took her face in his hands and pushed her into the wall, his lips finding hers immediately. They both moaned the moment it happened, and it was so much better than Sparrow remembered it.

It was like breathing in a life source. She was intoxicating and he needed to have all of her.

His hands moved of their own accord, slipping from her face to the backs of her thighs and hefting her up so her legs wrapped around his waist. This time when he slammed her into the wall, his cock fit perfectly into her cunt and he groaned at the pure pleasure of it. It was moments like these that he loved that she preferred trousers over dresses with their thicker layers.

And finally, he allowed his tongue the chance to make its way into her greedy, ready mouth.

Her fingers messed into his hair, and she pulled at the roots as his tongue fucked her mouth the way his cock wanted to fuck her pussy. It was a ravenous need to taste every bit of the inside of her mouth, memorize every little bit about her to dream about when he went to bed that night and every night following.

"Oh, my!" A shocked yelp came from beside them and Sparrow instantly pulled away to find two servants wide eyed at the door. "I am sorry, Master. The King told us to clean the tea from the tables. We didn't know..."

Her friend was pulling her out as they both bowed in apology and closed the door behind them.

Evony's giggles broke the moment and Sparrow turned to her, his mind coming back to him and telling him how stupid of an idea this had been. "At least Alexei will definitely have nothing to doubt now."

Sparrow grumbled and finally released the hold his hips and hands had on her so she could drop back to the ground. "We shouldn't have done that."

She didn't look perturbed by the rejection as she smiled seductively up at him. "On the contrary, we shouldn't have stopped."

"Evony," he growled.

She stood on the tips of her toes so her lips pressed against his as she smirked. "Behave?"

He nodded because he couldn't find it in himself to speak. But he made sure his eyes held no joking manner to them.

She nibbled on his bottom lip before finally pulling away with a chuckle as she took his hand and headed out. "I'm so glad you're mine."

CHAPTER 15

SPARROW

Sparrow normally didn't train at night. But he couldn't get the feeling of her body pressed against his, her legs wrapped around his hips, her hands in his hair, out of his mind.

So he would punch the hanging sandbag until his hands were raw and his mind too tired to think of anything but sleep.

"Rumor has it you two were caught in the King's suite." Tristan's joking voice filled the air. Of course the moron twins had found him.

"You know"—Miels smirked as he threw an arm up to lean into and watched Sparrow. "When we thought she may like companionship and you might be her option, I never would've fathomed it to be true. And best of all, you want her back."

"Oh." Tristan moved to Sparrow's other side so they could both watch him. "Looks like he's ignoring us again, brother."

"Yes, he seems to always do that when we speak of the Magician." There was that cocky grin that normally got women puddy at his feet. "So tell me, Tris, do you think the rumors are true? He got caught in the King's suite?"

"I would have to believe so," Tristan boasted and Sparrow continued punching the bag and trying to ignore them. "They were caught. I mean, it's not like it could have been misinterpreted like the other rumor of them sweaty and barely dressed when my missive was sent."

"Ah, yes, the one that made it adamantly clear that the Master Assassin and the Princess's cousin were definitely fucking in that suite."

"Fuck off," Sparrow finally spit out because he knew that they knew it wasn't true.

Tristan crossed his arms before his chest and grinned. "So it is not true that my letter was delivered to you as moans and laughs were heard, then sweat and barely clothed individuals seen?"

Sparrow didn't want to entertain their line of discussion, but he couldn't help it as he punched the bag with his bare knuckles. "I had just come out of the baths so I wore only my trousers. I wasn't sweating, it was water. And we weren't moaning, she hit the table and fell."

Miels tsked as he crossed his arms. "From what I hear she was in *your* shirt."

"So she likes wearing my shirts. It does not mean anything."

"Like the kiss in Edmund's suite didn't mean anything?" Tristan asked.

"Exactly." Sparrow had to grit his jaw to force the word out.

"He's back to denying it, brother." Miels threw his head back. "What are we to do with you, Spar?"

"Fuck off," he said again because talking about his time with her was definitely not aiding in forgetting about his time with her.

"And now you're betrothed," Tristan continued. "You have the servants in a tizzy. I cannot tell you the excitement that is going about. Some are saying they knew it was more than just sex from the beginning, others are saying they cannot believe anyone would interest the Assassin."

"And others say they cannot believe anyone so unafraid of him as Miss Evony." Miels watched him. "Those are my favorite."

"Mine too," Tristan added. "Though I am a bit perturbed that the lord was told before I was of such a betrothal."

Miels laughed.

Tristan's tone grew a bit more serious—but only a bit. "It is a high claim, brother. And not something that can be brushed aside when Alexei is gone."

Sparrow knew that much. And hated his treacherous heart for loving that it meant Evony was stuck as his.

"I believe that is *his* favorite part," Miels suggested.

"Will you two fuck off," Sparrow growled as he punched harder, one after the other after the other.

"If you answer me a question." Miels's smirk was so wide, it was blinding even from Sparrow's periphery. "Does she taste nice, brother?"

Sparrow felt the fumes coming from his nostrils but didn't interact.

"Does she feel nice, brother?" Tristan joined.

They both laughed when Sparrow's punches became more animalistic.

"He won't tell us, Tris. But let me tell you"—Sparrow could feel Miels's stare as the next words hit home—"I do wonder what those *lips* taste like."

His body froze on its own accord. He knew Miels was joking, knew he would never attempt such a thing, but all he could focus on were the flames that sprung before his eyes. Because he was going to kill his brother for even suggesting such a thing.

He didn't realize he'd moved until Miels was pinned against the far wall, Sparrow's hands tightly wound around his throat and cutting off circulation. The teasing glint in his eyes quickly turned to fear as he fought against Sparrow's hold but couldn't get out.

Sparrow felt another pressure from behind him. Two hands gripping at his shoulders and trying to pull him off. But all he could focus on was the rage that entered him every time *anyone* tried to touch his magician.

She was *his*. And that strength that had kept him from killing Alexei out on the steps was only because she'd been holding him. He didn't know if he could control himself otherwise.

Miels was turning white under him when he felt a kick to his balls. It still wasn't enough to loosen his grip, but it got him out of his thoughts and back to the present. Where Tristan was yelling at him to release Miels.

And that's when Sparrow realized he'd been using his Master strength—something he never actually used on his men—on Miels. His brother.

His grip went limp immediately and he watched Miels take in large inhalations against the wall. But all Sparrow could think to say was, "Those lips taste like mine."

"Understood," he rasped out.

Tristan pulled Sparrow away from Miels and moved to stand between the two of them. "Calm down, brother. You know he didn't mean it. We could see she's yours, has been since the moment she revealed herself in that meeting."

Sparrow didn't answer because he couldn't. He felt ashamed for almost killing his brother over a meaningless comment. And he felt annoyed at the Magician for making him feel this way about her. And angry with himself for allowing himself to feel anything at all for her.

Miels stood up tall again, the smirk beginning to blossom once more. "And all I did was threaten to kiss her. What do you reckon he would've done to me if I'd insinuated at any more?"

Sparrow growled but didn't move for him. He knew it was all jokes and with a clear head, he could stop himself from the jealous urge to eradicate the blonde's existence.

Tristan laughed and punched his arm. "Don't you think you've come close to death enough as it is for today?"

Miels laughed and moved up to Sparrow, his hand resting on Sparrow's shoulder so that their eyes met. "You know I am only joking, brother. I would never take her away from you— couldn't even if I wanted to, that woman only has eyes for you. But even if I could, she's given life into you that I would never play with." His other hand gripped his shoulder so he forced Sparrow to meet him man-to-man. "And more importantly, you need to know that when I call her sister, it is for a reason. That is all she is to me."

"I know," Sparrow finally breathed.

And he saw the understanding in Miels's eyes that he couldn't help the reaction. His brother wouldn't be angry with him, but fuck, Sparrow hated this reaction he had.

✝

IT WAS ALMOST therapeutic that Sparrow needed to leave on a mission the next day. That much needed time away from the magician. It was more than therapeutic. It was vital.

He was with three of his men on a—presumably—non-rebellion related matter. They were following a lead one of Sparrow's spies had found regarding the day-to-day burglaries and smugglers that every nation had to deal with. And when a rebellion wasn't brewing, and fuckers like Romanchi about, they were the things Sparrow dealt with.

And they were the easiest of jobs.

Sparrow had secretly wanted a more straining task. Something that would allow him to blow through the anger that still riddled within him at the scar that forever marred Evony's stomach.

The smugglers always believed themselves hardened criminals until they were face-to-face with the Master Assassin. Then they weren't so tough. They were begging at Sparrow's feet.

Sparrow and his men were currently hidden in large bushes as the rumble of wagons came at them. Part of the job was finding them in the act, and patience was a very important key.

Two men led the group—obviously the ringmasters of this escapade—as they laughed at some inane joke.

And the smell of ale was strong.

Northerners didn't normally drink alcohol. But smuggling Northerners didn't always follow the same customs.

Five men followed the first two, in position and stoically marching. The wagon behind them was much larger than any Sparrow had been expecting. And surrounding it was another ten men. Smugglers weren't normally this large in order to avoid getting caught. So this could be legit.

Another ten followed around a second large wagon behind that one.

Then another ten on horses carrying tents and food.

This felt too organized for a smugglers group. There were only two groups ever like this. The first were the genuine merchants of luxuries moving from village to village to drop off items, and even they didn't have so many guarding their things.

And the second left a sick feeling in the pit of Sparrow's stomach as he watched them.

One of the leaders made a pause and turned with claims of hunger.

It was the smirk from one of the standing guards that solidified this as option two in Sparrow's mind. "For what?"

The responding smirk was just as sickening. "Meal first." He turned to the wagons. "Dessert after."

That more difficult job Sparrow had wanted? Check.

And maybe it was the fact that these fuckers were the exact kind that had taken his magician—because they were always calm on the outside and savages once they got the women alone—that got Sparrow's blood boiling more deathly than usual.

And that meant something because he was always the most deathly when he was stopping these fuckers.

Sparrow threw their entire plan aside and stepped out of the bush, knowing his men would be confused but would play along.

"Take the wagons," he called to them, knowing they would wait for their opportunity before allowing themselves to be seen.

The leader that had been joking of desserts grinned at him, though the look in his eyes was pissed. Almost like he was attempting to be terrifying, but it was merely humorous to Sparrow. "And who do you believe yourself to be?"

"An assassin." Sparrow's lips quirked up as he met the man's stare.

He laughed, obviously believing himself superior with his forty men against Sparrow's lonesome figure. "Does the assassin have a name?"

He was only a foot away when Sparrow's eyes shined. "You may call me Master."

The man narrowed his gaze, the obvious affront to being ordered to call him *master* clouding his thoughts.

But it didn't take long for those thoughts to come together.

The man's eyes widened just as the quirk of Sparrow's lips turned to a smirk and he jut his fist out, hooking the man up the nose, knowing he would be out immediately.

Easy fucker.

When Sparrow looked up to the others, they were stupid enough to have their swords out as if they could actually fight him. As if the fury of what had happened to Evony because of lowlifes like them wasn't thumping through every fiber of his body.

His Master speed and strength had him before three of them in a moment, taking the sword from one and skewering all three of the others with it. He was on another two before the attack could even register to the fuckers.

He had ones neck snapped back as the other tried to swing at him. Another three were coming fast.

The rumble of joy spread through Sparrow as he waited for all four to get close enough before moving out of the way and watching them skewer one another. Only three fell.

More were coming at him as his periphery picked up that the smarter—and more cowardly—of the lot were beginning to shuffle back, obviously preparing to run.

Sparrow made his way through the masses in moments. Neck snap, punch to the face and crack of the skull, kick to the balls and punch up the nose, swiped kicks to their heads that would crack their skulls with the sheer force of his Master strength. More snapped necks because he especially loved the feeling of the crack beneath his hands. These lowlifes deserved far worse. Every asshole who dared put his Evony in danger deserved far worse.

The episode ended with a final hook to the nose that blew the fuckers brains back.

All in only a couple of minutes. It was easy when his victims were useless fighters.

Sparrow could see his men coming out of the bushes then, moving for the wagons.

He opened the pocket by his thigh and pulled out the throwing stars for the runners. He only had five, but that was all he needed. They were like boomerangs the way they swung in the air and took two or three out each.

And just like that, Sparrow had them all dead. In minutes.

Though he was sure his men could've easily handled this mess of cowards. They were so undertrained that even had Sparrow not been a Master, he would've been able to kill every last one of these scumbags. Just would've taken longer.

He turned in his spot, eyeing the bloodshed around him and felt a breath of relief to have them out of this world. Not only for Evony's sake, but for that of every woman in the lands.

When his attention finally landed on the wagons and the women cowering as his men helped them out, he could only say one thing. "Take them to safety."

There were at least twelve in each wagon and he couldn't force himself to look at them. It would bring up the nightmares of Evony back to the forefront of his mind, and it already took everything in him to suppress those images.

When they were gone, he found a tree so tall he would be hidden without any efforts and sat atop a branch to view his handiwork laid out on the forest grounds.

He forced his mind not to hang on to anything and to clear of everything but the scene around him as he crouched on a branch. And it was working to calm him, a gentleness entering him that he hadn't felt since before the Magician's appearance into his life.

He's trying to convince me to drop you and take him instead. A more advantageous marriage apparently.

Sparrow nearly fell off the branch, catching himself on the branch beside him before he completely toppled over. What the fuck. That was Evony's voice in his mind.

I'm sorry. Did I distract you? Please don't hurt yourself. I need that body primed and ready when you get back.

Definitely Evony. But he was nowhere near the palace.

Could he talk back? *Evony?*

Mm, I love when you say my name.

Sparrow sighed and tried to relax back onto his branch. *Evony, what are you doing?*

I'm telling you, my betrothed, that Alexei just sat me in the dining hall to convince me to drop you and marry him instead.

Oh, the moron was lucky he was far, far away from the palace. It would take him hours before he made it back, but fuck, did he want to bludgeon the man for his attempts.

Especially to *his* Evony.

No. She wasn't his Evony. It was a fake betrothal.

And what did you say?

Aw, love, no need to worry. I'm all yours.

A growl vibrated out of him without his realization, but he couldn't control it. He loved the sound of that from her. Loved the acknowledgment from the Magician herself declaring that she was his. He hated that he loved it so much.

I'm working, Magician.

He even heard her laugh in his mind. That beautiful fucking laugh. *Just get home soon, my assassin.*

She was gone and his mind was entirely his again.

Now he felt an urgency he hadn't before to finish this and get home. Soon.

CHAPTER 16

EVONY

Sparrow arrived back to the palace just before dinner, blood and sweat still sticking to him when he entered the dining hall. He should've gone to the bathing rooms then had dinner sent to the suite, but Evony had watched his dark and brooding form enter as she'd stood off to the side with Gemma and James.

They'd been laughing about Alexei's attempts when Sparrow moved for her and his hand rested at the small of her back. She'd merely smiled at him like the action didn't cause a million little butterflies up her every inch.

And he'd glared at Alexei.

All.

Through.

Dinner.

The little lord had been perplexed through the entire meal at the glares he received. Probably considering Sparrow had just arrived to the palace, so there was no way for him yet to know about Alexei's attempts at taking his bride. He'd squirmed and Evony had enjoyed every moment of Sparrow's jealousy.

But she'd sent him to the bathing rooms after dinner. He needed the wash, the fresh feeling on his skin.

He'd walked back into their suite in his sleeping trousers and nothing else. Evony loved this look.

Then his gaze dropped to her form as she sat before the hearth—in his shirt and nothing else—and walked right up to her.

She didn't know how she'd done it, but Evony had somehow convinced the Master Assassin to play a game of thumb war as they sat cross legged before the hearth. The game had gone from one to two to three and now she'd stopped counting.

Their conversations had moved as well, from playful and teasing to genuine and telling. And somehow led to a place Evony always thought she would only have with Gemma and James.

"Why is it only the three of you, Magician? Why has there never been anyone else?"

"Our relationship is an anomaly to me. I cannot form real relationships without the person knowing I'm the Master Magician." Their thumbs fought for dominance, their knees lying atop one another as they moved closer with each game. "And once people know, they want to use it to their advantage. Or they get scared of me. That didn't happen with Gemma and James. Shit, Gemma knew me before I was considered a Master and she's always treated me like a real sister. Though she likes to play the older game a little too much sometimes." She laughed. "But others, they don't. James was different, it clicked with him, but it's not like that usually. He saw me as a sister instantly and he's protected me ever since. But I've had to wipe a few memories because of it. Because we think there's someone else we can trust wholly and it turns out we were wrong. It's not something I like to do, I feel like it gives me *too much* power. But I had to. And it's taught me that if I don't try to form relationships, my trust cannot be broken. We've all learned it, but I think me especially."

Their thumbs fought before his inevitably won. "Do you trust us?"

She didn't look at him as she answered, focusing her attention on the new game they were starting. "I don't want to."

"Because it scares you?"

She nodded though she wasn't sure if he was watching her or their thumbs. She felt the weight of revealing that side of her in the silence that followed, and she didn't even try to fight before he won the next round.

They were starting the next round when he said, "I was orphaned. That's how I got taken in by the King." He took a large breath. "And how my assassin skills came out."

Evony's eyes shot up to meet his and watched his gaze lower to their hands. No one truly knew the story of how the Northern Lands King came into possession of the Master Assassin.

And absolutely no one knew how the Master Assassin came about his skills. He'd been more forthcoming than her at his Masters interrogation, but not entirely so.

"My mother left when I was a baby. My father went to the King for employment not long after that and received it. He was the land's best sword maker and always got personal visits from the King."

Evony dropped her gaze to their fingers and watched them dance around each other.

"I was eight years old when he was killed. A group of ten from the Island Nation going after the best sword maker. When I came out shaking and crying, they looked to me almost like they didn't want to, but they'd get rid of me too. But I didn't care about that. All I cared about was that my father was lying on that ground and his chest was no longer rising and falling. I slayed ten grown barbarians and barely broke a sweat. Then I stayed in the house with all the bodies around me, with my father's bloodied body, for a week before the King came for a visit. He had five men with him, who carried out my father and cleaned the house. Edmund carried me out so gently. He gave my father a proper burial and took me in as his own." Unsurprisingly, his large thumb overtook hers once more. "And not only because of the assassin skill, though that's what everyone assumes."

She pulled her thumb out from under his and got ready for the next game but didn't start it. Instead, she dropped their joined hands to lie on their legs. She looked up to find his attention on her. "I know he loves you."

His lips didn't quirk, but his eyes shined down at her. "It was a month after the Queen was taken. You were taken."

Evony's heart raced at the attention and she dropped her gaze to their joined hands, moving her free hand to hover over the top of his and draw on it with a finger. She didn't meet his stare as she asked, "What happened to the home?"

His free hand fell to rest on her bare knee while his fingertips grazed her skin in small circles. "It's still mine. On the coast by the Southeast of our lands."

Her lips twitched in a grin she tried to suppress as she looked up at him. "By the castle I was offered?"

His eyes shined and he didn't try to hide the smile. "A mile north."

She shook her head and laughed. "I knew you were lying about no spies."

"Was not. I would not be a spy, just a neighbor."

Her finger stopped drawing on his hand and dropped so

that both of her hands clasped his as she watched him. Just watched. He was beautiful. She hadn't been lying those weeks prior when she'd said he was hypnotizing.

And the way he watched her sent shivers down her spine.

Her voice was low, barely over a whisper, when she spoke. "Do you find me hypnotizing, Assassin?"

His breath hitched as he stared into her eyes but didn't answer. Seconds passed. Then minutes.

Eventually, in the silence of the room, he said, "I do."

CHAPTER 17
EVONY

She fell asleep to the sound of his admission on repeat in her mind. *I do. I do. I do.*

Breakfast had been quiet and she'd given Sparrow the reprieve from her flirtations, too in her mind about their confessions to play with him.

Now, she sat in the private training room and waited for Rosaelia to enter.

She was shocked to find her twin show up with the King at her side. "Did you need to cancel today's session?"

"No. Why?" the Princess asked with furrowed brows.

"I just wasn't expecting the King's appearance," Evony explained as she moved back to allow Rosaelia the space on the mat to begin her stretches. When she wore her training attire —a trouser and vest set—she looked so much more like Evony.

"I merely would like to watch the lesson," he replied in a relaxed manner.

Evony didn't know why she was shocked to hear that but nodded and motioned for him to take a seat off to the side.

Evony joined her twin on the mats and stretched alongside her. Then joined her in the warm ups and even did a few of the exercises. But eventually, her muscles screamed at her from the solo training she'd done before Rosaelia and Edmund had arrived, so she stopped and instructed Rosaelia on her own.

These sessions were always fun. They always moved from stretches and warm ups to pure exercise to actual trainings for hand-to-hand and weapon combat. She loved bossing the Princess—her older sister—around.

But today, it felt a little more awkward. Usually, she didn't mind being watched, but she'd never considered her father's attentions. Especially when she felt them burning into her neck.

She allowed Rosaelia a break and turned a smile to the King. "Observing normally means watching the one training, not the one instructing."

"Just keeping my eyes on you, young lady." His tone was teasing, but something about it set Evony off.

She quirked a brow she hoped looked playful. "Is there a reason for this attention, Your Highness?"

"You are trying to seduce my assassin, my best spy."

She laughed with a spark of joy as Sparrow's words from the night before came back to her. "It is not my fault he is easily manipulated."

"I would say it is the looks, but he's known me all his life and never once wanted more," Rosaelia interrupted with a breathy comment.

"It's the eyes, baby, they never lie. And mine are calling to him like a siren to seamen, my twin." Evony's heart jumped as she spoke the words. At least she *hoped* she called to him the way he called to her.

But Edmund still looked suspicious, though he attempted

to hide it. Evony couldn't tell if she was reading too much into his expressions. There was no reason for the suspicions regarding her, but she supposed she could do more to convince the King not to worry about her.

Rosaelia laughed and Evony turned back to her. "Jumping jacks, Twin. Easy."

"Yeah, real easy when you're only watching," Rosaelia muttered under her breath.

"Are we getting mouthy?" Evony's lips twitched up. "I can always change it to burpees."

Rosaelia narrowed her eyes on Evony but didn't say another word as she began jumping. Her eyes though, they didn't lie. And they told Evony exactly how much Rosaelia hated her in the moment.

Evony laughed. "Count."

✝

SHE WAS CLEANED and the last to the dining hall. Sparrow had come straight from his meeting with the King, so she hadn't expected him to be around to walk her, but it had felt oddly empty to not have him at her side. It was scary, how quickly she'd become accustomed to his presence.

Sparrow's gaze was sharp on their guest when she took her seat beside him. The chair already pushed closer to him than it should be. Odd, she was normally the one to push closer to him.

Staring at his profile, she wondered if he'd done it, and that hopeful heart of hers beat a little faster knowing the answer was yes.

Dinner was set about and the doors left open—as they

almost always remained when guests were visiting—but the hour passed slowly. With Alexei seated among them, they couldn't be the same joking group they normally were. Maybe that's what was darkening her assassin's mood.

And another even more intriguing question popped into her mind when she noticed the bruising around Miels's neck. Those were most definitely not sex related and they looked large and deep and she needed to know the story behind them. Fucking Alexei, she'd have to wait until later for that one.

Sparrow was leaning back in his chair at the end of dinner, his head tilted in the general direction of the majority past Evony, and she noticed that his gaze shot in Alexei's direction every few moments. And every few moments, Alexei would flinch under the scrutiny of such attention from the Master Assassin.

Evony leaned into Sparrow so their faces were only a couple of inches apart, tucking one hand under the arm he had resting on the chair and the other over the hand that laid there. "Jealous?"

He didn't acknowledge her. "Of?"

"Alexei."

His gaze shot to her. "Why would I be?"

"He tried to take me from you. I should marry him rather than you."

He scoffed. "We aren't truly betrothed."

"Then why the constant glares in his direction?"

Sparrow's eyes moved to watch the others again, ignoring her question entirely. She smirked to herself as she did the opposite and ignored the rest of the table.

She rested her chin on his shoulder and gave him her full attention, her smile soft and glowing, as she leaned in and gave him the barest of pecks against the lips.

His gaze shot down to hers and narrowed. "What are you doing?"

"Considering I'm doing it to you, I'd think you'd know."

A thrill passed her as his jaw clenched and eyes turned to slits. "Evony."

"I'm kissing my betrothed. A daily common and expected occurrence."

"Maybe in the South."

"Well, I'm from the South."

"Alexei doesn't know that."

Yet he wasn't pulling back, so every word that passed between them tickled her lips in the most delightful of ways.

Evony fluttered her nose against his in an Eskimo kiss. "He believes me from the border. Those along the border are so like one another that I would have surely picked up Southerner behaviors. I'm sure he's caught on by now. Especially considering I'm supposed to be half Southern, since Gem could never pass off as a full Northerner."

Her fingers danced over the hand he rested on the arm of the chair, the fingers of her other hand beginning to graze his forearm for any chance to constantly be touching him.

She couldn't help the joy that pierced her when he didn't pull away. It was not in his customs to be so public in his affections, yet he wasn't pulling away.

She also saw that he was thoroughly unconvinced at her little excuses, and leaned in to kiss him again. Just because.

She didn't pull away before planting another. Then another.

And still, to her surprise—and joy—he wasn't pulling away. But he also wasn't reciprocating.

She pecked him again.

"Evony," he demanded. "Behave."

Her blood rushed as she pressed her thighs together,

feeling how wet she got every time those words left his mouth, and leaned in for another kiss. And another. And again and again and again. She smiled against his lips. "I just might continue until you kiss me back."

Her fingers stopped dancing on his skin, rather resting over his forearm and the top of his hand and intertwining with his fingers as she leaned in for another kiss.

At the next one, Sparrow surprised her by leaning in and pressing his lips to hers in plain view of the entire room. And it wasn't a stoic press of lips to get her to stop either. There was passion behind it that Evony knew meant more.

His fingers tightened around hers in the brief seconds of the kiss before he pulled away, disguising his features but unable to hide the pleasure in his eyes. Her smile was wide as can be as he muttered in a thick voice, "Behave."

"Yes, sir," she whispered without realizing it. His fingers tightened around hers again as a growl escaped from deep within him.

A thrilling, throw-you-against-the-wall type of growl.

But before she could play with him anymore, he turned back to the table and Evony followed along, allowing him this small reprieve from her antics.

The second she turned back to the table, she saw the shocked expressions of a group trying horribly to hide them. They wouldn't bring it up now because of their guest, but it was obvious they wanted to. And it was obvious Alexei was not accustomed to this sort of display in the uncomfortable way he glanced their way.

Or maybe that was because Sparrow's glares were back on him.

As Evony snuggled into his arm, holding on as her head rested on his shoulder, she felt Sparrow's head tilt over hers and plant a kiss to the crown of her head. The gentleness of it told her it wasn't for any other reason but that he wanted to do it.

She breathed in the moment and listened to the mundane topics as her heart beat at an abnormal rate, her smile too wide to even attempt to hide.

CHAPTER 18
SPARROW

She was wearing his shirt again.

He walked barefoot into the room and fell back on the couch in his usual sleeping trousers and nothing more.

She didn't turn from where she stood in front of the fireplace. "You're teasing me, Assassin."

One foot skimmed up her bare leg and all his attention snagged to that movement. Her skin shined and begged for his touch and he was barely able to peel his gaze up in order to catch the mischievous glint in her eyes as she watched him.

"High compliment from the Master herself."

Her laugh was intoxicating the way it made every cell in his body stand to attention.

"You borrowed my shirt again."

She turned from the fireplace, her skin shining off the flames that illuminated her. It was just coming on midnight, and she'd harbored a habit of waiting for him to return to the suite before she went off to her room.

She tsked. "That implies I intend on giving it back."

He chuckled but didn't break his gaze.

She waited, long moments of every cell in his body singing with a plea to touch her, then moved for him. Like an animal on the prowl. Sparrow felt like the antsy prey that wanted to get caught.

She didn't hesitate to straddle his lap, the shirt she wore rising higher so it barely covered the tops of her thighs.

He wanted this. Wanted every inch of her. But still, he growled, "Magician."

Her hands looped around his neck, grasping the bottoms of his hair. "Yes?"

"Behave," he groaned as her hips rocked against his.

There was a seductive softness to her laugh as her lips leaned in to meet his. Though he knew he should fight it, he reciprocated immediately, hands finding their way into her hair again. He'd dreamed of doing this—plunging into her dark waves—a million times since that night against the window.

His tongue was greedy, unwilling to wait for her to make the claim. He was especially glad to find a wanton response as her lips parted for him.

Their tongues fought for dominance and she pulled at the strands of his hair, her nails scraping against the back of his neck and causing groans to escape him. That scrape against his neck and the way her hips had begun grinding against him. All of it made him groan and want more.

She was inexperienced, he knew that much, but she definitely wasn't innocent.

His hands moved of their own accord, finding their way beneath the shirt she wore and onto bare thighs.

Smooth.

She was so smooth.

"Sparrow," she moaned and he didn't even try to fight the urge to thrust his hips up to meet hers.

His fingers danced beneath the shirt, an involuntary growl forming when he realized she was completely bare under it, even though he'd known she was. She laughed into the kiss, biting his bottom lip, hungry for more as her hips bucked into him.

He gripped her hips and a sick part of him hoped his hands left bruises. "Keep going, baby," he groaned. "Don't stop..."

Their gazes caught for only a second before she was pulling his hair so his neck opened to her, and softly kissed his collarbone. When he ground his hips up with a groan, she laughed again and kissed him just below the ear, across his neck to the other ear, and nibbled softly at it as she whispered, "This feels so much better than anything my virgin mind could imagine."

He chuckled against her skin, his fingers biting as they held on to her hips and rocked her against him, fixing the rhythm to one that made her moan out with every single movement. "That's right. You're almost there."

Then her lips were on his again and there was a divine fulfill-ment that sparked through him when their tongues molded together. As she clung to him, her hips almost thrashing over him, his hips bucked as the pleasure hit his spine and made its way down, curled at his toes and shot up his body.

The desperate need to be inside her pumped within him as he guided her, her moans filling the air he breathed. "Don't stop, baby. You're doing so good..." He bit her lip, knowing she was getting close and finding life in the knowledge that it was because of him. "Fuck, Evony, don't stop, baby."

"Sparrow," she cried out. "I'm going to come."

His hips bucked up, but he forced himself to control the urge to change the pace and thrash into her. This was the rhythm for her and he wouldn't stop until she was crying out his name.

"Good," he growled. "Come, baby. Come for me, Evony."

He knew it was the name that broke her. She was thrashing above him, riding his trouser clad cock as her body reveled in every pleasure it deserved, head falling back as her nails dug into his neck. He groaned along with her, because witnessing this was a heaven send. Hearing his name echo throughout the room was torturous delight.

When she came down from her high, he pushed the stray, sweaty hairs off her face. "Good girl."

She moaned again as her forehead fell over his.

Sparrow shook himself out of his memories from the night before as Edmund walked into the training room and moved to the weapons table. The last thing he needed was a full erection while with the father of the woman he was fantasizing about.

But fuck, the memory was strong.

And the swiftness of his own ejaculation that had come when she'd gone to her room and he'd pushed into his own was still fresh. The dewy evidence of her arousal was all over his trousers before he peeled them off and touched himself. And it was still lying at the edge of his bed when he'd awoken that morning, giving him the proper reminder of their night as he touched himself again.

And came so fucking hard he struggled to keep quiet.

But he couldn't think of that, any of it. He had training with Edmund, and the very last thing the man needed was to see him aroused. Especially toward Evony. Even if he didn't feel for her the fatherly affection he felt for Rosaelia, it still wasn't right.

Plus, Edmund had enough to worry about with the rebellion in the lands, and Alexei bothering their group's peace, to also now be focused on this particular relationship.

"Ready?" Sparrow jumped up and down in his spot to get the rush of the memories out of his mind.

Edmund looked annoyed. "If I pretend you're Alexei, I might win, Sparrow."

Sparrow laughed. As the Master Assassin, it was impossible for any of his men to beat him since he had the upper hand without trying. But that also meant training with him made them the best of swordsmen. And Edmund liked to keep polished with his skill, unbothered that none of his attacks ever stuck. "He bothers you that much?"

"He's a nuisance to the servants. At least your threat about Ro keeps him away from her." Their swords collided, but Edmund didn't break phase, switching tactics and continuing his movements seamlessly. "But apparently, now he's insisting on talking to us at breakfast about his *true* nature for being here."

"At least he has one and we won't have to endure his 'just a friendly visit' nonsense."

Edmund circled the mat, but never stopped attacking or defending. Sparrow would say he were proud if the King hadn't always been a dedicated swordsman. It was one of the many things Sparrow respected about the man—he didn't sit back and allow his men to do all the work. If it came down to it, Edmund could fight.

"Have you found anything else regarding the rebellion?"

Sparrow shook his head, noticing the sweat begin to spring on the King's forehead. "They've quieted down since Evony's arrival. Really makes the whole asking for her help a moot point."

"Yes." His sword rang against Sparrow's with the force it hit. "Or maybe they see the distraction she may be. If word has gotten out that she is your *betrothed*, and before that, that she was sharing your rooms, the rebellion may find it in their best interest to wait for you to be thoroughly distracted with her."

So he still wasn't happy about the betrothal announcement. Tough. It was one of the best rash decisions Sparrow had ever made. Every man would now know to stay far, far away from her. Even though technically it was all false.

"Good," Sparrow responded. "Let them believe me distracted. Even better if they're not expecting us to respond.

Let them believe her distracted too. She still has her magic around, that hasn't stopped just because we haven't given her cause to use it yet."

"Yes, yes," Edmund muttered as he pushed against Sparrow's defense. "It was quite a good plan, even though you blurted it without considering the outcomes."

Sparrow rolled his eyes. He doubted the man would ever drop this.

Edmund stopped for a water break, dropping his sword on the mats and picking up his jug. Sparrow joined him. Even though he hadn't broken much of a sweat, hydration was still important to keep him in top shape.

He was putting his water back and turning for a new weapon when Edmund asked, "What happened to your neck?"

Sparrow's hand shot to cover the back of his neck, skin flushing as a flash of Evony writhing above him crossed his mind. "Nothing."

Edmund's eyes looked tired as he watched Sparrow. "You used to be better at lying, Sparrow."

Sparrow sighed and moved to the mat again, choosing no weapon instead, and waited for Edmund to join him.

When the King did, he had a heavier sword in hand to combat Sparrow's lack of one. Then he was attacking again, Sparrow easily moving out of the way, and the frustration was clear on his features.

But it couldn't be the frustration of missing his target. He never nicked Sparrow when they trained.

Finally, Edmund let that frustration out, stopping in the middle of the mat and dropping his hand so the sword tip hit the mats. "You've entertained her flirtations. Allowed the rumors to spread of your activities in your suite, were caught kissing—and from what I hear, getting ready for *said* activities —in *my* suite. Then you go on and kiss in front of everyone—in front of Alexei—at dinner. You didn't answer when I asked about you two before and I dropped it, but now I want to know. Is there something between you and Evony, or are you just getting your dick wet?" It was a lewd way of speaking of his daughter, but Edmund didn't necessarily see Evony as his daughter.

Sparrow's breathing was growing louder, but it was more from his own frustration of not knowing how to answer Edmund than from the training. "Alexei believes us betrothed. It makes sense to have kissed before him."

Edmund scoffed. "Do not play with me, Spar. We're in the North. Alexei is a Northerner. He did not need a public display to confirm your betrothal. Especially with all the rumors already spreading about the noises coming from your suite. And, might I add again, what you were caught doing in my suite."

"He watches us. Has tried to pursue Evony. It is important he understood."

"Important for whom, Sparrow?" Of course the King was onto him.

And the blood boiling under Sparrow's skin answered the question. It was important to him. Important that Alexei and every other male in the lands know Evony was not to be touched, thought about, or breathed around. That she was his.

But he wouldn't say that to Edmund, and he also wouldn't lie. So instead he said nothing.

"Do you deny it? The rumors?"

"How can I deny something that was clearly seen by two others?"

Edmund's eyes narrowed on him. "And the others. What happens in your suite, Sparrow? Are you fucking her?"

"Stop talking about her like that," Sparrow couldn't help but grit out. He was tired of hearing Edmund's disregard for the way he spoke of his second daughter. "Most of the rumors are false and you know it."

Most. Edmund caught that. "Why did you kiss her last night? And do not say it was for Alexei's sake. Evony's flirtations and kisses made it abundantly clear you two were spoken for. I want to know why *you* kissed her."

Sparrow's anger was rising. And not at the King, but at himself. At not being able to interpret what was happening to him when he was around the Magician. Or simply thinking of the Magician. "She said she'd stop if I kissed her back." It was weak, but it was all he had at the moment.

Edmund made a tired laugh.

"What do you want from me, Ed?" Sparrow was tired too and still, he could not bring himself to voice this relationship with Evony. Like if he said it to Edmund, it was absolute.

"I want the truth, Sparrow."

And he couldn't give that. Not fully. But once he figured it out, Sparrow wouldn't hide his thoughts from the man who had raised him.

So instead of answering, Sparrow simply left the training room.

And that much was answer enough.

CHAPTER 19
SPARROW

The annoyance at Sparrow for refusing to answer his questions yet again was surprisingly not on the King's face when Sparrow walked into the dining hall for breakfast less than half an hour later. Just enough time for a wash.

And even more surprisingly, Edmund didn't narrow his eyes at Sparrow when he walked in with Evony on his arm, her lips pressed into his bicep as she muttered about the annoying way the tailors looked at her every time she wanted trousers instead of dresses.

"Sparrow." She pulled on his arm to garner his attention as they reached their seats. "Are you even listening?"

His lips twitched up involuntarily as he cradled her face in his hands. "I'm listening and I agree. Blasphemous the way they look down on your trousers."

She laughed and pushed him away, taking her seat as he took his. "Fuck off."

But he hadn't been joking. It was blasphemous that Evony was considered unladylike for wanting to wear trousers. Especially since those trousers gave Sparrow the most exquisite view of her ass. The only reason he would agree with the tailors was to keep others from staring at that delectable bit of her.

A thought he should definitely not be thinking. He needed to get away from her. She was taking up too many of his thoughts and he didn't know how to handle that.

Miels threw his arm over Evony's chair. "You two look cozy."

"You should see us in our suite," Evony retorted with an innocent smile.

Alexei coughed into his cup as he drank, and Sparrow involuntarily glanced up to Edmund who was eyeing him with an 'I knew it' look.

Miels leaned into her. "Is that an invite?"

She pushed back in her chair so she fell onto Sparrow's chest. "Only Sparrow's."

Miels smirked. "I'll watch."

Sparrow growled even though he knew the man was joking. "Fuck off, asshole."

Miels's glinting eyes caught Sparrow's, and the look there said he remembered the way Sparrow had thrown him against the wall and he didn't care.

"Fine." Miels turned back to his plate. "Maybe I'll just listen." He picked up his knife and fork and spoke casually without looking over to them. "Maybe I'll come by to invite you for a late night with me and Tristan and I'll just stand outside the door and listen."

Sparrow froze.

The knife was flying from his hand before he thought to control his anger. But Miels was ready. He caught it and laughed out loud, Tristan and the married duo joining in quickly. Even Rosaelia's lips quirked up.

And Evony, of course, not to be left behind from the teasing as she laughed with the others, turned her face into Sparrow's neck as a light flush rose up her neck.

At least Alexei looked even more petrified of him now.

"I'll kill you next time," Sparrow growled.

Of course Miels caught the use of the phrase "next time." Everyone had.

Miels's lips quirked into that cocky, annoying smirk of his. "You be any louder next time, and I won't even have to leave my rooms."

Sparrow didn't have time to threaten him again as Evony's hand held his jaw and forced him to focus on her. "He's teasing, my love. Calm down, we have a guest."

With the way she looked up at him, all Sparrow wanted to do was lean down and kiss her and never stop. But he didn't allow himself the pleasure.

He swallowed back his rage and turned back to the table, catching Edmund's eyes. Sparrow scoffed beneath his breath. He wouldn't have to tell the King anything, his actions were far too telling, and it was obvious Edmund was picking up that this wasn't just Sparrow *getting his dick wet.*

Even though Sparrow didn't want this to be any more than that.

He didn't want to want Evony. Didn't want to allow her into his life, into the lives of the King's Posse. Didn't want to trust her. Didn't want to desire her opinions. Didn't want her.

But he needed her.

And thankfully, Edmund didn't try to push the matter before the rest of the table. Instead, he turned to Alexei. "You said you had a purpose for traveling down to the palace."

Alexei sat up tall, obviously trying to act like the manners of the table—and Sparrow and Evony especially—were not throwing his mind for a loop. "Yes, Your Highness. I have come with a most advantageous proposal."

Sparrow grumbled under his breath as the eggs filled his mouth, and Evony tried to hide her responding giggles behind a chunk of bread. He caught her shining eyes and had to force down his grin.

"As we are all aware," Alexei explained, "I run the towns harboring the borders to the Island Nation. I was offered a treaty."

Sparrow looked down to suppress the eye roll. This was why he hated politics. The last thing he wanted to do was sit about with a stoic expression when ridiculous things were being said. But alas, politics.

"The treaty explains that the Island Nation will send a couple of sorceresses to each of my three towns in order to aid with ailments. Given the plague in the north of the lands, I believe it a most valuable offer."

Of course the moron did.

"And in turn?" Edmund entertained.

"They only ask to be allowed to travel to my three towns. No more. They do not wish to stay for long, but they currently have no rights to travel the Northern Lands and hardly any for the Southern Lands given they cannot step onto our lands."

"And how will you control what these sorceresses actually do, Lord Alexei? What they do on their free time?" Edmund tilted his head at him.

Alexei stuttered. "They would not betray the treaty. Doing so would relinquish the travel allowed."

If Alexei didn't do such a good job keeping his towns in order, Sparrow would throw the idiot off his lordship and appoint a new one.

"But if they already have sorceresses here converting our

people, do you believe they'll care for an allowance?" Edmund's smile was condescending.

"I'm sure they wouldn't."

"Unfortunately, Lord Alexei, I cannot take *your* certainty in regard to the safety of my lands. Permission for a treaty is denied. We will have no such deals with the Island Nation."

Alexei didn't look happy, but he would not argue with his king. "Of course, Your Highness."

Breakfast passed quietly for the remainder of the period, until Alexei rose for his late morning ride out on the greens. A servant was quick to close the doors behind him so their group had their privacy once more.

"Clever distraction." Tristan was the one to break the silence.

"But they had to know we'd never take it." Rosaelia looked confused.

"They do," James replied. "But it's still worth a try. It's like when you're training and you know the sword will be too heavy, but you still try to heft it even though you're almost certain it will fail. If by chance you succeed, it will all have been worth it. Especially when you're not losing anything in trying."

"What we have to worry about now"—Sparrow leaned back in his chair—"is whether we should suspect the Islanders with this plague as well."

"You think they had a hand in it?" Rosaelia sounded thoughtful.

"I wouldn't rule it out. Especially as a perfect excuse to bring sorcerers in," Sparrow answered.

"We'll look into it." Tristan leaned back in his chair.

Somehow the silence didn't last long, almost like the peace of not having Alexei at the table pushed their normal behavior out. Gemma and Evony were arguing across the table with

Tristan joining in as James, Miels, and Rosaelia started their own conversation.

Sparrow caught Edmund's gaze and leaned onto his forearms over the table.

Edmund followed and caught his eyes again. "I'm sorry, son," he said softly so no one else would hear. "I won't bring it up again. When you desire to tell me, I'll listen."

Sparrow didn't respond, but he wanted to say thank you. Instead, he just gave a nod of acknowledgment.

Thankfully, Evony had him pulled back into his chair so he wouldn't feel the need to confess all his confusing feelings to his father figure. She hugged his arm as she looked up at him with those beautiful blue eyes. "They're being mean, Assassin. Kill them for me."

He smiled down at her. "Right away, Magician."

✝

He refused to go back to his suite. He had work to get done and there was no way he could sit in that room and not remember the night before.

He'd thought about reading his missives in the dining hall but figured Evony would too easily be able to find him there. He'd then considered Edmund's suite or office, but again, figured Evony may be able to find him too easily there. Not to mention, if he began thinking of her, he didn't want to be aroused in her father's suite.

Up in this room—the one he had been in the first time she was at this palace—he should be safe. She didn't know about this room.

He'd just finished writing a missive back to one of his men in the coasts borders and picked up another—this one from the southern border—to lean back into his chair and read when the doors opened.

He definitely hadn't expected her to find him. "How did you know I was here?"

She gave him that sneaky grin as she strut over to him in her normal trouser-vest attire that gave him a beautiful view of her body. "I *am* a Master, my love."

Naturally. He should have guessed she could use magic to track him down.

She plucked the letter from his hands, placing it on the table and ignoring the annoyed expression Sparrow forced onto his features as she seated herself onto his lap. "I've missed you, my love."

Her position reminded him of their night. "You saw me a couple hours ago at breakfast."

Her fingers played with his hair. "So we're in agreement. It was too long a separation."

"Evony." Even as he voiced the reprimand, his fingers played with the bottoms of her vest.

"Sparrow," she whispered in the most seductively innocent tone Sparrow had ever heard. Her lips grazed his and it was only a lifetime of training that kept him still against her.

"I'm working," he bit out with no conviction.

Her brows furrowed in feigned consideration as her hands slowly slid down his arms. "Yes, I know." She leaned in closer, kissing him soft and sweet, before pulling away and moving to the laces of her vest. "But I figured you may like a feast." She slowly and skillfully unlaced the vest.

"Evony." The restraint was evident in his tone. He didn't like the control she had on him.

She ignored him, her fingertips tracing up her breasts to the top of the vest. Then she lowered it off her shoulders and presented him with the two most beautiful, puckered brown nipples.

He gripped the arms of his chair, his breath hitching as he involuntarily licked his lips and refrained. "Evony."

"You're my betrothed, Sparrow." The teasing in her tone mixed with a wantonness that affected his body instantly. "Take advantage of what's yours."

She'd left the vest bunched beneath her breasts giving them a perfect purchase. Sparrow looked her over, giving every exposed inch of her the attention it deserved, and found the desire heavy in her eyes before dropping his gaze back to the twins.

His hands grasped her hips to bring her closer before he realized he'd made up his mind. Her smile matched his and he didn't know what he'd done to deserve this, but he wasn't going to question it.

His hands traveled up her back, lingering along the arch and bringing her chest up to his mouth so his lips grazed against the hardened tips and his breath sent shivers down her body. He caught her stare and held it as he plucked his tongue along one breast, circling the nipple but never giving her what she wanted.

He teased her skin, tasting his way from one breast to the other in a figure eight, but never getting the taste they both desired. Her hips bucked against his like they had the night before and he smirked knowing it was all because of him.

When she finally let out a moan, not just a haughty breath, he stopped torturing the both of them and latched on to a nipple. Her hands fisted into his hair as her hips chose their rhythm and Sparrow groaned as he grew harder by the second. She tasted so good, felt so good, it was exhilarating.

When he licked over to the other breast to give it the same attention its sister had received, she released him and leaned back. Her back arched so her chest took up the air he breathed and her hands clung to the wood table for balance. And Sparrow had never been hungrier.

He took a breast in each hand, allowing himself the pleasure of feeling them bare beneath his hands. His thumbs skimmed her nipples teasingly as he watched her. Watched the way her chest rose and fell as she clung to every breath, the whimpers escaping her as she rode his hard length.

He leaned in for another taste, twirling his tongue around her nipple while his thumb played with the other. He bit lightly and felt a rush course through him as she bucked against him, her moans picking up volume.

"I want to hear you whimper my name, Evony. I want it to be the only thing you can say." He moved to the opposite breast, giving it the attention it deserved.

She ignored him, continuing to moan the incomprehensible cries as her cunt rocked against him and his tongue and thumb worked her nipples.

He kissed the valley between her breasts. "Do you want me to stop?" he teased.

"No. Please no," she called as she forced her eyes open to look at him.

"Then say my name, love."

She loved when he called her that. He knew that much. And it was further proved when she cried out his name.

He was about to continue his feast when a loud chorus came from just beyond the doors. Sparrow froze. From the sounds of it, they were at the tops of the stairs, only a few yards from opening those doors.

He pulled away and pushed her vest back into place, hands already beginning the laces when she righted herself and watched him, her breath still coming in hard.

This room was much better with the sound than their

suite, so he doubted whoever that was had heard her, but there was absolutely no way they were going to see her bared.

"I'm going to kill whoever that is," she managed breathlessly.

Sparrow chuckled. "We're of one mind about that, Magician."

He'd just finished with the laces and settled his hands on the arms of his chair when the door opened and in walked the King with the idiot twins.

They froze at the scene, Tristan and Miels quickly smirking as Edmund quirked his brow. "Well, if it isn't my daughter seducing my assassin once more."

He didn't look angry or suspicious. Sparrow didn't know why he was surprised, Edmund had said he would leave this *relationship* alone until he was ready to speak of it.

In true Evony fashion, she smiled unashamedly as her hands settled around his neck. "And it would have worked had you not interrupted."

"Oh, I do not doubt that," Edmund said as he took the seat across from them.

She bit her bottom lip softly—effectively distracting Sparrow—as she met his stare and moved to roll off of him.

His hands immediately shot to her ass, staying her. "Don't you dare move right now."

He was still completely hard, and with the attention from the others at the moment, if she moved, he wouldn't have enough time to cover himself before they saw it.

She horribly tried to stifle her laugh as she softly rocked her hips over him and felt the strain of his cock trying to get inside her. She laughed softly and leaned in to peck him on the lips.

Then she hugged him.

Remained in her straddle position and hugged him.

Sparrow wasn't sure why, but this was almost more intimate than what they'd just been doing. And he couldn't stop himself from reaching around her and bringing her in closer to him. He felt her smile against his neck as she tightened her hold.

This was Sparrow's definition of perfect.

And that was a dangerous thought.

So he forced himself out of it. "What are you lot doing up here?"

"Sorry, Spar." Tristan's tone was the complete opposite of apologetic. "Interrupt your time with the Magician? Isn't that what your suite is for?"

Evony giggled against his neck as he narrowed his eyes on Tristan. "You want the same bruises your brother has?"

The moron twins laughed as Edmund said around a grin, "We just wanted to hear what your men are saying."

CHAPTER 20
EVONY

"You know he refuses to tell me how you got those bruises." Evony smiled to Miels in hopes he would give it up.

"He's a territorial motherfucker. That's all I'll tell you." He moved past her like he knew what she was doing and he wouldn't fall for it.

"Does that mean it was because of me?" She gave an encouraging smile. And her heart beat hopefully.

He didn't fall for it. "Ask him."

She gave him a disgruntled pout. Then quickly brought the smile back as Tristan entered the library. "Tristan! Hey!"

"Whatever you want, ask Sparrow." He didn't even look at her.

"Tristan," she cried.

He sighed and met her gaze. "Your Highness?"

She smirked. "Tell me how Miels got those bruises."

Tristan laughed. "Spar won't tell you?"

She gave a sad pout with the shake of her head.

He smirked. "I'm definitely not going against him. My body

needs to remain in pristine condition for my lady's nights, dear Evony."

She fell back into her seat. "You guys suck."

"There you go." Miels gave her a cocky grin. "Go suck him and he might feel in a more giving attitude."

Evony didn't want to allow the grin, but those were the kinds of comments she usually made so she definitely found humor in them. "Fuck off."

"No," he teased. "Fuck *him*. Evony, learn faster."

"I hate you," she grumbled through a grin.

"What are you doing in here anyway?" Tristan asked. "I thought you didn't like libraries. They're too stifling."

Evony leaned back into the table with her still open books. "You guys called me here for a reason. I want to be useful."

"Eve," he said softly and Evony froze at the nickname only her two best friends used with her. "You're part of the family. We called you because we thought your magic could get rid of the Islanders without them actually being caught. If we cared about your usefulness, you would've been booted days after you arrived."

"Plus, now that you've stayed so long, Sparrow would never let you go," Miels added earnestly. "And if he tried, we wouldn't let him. He's happier now. With you."

She smirked. "Those bruises mean happier?"

He wasn't falling for it as his lips quirked up. "So he's never used his Master power on me before you came around. I can live with it if it means he's got you."

She gasped. "He used his Master power on you?" She'd guessed that, but instantly pushed it aside, knowing Sparrow would never hurt his friends like that. "Now I have to know what you did."

"So go suck him, fuck him." Tristan grinned from across the table. "And find out."

She grumbled. "Assholes."

"What're you researching?" Miels changed the subject.

"The past wars with the Island Nations. I'm trying to see if there're any similarities to our situation. There's also the complication of whether this is a sorcerer's war or not. It could just be a woman using a sorcerer, or it could be the sorcerer herself who wants the throne." She flipped the pages again as if they'd show something new. "If I can figure out more, if there is something I can do with my magic, I want to find it and help."

"If you figured out more, maybe more on the specifics, do you think you'd find a way to use your magic?" Tristan asked.

"My magic is very dynamic. I can manipulate it into doing just about anything I want—apart from the changing features thing—so if I know what I'm aiming for, yeah. Even if they're not around, I can set precautions around to stop them. Or to warn us ahead of time."

"So there's nothing you can do now?" Miels asked.

"All I have now is the same protection around us that I had on James, Gem, and I before, just to a larger degree. I don't have anything specific up because I don't know what I'm trying to do, and even as a Master, if I tried to do everything plausible, I'd be out."

Tristan's hand took hers and squeezed. "We'll figure it out. And with Alexei about gone now, that's one less thing taking our attention away from this rebellion."

Evony smiled warmly to him. Moments like these made her feel like part of the King's Posse, even if the King himself was still standoffish. Moments where Miels and Tristan treated her like an actual sister.

Miels broke the tension speaking of the Islanders had brought down. "I'd let go, brother, before you end up with the same bruises."

They all laughed and she looked between the two, annoyed that they still wouldn't tell her what had happened between Sparrow and Miels.

But that comment kind of signified it definitely had to do with her.

And even though she should be angry with Sparrow for hurting his brother on her account, she couldn't help but feel giddy at the thought of his possessiveness.

†

ASHTYN WAS in a beautiful mood that afternoon.

Evony sat with Gemma and watched as the medic readied Lord Alexei—who had been sent to the infirmary after a sparring match with James—who hadn't known the lord was a poor sport—for release. The man was whining like a child rather than a man entering his thirties.

Ashtyn tightened the wrap around his injured arm, her lips twitching up when the man let out a cry.

Old Lady Arba came out from the curtains she'd been helping a woman behind, and her livid gaze shot straight to the young medic. "Ashtyn! What do you think you're doing?"

Ashtyn rolled her eyes at the woman and tightened the wrap a final time before beginning to tie it off.

Alexei gave a dramatic welp which gave Old Lady Arba all the ammunition she needed to attack the younger medic. "You are to help the patients, not hurt them any more than they've already suffered!"

Ashtyn scoffed. "Please. It's a graze. He doesn't deserve the title of lord with such a weak demeanor."

Old Lady Arba gasped. "Keep this up and I will make sure you're let go of."

Ashtyn's smirk held no pleasure. "Please. Try it."

"Do not mock me, young lady."

"Medic," Ashtyn corrected, her agitation climbing.

"Excuse me?"

Alexei looked like he wanted to jump out of his seat to get out from between the two medics, but he was stuck between them so he just backed away from the argument.

"I am a medic," Ashtyn stated matter-of-factly. "Best you remember that."

"Not in the eyes of this infirmary," Old Lady Arba spit.

"Funny. Should I let the Master Assassin know you're blatantly ignoring his calls?"

Old Lady Arba barked and stepped back, her eyes all too telling of how much she despised Ashtyn. She turned away and made an angry stride back behind the curtain to the patient she had been helping.

Ashtyn's fury-filled gaze moved to the lord on the sickbed and he blanched, quickly jumping off. "Right. Well, I'll be off now."

He was gone in seconds.

Evony and Gemma applauded as the lord scurried out, Ashtyn turning just as displeased eyes on them. "What do you two want?"

"You're just in such a lovely mood all the time, we wanted to be around it," Gemma answered.

Ashtyn moved to her so-called office in the back, and the two of them followed as she fell into the chair behind her desk. She grumbled when she saw them and grimaced at Gemma. "Don't you have a warrior to shag?"

"He's training." Gemma seated herself on Ashtyn's desk.

Ashtyn turned on Evony. "Don't you have an assassin to shag?"

Evony took the other end of the desk. "He's training."

She rolled her eyes before fluttering them closed as her head fell back. "Well, then go bother your twin and leave me be."

Evony froze. "Excuse me?"

One of Ashtyn's eyes opened. "Did you truly expect me to believe you were cousins? That you two are sisters? Please."

Evony's gaze narrowed on her. "Everyone else does."

"That's because they're all morons."

Scary Medic Ashtyn knew she was an heir. And she didn't look like she gave a single fuck. If she'd known this entire time, she apparently hadn't mentioned it to anyone, because there was no way that rumor wouldn't have spread like wildfire.

"Okay," Evony simply said.

The medic watched her closely. "Okay? That's it? You're not going to tell me to keep it to myself?"

"I trust you."

"And why's that?"

"Intuition."

"Is that so?" Ashtyn watched her slowly, gaze gliding over her seated form.

"You don't believe me?" Evony asked with an innocent smile.

"You're shagging the man who holds my job wouldn't have anything to do with it?"

Evony's eyes twinkled. "We're not shagging." She clutched at the edges of the desk at the simple thought of it. "Yet."

Ashtyn quirked a brow. "Word around the servants is they've heard quite the noise coming from your suite. Not as bad as that one's"—she nodded to Gemma—"but still telling."

Evony beamed proudly. "And we weren't even naked."

Ashtyn grimaced. "Didn't need to know that."

Evony smirked. "And you said it wasn't good. We've barely

scraped the surface and I'm already bubbling with need for him constantly."

She rolled her eyes. "Like you said. You haven't shagged yet, it's not all it's said to be."

Gemma leaned in. "Or maybe you just haven't done it with the right person." She caught Evony's stare. "Maybe Gabriel can show her what she needs."

Evony leaned in and watched Ashtyn's annoyed tick of the jaw. "A little tussle in the hay. Though maybe your screams will scare the horses. Tussle when they're not around."

"Will you two get out of my office." Ashtyn wasn't asking.

Evony gasped. "Is that any way to speak to your Princess?"

"Fuck off," Ashtyn eyed Evony, and though she tried to hide it, there was a twinkle of amusement in her brown eyes.

Old Lady Arba's voice interrupted Evony's response. "Ashtyn! Now!"

The young medic mumbled a wagon load of expletives under her breath as she moved out of her makeshift office.

Gemma laughed while she took Evony's elbow and pulled her out of the infirmary while Ashtyn grumbled to a few kitchen children for being so stupid. "Oh, I really like her."

They were headed in the direction of the training yards where all but Sparrow would be. Though she'd told Ashtyn he was training, Evony was fairly certain he had only been there half an hour—enough time to instruct what he wanted done— before heading away to look over some more missives he'd gotten. And because she was feeling in a giving mood, Evony would allow him the reprieve from her perfect presence to actually do his job.

"She'll kill them all," Gemma joked about their medic friend.

"And she'll rule over them. Deservedly so." Evony basked in the image of Ashtyn being rid of the assholes in the infirmary when she was head nurse. Or keeping them and ruling over them, forcing them to be respectful even though every fiber in them didn't want to be.

"The world will fear her and we'll be right there by her side." Gemma sighed as her gaze glazed over as well. "A beautiful future if I'd ever known one."

"The palace will be ours for the running!"

"And the King will cower at our feet!"

"And we will run the world!" Evony laughed with her sister as they came around the corner.

Right into Princess Rosaelia.

Who looked rigid as she stood before them.

"Princess," Gemma said softly. "Are you all right?"

Rosaelia looked at them almost...suspiciously? "What were you two talking about?

"The infirmary," Gemma answered. "Old Lady Arba's name should be changed to Old Lady Arseba."

Rosaelia's eyes narrowed. "Right."

"We were just headed to watch the boys." Evony tried with her twin—their relationship was better than her relationship with Edmund, but still the weakest compared to the others. "Did you want to join us? I'm sure Miels is there."

Rosaelia's cheeks grew warm, but her eyes did not budge from the suspicious look. "No. Thank you."

She brushed past them, but her rigid stance never settled.

Evony and Gemma looked to each other. Gemma shrugged though it was obvious she was thinking the same thing Evony was. "Right. Well, let's go."

The mood wasn't as high spirited any longer because Rosaelia's stance had told them one thing—they were still strangers in the palace. Still untrustworthy. Still not part of the family. And it almost felt like no matter what they did, that's where they would remain.

When they got to the yards, James threw a sweaty arm around Evony's shoulders, bringing her into his side and covering her with his sweat.

"James!" Evony yelled at him. "You know I hate when you do this!"

She pushed against him but he tightened his hold, hugging her closer. Evony laughed as she pushed against him.

"You deserve it."

Evony scoffed, still fighting in his hold. "Why!"

"Your betrothed tortured me this morning." His smile was wide as he looked down at her.

"So go hug him." She finally got out of his grasp and watched him stand there and throw his head back, a villain's laugh bubbling in his throat.

Gemma strolled up to her husband and wrapped her hands around him as she purred against his lips. "Or hug me."

James's eyes twinkled down at her. "Yes, ma'am."

Evony feigned vomiting noises and they all laughed before she said, "How could he have done anything to you anyway, he's not even training with you guys today."

"He left instructions. And we were forced to follow them. Pure torture, woman."

Evony rolled her eyes, then smiled at her friends. "Let's go back to your suite. Have a night just the three of us. We'll order food in and just be us!"

Gemma's wide smile answered for them. "Perfect!"

"All right, let's—" James was cut off as Sparrow came running out of the castle, Miels and Tristan on his heels—only then did Evony realize the two hadn't been out either, having two others lead training for practice.

They didn't look like they were fooling around or training. Sparrow had worn the same features when he'd caught Evony and Gemma on the grounds years ago and come running for them. Something was wrong.

All three looked immediately in the direction the others were running toward but found nothing. Evony reached out with her power as dozens of guards went running after the men.

James turned to her. "What is it?"

Evony felt it then, the air pushing against her power, the scent her magic carried back to her. "Explosion. There are deaths."

None of them hesitated as they turned and ran after the dozens of men for the town two miles out.

CHAPTER 21

SPARROW

Sparrow was the first on the scene, the scent of acid hitting him the instant he stepped within twenty yards of the explosion site.

He'd been at the top of the tower again when Evony's presence outside caught his attention, and he watched her through the window as she hugged her friends. Then it had happened. Whatever *it* was had blown up like a shimmering of air, not the natural fire that would envelop the skies with smoke. He'd known it was an acidic explosion in that moment, and hadn't bothered a second's thought before running out of the room and calling for his men to follow.

Acidic explosions were only possible by one source. A source he'd allowed to remain within the public so that the rebels wouldn't know they were on to them. This was his fault.

They were created when a vial of potion was placed in the center of where the explosion was desired to occur, then pierced to allow the air to penetrate and send the acid everywhere. Whoever had done this would have shot an arrow into the vial, making sure they weren't hurt along in the process. The only consolation Sparrow had at the moment was that the victims didn't suffer. Acidic explosions killed instantly.

But this was his fault.

All around him were bodies of dozens of men, women, and children, and he couldn't tell the dead from the injured. But that didn't matter to him. What mattered was finding who had done this. His men would take care of everyone else.

But Sparrow had to work fast. If intuition was anything to work off of, that was only the first explosion. At only two miles out of palace grounds, this village was chosen specifically to get his men out here. He would not allow anyone else to get hurt because of his stupid decisions.

He scanned the crowds of chaos, searching for those who looked a little too calm, those whose tears felt a little too forced.

As his men joined the crowds, Sparrow noticed two men crouched behind a wailing set of girls. And they looked damn ready to piss their pants with glee.

He knew the chance of another vial exploding at any moment was high. Knew this was likely done to get him out here more than it was done to get to his men. Knew that the main goal here was to kill him, taking the lives of these villagers as casualties. And he hated himself a little more for it.

But he didn't care. He wouldn't allow any more people to get hurt for him. If another explosion hit, he'd be here fighting to the very end.

Then a tingling shot down his spine and he stiffened. It was a phantom touch, but he recognized it instantly as Evony's.

I'm here, my love.

That's all she said to him, but that was all he really needed. Now he would have absolutely nothing to fear because she wouldn't allow another vial to explode. She'd protect the people of this village even if he couldn't.

Sparrow moved slowly, walked in and out of the crowd so expertly, that even those around him were unable to detect the Master Assassin in their midst.

All around him there was heartbreak. Children crying for their parents, sisters crying for their brothers, brothers holding their little sisters, and worst of all, parents crying for their children. There were tears over lifeless bodies, wails against unhelpful embraces, and the misery of a village that did not deserve this.

His nose tickled with the sweet smell in the air that was just muffled with the scent of acid and blood as he neared the crouched men. Their joy looked to envelope the space around them. Theirs were the only smiles in this wreckage.

Sparrow fisted their shirts from behind and dragged them to standing. They jumped, and when they realized who held them their eyes widened horribly large, but there was no way out of Sparrow's hold.

"Enjoying the show?" Sparrow wasn't sure how his tone remained calm.

He walked them off to the edge of the village as they attempted time and again to get out of his grip. "M-M-Master Assassin."

Only those around the palace recognized his face which meant they were locals.

Even worse.

His stomach soured. These fuckers knew the people in this village, even if not personally, and allowed this to happen. Grinned enthusiastically at the outcome.

He laughed with no humor and threw them to their backs. "You didn't truly believe you'd blow up the village and I wouldn't show up, did you?"

They looked like they did, which meant they weren't the masterminds of this ploy. Though the way they shit their pants in his grip would've told him that much.

"You were meant to be out to the borders," the other said as they crawled back.

"Was I?"

The stuttering one tried to jump and make a run for it. Sparrow's laugh darkened as he grabbed the man and threw him back down, a foot landing on his knee and smashing hard enough to shatter the bones within.

The man cried out, though it was blocked by the sounds around them, and his companion literally pissed his pants.

Fucking cowards.

"Now, boys, let's chat." Sparrow watched as the one who cried he held his shattered leg while the other searched the crowd. Looking for the boss.

"We'll start with an easy one. Who're you looking for? Who's the real mastermind behind this?"

"We-we-we're not allowed to meet the heads of the rebellion." The second was stuttering now too.

"And your leader here? You boys do not have the courage to attempt this on your own."

They shook their heads. "We don't have one."

"Oh?" Sparrow feigned a furrow of the brows as he walked over to them and casually stomped on the uninjured one's hand. The snapping of bones was thrilling to Sparrow's furious body. He turned on the broken knee as the other screamed out and raised his foot.

"No! No! Please, I'll talk," he sputtered as snot mixed into his tears.

"I knew we'd see eye to eye."

"I don't know where he is." He glanced around the crowd, but it was obvious too much of his attention was on the pain in his leg. "I don't see him, but he was just here. His name is Heron."

"What does he look like?"

"Blonde hair, thirties, almost your height," the other stuttered.

"Not good enough," Sparrow sang as he neared them once more.

The one on the left raised both hands. "He told us to act like we're part of the crowd. I think he was acting like the others. Like, like he lost someone too."

Now that sounds like a sophisticated rebel, one capable of managing this outcome.

A blonde.

The same blonde who had been crying over the elderly man?

Sparrow shot his gaze behind him and searched the crowd. Lying there was the lifeless man, but nowhere beside him was the crying companion. Instead a few tearstained children crowded him.

Fuck. Sparrow's gaze narrowed on the crowd. How had he missed that?

He turned back to the goons on the ground.

"Please. Please, let us go." The one on the right cried.

Sparrow laughed so dark, he didn't recognize the sound. He whipped his sword off his hip and watched them blanche, but he didn't have time to play with them. He had a fucking blonde to find before he hurt anyone else in this village, his men, Evony.

Evony.

She was here too.

No. No, no, no. He wouldn't let the fucker hurt her.

The one with the injured knee was simple since he couldn't move to run, so the sword was in and out of his chest in seconds, blood already sputtering out of his mouth and the life gone from his eyes.

The other wasn't all that much more work. He ran, but Sparrow was fast.

He stabbed the man through the gut, blood sputtering around him as Sparrow growled through his teeth, "Do not attack"—he pulled the sword out and watched the man crumple—"if you are not prepared for the consequences."

He turned back to the crowd. The blonde would be around, waiting for the perfect moment to send his arrow flying and kill Sparrow and his men.

Evony was at the top of a tree at the edge of the center, her hands wide and gaze focused. Using her magic away from prying eyes.

Good. Her place at the edge put her just out of reach of getting hurt by the explosion. But Sparrow still hated that there was a chance anything might happen to her.

He stood in the middle of the wreckage, exactly where the vial would've had to have been. And where he assumed the second one was.

But he didn't search the area for it. Instead, he searched the crowd.

At the very edge of the crowds, by the ramshackle shop, he found the man he'd been looking for. Blonde, thirties, almost Sparrow's height. And fake tears dried upon his face.

He stared at Sparrow directly as he lifted his bow and arrow and released.

The arrow shot clean through the crowd aiming for a spot just to the left of Sparrow when his hand shot out and caught the long piece of the arrow, burning the flesh on his hand as the speed stopped abruptly. He knew Evony was there, felt her magic on his skin, knew she would take care to make sure the arrow didn't hit or that the vial was removed altogether. But he didn't care, he needed to feel that burn.

Sparrow dropped the arrow where he stood and began the stride toward the blonde. Heron, his name was.

Heron's eyes widened slightly as he strapped another arrow and released. Sparrow barely felt the burn of catching this arrow and released it to the ground. His heart pounded too vigorously within him to care.

Heron's gaze began to waver as he tried a third time. When Sparrow allowed this one to fly past him, trusting Evony to take care of it, and nothing happened, the man's confidence drained completely.

Like the fucking cowards all these fuckers turned out to be, he dropped his bow and made a run for it.

Sparrow caught up faster than he would've liked, but the adrenaline in his body needed to be expended so he had no control in holding back and allowing for a chase.

They were only a few feet into the forests surrounding the village center when Sparrow reached the man's shirt and rung him backward and onto the ground.

Sparrow's head fell back, stretching the knots in his neck before turning to face the man. "I would have enjoyed a more exciting chase, *Heron*."

The man blanched like he hadn't expected Sparrow to know his name. Why that part was important when the man was about to die, Sparrow couldn't fathom.

The man crawled back on his hands like his two little friends had. And when he peeled himself up and made another run for it, Sparrow tripped him and watched as he tumbled to the ground.

Again, he allowed the fucker to crawl back and get to his feet.

Seeming to realize he wouldn't be able to run out of there, the blonde faced Sparrow with a foolhardy expression.

Heron pulled his sword and got into position. Sparrow didn't reach for his own weapon. It wouldn't be needed. Not yet at least.

Heron attacked and Sparrow dipped out of the way. Again and again.

When Sparrow dipped out of the way and ended up behind the blonde, snickering in his ear, the fear seeped off the man's skin. Especially when he swung around to find no one behind him.

Sparrow leaned against a tree with his arms crossed against his chest when the blonde slowly turned on shaking legs. "Tell me, the plan here was to what? Get our attention? Verify that you're working with the Islanders?"

"It was to kill the lot of you. To kill her." Impressively, there was no shake to his tone. "To kill *you*."

"So you killed a bunch of neighbors first?"

"Casualties."

"Mm, yes." Sparrow watched the blonde and knew Heron would see the shine in his eyes. When his Master Assasinary turned on, there was a twinkle that shined brighter than the stars in the sky in his pupils.

Sparrow casually pushed off the tree when the realization struck the fucker and he turned to make another run for it. Sparrow caught up in two strides and rung him back at the same instant he pulled the sword from the blonde's hands.

He pushed Heron against the tree and plunged the sword into his gut, exactly where it would take hours to bleed out and kill him.

Heron tried applying pressure to the wounded area, smart enough not to try to remove the sword.

Sparrow smirked as he pulled his own sword out and flung

his wrist casually, watching the gash open on the blonde's forearm from the nick his sword had made. "Oops."

Heron was beginning to beg.

This was what Sparrow hated the most. They were always tough guys until it was actually time to be the tough guy. Then they gave up like the fucking chickenshits they were.

He made another swipe of his sword so it nicked the man's leg. And another straight through his dick—that one got a cry like no other.

Again and again and again, he nicked small areas of the blonde's skin until he was bleeding out too much for his body to withstand it. The sounds of Heron's cries for mercy were like music to Sparrow's ears as gashes opened on his legs, torso, arms, face.

When the fight was gone and the man hung limp against the tree, Sparrow cleaned his sword as much as he could at the moment.

He left the small area of the forests they'd been in with the man hanging on that tree, something his men could clean later. He moved back to the mess of the village center and merely stood at the edge.

The crowds were spaced out and controlled now, his men doing an amazing job at calming the chaos and helping the grieving. As he stood there, blood stained and raging, the pain crashed into him.

This was his fault.

They'd done this to kill him.

He'd allowed fucking Northerners to keep vials of what he'd believed to be pain relief potions. And though he was sure most of them were, he should've still taken them away and at least had Evony test them.

Catching Evony's gaze from across the field, Sparrow saw something he did not deserve in those beautiful sapphire eyes.

This was his fault. If he had paid better attention to the rebellion, searched the houses, confiscated vials, this wouldn't have happened. Anything instead of passing his nights dry humping the Magician and his days dreaming of her. If he'd done his job.

As his mind killed him from the inside out, he could feel her magic on him, trying to protect him even as she worked through the rest of the village center. *I'm here, my love. Always with you.*

She was too good. And he deserved none of it.

CHAPTER 22
EVONY

Evony wanted to soak in the water all night long. If she weren't in danger of drowning, she'd even consider sleeping there.

Through the chaos of the day, using her magic to ease the air while finding the vial of acid the rebels left for the second round of explosions had knocked all the energy out of her. Not to mention getting it out of there before the blonde threw his arrows directly at it.

She'd just gotten it away the first time Sparrow caught the arrow and was holding the vial the second time an arrow scorched his hand. She'd felt the pain cripple through her at the sight, but he hadn't seemed bothered. Hadn't even seemed to register any of it.

When the third arrow had flown through the air, she'd been glad he'd allowed it to fly past him. Because it meant he wouldn't be hurt again, but also because it meant he trusted her to keep him and his men safe. She'd stopped it before it touched anyone, but all she cared about was whether or not it touched him.

Then she'd allowed her magic to follow him as he disappeared into the forest, because as much as she needed all of it to help the chaos of the village, there wasn't even an ounce of her that had considered leaving him.

But the pain in his eyes when he'd come back out, blood stained all over as he stared out at the crowd, had pierced a deeper ache than Evony had known possible into her soul. He was hers, and he was hurting and there wasn't a thing she could do about it.

When he'd left the village, he'd looked like he needed time to think everything through on his own, so Evony hadn't followed him. She'd stuck around and helped her friends, Miels and Tristan, giving the latter the vial she'd taken.

Now, with the water running cold around her, Evony couldn't stay away from him much longer. She'd searched for him with her magic when she'd gotten back to the palace and found him in the men's bathing chambers. She knew he should be out by then. He would most definitely need the rest.

She stood before the fireplace in the bathing chamber to dry off rather than use a towel. She preferred the way the flames licked the air that heated her and had the time to pass.

When her skin was dry enough, she wrapped a long silken black robe around her naked body and moved for her suite, her mind too clogged with thoughts of the Assassin.

She'd expected to find the common area empty, expected him to be in his bed already, but that was far from the case. She'd been too optimistic to believe he'd allow himself the rest he deserved.

Sparrow was sat before the lit fire in only his sleeping trousers, knees bent before him and head fallen into the space between them.

Evony sighed softly, then closed the door behind her without a sound. She stopped behind him and got to her knees, sitting back on her legs as she ran her hands up his bare back.

She moved slowly, massaging out the tension in his shoulder blades, but he didn't show any indication that he knew she was there.

But he was aware. She knew he was.

His fingers thrown over his knees fought one another, like they were trying to peel the skin right off his hands.

Evony kissed the base of his neck, ignoring the slight stiffening as he felt it, and crawled around so she faced him. She had to pull his head up so he'd look at her and force herself to remain calm as she looked into the broken eyes of her assassin.

It was so interesting. He wasn't simply an assassin, but the Master. And he was the one feeling so much sorrow for those who were hurt.

It just went to show that he was only the Assassin when he needed to be. That he only used his skills when they were needed—like for fuckers like Romanchi—and Evony's heart squeezed a little bit more at the knowledge.

She pulled his hands apart so they'd stop scraping against each other and gasped at the palm of his hand. He hadn't gotten his hand checked. "Sparrow. You should've gone to the infirmary."

"I deserve it. I deserve to be reminded every day."

"Sparrow," she whispered as she brushed her thumb across the raised skin on his palm.

That simple word seemed to break him. "This is my fault."

Stiffening, Evony looked down. "What?"

"If I had confiscated the vials, they wouldn't have been able to do this."

She moved again, feeling her robe open as she straddled his lap. "Sparrow, listen to me. This is not your fault. We were all trying to play it off as if we didn't know the Islanders were working with them. None of us would have assumed this would happen. This is no one's fault but those rebels."

He shook his head, and looked like he was holding so much in.

She allowed him the moment to stare into her eyes before she took his hand again, unable to leave it injured.

"Don't." He tried to pull away.

She didn't let him, so he fisted his hand so she wouldn't be able to get to the injury. "I can't, Sparrow. I can't leave you hurt."

"I deserve it." His voice was raspy, nowhere near the hard edge she'd grown so accustomed to.

She met his gaze. "Would you allow me to remain injured?"

His jaw ticked, but he opened his hand. Her heart raced with what that meant, in more than just this situation.

Healing always knocked her out, but this one wasn't so large a problem and it was about time for bed anyway, so she didn't care.

When it was done and she looked back up at him, he was staring at the light hold the belt had on her robe. His hands shook as they settled on her thighs beneath the silk. "I'm meant to protect them. This is my fault."

Then the impossible happened. Something Evony never expected to see from the Master Assassin. A single tear fell down his cheek.

Her hands skimmed their way up his arms and into his hair, around his neck. She snuggled up closer to offer her comfort as another tear fell down those cheeks.

His hands moved farther into her robe, exploring her skin before settling at her back and bringing her in closer. Then his face fell into the opening at her chest. She held him as the tears stained her chest and his fingers bruised into her skin as he kept pulling her tighter into the embrace, almost like he was afraid she'd pull away because of everything that had happened.

"I'm here, Sparrow, and I'm not going anywhere. Let go of the pain. It wasn't your fault." She kissed the side of his neck, the top of his head, the edge of his temple over and over and over again. "I'm yours, my love. And I'm here, and I cannot fathom a life without you. This isn't your fault."

His tears subsided eventually, and his breathing grew calmer as the evening grew darker. The exhaustion was so clear in his eyes, Evony used her magic to pull a pillow and throw from the couch over to the ground and slowly moved Sparrow back.

He settled on his side looking into the flames as the small clock on the mantel struck midnight. Evony threw the throw over him and knew sleeping on the ground, especially this plush rug, would not be so bad.

Before she could move away, he opened his arms wide and his eyes beckoned for her to join him. That heart of hers was ready to explode into its own million little pieces at the sight.

She settled her back into his chest and felt him tug the throw over them both before his hands found their way into her robe and settled there.

He was out in no longer than five minutes, but not before he mumbled into her ear, "I cannot fathom a life without you, my Evony. You are everything to me."

Her heart was working far too fast to be able to handle all of this, but she wouldn't think too much on it. At the moment, he needed the comfort, not a discussion on what this was between them. But she wanted this.

Wanted to be by his side always.

She shut her eyes and squeezed tight as the feeling within her grew. Opening them back to look into the flames, she finally understood fully what Gemma and James were always going off about and didn't know if she could live without it.

But she also wasn't sure if Sparrow would ever acknowledge this—what they were—publicly and take her as his. And that scared her far too much to allow herself to think about.

†

WITH THE AFTERMATH of the village's explosion, the entire palace was in an uproar of damage control.

With Edmund and Sparrow making their formal appearances to the village in order to make sure the people didn't take this as ammunition that the King didn't care for his subjects, the rest was left to the others.

Gemma left with Tristan to oversee damage control within the town's people. James with Miels to lead training of the palace guards. And Rosaelia was aiding the servants in preparing aid packages for those in the village.

That left Evony with nothing to do. She didn't excel in damage control, was completely inappropriate and unconventional for political roles, and didn't want to be a bother to the system the servants already had with the Princess.

The last thing left was helping out in the infirmary. And as the Princess's cousin, she should be freely able to, but something in Evony told her that didn't matter much to Old Lady Arba and her minions. No, it was being the Master Assassin's betrothed that would give her free access to help.

Those who had survived with major injuries had been brought to the palace infirmary in order to receive the best treatment they could offer. It was the best part of being the closest village to the palace—if they needed it, they could use the palace infirmary.

The infirmary was a mess of bodies, and although she wanted to help, Evony didn't want to get in the way of the medics who already weren't too sure of her. So she made her way to the back for Ashtyn's makeshift office. The feisty woman could give her work.

When she made her way past the curtains, she was surprised to find Papa Ignatius, the man who had been stabbed in the courtyard, sitting patiently on the sickbed as the dark brown, floppy-haired stable boy, Gabriel, fought with Ashtyn.

"Tell him he is in no shape to be doing any work!"

"Are you questioning my methods?" Ashtyn looked indignant.

"I am not questioning anything. I'm telling you he is an old man with very recent injuries. He needs rest!"

The two stood nose to nose, Ashtyn's eyes narrowing on the man a foot taller than her. "I've taken care of him and there should be no reason why he cannot do some light work. It'll do him better than allowing his body to shrivel up. Light work will give him the necessary exercise."

"Necessary exercise my ass. He's an old man, and he needs to rest."

Gabriel was such a sweet man that hearing him speak like that was a shock to Evony.

Ashtyn's hands clenched at her sides as her anger rose. Gabriel was only trying to care for the man he saw as a grandfather, but all Ashtyn would hear is just another criticism toward her work. The poor girl was so used to expecting them at this point that it was probably all she assumed this to be.

"Enough you two." Evony stepped up, signaling her presence in the room.

Gabriel immediately took a large step back and bent low at the waist. "Miss Evony."

Ashtyn grumbled and turned to her seat, plopping into it as Evony quirked a brow and stifled a smile. "Just Evony, Gabriel. Everything okay?"

Gabriel looked hesitant to speak up.

"Is there a reason you won't speak to me as plainly as you did Ashtyn?" Evony asked.

A blush erupted across his cheeks as his chestnut brown eyes sheepishly met her gaze. "You are the Master Assassin's betrothed, I cannot speak to you in any way I wouldn't the Princess."

Evony scoffed at the same moment Ashtyn did from behind him. "Speak to me plainly, Gabriel," and with emphasis, "*Please.*" When he didn't look convinced, she added, "Sparrow will not mind as long as I do not. Please."

He breathed in a few moments like he was thinking it through then started, "I just think it irresponsible to put an elderly man like Papa Ignatius to work so soon after his injury."

"So don't allow him to do any work."

"He doesn't listen!" He turned on Ashtyn. "And he won't listen until you tell him to stop!"

"Tough." Ashtyn stared him down even from her seated position.

Evony laughed. "Enough." She turned to Papa Ignatius. "Just do as the poor man says and take it slow. Another week before you continue. For everyone's sanity."

Papa Ignatius grew pink with a slight blush. "As you wish, Miss...ah, Evony."

Evony smiled. "Good. Then you are dismissed."

Gabriel turned to her, the fury in his gaze turning to gratitude. "Thank you."

Evony gave a simple nod and watched them walk out, Papa Ignatius stopping by her ear as Gabriel waited by the infirmary doors. "I'm onto him. He just wanted to see the pretty medic."

Evony laughed, her gaze moving to said medic as the men left the infirmary. "Aren't you helpful."

"What do you want?" Ashtyn never beat around the bush, Evony liked that about her.

"He's cute, no? Gabriel."

"I thought you were into the Assassin."

"I am. Entirely." Evony sat on her desk, blocking Ashtyn from doing any work and forcing her to pay attention. "But you're single."

"Evony." Ashtyn tried to pull her papers from beneath Evony's ass. "Go away."

"You're not denying it."

"I'm not entertaining you either." Ashtyn gave up and threw her head back to rest on the chair.

"You must! *I'm* the Master Assassin's betrothed."

She scoffed in response. "Just because you suck his dick doesn't mean I have to suck yours."

"Then you'll be pleased to know I came with a true purpose today."

She popped one eye open and looked to Evony expectantly.

"I want to help with the injured. Tell me what to do."

Ashtyn sighed and there was a tired resignation behind it. "You'll have to ask Old Lady Arba. I'm not allowed to help. She says if I'm so high and mighty then I should worry about palace problems only."

"You're not going to fight her?"

Her smile was also tired. "I know it doesn't always look like it, but I do pick my battles. And right now, it's more important that the injured get the help than for any of us to be distracted in petty arguments."

"Do you think she'll allow me to help?" Evony asked.

Ashtyn's lips turned down, but she said, "Like you said,

you're his betrothed. They'll have to allow you whatever you want."

"But I'll distract them from helping."

"Helping to their fullest, yes. They'll be too caught up with checking on you."

Evony studied her a moment, then sighed. "Great. Back to being useless I go."

Ashtyn shrugged because there was nothing she could really say to that.

In the bout of silence that followed, Evony swung her legs from the desk. Then the words were out before she realized it. "You've been here a while right?"

Ashtyn opened both eyes, blatantly staring in question. "Just over a year. Why?"

"Sparrow's interests... have they ever wandered about the palace?"

Ashtyn sat straight up. "Are you insecure, Sapphire?"

"Sapphire?"

"Your eyes. I call your sister Emerald. Well, not to her face, but given I never talk to the girl, that's not too hard."

Evony smiled at the nickname and shrugged in answer. "I guess I am."

Surprisingly, there was no mockery in Ashtyn's features as she answered, "He hasn't shown interest to a single person the entire time I've been here. From what I've heard, he's never shown interest to anyone at the palace. Apparently, he would get his release when out of town, and even then, rarely. The man is too secretive and suspicious of everyone to let his guard down."

Evony felt a slight ease to her anxieties but got stuck on the prickling question she didn't want to ask tickling her throat. "And... Rosaelia?"

Ashtyn stiffened a moment before relaxing into her seat.

"Ah, now I see where the insecurity is coming from. You think because you two look exactly alike, he'd have been interested in her too?"

Evony shrugged, knowing a blush was beginning as she looked down to her interlaced fingers. "It would make sense."

"It's never been like that between them. And before you quirk your brow at me because I've only been here a year, it's well known that they're like brother and sister. When he was adopted into the family, he immediately looked to Emerald as a sister and that's never changed."

Evony nodded slowly, though she knew her features gave away that she wasn't convinced. "That's good." Her tone was even less convincing.

Then the unexpected happened—Ashtyn took Evony's hands in hers.

Evony shot her gaze to meet the medic's and saw nothing but kindness there. It was so different for Ashtyn that it caught Evony completely off guard.

"The day you showed up was an uproar in the palace, and I'm just as curious as the next guy. I was out there when you arrived. No matter what he did, he wasn't able to keep his gaze off of you. He looked like he was fighting himself the entire walk to the King's wing, like he was trying to convince himself to stop finding you in his periphery."

Evony grimaced. "That's because he didn't trust me."

"Maybe. But it's also because he's been fascinated with you from the beginning." Her hands tightened as she smiled up to Evony. "You two may be twins, but he found a striking differ-ence in you. Emerald will always be his little sister, but you? You're far more."

Evony felt her heart crack and her anxiety shrivel away as she gave a weak smile. "You should tell him that."

Ashtyn's annoyed smile came back as she pushed away

from Evony and leaned back in her chair. "He knows damn well."

✝

EVONY LEFT the infirmary feeling better—if only for hearing the reassurance of Sparrow's actions. She'd spent the rest of the afternoon in the library, reading more books in the stifling room as she tried to figure out if there was anything more she could be doing. Especially now that an attack had been aimed, the very last thing she could endure was watching Sparrow live through blaming himself again.

She knew everyone was back when the sun was beginning to drop, casting the skies in beautiful oranges, and the servants she'd asked to inform her of their presence came to her.

She'd left the library only then, heading for her suite to wait for Sparrow to finish his late training, clean up, then meet her there. All in hopes she'd be able to take his arm to dinner.

It was on the walk to the suite that she felt a shift in the air of her magic around the palace. She'd learned the peoples of the palace grounds so her magic wouldn't be disturbed if any one of them had moved about within it, which only meant there was a strange disturbance.

Evony froze in her spot in the middle of the palace hall, letting her concentration settle around her magic as her mind moved with it in the air, finding the point of contact.

It was hard to tell sometimes when the disturbance was innocent—a young couple from the local village trying to find a secret spot to be together for an hour or two—or quite the opposite.

She focused her attention to the spot her magic took her to and let it wander, looking for minds to infiltrate. She would only be able to remain in their mind for a few seconds before they were aware of something amiss, but seconds were all she needed.

She'll be happy. Infiltration is simpler than I thought.

But worse than the confirmation that these were rebels was the image that popped into Evony's mind—one of a potion left off to the edges of the palace to slowly bleed into the air.

She knew exactly what that was. Knew that sorcerers made it specifically to hide and allow the winds to carry the contents into the air, slowly poisoning everyone within its vicinity.

She needed to stop it.

But first, she needed to get to the men, get them to the bunks where the six rebels were headed. Get them to stop the men and learn something from an interrogation.

She was running before she knew it.

Running, sprinting, flying to the outdoor training grounds she knew Sparrow, James, and the whoring twins would be.

To her shock when she arrived, Edmund was also out with them, training as an equal under Sparrow's command.

Her speed picked up, and she was more thankful than ever that she wore tight fitted trousers rather than a skirt that would hinder her movement.

James turned, almost like he knew she was in trouble, and caught her eyes. He was breaking from the group and moving to her as he shouted, "What, Eve? What happened?"

She realized in hindsight that the fear had a lot more to do with something happening to Gemma than anything to do with politics or anyone else's safety.

His yell got Sparrow's attention and he was moving to her just as she skidded to a stop before them. "Infiltration in the west grounds. Around the men's bunks. At least six. Right now they're not backing down because they think they've gotten an easy way in."

The words were out of her mouth in a single breath, and it took about as long for the men to process the information before Sparrow shouted instructions for his men to get to the west grounds. He'd undoubtedly have them check every nook and cranny of the area.

And that was all he needed to know, she could take care of anything else as he worked to keep the palace and his men safe.

When it was just their little group, Sparrow stepped even closer to her. "How do you know?"

Sparrow watched the spot James held her like he wanted to do it, but Evony couldn't think about that at the moment. "I have a ward around the palace grounds. The magic recognizes all the palace inhabitants, they're not one of them."

The weariness was evident in Sparrow's eyes, especially after what had just happened at the village center.

"It could be village people," Tristan suggested.

She shook her head. "Got a glimpse into one's mind, that's how I know they think the infiltration will be too easy."

Edmund breathed through his nose as he grit calmly. "Let's catch up with the others."

Good, they needed to go so Evony could go.

He and the brothers were gone in seconds. That was the one thing she really liked—respected—about her father—he was a King who worked with his men rather than cowering behind them.

James took her face in his hands and looked to be analyzing her emotions. "Evie…"

"I'm all right, James. Gem's okay." She grabbed his wrist. "Go. Go check on them."

He watched her another moment before leaning in to kiss her temple. Then he was running for the bunks.

Evony turned to Sparrow who still stood rigidly at her side. "You too. Catch up with them."

She didn't know if she was imagining it, if wishful dreaming was getting to her, but she swore she saw a mix of desire and concern in his eyes. Like he thought her fragile and wanted to hold her and never let go. It's exactly what she wanted him to do, even though she was far from fragile.

"Go." She nodded back in the direction the others had gone.

He stepped forward, cupping her face in his hands and taking in her every feature. "You weren't touched?"

Her brows furrowed. "No, of course not."

"Then why is there fear in your eyes?"

Because I still need to stop the powder from filling the air around the palace. Because I will not have you blaming yourself again, and I definitely won't have you dying because of the winds.

He was reading her too well, and she didn't know how she felt about that. If she were to remain here, be accepted and stay by his side, then she didn't mind. She loved how well he knew her. How well he could detect what she needed.

But if she were to be pushed aside after they were through with using her like she was accustomed to, then the very last thing she wanted was for the Master Assassin to know her so well.

"I had to make sure you were okay." It was the truth. She feared what would happen to the palace, but more than anything she feared for him. His safety and his sanity. "All of you, but especially you."

His lips quirked up ever so slightly. "I'm the Master Assassin, love. It'd take far more than six men to hurt me."

She nestled her cheek into his hand, closing her eyes to

breathe in his scent—her newest form of oxygen, she needed it to survive. "But you're still my assassin, and I cannot help but worry."

She opened her eyes to see a shine in his as he looked down at her, and his thumb brushed her lips. "I'll catch up with the others, go inside and make sure everyone else is all right."

She had planned on doing just that.

But she liked that he didn't send her off to the rooms like a damsel. He was using her to protect the others, knowing she could protect herself.

Her hand reached up to hold the wrist that cupped her face. "Be careful, Sparrow. And before you begin with that Master crap, remember that I don't care. I need you to be careful for me."

He leaned down and gave her the lightest of kisses on the lips, so brief she barely had time to process it before he pulled back. "For you, anything, my love."

Her breath hitched. He so rarely called her anything but her name or her profession, and every time he did, her heart sank a little more into that pit made specially for him in her stomach. The one that was always fluttering at this point.

CHAPTER 23

SPARROW

It was the briefest of touches of the lips, but Sparrow felt her on his mouth the entire way to the men's bunks. Felt her body molding into his and her eyes shining up at him with all the trust in the world. As guilty as he still felt for what had happened at the village because he paid more attention to being with her than the rebellion, he couldn't help but know he wouldn't stay away. She was his, and he would remain by her side, keeping her safe and happy, even if the entire world went up in acidic explosions.

When Sparrow reached the bunks, the six men were on their knees in a single file and everyone was awaiting him. The other palace guards would've already been sent by Miels and Tristan to check the rest of the palace. Only two stopped at the end of the room—too far to hear—to aid if it were required.

He sighed. "Should I open or would you lot like to speak?"

The leader of the little lot snickered. "You're wasting your time."

"In your acquaintance? I know, but some matters must be dealt with whether we like it or not."

"It's as much a waste of my time as it is yours, Assassin," the man spoke as if he'd have very much time left.

"So why don't you start talking, and we can cut this short?" Tristan interrupted the man's rudeness.

The man shrugged, smug. "I don't know shit. But I do know the real people you should be focused on are up in those pretty trees that line the palace. Convenient."

"Is that so?" James quirked a brow.

"Hey, whatever they were looking for, you lot gave it to them." The man laughed like he was enjoying their downfall rather than his own. "They thought whatever you have going on would detect us. But we never would've imagined it to work this quickly. I'm impressed. What is it?"

Though he made Sparrow sick, Sparrow could still give the man props for not backing down and cowering like these so-called rebels tended to do.

"Does it matter to you?" Sparrow answered. "You will not be making it out of here to inform your leaders."

The man smirked proudly. "I guess I'm just curious. I heard it's a magician, but that would be impossible. The Northern Lands don't allow magicians."

Sparrow didn't show any reaction, but this complicated things. If the Islanders knew they had Evony—even if they didn't know she was a Master—then the North didn't have the leverage they'd thought.

The man ignored his friends telling him to shut up. The thing about some of these less cowardly ones was they tended to be cocky. "I guess I'm curious, will your magician be able to stop it?"

Sparrow narrowed his eyes, but the mirth in the man's eyes said he wouldn't give it up, no matter what Sparrow did to him.

So instead, Sparrow grabbed the shoulder of one of the others, and pressed into a pressure point. "Should I ask?"

"Slow powder," he cried, his back arching backward. "At the edges of the palace. Carried into the winds to poison."

Their little leader looked annoyed, but now that it was out, he didn't hold back. "Yes, I think we were told they were curious whether your magician would die trying to carry away all that powder." Sparrow's heart stopped. "You see the powder needs to be distributed in a contained space and if I'm guessing correctly, I'd say this magician is using her power right about now to wipe that powder out so thinly into the winds that it would die out, unable to poison anyone. Except herself, of course."

The fear in her eyes.

It hadn't been thinking these fuckers had gotten to them. It was the possibility of that powder getting into the air.

He didn't care about holding in his reaction anymore because breathing was getting harder and harder.

The leader's smirk grew. "Am I to believe this reaction? You know, I have heard of your betrothal, but it would be blasphemous to be with a magician."

Sparrow couldn't listen to him anymore. He caught Miels and Tristan's gazes. Then James's.

Then they were all running.

Edmund would take care to make sure the men standing off to the edges would hold the fuckers in the dungeons, but all Sparrow cared about was getting to her.

He needed to get to her. To those calming blue eyes and that sweet, beautiful smile.

He screamed to the servants for her location and they all huddled to the edges as they told him she was in the library. He didn't care. About anything. He just needed to get to her.

The doors to the library slammed so hard, he heard the

wood splintering, but couldn't pay attention to any of it. Evony stood in the middle of the library, her arms spread around her hips and her skin growing white as her eyes popped open with the sound.

"I got it all, love," she muttered with a weak smile as her eyes fell again and her body limped.

Sparrow was at her side, catching her into his arms and bringing her into his chest before she could hit the ground. "Evony. Evony, baby, look at me." He lifted her into his arms and turned for their suite. "Get Ashtyn. Now," he demanded of no one in particular.

He got to their suite quickly, all the while begging her to wake up, to open her eyes, to make a dirty joke, anything. But she was limp in his arms, her chest barely rising and falling.

He didn't hesitate to move to his room, wanting her in his bed where she belonged.

"Get out," he bit out to the three men who had followed him in. When they went to argue, he grit his teeth, "I'm changing her. Get. Out."

James was a little more hostile about leaving her side, but all three complied.

Sparrow took no pleasure in removing her clothes. Her skin was lightly mattered in sweat and every bit of it ashen. Not to mention the scar that ripped across her stomach added to reminding him of everything she'd suffered.

He tried not to look—to give her that bit of dignity—as he stripped her by placing the blankets over her before throwing one of his oversized shirts she loved so much over her head. When she was covered with the shirt, he brought the blanket back over her body and took the chair beside the bed.

There was a soft knock on the door before Ashtyn walked in with the others behind her, Gemma included in the mix, but he couldn't focus on them. He brought the hand he had in both of his to his lips, kissing it softly an infinite amount of times.

Ashtyn sat at the edge of the bed between them and as much as Sparrow didn't want to, he pushed back, releasing Evony's hand to allow the medic to do her job. That mattered more than any of his desires.

"Don't," she stopped him. "Hold her. It's what she would want and even unconsciously, it would calm her and make my job easier."

The selfish part of Sparrow didn't consider questioning her. He had the excuse to hold Evony and he wouldn't throw that away.

Her hand was back up to his lips and he unconsciously kissed her as Ashtyn worked. When she checked her over in every way she could, she closed her eyes and held her hands over Evony's chest like she could magically make the second heir better.

She let out a soft breath when she opened her eyes and pulled her hands away. "She's going to be okay, Sparrow."

The crazy, possessive, protective side of him couldn't believe that. Needed her to do something because he felt too helpless and he needed Evony to open her eyes.

"I don't know what happened and I have a feeling I'm not going to find out, but she *is* going to be all right. Her body's just exhausted, it needs to rest. Honestly, she kind of looks like she's been healing for a week straight. That's kind of how I looked that month before you found me." Ashtyn's hand fell on the ones he had clasped around Evony's. "She's tough and her heart is strong. Plus, let's be honest, she's not giving you this easy out. She's going to be okay and she's going to stick around to drive you crazy for a long while, Assassin."

He couldn't look to Ashtyn or anyone else in the room,

hadn't been able to remove his gaze from Evony, but his lips tipped up. "That does sound like my girl."

"You should tell her that when she wakes up."

"That she drives me crazy? I think she knows."

She laughed, softly and barely audible, but still a laugh. "That she's your girl. I know she'd like to hear it, doesn't matter if she knows it or not."

The medic wasn't wrong.

Sparrow peeled his eyes off of the beauty in his bed and caught Ashtyn's gaze. "Thank you."

†

HER COLORING WAS COMING BACK. Slowly.

But she was still unconscious.

Gemma lay asleep cuddled into James in an armchair at the corner of Sparrow's room, but the others had left. As much as Miels and Tristan had wanted to stick around, with Sparrow busy at Evony's side, they needed to lead the matters of the palace.

Rosaelia stopped by after they'd gone, hugging Sparrow from behind as she tried to comfort him. Then Edmund, who leaned by the door jam and looked out to his daughter in the bed. They'd left together not too long after.

And though Sparrow couldn't blame them for not feeling the instant connection to Evony, he hated that they were her blood and they treated her worse than everyone else. Treated *her* like she was the outsider.

All the while, Sparrow stayed by her side.

He clutched her hand in both of his and laid so many kisses upon it, her palm was probably numb from all the pressure.

Her coloring was coming back even though it was nowhere

near the tanned lightness of before and that helped his restlessness settle, helped him believe Ashtyn's words from earlier.

"I don't know if I like you by her side like that, Assassin," James broke the silence.

Sparrow froze. He definitely hadn't expected that. Somehow, he thought since Evony flirted so outwardly with him, her friends were on board with their entanglement.

Apparently not.

"I won't leave her." His tone was clipped. James was her brother so his job was to protect the Master Magician, but Sparrow could not imagine leaving her. Not unless she asked him away.

"How can I be sure of that?"

Sparrow's brows furrowed as he looked over to the man hidden beneath his wife's body. That question made it sound like he wanted Sparrow to remain by Evony's side, completely at war with his original comment.

"She acts so often like she's free spirited, and at one point she was, but she's been hurt too many times. But never has she been so invested in a relationship as now. How do I know you won't raise her spirits only to pull them away?"

"I'm not prone to games, warrior," Sparrow had to grit out.

"I know," he answered calmly. "But she is my sister, and I care more about her than how angry you may get hearing this. She's been hurt so many times in the past and as much as she's tried to come out of it, it's crippled her heart a little more each time. And never had those relationships been romantic. I cannot imagine the agony if you were to deposit of her when she was done being useful."

Sparrow's heart ached as he turned back to the woman in his bed, her chest rising and falling normally now. He pushed some of the locks out of her face and softly skimmed her cheek, needing to touch her more than just holding her hand. "What happened before? She's said she's had to wipe a few memories."

James sighed. "Which time?"

Sparrow's jaw clenched. To think there were more than one. He wanted—needed—to hear all of them, but one more important than the others. "The worst one."

James didn't respond for some time as Sparrow caressed his magician's face, memorizing it all. Finally, he said, "Three years ago and the last time she'd allowed herself to trust anyone outside our group. Except your lot now."

"What happened?" Sparrow's voice was lower than he'd thought, but it was all he could manage, already preparing himself for more of the hurt that made up those ocean blues.

"We were in the southernmost part of the Southern Lands, had been there for a few months, which is kind of a lot for us. Before coming here, we would travel as Gem and Eve as sisters or cousins and Gem as mine. So we were considered family and always had a little cottage to ourselves. There were these two girls across the way of our cottage, their father was in the militia I was helping with. They were all about the same age and their personalities were so similar that they kind of gravitated to one another without trying. Even as Gem and Eve tried to keep a wall because that's what we've always done, those two girls—Maria and Marta—broke it down.

"They were the sweetest, most pure girls, and when I saw them with Gem and Eve, I would kind of get excited. Because they've always wanted more people they could trust. When I met them in the forests, they would talk about futures where they married a man and would finally have a family, a large expanse of relatives to be crazy with. It obviously didn't work out that way after Gem and I fell for each other since I'm also an orphan. And since Eve never seemed particularly interested in any of the men we saw, we kind of lost hope for that picture.

So we started thinking of friends, like what we were to each other. Friends who became family. If we could find a few more and possibly have kids, we'd make our own little big family. It's naïve really, and since then we've grown content and happy with it just being the three of us, but we were teenagers and dreamers.

"Before moving down south, we were actually happy with our little circle. Because of the times we'd been betrayed before, that was when we'd decided to be happy just us. But then we met Maria and Marta and they were so sweet and welcoming and they made us feel so wanted. We met their family and the friends who were like family to them. We basically got what we'd wanted our whole lives—a large family to call ours. So eventually, we were maybe three months into seeing them every day, when the girls decided it was time we tell them. They'd brought us into the family, they deserved to know us completely. So we invited the two of them to dinner and told them everything—that none of us were actually related and that Eve was the Master Magician."

Evony moved in her sleep, turning completely to her side and bringing the hand Sparrow still held up to her chest so she could cuddle his entire arm. Sparrow wanted to smile at the movement, but the fear of what was about to happen gripped him as he pushed his chair right up to the bed so he could be closer to her, lest she wanted more of him to cuddle.

He didn't stop playing with her hair or face though. It was his tiny reprieve at the moment.

"They were calm when we told them. Shocked, understandably, but they promised to keep it to themselves and we thought everything was working out. We didn't realize it right away, maybe we were blinded by the joy of finally having more friends, I don't know, but things began to shift afterward. We'd still see each other every day, but slowly requests began being made. Little things the Master Magician would have no trouble with and again, we were naive not to see it, but we didn't think much of it. We—Eve—helped.

"But those girls, they were slick. Cunning, wicked. They knew what they were doing. The very least was that they kept their promise all the while and didn't mention it, but I know that was only to keep the Master Magician for their own personal use. Greedy fuckers. The reason this was the worst was because of how gradually it happened. They actually manipulated us into thinking using magic was our idea. They started expecting magical use, our relationship began being all about the magic. And we were blind to it all."

"How'd you realize?" The night playing thumb war was coming back to him.

"Gem had gotten hurt so Eve healed her. It's the one thing that wipes Eve out—healing. Somehow her Master skills don't expand there. So she was wiped, kind of like she is now, and resting. She'd just woken when Maria and Marta came by, and even though she'd slept it off, after healing she normally needs to take it pretty easy with the magic. We told them what happened because they were our friends and knew the secret so they'd understand. But they insisted. They'd gotten so used to hearing yes from us for the magic that they kept insisting she wasn't too tired—that's when I realized. When I fought for Eve, they tried to turn it, said who was I to dictate what *the Master Magician* did. Tried to make it sound like I was the bad guy rather than them. That's when Gem and Eve realized what was happening so Eve played along with them. Spoke to us in our minds so we knew what she was doing when she acted like she agreed with them, so we knew what we needed to do to make it believable. So we made it sound like she was pushing away from us and toward them and when they told her it was okay, she could use her magic, she did. Used it to force honesty out of them. I was angry with her for it because it's a hard thing to do and as wiped as she was, it would knock her out again. Even completely healthy, it's a hard thing to do. But she needed to know. They said they were trying to take Eve for themselves. As if I was controlling Eve's actions and this whole ploy was to take that from me and use her themselves. *Like Evony is a fucking puppet to be played with.*

"She lied to them then, told them there were some things she needed to take care of to make sure her magic was in top condition for them. Asked if she could move in with them so she'd be away from my manipulation. Those two were so giddy, they immediately agreed and gave her the two days she'd told them would be required. She spent those two days resting so her magic would be in top condition. When they came to bring her over to their house, she wiped their memories of us. It was harder since she had to expand her magic to wipe the memory of everyone else there that we'd been around, that they'd ever introduced us to. But Maria and Marta, she had to wipe the secret from them too, everything her magic had gotten them. All of it. We left after that and stuck to ourselves, taking on requests for the Master Magician whenever we wanted to, but mostly sticking to the shadows and not risking it any longer."

Sparrow leaned down to kiss Evony's nose and couldn't get himself to pull away. She was so innocent and pure. He hated how much pain she'd gone through, in all ways—physically, mentally, and emotionally.

When he finally got himself to pull away after another kiss, he only got a few inches before it felt like too much. "I can't tell you much, James, but one thing you can be certain of is that I am ready to protect Evony with my life. She *is* my life." He hadn't realized how true those words were until they were out.

"Fuck, if I thought she'd listen to me, I'd ask her not to use her Mastery because look at what it's done."

A light chuckle left the corner. "The reason I said I didn't *know* whether I liked it, Assassin, was because that's not true. You wouldn't ask her not to use her Mastery, even if you want to coddle her up and protect her from the world. You respect her power too much, the way everyone respects yours."

That was true. She was a goddess and he wouldn't stifle that. But he also hated how vulnerable that left her.

James sighed. "It's what she's most scared of—how hard she's falling for you. So, as her brother, I need to tell you that it makes me wary of you, Assassin. Though I'm sure it goes without saying that I don't care that you're a Master, my skills are enough to kill you in your sleep. Or gradually. It's one thing to hurt us, but to hurt her heart, it is the single thing I will not allow."

Sparrow nodded because he respected the threat. "Understood."

James got up to his feet with his wife tucked in his arms. "I may be considering your worthy-hood, assassin, but I know she's safe with you so I'm going to take my wife to bed. If *anything* happens, we're a breath away."

Sparrow nodded to him, knowing what James felt for Evony was what Sparrow felt for Rosaelia, and so he understood the need to protect. But he also loved that as protective as James was with Evony, he trusted Sparrow with her. It meant his actions, not just today but overall, had shown the man what Evony meant to him.

Hopefully Evony saw it too, because Sparrow wasn't the best with his words and he'd never been in this type of situation before. One where he wanted—needed—a woman to know how he felt about her. Maybe that was because he'd never felt for anyone what he felt for his magician.

His crazy fucking magician who had gone off and almost killed herself distributing poison into the winds. All to protect the fucking palace.

And though reasonably if he'd been in her position, he knew he would've done whatever he could to protect the palace—his home—the thought that it had brought Evony down was too much to process.

She'd somehow become his reason for breathing.

CHAPTER 24
EVONY

There was a reason Evony avoided healing as much as she could. It knocked her out like crazy, but this felt worse than normal. Though to be fair, she'd used every little bit of her magic to distribute those grains of powder as far as the Rivorbant Waters.

And this was a form of healing. Like healing the air.

So it made sense that she felt wiped out in the same degree.

But all it really took was a good rest for her to be back to normal and with how comfortable she was feeling, she'd gotten the perfect bit of rest.

As her eyes fluttered open, Sparrow's scent assaulted her in the most delicious of ways. And the strongest of ways. How was his scent so strong? Even when she stole his shirts to sleep in, the scent didn't hit her as powerfully as she would like.

Her eyes adjusted to the small amounts of candlelight around the room and realized why the scent was so strong.

She'd been in his room before—every time she stole his shirts—but she'd never stayed long and never had she gone onto his bed, even though every bit of her had wanted to.

But that's exactly where she was—in his bed.

In his shirt.

With him in a chair by her side.

And her hand in his.

She squeezed her eyes tightly, then opened them again. And tried it once more.

"Is there something wrong with your eyes?" His hard tone cut through the silence of the room.

She opened her eyes again and he was right there beside her. "I'm just trying to wake up. Because I must be dreaming. Real life Sparrow would never allow me into his bed, better yet sit by my side."

His lips dipped into a frown, the furrow between his brows deepening like he was upset with something she'd said, but none of it had been a lie. He fought her flirtations. And though sometimes he entertained them, he was mostly on the opposite side.

He pushed the frown away and moved a hand to cradle her face. "You're awake, Magician. And I'm right here. *Always with you.*"

"Prove it," the whisper left her lips before she could stop it.

His lips tipped upward this time and he leaned in, kissing her delicately. And he didn't pull away right away either, allowing them to bask in it for long moments.

When he did finally move to pull away, her free hand shot to his nape. "More."

He laughed. "You need rest, Magician."

She pouted. "Just one more."

He relented and kissed her a little more passionately this time. "Now rest, love."

She grumbled but cuddled in with his arm and stared up at him. "Why am I in your room?"

"What happened out there, Evony? Why would you go try

distributing poison knowing it would be too much for even your magic? Why would you do it without telling me? I would've been there for you."

"No." She loved the passion as he spoke to her. "You would've tried to stop me. You would've kept interrupting me before I could finish."

"And I would've sent my men to take care of the powders so they didn't get picked up in the winds," he argued.

"And risked your men? Don't be ridiculous, Sparrow."

"Better than risking you." He breathed in abruptly, obviously trying to control his anger.

"Why are you angry?"

"What would've happened if those fuckers hadn't baited me with your safety? If I hadn't come running to you the moment I found out?"

The moment he found out? Running to her? Baited him? The words teased her with how much she wanted them to be true.

"I would be resting, the same way I did here." She still needed to know what this reaction was. "Why are you so angry, Sparrow?"

"You almost killed yourself and you're as—"

"I wouldn't have died. I'd be exactly as I am now, tired and in need of rest, but that's it. I'm a Master, things like that are exactly what the Mastery is needed for."

He inhaled sharply. "You almost killed yourself and you're asking why I'm angry? Evony, what if you'd hit your head on your fall? What if you bled out and no one was around to help you? What if something happened while you were working your magic and there was no one around to stop you before it got too much? What if...Evony..." His voice broke. "You could've been hurt, past exhaustion."

"Why do you care?" she asked it softly because this Sparrow sounded different. Sounded vulnerable.

He scoffed, taking his hands away from her and leaning over his knees as he stared at them.

Evony swallowed, missing the feel of him, and looked down. She was wearing his shirt.

Her brows furrowed. "Who changed me?"

He inhaled and lifted his head just enough to look at her. "I did. You were sweaty. I wasn't sure if it'd get worse."

It didn't. She normally had a light sheen when she healed because of the amount of energy it took her, but it wasn't much.

She eyed him and felt little sparks come back to her as the flutters made themselves known and she smirked his way. "You like what you saw when you got me naked?"

He bit the inside of his cheek, obviously trying to hide his amusement, even though there was still an edge to his eyes. "I didn't look. You deserve your dignity."

She grimaced. "Not with you. You could have your eyeful."

"Behave, Magician," he growled, but the edge was slowly dissipating from his chocolate browns. He pushed his chair back as he stood. "I've entertained you enough. Rest."

Evony didn't hesitate in moving over. "Okay, c'mon. But take your shirt off."

He eyed the empty space, then her. "I'll sleep on the couch. Rest, Magician."

She crossed her arms before her chest stubbornly. "Only if you rest with me."

He looked well past exhausted and that hopeful part of her wondered if he'd spent the entire time she'd been out by her side.

"Evony," he warned.

She interrupted him before he could say much more. "How long have I been out?"

"All last night and today. Ashtyn kept insisting you just needed the rest and I see now she was right."

Ashtyn. He kept calling for Ashtyn. Why?

"You have my final offer. Get in here if you want me to rest."

He looked heavenward as he took in a large inhalation but relented and moved for the spot beside her.

"Ah, ah, ah." She stopped him with a hand to the chest. "Shirt, Assassin."

"Evony," he growled.

"Fine." She began to move for the edge of the bed. "Then I see no reason to be here."

She was about to step out of the bed when his arm reached around her waist and threw her back onto the bed. "Fine. Just, stay in the bed."

Her crooked grin was probably too wicked, but she didn't care to hide it. He single handedly reached for the back of his shirt and pulled it off, causing those flutters in her stomach to fly down south and make her as wet as the oceans.

She stripped her shirt off before he could move and he froze at the sight. His unmoving chest told her he wasn't breathing either.

She felt his eyes on her body—no longer trying to give her any dignity—as she reached for the shirt he'd just discarded and threw that one on.

"What"—he was controlling himself as he got the words out through a clenched jaw—"was the point of that?"

"This one smells more like you, the other has been cleaned so the scent is lighter. And this one is warm with your body heat." Her grin held the mischievousness she knew angered him. "And I just wanted you to get the eyeful you missed out on before."

He grumbled, but still got in when she moved back over for him.

They were staring at each other when she finally asked, "Why do you keep calling for Ashtyn? With all the medics here, why always her?"

"It's not always her. It just so happens that when you're around, the best is always needed."

"Ha. Ha. Very funny, Assassin."

His lips twitched up and she took that excuse to move in closer to him. He didn't move away, allowing her legs to tangle in with his.

"I think she's a Master."

Evony gasped. "What?"

"She hasn't been identified, but that doesn't mean she's not a Master. She's secretive so it makes sense that no one would've suspected it of her."

"A Master Medic?"

He shrugged. "Healer, but same thing I guess."

"Incredible. I've had the same thought, but figured since she's older than me and hasn't been named…"

"I know. We've spoken of it. Briefly. She's still unsure if she wants to find out." Evony was about to speak when he said, "That's enough, Magician. You said you'd rest if I got in with you."

She pouted.

"What else do you want?"

"You."

He smirked though the amused annoyance was in his eyes. And instead of telling her to behave, he grabbed her and pulled her into his chest. Flush. His body against hers with the shirt she wore and the trousers he wore the only things separating them.

She gasped.

His cocky grin pressed into her forehead as his arms wrapped around her. "Now rest, love."

Her lips quirked up and instead of flirting any more, she kissed his chest and snuggled into him. As much as she loved talking to and infuriating him, she was still a bit tired.

Before sleep overtook her, she mumbled against his chest, "Thank you, Sparrow. For holding me."

His arms tightened and pushed her closer. "You're welcome, baby."

†

She never wanted to wake up, because doing so meant giving in to the possibility that this would fade away. This warmth of being in Sparrow's arms. This intoxicating sense of breathing him in. This feeling of safety at being held by him, like even nightmares wouldn't be able to frighten her.

But she had the sensation that she was being watched, so her eyes fluttered open and found Sparrow still sound asleep with his arms tightly bound around her. He looked so calm, so at ease.

When her gaze skimmed past his shoulder, she found her father standing above them and her heart stopped a moment from the shock. "Edmund," she stuttered. It was still weird trying to figure out what to call him.

"You're awake." He eyed the two of them. "And comfortable, I presume?"

A blush found its way to her cheeks even though she was always more careless with her flirtations. This felt far more intimate than anything else the King had ever seen between them. Or maybe it was the feelings confusing Evony at the way Sparrow had acted before they fell asleep.

She could hardly move in his grip so her breath still hit Sparrow's chest as she spoke to her father. "I would tell you to sit, but then you'd be talking to his back. I mean, if you'd like…"

"I don't mind standing. Sometimes I think I sit far too much."

She felt awkward. It wasn't a normal feeling for her. Usually, she could remain in silence with anyone and be fine, but something about that moment was throwing her off. Maybe it was being stuck in her position of not being able to properly look at him or maybe it was the *intimate position* she was stuck in.

"Did you need me to wake Sparrow…"

"No, no, allow him his rest. Poor man hasn't slept in two days. Not to mention I don't believe I've ever seen him so at ease."

The flutters were back with full force.

She sighed when he put her out of her awkward misery, a feeling she supposed he was used to putting people in as the King. "I am simply here to thank you. For protecting the palace when you did not have to."

"But I did. I was asked here to help against the rebellion with my magic and that's what I did. Not to mention, as the second heir, it's my palace too." His eyes sparked, but he allowed her to continue. "And throwing all that aside, there's no way I would've allowed the winds to bring the powder anywhere near Sparrow. So if nothing else, be thankful I have the hots for your assassin."

His lips tipped up, but his eyes didn't look entirely amused.

After a minute, Edmund's gaze settled on the shirt she wore. "You are in his bed. In his mind."

"And he is in mine."

"Not in the same way, I suspect."

What did that mean? "Possibly not. I am very open about my intentions, I have yet to determine what his are."

"Yet you remain in his bed." There was almost an accusation in the way he said it, which struck odd since she knew he didn't have a problem with bedding. Northerners held no more purity concepts than Southerners or Islanders. All the lands believed individuals could do as they pleased, so his tone wasn't a difference in their upbringings.

"I do."

"Am I correct to suspect you'd do a great many things for Sparrow's attentions? Even if that makes them waver from the rebellion?"

She knew she was getting attacked, but she tried to remain calm. Even though she didn't feel a fatherly affection for him, Sparrow still looked to him as a father and she didn't want to upset her assassin.

"You are correct that I would do a great many things for Sparrow. But none of it to cause him any harm, and distracting him would cause him emotional harm when the outcomes turn out like that village." She kissed Sparrow's chest because she needed the bit of strength it gave her when having this conversation—the one that clearly drew the line with her on the *not one of us* side. "But I also respect myself too much to do *anything* to get his attentions. If he does not want me as I am, then he will not have me. I will not make myself anything else in order to please him. He will have me as Evony, the girl who happens to be a magician, or he will not have me at all."

"And if that means he will not have you at all?"

She wished she could've hidden the gasp of pain at the prospect, but it was too sudden. And it was also a fair question. "Then I will not bother him any longer. I will complete my end of our bargain, and you will hold the leverage of knowing my identity, but I will no longer be a bother to the palace."

His gaze studied her for long moments, and Evony wanted more than anything for her father to get out, to leave her. She already had the fear of not being wanted, and having him blatantly put it into the air around her made her heart race in panic that this may be her warning that they would soon be rid of her. That they'd be done using her.

Sparrow unconsciously brought her closer, like he could sense her unease and wanted to settle it, even in sleep. She huddled deeper into his hold, feeling cowardly under the scrutiny of her father's eyes and needing the protection Sparrow offered. Needed to believe that he wouldn't throw her out of his life, that he'd meant it when he said always.

"I will leave you to rest, *daughter*." The way he said the last word spiked another shot of trepidation within her.

She was glad to have him gone and, to finally allow the tears she'd been fighting to fall. She hated how much those few minutes with him had affected her, but she couldn't help the helplessness she felt in the outcome of these relationships she'd established.

Was she naive again to allow it to happen? Was she stupid enough this time to allow it to happen with her heart too? Were they thinking about getting rid of her? Throwing out her uselessness? Depositing themselves of the trouble a magician in the palace could bring them?

And most importantly, was she reading too much into the way Sparrow treated her? Allowing her hopeful heart to feel the love that wasn't there?

The tears were light, but they continued to fall for long minutes as she hugged Sparrow tighter, never wanting to let him go, and told herself he wanted this—her.

✝

WAKING up next to Sparrow was a superior experience.

But convincing him—which took absolutely no effort—for a little morning make out session? Even better.

The feeling of his smile against hers as they'd kissed, as the passion had grown to such a high, he'd pushed her to her back and gotten between her legs. The reminder that she was only in a shirt that was hiked up from the movements of sleep and he was only in his sleeping trousers. The ecstasy of his tongue in her mouth as his hips ground down on her. The way their hands reached for any bit of skin, hers raking down his back while his skimmed over the borrowed shirt.

All to be interrupted with Miels barging into the room to wake them up—apparently the twins had taken to checking on Sparrow after her fall in the library.

Yeah, the interruption hadn't been the best, but the wicked gleam that had entered Miels's eyes in finally *catching* them mixed with the fury in Sparrow's? It was coming up to her favorite morning to exist.

She had breakfast with Gemma and James in the privacy of their suite so that they could have their alone time with her. Evony could only imagine how much she scared them.

It was on their way to the private training rooms to meet with Rosaelia for her training that Sparrow intercepted her with a grumpy *Where do you think you're going?* and *You need to rest.*

When she shrugged him off and continued on her way, he took her hand and followed—well, led, with the length of his double-her-size legs.

Miels and Tristan were already with Rosaelia when they

entered, and the grins they both wore as they faced their best friend were far too telling. Sparrow had growled at them and left Rosaelia in the middle confused.

Even more so when Sparrow took Evony to the edge of the room and pushed her onto the sitting foams.

"How am I meant to train her from here?"

"We'll train her," he grumbled down to her. "You're lucky I'm allowing you to be here."

"Sparrow, you're being ridiculous. I don't need any more rest." She looked to James for some help.

The ass threw an arm around her shoulders. "I agree, you don't *need* the rest. But I think I'll be on the Assassin's side here."

Sparrow smirked as she harrumphed. "Trader."

And he really made her sit there.

And watch as all of them—because even Gemma and James joined them—got to have fun on the mats. It wasn't fair.

She gave up listening to Sparrow's command about ten minutes in, moving to the mats and joining Gemma. She, of course, knew that Evony didn't need the rest—once the weariness wore off, she was always as good as new—but she still smiled to Evony with that knowing twinkle in her eyes that said this wouldn't last. The Assassin wouldn't allow it.

But Gemma still entertained Evony by allowing her to join in her flexibility training the minute and thirty-six seconds it took for Sparrow to get in her face.

"What do you think you're doing?"

"Making myself all warm and loose for you, my love." Evony wasn't foolish enough to think the flirtations would work, but she truly enjoyed the way his eyes flared at the insinuation.

"You expended too much magic, Evony. You need to rest."

"No. I don't."

"Evony," he growled and she felt everyone in the room quiet and take a couple steps back.

"Do you know the definition of overbearing?"

"Sit down." His teeth bared at her.

She crossed her arms in stubborn resistance.

A gleam awoke in his eyes. "Sit down and we'll see if tonight can mirror last. Or maybe we can mirror the morning?"

Her heart sped up. And she quickly put her ass back on the foams.

"Good girl," he purred and she had to glare at him to stop this effect he was having on her because she was far too wet for a training session.

The remnant distraction his praise had given her faded after a while and she was back to being grumpy about not being allowed to participate. This was her training session!

She grumbled under her breath as she leaned back on her hands. Sometimes she just wanted to smack her overprotective assassin.

Miels strolled over to her with a teasing grin already about his features.

"You better go away before he kills you," Evony opened, not bothering to look at him—unable to when Sparrow was directly in view and distracting.

"Yeah, that dagger he threw at me this morning was probably a warning, huh?" The blonde was enjoying himself far too much, and had Evony been in a more teasing mood, she'd be laughing with him. But that dagger throwing assassin was so frustrating sometimes.

Sparrow was well aware of his friend's presence beside her. He glared from across the room.

"C'mon, Magician, cheer up. Ro is still getting her training. Your session is not wasted."

She glared at him. "*My* session. Where *I* teach her."

He quirked a brow at her. "What exactly were you going to teach her that we cannot?"

"How to claw her prey." She smiled smugly.

He merely gave her a cocky grin back and nodded to Sparrow. "Kind of like what happened to his neck?" The marks were light, barely even visible anymore, but they were still there.

Evony's lips twitched up involuntarily as she muttered, "Don't remind me."

Miels feigned disbelieving shock as he settled beside her on the foam. "Not a good experience? After this morning, I find that difficult to believe."

She exhaled to keep her peace. "A world-shattering experience. But he is currently high up on my want-to-throttle list, and therefore, does not deserve any of the positive thoughts."

He shoved into her shoulder. "Like you're not ogling him now imaging him naked?"

Sparrow was before them in an instant, but there was no way he would've heard the blonde's remark. He had Miels gripped by the shirt and yanked up before Evony could process the movement.

Evony gasped. "There's no way you heard that." *Why was that the first thing to come out of her mouth?*

Miels's smirk grew past his eyes as he stared Sparrow down. "He didn't. Sparrow dearest just doesn't like me touching what's his."

Her brows furrowed, but with the fading bruises still marring Miels's neck, she knew he was most likely on the right track. She placed a delicate hand to Sparrow's death grip on Miels's shirt. "Let go of him, Sparrow. You're being ridiculous."

Sparrow's jaw ticked, but finally he released his friend. "I'm killing you next time. I swear it." Everyone joined Miels in his laughter as Sparrow turned hard eyes on her. "Sit. Down."

The backs of her knees hit the foam as she bit her bottom lip. "You're sexy when you're all possessive, Assassin."

He pushed her back onto the foam. "Last time I say it to you too." He leaned over the bent knees she'd brought up before her chest. "Move again and I'll tie you down, Evony."

"Onto your bed?" Her voice held sultry undertones.

His eyes turned an enticing black. "Behave, Magician."

At her smiles, he moved to pull away, but she grabbed for his wrists before his hands left her. "Fine. I promise, no more. But can I have a kiss before you go back to being eye candy?"

She knew the pout was beginning to win her pointers. It was slight, but there was a lift to his lips before he leaned down and gave her a chaste kiss.

Surprisingly, he didn't pull away from her after the kiss. Instead, he stared into her eyes like he was searching for something, then moved up to her forehead and laid a kiss there too. It was shocking to find that with everything they'd already experienced together, it was that one—that long pause on her forehead—that was the final straw. Her heart surrendered.

When he pulled back to search her eyes again, he said in a voice so low she barely heard it, almost like a prayer, "Those ocean blues calm my world."

CHAPTER 25

SPARROW

Because he was being an overbearing ass, so he owed her—and because he just selfishly wanted to—they did mirror the previous night. And the following morning.

Except this time, he made sure the door to their suite was locked before heading to bed. He hadn't wanted any interruptions when he rocked into her beneath him and made her come onto his trousers again.

It really went against his *You need to rest* argument, but that contented smile she'd given him afterward was worth it.

The memory of her moans circled the air around him as he stood in the library's balcony, looking out to the greens below. He forced himself to not barrage Evony for being down there, running around with Gemma, James, Miels, and Tristan. He knew she was fine, that she looked as healthy as ever, but the twinge of uncertainty still beat against his heart.

Her laughs echoed in the winds, reaching for him, as she ran from Tristan's clutches—another thing he had to stop himself from, adding Tristan to Miels's dead man boat. Especially because he couldn't blame his friends. It was her free spirit and playfulness that captured everyone's hearts. He couldn't blame them for becoming as enraptured as he was.

"She's beautiful, isn't she?" Rosaelia's soft voice startled him out of his thoughts as she stepped up beside him.

"Well, she is your twin."

Rosaelia shoved her shoulder against his. "Please. You've never once looked at me the way you do her. And don't get me wrong, I'm glad for it. Just gotta let you know that no one buys that bull you spew, least of all me."

Sparrow laughed and looked back down to the group, to that smile that'd become his reason for living. "She is...beautiful. Hypnotizing."

Evony was more than just beautiful too. Her features were enticing and called to him in every way. Her smile warmed his cold heart, her eyes shined into his soul to calm him, and those long black locks begged for his touch. Her body—which he had ingrained in his memory from her change of shirts—sent shivers through him. The fantasy of kissing her every inch, of worshipping that scar across her stomach, of pumping into that cunt that was made just for him.

But it was more than just the physicality of Evony's presence.

It was her carefree words and dirty insinuations. It was her mischievous manners and delicate comforts. It was knowing when to tease him and when to allow his overprotective nature to win. It was her vulnerable whispers and that salacious spark her eyes always showed for him. It was her every bit that was made specifically for him.

"Brother, are you in love with the girl?"

Sparrow's heart dropped to the pits of his stomach as he sputtered at the question. "Of course not, I've only known her a few weeks."

"Mhm."

"In any case"—Sparrow turned to her—"if we're speaking of being in love, you should be the one in question. Ever plan on telling Miels how you feel?"

Rosaelia didn't sputter—probably because she only had a crush on the blonde—but she turned a deep crimson and shot a warning glare his direction. "I don't know what you're talking about."

"Mhm."

"I was trying to be serious and you go and ruin it!"

"How am I ruining it?" He really didn't like being questioned about Evony, that was becoming evident by the situations he continued to find himself in with Edmund and now Rosaelia.

She rested a hand to his shoulder and they both turned back to the group on the grounds. They'd run about and fallen so many times, their clothes would be unfixable, but they were happy. "Last month, when we sent that letter, do you remember what I wished for more than anything?"

You deserve to find someone who will fill your life with contentment...be the reason you smile when you're alone with your thoughts and the center of every enraged and frightening moment you experience.

"I do."

Evony chose that moment to look up at the balcony, like his stare called down to her, and gave him the most soul-melting smile conceivable. She motioned for them to join, then exaggerated her furrowed brows when he shook his head down to her. She turned away from him in the most embellished motion possible and Sparrow felt the smile eat up his entire face.

Rosaelia snuggled into his arm. "Contented, Spar?"

Sparrow felt the tightening around his heart but didn't

want to think too deeply about it. With a rebellion in the kingdom, it was certainly not the time. Instead, he leaned into his sister and kissed the crown of her head. "I love you, Ro."

"I love you, too." She pulled away, the smile widening on her lips. "And I bet I could beat you down there."

Sparrow quirked a brow. A race? With Princess Rosaelia? He could win by walking. "You asked for it."

And she was off, running straight out of the library and into the halls that would lead them to the grand staircase, then eventually, the courtyard. Sparrow allowed her the moment's head start before chasing after her.

And catching up in seconds.

He allowed her the advantage until they reached the bottom of the stairs, then it was no more nice guy. As he made his way out, a weight hit him in the back and he realized the Princess's plan.

"You're cheating, Ro." He laughed, but didn't stop running.

"Nowhere does it say I cannot hitch a ride." She giggled into his ear as they reached closer to the group.

Evony caught sight of them just as Rosaelia jumped off his back and took two steps before him, throwing her arms in the air. "I win!"

Sparrow didn't have the chance to refute her as Evony jumped into his arms, legs wrapping around his waist and squeezing him tight into her as her hands messed their way into his hair. "You came!"

Sparrow laughed as his hands landed on her ass, effectively holding her in place. "Happy wife."

She gasped, the smile growing even wider as she leaned in so her lips pressed against his. "Happy life."

She kissed him and Sparrow wanted so much to take her to the palace, push her against the wall and ravish her against it.

"Now make that statement true, Assassin. The chapel *is* free right now."

He laughed, leaning in for another small kiss as he squeezed her ass before dropping her to her feet so they could join in the group's fun. "Behave, Evony."

✝

UNFORTUNATELY, duty meant they weren't allowed to enjoy the beautiful day out in the greens for too long.

Evony was off with Gemma, doing lords knew what, while the boys headed for training—today's wouldn't be physical, but priming of interrogation skills—while Sparrow met with Edmund fresh from his meeting with a lord's second from the east telling of the towns there.

They were in the King's suite, the dark wood of the room perfectly lit by the fireplace and the curtains half closed to block out the sun. It was how Edmund most preferred it.

"They're getting more dangerous," Edmund opened their meeting. "First killing the villagers in hopes to get the lot of you out there, then setting out poisons."

Sparrow tsked. "They knew about Evony. Probably not that she's the Master, but they knew the poison wouldn't work. They played us so we'd have to show our cards, show them that we have a magician and she cleaned the poisons they had laid out."

"You think they believe her dead?" Edmund asked. "If doing what she did knocked her out, then a normal magician, even one considered among the more powerful, surely wouldn't have survived."

Sparrow shrugged as he fell into a chair beside the flames. Being beside them made him think of the times he and Evony sat before their fire. "Based off what that rebel said, I'd have to presume that was their goal. Get rid of the magician. They figured out we had help either at the village explosion or sometime before and needed to get rid of her. The best course of action would be to allow them to think that, though I don't really know what we would do to convince them of it."

"I'm sure they're not expecting a reaction out of us." Edmund brought a glass of hot tea to his lips. "If it were true and our magician had been eliminated trying to clear the poison, there's no way we would've shown a reaction to it. Especially considering we're not meant to have a magician among us."

Sparrow grit his teeth. "In all my years...I can't figure out what they're going to do. I know it's going to be an attack on the palace, know they need me out of the picture to make it easier on themselves, but that's it. I have no indications on schedules or procedures. I don't even know if I should be leaving the palace."

Edmund's lips tipped out. "Someone's cocky. I'm sure we'd be able to handle without you, Master. The men *were* trained by you."

Sparrow rolled his eyes but wasn't able to hide the grin quickly enough and knew Edmund saw it. "I'll tell Evony to be extra careful with her magic. Not that she randomly uses it, but in any case, I'll have her be cautious."

The amusement in Edmund's eyes vanished. "Tell me, Sparrow, are you shagging the girl?"

Sparrow nearly spit the tea he'd brought up to his lips. But he did choke on the bit he'd swallowed. "Excuse me?"

Was he truly asking whether or not Sparrow was shagging his daughter?

"I believe you heard me correctly, son. Are you shagging the Master Magician?"

Sparrow analyzed the King but found no telling signs behind the reasoning to the question. "No."

He almost looked...relieved? "Good. I think it is a good idea to refrain from doing so."

Because Sparrow wasn't good enough to be with one of his daughters? One of the heirs?

"Why?" Sparrow had to know.

Edmund merely shrugged. "I saw you holding her in your barely dressed manors the other night. I was merely curious."

He definitely wasn't *merely curious*, but Sparrow had a feeling he wasn't going to learn the reasonings at the current moment.

"I'll give the others a chance at interrogating. As much as my Mastery puts fear into them, it's not always the most helpful."

Edmund nodded. "Good. I'd like to rid of this problem already."

Something in the way Edmund said that made Sparrow feel like he meant more than just the rebellion.

†

IT'D BEEN a while since they'd done this.

The three of them used to go out to the forests that surrounded the palace grounds at least once a month— usually once a week—and practice their targets out in the open. They trained well enough in the palace with the others, but it was something entirely other to be out in the forests and throwing daggers up a tree so tall they could barely see their supposed targets. Or to climb the trees then throw at specific leaves or branches while balancing on the bark they stood on. Overall, it was just another form of training, but it was something the three of them enjoyed in the privacy of their friendship.

And it gave them rein to speak freely without having to worry about anyone within the palace overhearing. Though they had plenty of private discussions within the palace, something about being outdoors and doing so made it feel more authentic. It was something Sparrow could not describe.

So when Tristan and Miels pulled Sparrow away from the palace a couple of hours before dark to go into the forests, he hadn't argued. But he was coming to regret that decision.

"Now that we're free of the royals and the little magician's crew," Miels started, "you can tell us."

Sparrow looked between the two of them. "Tell you what?"

Miels's arm flew around his shoulders. "Don't play daft, brother. It is quite obvious she is not just the Master Magician or a fake betrothed to you."

When Sparrow didn't answer, rather moved out of his friend's grasp to take one of the daggers they'd brought out with them to begin, Tristan started, "Oh, c'mon, brother. Just tell us, have you been shagging her this entire time or just after the betrothal announcement?"

Sparrow's blood boiled and he growled at the man. "I think you're jealous of the way I handled your brother last he spoke of her like that."

Tristan chuckled, but his grin held strong. "You won't hurt us. It'll upset her too much."

"I have ways of cheering her up."

Both men's eyes widened and they clapped his back as their laughs grew and both called out, "I knew it."

"Oh, would you two fuck off." Sparrow threw their hands off him. "I am not shagging her. Why does everyone care so much about our private matters?"

"Brother, I walked in on you two," Miels argued.

"We weren't shagging and I still want to skewer you for that," Sparrow grumbled as he threw the dagger in his hand high into a tree to land just shy of a squirrel. The little creature scurried away scared as the dagger embedded into the bark beside it. Sparrow smirked. Poor thing. If he'd been aiming for it, it'd be dead.

"No, you weren't shagging." Miels's tone was losing the certainty. "But you were definitely on your way. I know what I saw."

Sparrow grabbed for a heavier dagger this time, refusing to look at either one of them. "It's all been clothed."

Tristan settled against a tree. "Why?"

Sparrow didn't have to turn, his growl was answer enough. The morons had no place in his private life, least of all Evony's.

"You want to shag her and we're all *very* aware that she wants to shag you. What's stopping you?" Tristan's teasing was gone.

Sparrow looked down to the dagger in his hands and thought of his magician in the palace. Her place in the royal family. Her importance to the world as both an heir to the Northern Lands and as the Master Magician. Unlike Sparrow's Mastery, Evony's was useful to the world. And her free spirit and kind heart needed someone who mirrored it. She was all around too good for him.

He was undeserving of such perfection.

"Don't ignore us, Sparrow," Tristan called. "We have all day and you've taught us to be very patient."

The smirk could be heard off Miels's tongue. "Or we could always ask the Magician."

Of course the fucker knew what to say to get a reaction out of him. And he hated how much anything Evony related got a reaction from him. He'd have to train himself not to make it so noticeable.

"What do you two want?" he grit out.

"We just want to know what is happening with you two. We've never seen you so interested in anyone before. Definitely not so that you'd actually resort to the public displays you showcase to the whole of the palace." Tristan's voice was sincere.

"Yes, not to mention that smile that just about shined through your face earlier when she jumped into your arms. I almost didn't recognize you," Miels added.

Sparrow sighed and threw the dagger, this time aiming for distance rather than height. It struck a tree too many yards away for Sparrow to count. "We haven't spoken of it."

"But there is something?" Miels asked.

"You just said it was obvious there was something, of course there is something." Sparrow finally turned to face his brothers.

"Something that makes you *not* shag her?" Miels sounded like he was trying to figure out the complex equation.

He looked down to the basket of daggers sitting on the forest grounds because the confession felt too intimate to meet either one of their eyes. "I need us to be on the same page before I take her, because when I do, she's going to be mine."

The men watched him, like they were reading an entirely new book and they were trying to learn it's secrets.

"Are you in love with her?" Miels asked seriously.

"Rosaelia asked me the same thing earlier."

"And what did you say?" Tristan asked.

Sparrow shrugged, then looked out into the distance as his eyes glazed over and he thought of his magician with the infectious smile and shining blue eyes that called to him always. "I don't know."

Miels walked up and patted him on the shoulder, holding him as Sparrow met his gaze. He was still serious, but there was a shine in the man's eyes. Almost like an understanding. "I suppose we should expect a wedding soon then."

Sparrow felt the chuckle bubble out as he pushed Miels away. "Are you two done with your interrogations now?"

"For now." Tristan's smile was wide as he finally took a dagger and joined in on the fun. "But can you blame us? Today was interrogation training day."

Sparrow laughed with his friends as they finally turned their attentions on the competition of dagger throwing.

CHAPTER 26
EVONY

With Lord Alexei's visits closely followed by the rebellion's attacks, it'd been a while since they'd had one of their meals in their original group. And it was something Evony had come to cherish in her time at the palace.

Even with Sparrow not around to walk her—which she missed more than she cared to admit—they were getting back to some semblance of normalcy.

When she reached the dining hall, Evony found herself to be the last to arrive. And found Sparrow ignoring—or pretending to ignore—everyone else as he read his missives. The man could somehow pay attention to both the missives and the goings-on about the table simultaneously.

As she slowly strolled to her spot, she couldn't help but notice the deep flush on her twin's face. "What's wrong with you?"

"She walked in on us in the other room," Gemma responded with a mischievous grin.

With a mocking gasp, Evony shot a hand to her heart. "My poor twin's heart must've stopped."

Bright red, Rosaelia sputtered, "I heard groans and *screeching*. I walked in to find them tumbling against the walls!"

Evony laughed as she moved without hesitation between Sparrow's spread legs and took her seat on his lap, her heart rate jumping when his free hand immediately settled around her hip. She wrapped her hands around his neck and leaned in close. "Tell me, my assassin, should we also…"

"Evony." He didn't bother breaking his gaze from the missive as his warning sent liquid pooling at her center.

"What? It is completely expected for—"

"It is not the same. They are married."

"And we are betrothed. It's quite close enough."

He ignored her and her heart skipped a beat. He wasn't denying their betrothal. With Alexei gone, there was no real need to continue that charade—outside the fact that the rest of the palace still believed them to be spoken for—but really, the base reasoning behind the lie was gone.

"Sparrow," she slowly said his name as a single finger turned his attention from the missive to her. "I do not enjoy being ignored."

Evony heard the gasps as the servants began entering with their breakfast and felt the stares as they all took in her position on the Assassin's lap. To be fair, she doubted she'd ever been so blatant before the servants in this manner.

But she ignored it all as Sparrow whispered against her lips, "What can I do for you, Master Magician?"

Her lips quirked into a mischievous grin, not bothering with a whisper, "You can take me into the other room and rip my trousers off."

With the exasperated gasps coming from the servants,

and possibly Rosaelia, Sparrow narrowed his chocolate orbs at her though she noticed the tease shimmer through. "Behave."

She bit her lip. That simple word had the power to control her fully, to soak her to such lengths, he'd slip right in. Not to mention, the way his gaze latched on to her lips before moving back to the missive in his hand told her how much he wanted to do all the things she was requesting.

"Or what?" she stage-whispered loud enough for the entire room to hear as she leaned her forehead against his, her lips only an inch from his cheek. "Will you teach me to be proper? Maybe you can spank me into understanding."

With the sputtering from the servants, the King spoke up. "That's enough."

Right, the King. Her father.

She should feel more ashamed than to flirt so salaciously before him, but especially after his last conversation with her, she wasn't in the most forgiving of moods.

She pulled away and looked out at the table where all the plates had been placed but one.

Evony's servant stood at the opposite side of the table by the empty seat between Tristan and Rosaelia, the one Alexei had used in his time there. "It would suit propriety for you to sit across from your betrothed."

Now that there was another empty seat at the table, the servants were probably shocked she hadn't moved to it. Evony was surprised they'd been able to hold in their propriety crap this long.

Evony tilted her head as she looked the servant over, her fingers scratching the back of Sparrow's scalp through his hair as he pretended to be deep in his reading. "Hmm. I am quite comfortable in my seat."

"My lady, that is not proper."

A coy smile grew on her lips. "Shame for I believe this shall forever remain my favorite seat."

Astonishment filled the woman's eyes, even more so when no one in the room argued with Evony—surprisingly even Edmund refrained—and she reluctantly moved to place Evony's plates next to the one left for Sparrow before departing from the room and closing the doors behind her.

The King studied her and Evony attempted a genuine smile but did not move as she quirked a challenging brow at her father. "What?"

"What is it you're trying to do?" he asked with less accusation and more intrigue.

It was so baffling, how impossible it was to read him.

"I am merely speaking with my betrothed," she answered innocently.

"More like attempting to seduce your betrothed," Sparrow mumbled under his breath though his gaze never left the missive.

Evony settled her attention once more on Sparrow. "My love, let's not forget that I am *sitting* on your lap. I would call it succeeding rather than attempting."

A blush, light as it may be, shot across his cheeks as she turned to find her four friends holding back their laughs, and even Rosaelia wore a close-lipped smile.

"Now, Evony," Edmund tried for a teasing reprimand, but she knew, even if no one else did, that it was false. "I am your father, you shouldn't act like that in front of me."

"You are my father by blood alone. This doesn't truly bother you as it would were it Rosaelia."

His gaze told her it still bothered him and the flicker his gaze made to Sparrow told her why. Not because it was her, but because it was Sparrow. He was, for all intents and purposes, a father to the Assassin.

Edmund did not try to argue, rather turning to Sparrow as he finally put down the missives, his hand falling to rest on the leg Evony had strewn across his thighs. "Finally done?"

"Six letters. I had to reread a couple." Sparrow rolled his eyes toward her as if she were the reason. "Seems we have some problems by Brilfax Oak. I'll be heading out tomorrow to check on everything."

Evony didn't allow the thought to process before she said, "I'll come along."

Sparrow's gaze froze on the King. "No." He turned to face her. "You will not."

She stared into his eyes and couldn't help the smile that erupted as she cradled his face in both her hands and kissed him. He was becoming more comfortable with these public displays because he didn't even hesitate to respond, his hands squeezing her in closer to him.

After a few seconds, Evony pulled away and stared into his chocolate browns as she breathed in his scent. "Yes." She leaned in for a chaste kiss. "I will."

Not giving him the time to respond, she slipped from his lap and fell to the chair beside him, pulling her plate before her.

Sparrow cleared his throat and scooted into the table, effectively hiding his erection from the group as he began to fiddle with his food.

All the while, Evony felt her father's eyes on her, like he didn't trust her reasoning for wanting to accompany Sparrow. Her heart panged again in that gut feeling that she was about to get thrown out of the family.

✝

*H*IS BORROWED *shirt was barely buttoned, only the middle two doing any work in maintaining a semblance of modesty, as she glided to his bed.*

It was rare that she wore the button downs, but Sparrow had to admit, he appreciated this look.

"We're only sleeping tonight, Magician."

She furrowed her brows and nodded like she was in full agreement as she got onto the bed and prowled over to him.

"We must be up early for the trip, now is not the time," he argued, but she could hear the desire mixing in his command.

She crawled over him, dipping her head so her lips just skimmed over his trouser clad cock as she stared up at him through her lashes.

"Evony," he growled, hands fisting the sheets at his sides.

She kissed the skin at the edge of his trousers, feeling the hair of his happy trail tease her lips. "I think"—she moved up his chest with more delicate kisses—"now is the perfect time."

He didn't need to speak, even in the low moonlight of the room, Evony could see the blacks in his eyes.

When she was straddling him, hard length pressed into her bare cunt, she smiled warmly down to him, modeling the shirt she had on. "What do you think? It suits me, no?"

"Absolutely." His voice was rough with wanting.

She rocked her hips and delighted in the way his hands immediately grabbed her thighs. The way he looked up at her too, like she was a goddess, made her feel powerful.

"You're the second heir, Evony. I should have more respect for you than this."

She internally grimaced at the reminder. "This is the exact sort of respect you should have for me."

His hands slipped beneath the shirt and for the first time, his thumb found her slick folds still gliding over his cock. She bucked at the contact and the moan escaped her before she could recognize it.

"You deserve better. More than me." His breathing was

becoming labored as his hips moved beneath hers and his thumb found its spot on her clit.

It was all deliciously intoxicating, but he'd brought up her status and she hated how it wouldn't leave her mind.

She licked up his chest from happy trail to neck, suckled on a spot beneath his ear, then proceeded to his lips. She gasped from the expert way his thumb moved her, but there was a persistent conversation her mind insisted she have at that very moment.

"What's Edmund said about me?"

He froze for a moment. "What?"

"My father. What's he told you about me?"

"Evony," he grit out. "If you don't mind, I'd rather not bring you to orgasm while speaking of your father."

Her cunt clenched and she could feel how very close she was.

But she placed a hand to his and stopped him, raised her hips from his to remove the contact. "What's he said?"

He looked at her like she'd lost her mind. "Seriously? You'd rather talk about that right now?"

"He doesn't like me, Sparrow. Doesn't trust me. I need to know what he's said to you." Need to know if he's been telling you to leave me.

His brows furrowed. "You're being absurd. You're his daughter."

"Every time he speaks to me, I feel like he's looking for something, Sparrow. For a reason to get rid of me. Has he said anything?"

"No." He hesitated.

She caught her breath and moved off him, off his bed.

"Evony." He was before her, blocking her exit in seconds.

"You've never hesitated telling me something."

"It's nothing, love." When she crossed her arms, he cradled her face in his hands. "Love, it's nothing. He asked me the other day if we were shagging. He's not the only one either, so it doesn't matter. That's it."

She swallowed. "What did he say when you denied it?"

His eyes widened and she knew it was there. "We're Northerners, Evony. And as his daughter, he would rather you not be shagging just anyone. It's the only reason he was happy about it."

She scoffed. "No, Sparrow. He was happy about it because he doesn't want you getting any more attached than you may already be. He wants me gone. Once he's through using my skill. Maybe even before then considering a magician in the palace almost cost everyone their lives."

Now he was scoffing. "You're his daughter. He may not see you the way he sees Rosaelia, but you are his daughter and he would never send you away."

But he didn't say anything about trust.

And she truly didn't want to argue with him any longer, it was clear his mind was made up. "I'll see you in the morning."

He grabbed her arm when she moved around him and leaned into her ear. "Where're you going?"

"My bed. You were right, now's not the time. We should sleep, we need to be up early."

His jaw ticked. "You can sleep in my bed."

Her soul was sad when she met his gaze. "I can't, Sparrow."

She pulled her arm away and walked out before he tried stopping her again.

Remembering the night before, Evony watched Sparrow speak with Gabriel at the stables as the rest of his men readied themselves for the journey.

Speak was a relative word. Really, poor Gabriel looked like he'd rather be anywhere else. Sparrow had gotten her the best horse, one normally used for Rosaelia or himself on long trips, and badgered Gabriel to recheck the reins at least three times. Then checked himself twice in between. It was sweet.

It was annoying too. Frustrating. And poor Gabriel was left to deal with the impossible man.

Evony thought back to their night again as she watched the two men. It had been odd, being back in her room. She hadn't even realized when his room had turned into their room in the short couple of days, but being back in her bed alone had made it all the more difficult to fall asleep. Like getting a taste of what she most desired, then having it taken away.

She wondered if some of Sparrow's obvious frustration had to do with that. Sleeping in an empty bed.

"You're being impossible, Sparrow. The horse is fine." She'd been casual in her tone, but the annoyance was still there, especially detectible to his ears.

He turned violent eyes on her. He was angry. Truly? Because of a horse he knew she'd be perfectly fine on.

"You are to wait, Magi...Evony," he spit through his anger and Evony saw the blacks lining the edges of his eyes. The same black she had seen the night before when she'd been rocking her hips over his.

He *was* frustrated. Sexually frustrated.

Evony ignored the joyous hop her heart made at the knowledge and turned to helpless Gabriel. "You may leave." He looked grateful as he dashed out of the stables to help the others.

"Overruling my orders now?" Sparrow turned his blazing form on her.

She crossed her arms before her chest, a motion that captured his attention for a moment before turning angrier eyes back up at her. "How about you head to the stable loos and jack off before we head out. Your men don't need this right now."

Apparently those weren't the right words to say. Sounded right to her.

He threw her against the stable wall, his hand holding her in place by the neck as he leaned into her. "You chose to come on the trip so you should be made aware—on these trips, I am the master. Everyone follows my orders. *Everyone.* Understood?"

The way he hovered over her, commanding her around, had her center begging for him to rip off her trousers and take her against the stable walls at that very moment. "Yes, sir."

The blacks completely engulfed the brown as they met her gaze and she saw the amount of force he put into his body to peel away from her and turn around, heading out to the stable loos and slamming the door behind him.

Evony smiled as she brought her breath back to normal.

†

T‍HEY'D BEEN RIDING for some time and Evony assumed they were almost there. At least she hoped so. Sparrow hadn't calmed down much since their departure from the palace grounds with five of his men. He chose only a few since he had no reason to require more and the palace needed it's protection. But as they moved, his anger and frustration began to irritate her.

It was flattering, knowing that he was wound up because he wanted her, but she couldn't play this game with him. She needed him to see what she was talking about, to acknowledge that her father meant to have her thrown out of the palace. To believe Sparrow would fight for her to remain by his side.

And she wouldn't back down from that, no matter how appealing her throbbing clit found his domineering and commanding approach. No matter how much she wanted him to hold her against the wall again and tell her what to do, demand her to listen to him as master.

She had to stop thinking about it. This was no time to be getting wet over the man.

The bitter man who'd barely glanced her way in the hours they'd been on horseback, who'd ignored her as if she weren't worth his time when they stopped for their short breaks. The man was infuriating.

As much as he'd ignored her though, he'd stayed by her side the entire ride. Far more aware of her being than he let on. Infuriating was to say the least.

"You plan on ignoring me this entire trip?"

He rolled his gaze her way, then back to the grounds ahead, passive.

"Real mature, Assassin."

His hold on the reins tightened, knuckles turning white with withheld fury. "What do you want?"

"I want to know where all this fury has come from?"

He scoffed. "Don't play dumb with me, Magic..." He ground his teeth and kept forward.

"Oh, I have my theories, but I'd rather hear it from you. Especially considering I should be the angry one."

He turned scalding eyes on her. "Why should you be the angry one? Your problems with Edmund are unfounded. My frustrations are completely understandable."

"Excuse me?"

"Is there something you gain from psychological torture? From making me yearn for you, then peeling it all away?"

Evony felt his men shift uncomfortably on their horses as they kept pace surrounding them.

"I only peeled away because you refused to see my side of the argument, Sparrow. He doesn't want me and worse off, he doesn't want the lot of you to want me. The more I think about our interactions, the more I drive myself crazy wondering if I ever said anything that could make him so suspicious." It was driving her insane.

He scoffed again, anger truly beginning to fume from him. "That's because he is a good man, the best of men. What you're saying is unjustified and I do not understand your motives. What is it you want? You want the Master Assassin drooling at your feet?"

She scoffed this time, the anger rising in her faster than it had in him. "Drooling at my feet! You haven't shown an ounce of interest lest I wrap my legs around you. Tell me, Assassin, what sort of drool shall I expect at my feet?"

His men began to slow around them, putting little bits of distance between them. Evony wasn't sure if they were trained to do so in a private moment or if they were just beginning to feel uncomfortable, especially with the Master Assassin's anger rising by the moment.

She forced her anger to calm. "In any case, he is not the best of men, you are. You are the light in my darkness and I fear that that is all you'll remain. My light. Because you trust his intentions more than anything I tell you."

It's like he hadn't heard any of her last comments. "Haven't shown an ounce of interest? I've all but paraded you about! Evony, you share my suite. From the first day, I'd laid my interest."

"Oh, please, don't act like that wasn't in your personal gain."

But hadn't Ashtyn said the same thing? That his stare had kept finding her, and not in a suspicious manner, even at the very beginning. Was it plausible that there was another reason she was sharing his suite other than his original distrust of her?

He was about to argue when she turned on him knowing her eyes seethed the rage she felt inside. "He doesn't trust me,

Sparrow. And I wish I knew why so I could show him that *his* distrust is unfounded, but I will not grovel for his acceptance. I have come to gain Miels, Tristan, and you being myself, I do not need..." Her heart hammered, maybe that wasn't the case. Had her hopeful heart led her into a corner? *"Can I trust you, Sparrow?"*

His scoff mixed with an incredulous stare. "Don't be ridiculous."

It was sort of an answer. And she really needed to push the tears from watering her eyes. She kicked her horse and felt the gallop as he sped up.

But sure enough, Sparrow was by her side in half a breath. "Do not run off, that's a childish maneuver."

Well, that kicked the tears far, far away. "Oh, now I'm childish?"

His frustration was more than evident as he brought his horse in as close as he could to her and hissed, "Evony, the..."

His men raced passed them and they were both caught off guard.

Stopped at the top of the forest side they looked down to the town they were headed toward and a gasp passed from her lips. The group of the seven of them looked on for all of two seconds before they were racing down.

The town was covered in bloodshed.

CHAPTER 27
SPARROW

He'd been so caught up in the argument that he hadn't heard the clashes and screams coming from the town. Not until his men had passed him.

He'd been distracted. He was never distracted.

They all raced their horses down, Evony doing as well as any of his men. Hopefully that held up during the fight too because he didn't have time to be worried about her safety at the moment.

And yet, he knew half his attention would be distracted with making sure she wasn't hurt. Fuck, he really shouldn't have allowed her to come along.

From the few seconds he had to analyze the scene on the ride down, trained men had made their way to the town. Why would be the real question, but first he had to make sure there were some living left in the town. A town that wasn't known for its defenses, so why attack here?

The rebel fighters overpowered the townsfolk three to one, and that was fast becoming five to one. There had to be at least a hundred of the rebels scattered about the town center, and with three of his men already knowing to travel around and help the women and children, they were down to the four of them, hoping that Evony was more asset than liability.

As much as they'd all surely have liked to remain on horseback, it was too obvious the horses would not make it out if they went in there, so about twenty yards out, they all jumped off and ran into the bloodshed.

Evony was as quick as his men, not even needing his command to do so. That gave him hope for what they were running into.

Bloodshed.

It was a pastime for Sparrow, something that was well acquainted with his name. But he didn't like the idea of Evony being in it, or what it could mean for the town.

Sparrow made his way through three men easily, unsuspecting as they were to the new arrivals.

There were about twenty townsfolk left fighting, all injured, so technically, this would be down to the four of them. Realistically, it would be down to him. Even he had never fought so many with positive outcomes.

And these were trained rebels.

From his periphery, Sparrow noticed one of his three men pulling the injured out of the fight as the other two went toward the rest of the townsfolk. Good, keep them out of the way, this town didn't need to lose any more.

Then five men were on him at once.

His periphery told him Evony had two at her swords end and she fought them with the utmost training. So maybe his confidence in her should grow. Truthfully, he should've expected so, there was no way James would've left her defenseless. Especially after what had happened with Romanchi.

By the time Sparrow had slain two, four more had piled

onto the attack. He was getting through so many, it would set a new record. And it also meant he would be growing tired soon, because even Masters weren't undefeatable and he was taking on far more than his two men and Evony combined. As he shot out of the way of another attack and sliced through two throats in one swipe, he felt a shimmer run over him, momentarily freezing him in realization.

No.

If she was using her magic to protect him, she would be left open.

His sword made its way through the torso of one before he skewered another like a kabob, then pulled his weapon back as his gaze latched on to Evony, Master Magician.

She was truly a sight to behold. Breathtaking. *Hypnotizing.*

The wind picked up around her and her eyes glittered like the sun over the ocean waters as more attacks came her way.

Sparrow snapped out of it, rushing to her aid as more piled on him. He snapped around, barely noticing when he took the lives of six men with one blow. All he knew was that he needed to get to her.

Though he knew the aid was unneeded, for a single glance Evony's way showed bodies piled around her as she swung her sword about. Sparrow was sure either her magic was slowing the others down or speeding her up, but none of that mattered. She was getting through them.

And mesmerizing him in the process. He narrowly made it out of the way of a sword across the neck as he watched her kill two in one strike, blood splattering across her skin in the most exotic of ways.

Good, let her take care of them, he had some prisoners to round up.

Turning his full attention—or as much as he could muster,

no matter how much he tried, some of it would remain with the Magician—back to those around him, he began moving. Away from Evony.

When he was enough paces away, having killed off two along the way, he stopped and dropped his sword, watching as ten men surrounded him. He knelt to the ground, hands slipping into his pockets for the sharpened brass knuckles, as they all jumped him.

Fools.

He'd heard of this, the desire to hold the Master Assassin captive just to see what would happen. It's what normally signed their death certificates—the cockiness that they could catch him rather than just outright kill him.

A smile rose on his lips as he spun in his spot, both arms flying out as he bent back, slicing through the genitals of every man surrounding him. What easier way to get the high ground than affecting the genitals?

He watched them all drop, hands clasping around their centers to stop the bleeding as he rose above them and called to two of his men with the townsfolk. The numbers were dwindling down fast and he needed these fuckers taken care of so he could finish the ones running at his magician.

"Round them up." His men knew the protocol, the way to stop the genital bleeding and shackle them up enough for the ride back to the palace dungeons.

That was ten men, hopefully a good enough mix so he'd get some useful information. But ten normally tended to be all he needed. The rest could go.

He looked over to the carnage the Master Magician blew on her attackers. She'd dropped her sword too, playing with the sharpened brass knuckles and nunchucks she'd had hidden within her trousers.

She swung the weapon splattering one man's face into confetti without a second glance as she cut another man's face straight through the middle with the brass knuckles.

She didn't need the help, and in Sparrow's frozen position, he wouldn't be able to give it.

Awe.

Mesmerizing, beautiful awe.

He could stand out there and watch all day as she splattered blood onto that pristine skin, as she defended and attacked. She was a wonder he needed.

When a whip struck her leg—barely even enough to touch —he broke out of his stance and rushed into the fight. He had the remaining few finished off in the matter of seconds. Hopefully now she could retract her magic and not tire herself out completely.

As he looked around the carnage, he realized that after his massacre, her pile was quite impressive. Not quite as large as his, but as Master Assassin, that wouldn't have been expected.

It also made him realize that the two of his men in the battle had noticed as well and chosen to aid those who needed them—the injured—rather than continue on fighting. They'd realized that he and Evony were a team.

And he knew that she was his.

†

It was well known that Sparrow didn't handle damage control well. That was part of the reason he liked traveling with his men. They would help the families mend their wounded, which thankfully ended up being far more than twenty, meaning that far fewer had died in the battle.

While two of his men helped the people, Sparrow sent

another on horseback to the nearest town for their medics, and possibly another one after that. They would need all the help they could get. The more they could bring to this little village, the faster everyone would recover and try to move on. Because that's all they could do. Move on. They had to.

Sparrow helped his men get all the injured to resting positions, accepting the offer from one of the town grandmother's, a tavern owner, for two rooms ready for them to rest. She'd been thankful, but Sparrow couldn't help the desire to want to have done more.

While they aided the town, the two men who had joined him in battle chained the rebels into a wagon, but not before getting the slightest bits of information from them. Nothing that they revealed through their words, just things his men had been trained to pick up on.

Like when the attention of all the men went to the short, bulky one, they found the leader of the herd. At least of this little herd. The one who would know the most information and would likely be the most difficult to break.

Like when his men refrained from the gentle closing of their wounds, they found that the men weren't as tough as they acted. They enjoyed being bigger than the townsfolk, likely growing on more food and privilege, and they craved the power that gave them. But they were weak. Pathetic. And with the possible help of Nuhmed, easily breakable.

Like when the men threw curses their way, they heard the lilt of Southern upbringing. A Southern accent Evony and her friends didn't possess because they had always been traveling. A Southern lilt that was brought on only by the upbringing of a lifetime.

A possible problem.

They weren't necessarily from any one Southern place, but Evony, Gemma, and James considered themselves Southerners, and Sparrow was willing to bet a fortune they would not like the sound of their own people joining the barbarians of the Island Nation in this fight.

He watched his two men close the wagon doors, enclosing the rebels with extra chains, and get to their horses. They'd be taking the wagon from the townsfolk, but Sparrow would make sure it was returned.

When his men rode off, Sparrow felt a sense of ease at the knowledge that the prisoners would be in the dungeons when he returned to the palace. And a hopeful pang in his heart that soon, this fucking rebellion that made absolutely no sense would be over.

He turned and shot his gaze around the injured for Niel, the man who had sent him the letter.

Niel caught his gaze and slowly lifted himself off the bench many of the injured settled on, and hobbled off to the side. He kept his arm pressed to his chest and hardly allowed any pressure on his left ankle.

"What happened?" Sparrow had no time for niceties, Niel knew that.

"When I sent the letter, I had no idea it would turn into this. A few of them came into town, insisted on heading into the Sacred Gardens. When we didn't allow them entrance, they made a scene and argued, but that was it. They turned around and left. They came again throughout the week, and each time we fought, the Sacred Gardens started holding guards. Things were difficult, but manageable. Then maybe an hour before you got here, they showed up. *Insisted*, again, that they be allowed through. But they were more feverish with the need, almost like it was time sensitive. When we refused, they stopped asking and started killing."

"What did they want from the Garden?" Sparrow's gaze

washed over the people that resided in that small part of the Northern country.

Niel shrugged. "I couldn't exactly get that much out of them. I'm hoping you'll get it from the prisoners. But if I were to guess, it's the Sacred Gardens, where the soil is richest and some of the rarest plants grow. If this is part of the rebellion—which I greatly suspect it is—and they're working with Islanders, then I would presume it's to aid a sorcerer. Some of the higher-level sorcerer potions require plants from the Gardens."

Sparrow knew that much—it was the only real way this village made any money. They traded with the merchants sailing to the Islander borders.

Sparrow shook his head at the unbelievability of it all. If a sorcerer wanted a plant from the Gardens, they could have easily paid for it. "Do you have any idea which plant it could be?"

Neil scoffed. "I've been racking my mind for days. Tried forcing myself to figure it out while you and your lady fought them off." He gave Sparrow an impressed look at the mention of Evony and pride prickled through Sparrow. "I haven't come up with anything conclusive. It could genuinely be any of the plants, maybe even multiple of them. I'd have to have an idea of what they'd like to make."

Sparrow grit his teeth and looked out to the forest side his men had disappeared into. "I'll find out."

He stared another moment longer, then thanked and dismissed Niel to rest.

With his responsibility for the town taken care of for the time being, Sparrow's gaze shot around the mess for black waves and ocean eyes.

He found her resting on the other side of town's center with no one around her. And she watched him.

Her gaze was tired, likely depleted from the day's travels, the battle, and more importantly, the amount of magic she'd used during the battle. But even so, she didn't look nearly as tired as she should be, the same way he knew he didn't. That was the Master in them.

She was blood stained from head to toe.

And yet, she looked so beautiful.

He wanted more than anything to take her in his arms and have his way with her, and he noticed the desire he felt mirror in her gaze. But now was not the time.

She slumped in a little then and turned and walked off in the direction of the tavern they would be staying in. She disappeared through the tavern doors and Sparrow heard their earlier argument echo around him.

You haven't shown an ounce of interest lest I wrap my legs around you.

Don't act like that wasn't in your personal gain.

Can I trust you, Sparrow?

Sparrow stared ahead as the realization hit him that she wasn't playing with him. That none of this was a game to her. That, contrarily, this was the most important matter to her, something she hadn't allowed herself to feel in three years, and it was all for him. She was trying to give her trust and love to him, to make herself vulnerable, and he'd been too blinded by his loyalty to Edmund to see it.

He knew he'd been rash with his defenses. Knew as he recalled his more recent interactions with Edmund regarding the Master Magician, that they had grown less favorable. But was that because Edmund didn't trust her, or was it merely because he still felt uncomfortable with the knowledge that he was the reason he hadn't known of this daughter? He was the reason she had been hidden from him because a magician as a daughter would've surely been killed. He was the reason she grew up an orphan in the forests.

Sparrow knew him, knew how great of a man he was, so Sparrow was positive whatever gave Evony the idea that she wasn't trusted—and even worse, that she wasn't wanted—was just Edmund's insecurity about their relationship. Because there was no way *Evony* couldn't be trusted.

CHAPTER 28
EVONY

His gaze had shined like he would run across the town center and claim her. But he'd pushed it aside. Like he always did.

The magic she normally had surrounding the air around her, the one that took almost no energy and told her when he was around, was currently sitting dormant. As much energy as it didn't take, she'd wiped herself out against the rebels, so it shocked her more than she cared to admit when she felt his presence behind her in the tavern.

The tavern owner, an old woman by the name of Esta, led them to a table in the back with a small smile and thankful eyes. Evony didn't enjoy the look; as if she would have even considered not helping.

Evony sat facing the rest of the tavern dining space and watched as Sparrow sat beside her at the small circular table, both of them choosing to turn their backs to the walls rather than leave themselves open.

Wordlessly, three children ran up to their table with plates of potatoes, meats, stew, vegetables, and breads; a liter of water and two glasses were the final pieces placed before they went running off.

Evony had seen the two remaining of Sparrow's men take their food with the injured outside, glad that they were taking care of themselves alongside the injured.

She turned her gaze to the man beside her, then to the untouched plates before him. "Eat."

"Abide your own commands, Magician." His gaze allowed no room for argument, he would not touch his food until she began to eat.

She stifled the eye roll that begged to make a scene and topped a chunk of bread with stew and a small cut of roasted meats. When he satisfied himself watching her take two large bites, he began in on the meal.

Only a bite in, he turned to her again, this time to fill her cup. "Drink." She threw an annoyed stare his direction, but he ignored it and whispered through gritted teeth, "I don't even want to consider how weak you made yourself out there. That much magic should have killed you!"

"And fighting that many men should have killed you! We're Masters, Sparrow. I'll be fine."

Because she'd killed a lot, but nowhere near as many as he got through in seconds.

She should've learned from her fall a few days ago that even knowing she was strong and capable, he would be overbearing to the max. Even if all it meant was that he cared for her, and that made her insides sing, she wasn't in the mood to deal with his attitude.

He pushed the cup to her lips. "Drink."

She didn't stifle her eye roll this time, taking the cup from his hands and finishing the glass. As frustrating as he was, she was thirsty. He refilled her cup, then went to fill his own.

They finished their meal in silence, Evony stopping when

her stomach could take no more, and watching as Sparrow did their usual and finished off her plates as well as his own.

He made her finish her water though. And another one after that.

She was finally given reprieve when Esta came to them with the keys to their rooms.

"We'll be sharing, the other will go to my men," he told her with a gaze that said not to even think about arguing with him about it. She only nodded her acknowledgment. "I need to check on them. Go up and get cleaned, our room has a bath in it."

Again, she nodded, but said nothing. He looked like he wanted to throttle her, but just wrung his neck and turned to leave.

She didn't hesitate to move the moment he left the tavern, finding the stairs and climbing until she found her room on the top floor. She opened the door to find a small room with only a full bed against the wall, a nightstand on either side, a chaise at the end of the bed, and a chair in the opposite corner. There was a window opposite the door where she could look out at the forest grounds that surrounded this town. And beside the chair in the corner was another door.

She moved to it and found the bath.

A private bath.

It was still astounding that the Northern villages, no matter how small, all came with private baths. They were first given to the homes of the villagers, then provided to the inns. Something she had respected greatly about her father's rule. Still did. He didn't deal based on how much money he could make from the villages, he worked to give everyone fair ground.

She turned back to the room and found two stacks of

clothes on the chaise. She undressed in record time, wanting to get the dirt, grime, and blood off of her already.

The bath filled quickly, a steam of water escaping the faucet faster than she would have expected. So the King hadn't cheaped out on the private baths either. Good.

She filled the tub with the unscented bombs that sat to the side and watched the water lather up as she stepped into it and sighed as she settled in. A moan escaped her lips as she laid back and allowed the water to steam her muscles into a relaxed state.

She allowed herself the delay only a moment before dunking entirely into the water and beginning to scrub. She used a bar of soap that sat on a small table beside the bath and scrubbed at every inch of herself; hair, body, soul. She cleaned it all.

And when she felt like her skin was hers once more, she stepped out, emptied the bath, and refilled it. She wanted to think, but she'd like to do that in clean waters.

She didn't bother with bombs this time around, settling her limbs into the steaming waters and relaxing back. And immediately, her mind shot to the Master Assassin. Sparrow Lazarus Edvard Lefebvre.

The impossible, frustrating, amazing man.

The insufferable, incredible man.

She understood his desire to defend Edmund. It was the exact same way she would defend James if anyone spoke out against him. But she hated that he wouldn't consider her part. Hated that it showed her how much farther her feelings had fallen. Because she had no doubt in her mind that if he went to her with problems about anyone, including her two closest friends, she would listen. She would believe his feelings and go to her friends. She would figure it out, but she would never discredit him.

She scoffed to herself. *Is this what falling in love was like?*

If so, she wanted no part of it.

She fell deeper into the heated waters at the knowledge that she had no control over that particular matter. Her heart was already Sparrow's, and there was not a thing she could do to take it back.

Lords, to think this was what her friends felt for one another. It was infuriating.

Gemma and James, her brother and sister for all intents and purposes, were her rocks in life. She wished more than anything that her magic wasn't wiped out so she could call out to them. With the amount of distance between them, she would need a trained amount of magic to do it, and she was only just feeling her body recover from her earlier usage.

She missed them, needed her alone time with them when she returned to the palace, needed to speak to them about what was happening with her heart. Needed to vent, to rant, to cuss Sparrow's life within an inch of death for causing so much *feeling* within her. If this was what they felt for one another at all times, she regretted ever wishing for it.

And that brought Sparrow back to the forefront of her mind. Dominating, commanding, brilliant man.

Insufferable, incredible man.

She pushed out of the bath, not allowing herself the time to think about him, grabbed a towel, and headed out of the private bath. He hadn't come to the room yet. She'd left the door unlocked since he wouldn't have a key, and he hadn't shown up.

She moved to the chaise that held clothes for them and ignored the pile left for her, instead taking the large shirt that was meant for the Master Assassin and throwing it on. She loved wearing his shirts, even though this one technically wasn't his.

Dropping the towel where she stood, she glanced around the room drowned in the shirt, then moved to the window, looking out at the moon that had settled high in her time in the bath.

She heard the door open behind her, saw the outline of his form through the glare in the window as he closed the door behind him and took her in, dressed in nothing but the shirt meant for him.

He turned wordlessly to the private bath and closed it behind him.

Evony felt the breath leave her, unaware she'd been holding it, as she stared at the closed door through the reflection.

Pushing away from the window, she settled onto the bed and opened the nightstand on the far end of the room. The top shelf held loose sheets of paper filled with what she assumed were letters. Or poems. Or something of the sort.

Settling into the middle of the bed, she began to read.

Poems.

Long and elaborate poems.

She'd gone through three, only half paying attention, when the door opened and she watched from her periphery as Sparrow stepped out in only a towel wrapped low on his hips.

She ignored his presence and went back to the poem. Or tried to.

He wasn't getting changed. Wasn't moving at all. She glanced up to find him standing at the side of the bed, staring at her.

With her full attention now on him, he peeled the towel off and allowed to it drop to his feet. And still he didn't move to change.

Her gaze dropped instantly to his cock, which was growing harder by the moment, then back up to meet his gaze.

He stepped up to the bed as the poems slipped from her fingers and fell to the floor around the bed, and shot his hand out, grabbing hold of the back of her neck and pulling her up to her knees before him.

Evony's breath came in harsh as she stared into the eyes of the man she desired more than her next breath.

"You can trust me." His voice was harsh, raspy. "Please trust me. Because all I know is that I trust you. That I cannot live this life without you in it."

The thumb of his free hand moved in slow motions at the side of her neck as his gaze shot from her eyes, to her lips, and back. Then that thumb caressed up her skin to her mouth and settled there.

"That's the annoying part," she whispered against his thumb. "I've always trusted you."

"So don't stop," he begged. "Let me have all of it. All of you."

Her breathing hitched. *Was he asking what she thought he was?*

She nodded without a sound, unable to break her stare from those beautiful browns.

"There's something I've wanted to do since the moment I saw you in my shirt the first time, Magician." His voice was hoarse, like he was fighting his body for control.

"What's that?" Her nerves stood alert as she looked down to his lips, to the tongue that shot out to wet them.

His hand slipped from the back of her neck to hold her face, rough and commanding, ever the assassin. "To drown between those thighs."

The gasp was out of her as her gaze shot to meet his. To find the need there. His pupils entirely taken over in black. Pure desire.

He brought her into a kiss, his lips unforgiving as they took what they wanted, his tongue impatiently shooting into her mouth as his free hand found its way under her shirt. His tongue possessed her, pushed in and out as if he were fucking her already, and her center soaked at the thought.

He pulled away, reached for the bottom of her shirt and pulled it up and onto the ground beside the towels. He stepped back, out of her reach, and took her in. They almost mirrored the first time he'd seen her naked, after she'd awoken from scattering the poison.

But he took his time to enjoy it now. Allowed his gaze to rake her form, to stop at her peaked nipples and her thighs that wanted to clench tightly together but remained open to hold her up. He waivered at the scar that covered her stomach.

It was never something she'd been insecure about, the scar, and the way he took her in made it even less so. Like the scar almost made her more beautiful.

Finally, he pushed her back onto the bed and stood between her spread legs. He took in every inch, and her skin prickled with the knowledge that he was devouring her without a touch.

He pushed her farther up the sheets and got on his knees on the bed, his hands cupping the bottoms of her thighs and spreading her wider. Her breath hitched, back beginning to peel off the bed as he stared down at her, spread and dripping.

She moaned his name, fingers digging into the sheets. But he wouldn't move.

"I believe I approve of you this way—at my mercy." That raspy beg from earlier turned cocky.

Her back arched as he leaned over her and gently kissed the middle of the scar. She shivered with desire, her whimpers matching her need, but he acted like he noticed none of it.

He placed another delicate kiss to the edge of the scar, and another to the opposite edge. To the top, skimming her right breast, and the bottom, teasing her left hip so very close to where she wanted his mouth. But he never gave her what she craved.

Instead, he focused on the scar, whispered to it so low, she couldn't make any of it out, and she realized as she watched him that he needed this. Needed his moment with the scar, something he'd probably been aching for since the moment he found out about it.

So she tried to settle her body's needs—which was quite impossible, but she tried all the same—and gave him the time he needed.

Long minutes of his inaudible whispers and soft kisses passed before he peeled back and met her gaze, a thanks in his eyes behind the blacks of desire. She smiled, her heart falling impossibly deeper for the assassin the world was so afraid of.

His hands skimmed up her spread legs, finally giving her body the attention it wanted, and rewarded her whimpers with a kiss to the side of her knee. The cocky grin grew with another tentative kiss as he watched her body shudder in anticipation.

"Sparrow," she cried desperately.

"Evony," he teased her name out as he pressed a light kiss to her opposite thigh.

"Sparrow!" She shot a demanding stare his way.

"Yes?" he asked innocently.

"Drown."

His smirk grew along with the shine in his eyes. "As you wish, *Your Highness*."

His tongue found her center and licked up her folds faster than she took her next breath. He didn't touch her clit, rather licked around it, like he was purposefully avoiding it. Again. And again.

"I swear to the lords, Assassin!"

"Is there something the matter, my love?"

She growled. "If you don't suck me, I'm flipping us over and riding your face until I come." She was even astonished by the words that flew out, but couldn't care enough at the moment. She needed him at her clit.

He laughed with a gentle kiss to the apex of her thighs. "I think I like the sound of that." He kissed her right above where she wanted him. "No. I know I like the sound of that. Love it."

She whimpered his name as her head fell back and her hips rolled under his touch. Begging.

"But I believe I love the sound of you begging even more."

His thumbs spread her open for every drop as he licked up slowly, then flicked the tip of his tongue against her clit. Once, twice. On the third time, he suckled at the little nub. Her back came off the bed in the deepest bend she'd ever mustered without her permission, and her hands found their way from the sheets to his hair, taking fistfuls as he lapped up her taste. Pulled at his roots when he licked her again and ended the torture with the plunge of his tongue into her core. He tasted her, consumed her until her thighs were suffocating him between their softness as she came, her hips shooting off the bed as she saw stars.

And he didn't stop. Lapped up every drop as she came.

When her senses returned, her fingers loosened from his hair as her legs released from their death grip and fell to the sides. He looked up at her with wicked delight. "I didn't drown. We'll have to try again later."

Her desire grew as he kissed her hips.

Then her thigh, the other thigh, the other hip.

He softened again when he reached the scar and gave another bout of gentle attention to it.

When he reached the top of the scar, he turned to the valley of her breasts and pressed a soft lingering kiss there, his head bowed to her like he was vowing something unspoken under the beat of her heart.

He looked back up at her after a moment, and she found a renewed desire in his gaze. Something that told her what she already knew—she was his. Always.

She arched her aching breasts up to him, the hardened peaks reaching for his mouth. His attention settled onto the exposed pair and his hands rose to palm them, to knead them to his command.

He looked back up at her as he kissed the valley of her breasts once more before moving to a breast and leaving open mouthed kisses to the skin, then moved to her sister.

Her hands wrung around him, nails digging into his back as his lips drew closer to her begging nipples. His cock pressed against her hot core as she dug into his skin and all the sensations at once had her gasping through her moans.

The entire tavern would undoubtedly hear them. And she couldn't care less.

When his lips reached as close to her nipple without touching it, his hands found their way back up, capturing the swollen nubs between his thumb and forefinger and to play with her.

He watched the moans escaping her lips with a wicked smile. "It's erotic. Watching you lay there, waiting for me to ravish you."

"I hate you," she gasped out.

The grin grew. "Oh?" His tongue flicked out over one hardened nub before his fingers moved back to playing with her.

"Hate," she breathed, her chest rising and falling with such desperation, her nipple was basically being thrust into his mouth.

His smile grew darker as he moved to the other breast and circled his tongue around her nipple before taking it into his mouth and sucking. She thrust into him as her nails broke the skin on his back.

He laid an open-mouthed kiss in the valley. "Still hate me?"

Her eyes closed, unable to take all the sensations, and her breathing came out in moans alone, but she nodded her response to his question.

His hand moved down to her center, finding her clit and pressing tantalizing circles into her. "Can't have that, my betrothed."

Betrothed.

His betrothed.

That was all she needed to scream his name loud enough for the next town to hear as he found her nipple and began showing the girls their deserved attention.

The sensations built as her hands ran down his back time and again, knowing the resulting scratches would only build her desire for him more. She barely felt her own breaths escaping past her lips before another climax hit, arching her off the bed as he continued playing with her, tasting her.

Open-mouthed kisses laid up her neck were the first thing she was able to concentrate on as she came back from the stars, his hands caressing her body, getting to every inch of her form.

He stopped above her, a hand moving to gently hold her face as he looked into her eyes. His gaze was so sincere. And if she wasn't mistaken, filled with love. "You sure you want this? Me?"

She swallowed, trying to find her voice, finally able to get her words out. "It's all I've thought of this past month."

He smiled and leaned in to kiss her, his tongue—which had the subtle notes of her taste—invading her mouth again. He pulled away, and the way he looked down at her could've had her coming a third time.

He positioned himself to her center and slowly pushed in, inch by inch.

She felt the pain shoot through her center as he filled her fully, as her center clenched around him, made room for him. He groaned, but didn't move, his head falling into the crook of her neck as he waited for her to become accustomed to his size, to his being there.

She took a moment to breathe through the pain before nodding for him to continue. He was slow and caring as he pulled out to the tip, then pushed in. And when he pulled out the next time, it wasn't all the way but so much better. She felt the hard push into her core and the spike of pleasure that shot through her. The moan shot out of her before she realized that the pain had turned to pleasure. Delicious pleasure.

She throbbed around his cock as he pulsed inside her, their groans mixing, curses flying, and names echoing in the air as he pumped harder into her.

His thumb found its way to her clit and he found his rhythm of pumping into her and pressing against her.

The moonlight glistened off the sweat on his skin, and all Evony could think of was that she had it. She had him, and he'd made the move, he wanted her. As intensely as she wanted him.

"Evony," he groaned against her lips. "Come for me, come with me, love."

Those words off those lips were a dream come true, so she did as she was told. Holding on to him, she came for a third time that night as he released into her, his seed shooting into her in endless waves.

He convulsed above her until every drop was inside her, then he fell, barely catching his weight on his arms that caged around her face. He looked into her eyes, and she found the satisfaction she felt in his gaze, the smile as he leaned in to kiss her.

He pulled out slowly, and she felt her walls clench at the loss, felt his seed slide down her thighs. Her smile grew at the feeling of having him dripping down her legs.

He leaned in and placed a soft kiss behind her ear before pushing off the bed and moving to the private bath. It gave her a marvelous view of his ass, and all she could think was how much she wanted to bite it.

He was back in seconds with a small, dampened towel in hand.

Then he was between her legs again, cleaning their mess with the warm towel. She hadn't had a problem with it—feeling him dripping down her legs—but she also loved how much he cared for her. That he took care of her still.

That small towel was thrown over the ones they had lying on the ground already, and he fell onto his back beside her, eyes closing in post coital bliss as he took large breaths in and out.

Sweat still glistened off his skin in the moonlight as his tongue shot out to get the remnant tastes from his lips.

Evony's smile was as wide as it could be as she turned to her side for a better view, tucking closer and relaxing her fingers over his chest. "What made you decide you want me now?

"It was never a decision of whether I wanted you. It was always a decision of whether I'd allow myself to have you."

She closed her eyes and leaned into his bicep, leaving a soft kiss to his skin. *Allow himself*. Like she was a treasure. She internally scoffed, then asked, "So what made you change your mind?"

He was silent for a moment before answering with pure

honesty, "Watching you out there. You were captivating on the battlefield. I was mesmerized."

She couldn't help the soft giggle that breathed out. "Why am I not surprised? The way to the Master Assassin's pants was through murder."

"And to his heart?"

The question surprised Evony, and she opened her eyes slowly, curiosity stitching her brows together as she found him staring at her. "What?"

"What is the way to the Master Assassin's heart?" he repeated, his hand now playing with the one she had lain on his chest.

The answer to that question scared her more than anything else in the world. He had her heart wholly, but did she have any of his? Could she?

And because he'd been so honest, she answered him truthfully. "I fear to think of it, for I know I could not meet it."

His brows furrowed together as he studied her, and she closed her eyes to hide from the scrutiny. He'd said he trusted her, that he couldn't live without her, called her his betrothed. But for some reason, uncertainty still pulled at her.

CHAPTER 29
SPARROW

The sight of black lashes kissing tanned skin would forever become Sparrow's favorite thing to awake to. The even breaths of contentment and the easy tranquility of a body safe and satisfied could make him lose days laid out on his side watching the Master Magician curled into him.

His gaze traveled from the peacefulness of her face, to the black locks that fell haphazardly around her, to the lock that fell over her breast and the memory of the taste of that peaked nub still fresh in his mind.

He fingered the lock back, revealing her entirely to his sight. A tantalizing tip he yearned to suck, a tantalizing woman he yearned to relish in.

He watched her sleep, felt her breaths graze his chest and felt what he never expected to experience in its entirety—contentment.

She was his.

Finally, completely, and entirely his.

His gaze flickered to the hands she had curled by her head,

to the finger that lay empty. He would fill that spot, show the entire world that she was taken, that she was his.

"But why do we have to do this now?" he whined, wanting more than anything to run out with his father and play a game of guard against villain.

His father laughed at him. "Sparrow, child, be patient, it is almost done."

"But you could make that at night when I'm sleeping. Right now we could be outside!"

"It is important we make these today. It is an important day."

That got the six-year-old's attention. "Why?"

"I don't know," his father answered, watching him deflate, "but I know I must make these with the rains that fell this morning."

"If you don't know why, then how do you know you need today's rain?"

"Sparrow, behave, they are almost finished."

Sparrow slumped into his chair and rested his deflated face onto a little fist, watching his father work over the steaming cauldron.

Finally, his father stepped away from his work and lifted his gloved hand to show Sparrow what they had been sitting about waiting for.

Rings.

Two Rings.

One smaller and one bigger, but they were just rings.

"Father! We sat about all day for rings?" Sparrow jumped off his stool and stomped about the room.

His father laughed at him and got down to one knee, stopping Sparrow before him. "Not just any rings, Sparrow. These will be your matrimonial rings."

"My matri—what?"

"The ring you present your future wife."

Sparrow's little brows furrowed together. "Impossible. I'm never getting married."

His father quirked a smile. "Oh?"

Sparrow shook his head. "Never."

"Whyever not?"

"Marriage is bad. Falling in love is bad."

His father laughed at him. "Oh, Sparrow, my child, that is not true. Falling in love is amazing, finding someone you want to be with every day is thrilling."

Sparrow grimaced. "Ew."

His father laughed and lifted the hand that still held the rings. With his other gloved hand, he picked the smaller of the rings up. "This, this will be your bride's ring." He put it down and picked up the bigger. "And this will be yours."

Sparrow didn't respond but narrowed his little eyes at his father. "You cannot make me, I will never marry."

His father only laughed further. "I would never make you. Trust me, son, you will want to marry. You will have a bride that drives you crazy, but that you cannot live without."

"If she drives me crazy, why would I want to live with her? I could live without her if she's going to drive me crazy!"

"It's absurd, I know," his father agreed. "But trust me, you'll want her. You won't be able to live without her, without knowing she's safe and yours. Without knowing you will forever be hers."

Sparrow grimaced again. "Gross, Father."

"I know, I know." He lifted the hand with the rings once more, directing Sparrow's attention to the rings. "But know, when you're ready, these rings will be here for you."

Sparrow looked up into his father's loving eyes and nodded.

Twenty years had passed and he still found it ludicrous that a man would volunteer to live with someone who drove him crazy. And yet, he was finding his father's absurd words from his childhood reaping true.

He would not live without knowing she was safe and by his side.

Like his heart called to her, her eyes fluttered open and met with his, the ocean within them calming him in ways he hadn't known he'd needed.

"Morning." He lightly stroked her cheek.

Her smile was warm, but large. "Good morning."

"How're you feeling?"

Her thighs squeezed together under the sheets, but she looked happy as she snuggled in closer to him. "Amazing. A little sore, but amazing." She gave a light kiss to his bottom lip, then closed her eyes against him.

His hand wound up her naked back, feeling her shiver at his touch, and into her hair, taking a fistful and jerking her head back. Her eyes popped open to look at him, desire filling the pools. "As much as I'd love to stay in here all day, we need to get back to the palace."

They still had prisoners to interrogate.

She grimaced. "Will your men stay here? Help them?"

He pulled away from her, pushing out of the bed so he wasn't convinced to spend any more time in that room. "Yes, we'll be leaving alone."

He turned to find her blatantly watching him, taking in every inch of his skin like a child seeing sweets. He turned away immediately. "You will not seduce me with those looks, Magician. We must go."

She grumbled from behind him as he walked to the small bag he'd brought in with him the night before. The bag that held the clothes they'd brought from the palace. Pulling her bundle of trousers, top, and vest out of the bag, he threw them to the bed, refusing to turn to her.

Hands caressed his sides, stopping at his chest as he pulled his clothes out. He wrung his neck to control himself as her lips pressed against his back, her naked breasts pressing against his muscles. "Evony," he growled. "Behave."

She giggled against his back, teeth scraping at the little scars she'd left the night before. "You should know"—she kissed his back—"when you tell me to behave"—she rose to the tips of her toes so her breath was at his ear—"it makes me want to not behave. *Really* not behave."

His breaths were becoming labored as he growled once more. "Evony."

She laughed and pushed away, giving him the room to take in a few breaths before he could get himself to put anything on.

When he finally got dressed, he turned to find her finishing the lace of her boots seated on the chaise at the end of the bed. The sheets lay messed and a slight bit of red marked the spot they'd been when he'd entered her, a memory he would forever cherish.

She stood and walked to his side. "Ready and at your service, Assassin."

He narrowed his gaze at her and the things he could make her do filled his mind, but he pushed them out and stomped out of the room.

That woman would be the death of him.

†

THE TWELVE HOURS it took to get from the tavern in the middle of the lands to the palace were some of the most difficult Sparrow had ever had to endure, a fact Evony was enjoying all too much.

She'd been good when they'd gone down to the ground floor of the tavern to eat their breakfast, and their entire ride, but the couple times they'd stopped for a break had been the problem.

She knew exactly what she did to him and she had no cares

about extending their trip an hour or two. That intoxicating laugh bubbled out of her every time he'd cursed and walked away from her seductions. The woman was a minx.

But luckily, when they got home, she was her normal bit of flirty and inappropriate.

They'd gotten to the palace just as the group would be getting together for their dinner, so Edmund was waiting at the doors when they walked into the dining hall. His heart jumped when Evony's hand wrapped in his tightened a bit and he remembered the fears that still plagued her mind. He'd have to clear that up, show her that her father did care for her, even if he had a terrible way of showing it.

Edmund looked them over quickly, then stared at Sparrow. "The fight?"

Sparrow shrugged, knowing his men had informed Edmund of everything they knew. "I was lucky to have Evony by my side. I'm the Master Assassin, but without her, even I wouldn't have been able to handle it."

That was mostly true. He could probably make his way through that large carnage alone. He'd merely be far more injured at the end of it. But he was glad to have said Evony helped because he felt the small smile that graced her lips touch his bicep. It made his heart jump at being the reason for it.

Edmund looked to his daughter and Sparrow had to admit, there wasn't any welcome about the stare. "Good. Good, then let's sit for dinner."

Dinner was an array of stews, breads, cheeses, and vegetables, with cups of cranberry juiced for their delight. Among many things, Northerners weren't known for their drinking habits so no alcohol was present—not that it wasn't allowed in the North, most just preferred against it.

Dinner passed with no conversations of the visit to Brilfax Oak or the ordeal that took place when they'd gotten there. Nothing but the normal rambunctious laughter of everyone enjoying each other's company. James, Gemma, and Evony were quickly becoming an important part of their group's dynamic.

It wasn't long before the married couple made their departure, the fact that they were running off for a tumble in the sheets something they weren't discreet about.

Only seconds after their departure, Edmund turned to Sparrow. "Why don't we head into my office?"

Evony pushed her chair out and rose before he could answer. "No need. I'll be heading to the baths. I'm in need of a nice long soak, so no need to hide away from me." The last comment was an obvious knack at the King, but she was respectful all the same. He wondered if that was just her pleasant demeanor or if she did it for him.

She turned to Sparrow and settled a hand on his shoulder. It was nothing compared to the countless times she'd thrown herself at him, but after last night's events, his body flushed in memory. "I'll see you in our rooms."

Our rooms. He really liked the sound of that.

His hand stopped at her stomach and she looked down at him. He didn't do much more than sit up straighter, extending his form to reach for her, but that was all the incentive she needed. She gave him a beautiful small smile and leaned down to kiss him, her hair blocking them from the others in the room and giving him the privacy to delight in her taste, even momentarily.

"I'll see you in our rooms," he whispered against her lips.

He watched her walk out, wanting nothing more than to follow her and join in that bath. But he was still the Assassin, and he still had matters to discuss.

"You've shagged her," Edmund commented from his leisurely lounge at the head of the table.

Sparrow's gaze shot to the King's with incredulity. "I don't see how that's anyone's concern."

"Last time you were quick to deny it. This time it is no one's concern?" He looked tired.

The others watched on silently, as if unsure whether to question him about it.

Sparrow couldn't argue the King's point, didn't want to. And it didn't matter. What he and Evony did was entirely up to them. "You know of the prisoners? That some of them are from the South?"

Miels answered, "We were told when the men came in. Tristan and I locked them up, got a couple of them truly scared of a visit with Nuhmed."

"You're worried about the South aspect," Tristan stated rather than asked.

"Why?" Rosaelia asked. She was normally quiet during their meetings, taking in the information and not contributing much. But she was always there, always involved, ever observant.

"Evony is from the South," Edmund answered. "She may be a conflict of interest if she finds that the country she grew up in and considers her own might be involved."

"But that's like saying we're conflicts of interest because it is our people in the rebellion. There're bad lots in every people," Rosaelia reasoned and Sparrow had a feeling her recent encounter with the village men had taught her more in minutes than anything she'd learned over the years.

Edmund shrugged his acknowledgment and turned to Sparrow. "You think we should hide this from her for the time being?"

Sparrow met his gaze and found only sincerity, found the

man he knew the King to be. "No," he stated, a finger tapping away on his lips as he relaxed back into his seat. "I am merely checking that we are all on the same page that this may cause a problem."

"But you intend on telling her?" Miels asked.

"No." After a bound of silence as the others watched him for more information, Sparrow added, "I intend on having her with me during the interrogations."

CHAPTER 30
EVONY

Calling through the mind could be a tricky ordeal when she wasn't sure whether the recipients would be in the middle of a shagfest, but Evony had missed her friends and she wanted to check in.

She'd been so tired at dinner and they'd been having so much fun with the group that she hadn't done so then. And after dinner, she'd focused on herself with the long bath—plus they had just started the shagfest, and Evony definitely had no intentions of bothering them then. But enough time had passed where Evony felt better about trying.

Are you guys still going at it?

A soft laugh filled her mind and she knew she was in the clear. *All clear, babes.*

But not for long, I am getting hungry again.

Ugh, James, please! Evony grimaced as she sank lower into her bath. *I just wanted to check in. And tell you that I need some time alone with my two favorite people, it's been too long since it's just been the three of us and I miss it.*

Aww, little sister, James called to her. *Don't worry, I'll pull you away from that betrothed of yours and keep you tied to us for the entire weekend.*

Evony felt her smile come on. *Or just the day. Really, I'd like to return to Sparrow by nightfall.*

For what? He doesn't touch you. At least, not properly. Gemma's question was a bit bitter, like she was angry at the Assassin for not falling at Evony's feet and that made the smile on Evony's features expand.

He hadn't touched me. Things change, babes.

Two blasts of shock reached her mind and she knew a laugh was getting sent back to them.

What happened! Gemma asked just as Evony was pulling herself out of the water and drying off.

Oo, it's late. We'll talk when I see you next.

Evony, don't you dare, James began. *What hap..*

She cut off their connection and laughed to herself knowing the two were likely cussing her out at that very moment. She dressed in a frail light dress that was left in the bathing room and began the walk to her suite.

She should've guessed.

The two were stopped at the door of her suite, blocking her entry. Her smile grew wider. "Can I help you two? Did you need Sparrow?"

"That's not funny, Eve! You can't just leave us with noth-ing!" Gemma cried out to her just as the others made their way into the hall.

Sparrow looked like he'd gone off to the baths as well.

"Ah, Evony, perfect," Edmund called out. "Come. I have something for you."

Evony looked to her friends knowing her brows were deeply furrowed and found just as astonished looks from them. Sparrow's features gave nothing away.

But Miels and Tristan sighed as the latter said, "I'm telling you, she's not going to want it."

She turned and followed after her father, feeling the presence of everyone else following close behind. They stopped at a door across from Rosaelia's suite and followed Edmund in. He turned to face her with a warm smile.

She looked around before settling on him. "What's this?"

"Your own quarters," he said matter-of-factly. "We trust you, I trust you, there is no need for you to be under supervision at all times. You should have your own space."

What was happening? An hour ago he didn't want her to listen in on a conversation, now she was getting her own room. She wasn't naive, he could lie to the others all he wanted, but she knew he didn't trust her.

Which meant the only reason he would be giving her this space was because it was requested. Her heart panged in memory of the previous night. Had it just been Sparrow getting off while he was out of town?

She turned to Sparrow and did a surprisingly splendid job at hiding the pain from her voice. "Did you request this?"

He stood stiff, expression unreadable. "I had no idea of it."

The crash of relief was so immense, she could hardly breathe as a million butterflies released into her stomach. Thank the lords.

The King shook his head. "No, no. It was my idea. You are my daughter and I wish to give you your own space, as you deservedly should have."

Evony watched him a moment, trying to figure out what he was playing at. "I'm fine with my current arrangement."

"We told you," Miels sang from the corner.

"But this would be your own suite," Edmund argued.

"I already have a suite."

"No, you are a guest in Sparrow's suite, you can each have your own space now."

"Sparrow and I are comfortable in our suite, there is no need for a change. Thank you for the offer, but I am happy with my current living arrangement." She turned to the man in question, stopping a foot away from him. "That is, as long as you're okay with it?"

It was a chance for him to state where he stood. Was last night just a random fuck, or did he want something? Albeit Evony knew a positive answer wouldn't necessarily prove he wanted more, but it would tell her plenty. She could speak to him about their relationship later, when everyone's prying eyes weren't on them.

"I see no problem with our quarters, Magician."

I told you, she sent to his mind.

He's only offering you a room. That doesn't mean he doesn't trust you.

He's doing it because he doesn't want us sleeping together, especially after our trip.

Sparrow rolled his eyes. *He had this planned with the moron twins while we were away. He trusts you.*

Turning back to her father, Evony finished the conversation. "Thank you, but we'll be heading to our room now." She grabbed Sparrow's arm and pulled him out of the room and back down the hall to their suite. She knew everyone's eyes were on them and she really didn't care.

They'd just made it into the suite, the door barely closed when he threw her against it, his arms locking her in and body hovering only a couple of inches away. Her fingers clutched the lapels of his jacket, holding him close as he whispered against her lips, "I was scared you would accept the room."

Good. She wanted him just as afraid of losing her as she was of losing him. "And miss having you inside me every day? Never."

Sparrow laughed against her lips, their breaths mixing in happiness. "Is your mind always in the Rivorbant Waters?"

"When thinking about you."

His grin grew. Then those luscious lips were on her.

Evony kissed him back, passionately and fervently, before pulling away for a breath and staring up at him. "What is this, Sparrow? I need to know."

If this was just a game to him, she had to break things off now. If what happened at the inn was just him getting off, she had to turn around and accept the room from her father, no matter how much the thought hurt.

His hands cradled her face in the softest of caresses, pulling away another inch to stare down at her. "There isn't much I'm sure of, Evony, but that I am in love with you. That I have fallen irrevocably for your inappropriate manner, your cheerful smile, and your shining eyes."

She stuttered, "You're in love with me?"

Impossible. He couldn't love her. It was too much. It was everything that hopeful heart had ever wanted, and she was afraid that she was actually lucky enough to be receiving it. That this wasn't some trick, but that she was finally getting the man she'd waited her whole life for.

"You're compassionate and playful and sexy and everything I tried to force myself not to want, but cannot deny that I need. The depths I've fallen for you, the lengths my love expands, none of it is measurable. I'm completely at your mercy, Evony."

The tears brimmed at the edges of her eyes. "Good, because I've been in love with you for weeks and it's been torture not admitting it."

He smirked down at her. "You're my betrothed, Evony. And I mean that."

Her breath caught at the proclamation.

As the seconds ticked by, she realized that Sparrow still held her, waiting for her answer. For all intents and purposes, this *was* a proposal and her acceptance was imperative on it being set.

Her grin was wide when she took his face in her hands and brought it closer. "Good."

His smile was wolfish, his groan primal as he pressed into her, their tongues meshing. His hands were no longer soft as they held her, tracing down her every inch, his fingers pulling apart the ties to her dress.

Her hands reached for the loose shirt tucked into his trousers and pulled it free, her fingers finding their way inside to graze his chest and feel his skin beneath hers.

A moan rang from the back of her throat as she pushed him away and pulled at the shirt to get it over his head. Starvation was the only thing she felt at the sight.

He growled as he caught her stare and moved in close again.

She thrust her hands out, catching him at the tops of his trousers and stopping him. Her fingertips grazed the inside of his trousers as she stared up at him, a wicked smirk gracing her lips, before she pushed him back.

She followed him as she continued to push his pliant body until he hit the couch at the end of the room and fell back onto it. He sprawled lazily, the hunger in his gaze boosting her confidence to unparalleled dimensions.

She moved slowly then, her fingers grazing her sides as they slowly found their way to the ties at the front of her dress, his stare following them closely.

Her fingers pulled slowly, tugging them apart so that the valley between her breasts was open to his viewing.

He growled, shifting in his spot as he rubbed his hands down his thighs with hooded eyes. "Magician," he grit out through clenched teeth. "If I have to wait any longer, I'm going to rip that dress apart."

She let a seductive giggle slip her lips as her fingers edged the top of her dress and slowly—ever so antagonizingly slowly—peeled it from her skin, letting the fabric fall to her waist before shimmying out altogether.

He was so hard, the tent in his trousers visibly straining against the fabric, but he remained still, his hands clutching at his thighs to hold back as he watched her.

She stepped out of the dress, feet pointed like she were performing a dance for him, and slowly strut into his spread legs.

"Are you ready to play now, Magician?" He looked up at her with a cocky grin.

She furrowed her brows in a playful tease and tsked as she began to drop to her knees, hands finding their way onto his trouser clad thighs. "I was thinking I might tease you a little longer." Her fingers reached for the folds of his trousers, beginning to undo them. "Get a taste of what's going inside me."

He growled, his hips bucking up to give her the space to pull his trousers off as he gave her a pleased look. His cock sprung out, calling her attention as it stood large and demanding.

She didn't touch him, just pulled his boots and trousers off until he was fully naked before her. Then her hands started at his ankles and softly skimmed upward as she watched him.

Her fingertips reached the bottom of his thighs when his hips bucked up again, his cock frustrated and crying out for attention now, leaking with his arousal. She smirked as she looked between Sparrow and his cock, her tongue jutting out to wet her lips in anticipation.

"Evony, I swear to the lords, if you don't wrap those lips around my cock..." He broke off in a strangled moan as her fingers edged upward still, finding the insides of his thighs and skimming, playing.

"You'll what?" she insisted, eyes sparkling with the need to hear that answer.

"I won't allow you to come tonight, Magician. Keep playing."

Her eyes widened at the threat, and she grew wetter still at the sound of it. She could probably come just watching him like this, but the warning was still taken seriously. She wanted him inside her when she came, not just the picture of him. She'd come to the picture of him too many times already.

When she finally wrapped her fingers around his cock, a bit more pre-cum sprang free from the tip, and she smiled up at him as her thumb rode up his length and spread it over the entirety of his tip.

His hands strained at his sides, clutching onto the couch as he watched her.

And finally, she gave in.

Her gaze settled on him as she licked the tip once and delighted in his hiss. Then, she took him into her mouth for the first time. It was different, an intrusion almost, but at the same time astonishing at how much she loved it. She'd expected to enjoy it, couldn't fathom a part of Sparrow she didn't enjoy, but she hadn't expected *this*. This need that pushed through her body, her cunt clenching as if he had entered it rather than her mouth. No wonder he'd been so happy between her legs the night before, she could happily die between his legs.

She pulled it out of her mouth and looked up at him through her lashes knowing the sight would drive him crazy by itself, then leaned in again, taking him deeper this time.

His hand shot into her hair, fingertips scraping at her scalp as he slowly guided her, and lords did that make her wetter.

She let him set the speed and took in as much of his length

as she could manage down her throat while her hands gripped the base that would not make it to her mouth.

She moaned as she took him in, knowing the vibration would only add to his pleasure. Lords, she loved the taste of him.

He pulled her off, his cock popping off her lips as she sucked the tip. He growled down at her, the color completely drained from his gaze. "Stop!"

Her hands still gripped his base and began to thrust up. "I don't want to stop."

He growled, pulling on her hair. "I want to be inside you when I come, Evony."

She couldn't argue with that.

His fingers released her as she stood and straddled him, taking his cock in her hands again to lead him to her opening. She clutched her hands around his neck and stared into his eyes as she slowly lowered herself onto him.

His hands were quick to hold on to her sides as he growled up at her, "You have a talented little mouth, my magician."

Her heart sang at the praise while her insides clenched around his cock as it filled her to the hilt. They moaned in unison, breaths mixing and nails scraping as she moved above him. "It's easy when you taste that good, my assassin."

His fingers tightened at her sides as he decided on the pace again, controlling the way her body pounded onto him. Controlled the rhythm her breasts grazed his chest and lips as she fell again and again.

He took a peaked tip into his mouth and suckled and had her screaming out for him as he quickened his pace beneath her and bit onto her other tip, teasing the pleasure out of her.

She didn't have time to react before he was flipping them, her back hitting the couch as he rose above her.

CHAPTER 31
SPARROW

Her moans were loud and filled with ecstasy as he attacked her neck, biting and kissing and leaving his mark. He'd have to be careful, no need in broadcasting to her father about their private activities, though he couldn't help leaving a slight mark at the base of her throat.

His hands strolled her form, one hand cupping her throat and forcing her to stare up at him as the other moved to her core, fingers slipping between her folds. She was so mind-numbingly wet. He wanted to taste her. Drown.

But now wasn't the time for that.

He couldn't fight it though. Sparrow slipped his fingers through her folds then brought them to his lips and sucked. His fingers popped from his mouth and moved for Evony's. "Suck."

She took his fingers hungrily, her cunt squeezing the life out of him as she sucked his fingers, gagging on them slightly.

He moved down to take a nipple in his mouth, his tongue toying with the peaked nub before pulling away and letting his breath tease it to straining tips as his hips continued their onslaught, slamming into her at a perfectly slow rhythm that made sure to hit her hard and deep every time.

His hands found their way to the ones she had around his back, nails digging into his skin, and pulled them over her head. He held her wrists down with one hand as the other moved back down to the nub between her legs.

His fingers set a leisurely pace, rubbing softly into her most sensitive area and watching her arc and squirm beneath him. Every time her body pressed into his, he moaned with the need to give her pleasure, to watch her receive it.

"You're so fucking beautiful like this, Magician. So perfect." He licked her neck, needing to taste her skin as the need to finish began climbing down his spine.

Her whimpers begged him—to send her to the edge, to use his tongue, to allow her to touch him—and lords above did he want to comply. Those whimpers turned to harsh moans and he redoubled his attention to her clit, her wetness dripping around his cock, milking it with her juices.

She cried and arced into him as she came, her insides squeezing the life almost entirely from him. He could die in that moment as the happiest man to walk the lands.

But he didn't stop. Didn't release his pressure against her until he was so close and couldn't take it any longer. Then he released her wrists and gripped her hips so he could thrust into her in the animalistic way he wanted to.

And before he could tell what was happening, they were falling.

Sparrow landed on his back, hitting the ground but never breaking from Evony's folds. She leaned in until their breaths mixed and laughs bubbled together as he once again flipped them so he was above her.

On his knees, he brought her legs to his shoulders and

slammed into her, harder and harder until the way she tightened around his cock was unbearable.

Her clit was so sensitive, when he touched it, she spasmed beneath him and he knew she was close again. He leaned into her ear, stretching her legs and giving himself a perfect new angle. "Come with me, love. Lords, Evony, come with me. Milk my cum for that perfect little pussy."

He strained his neck to hold on for dear life but couldn't stop himself as he erupted inside her. The rush was incredible as he emptied himself completely into her, only barely feeling her nails rake his shoulders as she came around his cock again.

"I love when you do as your told, Magician," he groaned into her ear and received an elated in the whimpered response.

When he got his breathing in order, Sparrow rolled off of her and looked back to the hearth still flickering away with firelight. He shakily got up, caught a glimpse of her lifeless body lying on the ground and picked up a small pillow and two blankets from the couch.

He laid one flat in front of the hearth—the rug in the room was comfortable, but definitely nowhere near the blanket's level—then dropped the other beside it.

He then picked up a smaller towel left by a water bowl at the end of the room for his own personal uses and warmed the damp towel by the fire. He was between her legs in moments.

"You know you don't have to do that every time. I like feeling you drip down my legs."

His lips twitched up and as he looked into her drowsy eyes, he knew she was serious. But he didn't respond. He enjoyed doing this for her. And sure, other times he'd also enjoy watching his seed glide down her perfect legs, but not at this moment. Now, he wanted to take care of her.

When he finished, he tossed the towel to the edge of the room and took Evony's lifeless body into his arms. He moved them to the blanket and sat with her still in his arms. He didn't release her, rather laid on his back and delighted in the feeling of her stretching over his form so their naked flesh pressed together.

He rested his head on the pillow and threw the second blanket over her and watching as she settled her hands onto his chest and rested her head over them as she looked into the fire.

He played with her long black locks with one hand as the other caressed her arm. "You didn't have to leave dinner tonight," he opened with the one thing he'd wanted to tell her before Edmund decided to offer her new quarters. "I have nothing to hide from you."

"Oh?" She didn't turn to face him, and somehow, he knew it was the fear of showing how vulnerable she was feeling rather than anything else that kept her from looking up.

"Yeah." He didn't force her to look at him. "The others were only nervous about how you would react in finding out that some of those rebels we stopped were Southerners."

She stiffened above him. There was the reaction they had been expecting. Now to see how she processed it.

"What did they think I'd do? Break the rebels out and help them because we were raised in the same country?" She sounded almost tired, like she wouldn't be surprised to learn the worst was expected of her.

That caused a pain to spike through his chest. How unloved she must feel, must always have felt, to accept that the worst would be expected of her.

"I think they were just scared that you would be in denial." He wouldn't lie to her.

She lifted her head to look at him. "And you?"

His lips tilted up at the sight of her beauty. "I told them I would be taking you to question the prisoners with me." His hand moved from her hair to cradle her cheek. "I told you, I have nothing to hide from you."

Her smile was soft. Small. Her gaze looked hopeful and Sparrow wanted to burn the entire world down for ever making her feel undeserving.

"Thank you," she whispered almost inaudibly and laid a light kiss to his chest before resting her head again and looking into the flames.

✝

Rosaelia was seated in her favorite seat at the end of the library, cushioned into the large armchair that swallowed her whole. In her hands was a small book that Sparrow had a feeling was one of those romances she loved.

In a few hours, he had to be back downstairs to take Evony to see the prisoners, but until then, Sparrow wanted to talk to his sister. Allow her to grow cocky that maybe the words she put into the air about his contentment may be coming true. Had already come true.

"What is this one about, sister?" He knew his quiet entrance coupled with the question startled her.

She jumped, but only lightly, before smiling up at him. She closed the book instantly, a little marker keeping her place as she blushed. "Spar, aren't you supposed to be inside a certain blue-eyed beauty?"

Sparrow smirked. He knew everyone would've heard her the night before and loved that it would be irrefutable that she were his.

He also knew this was Rosaelia's way of distracting him from the matter at hand, so his eyes narrowed on the book and Rosaelia's pinking cheeks.

He snatched it out of her hands and kept it high as she tried to reach for it, pushing her into her seat so she could not move.

What he read shocked him more than anything. Little miss innocent Princess was reading a dirty book.

Sparrow cleared his throat and smirked down to her. "'Javi,' she moaned, 'please come in my mouth.'" Rosaelia burned crimson and covered her face. "Javi ground into her, sucking on her neck to mark her. His cock desperate to be milked by his beautif—"

"That's enough!" Rosaelia screeched as she snatched the book from his hands and sat on it.

Sparrow laughed and took his spot on the arm of the chair. "C'mon, Ro, you know I'm teasing. It's not embarrassing to have those desires. Not something I want to know about as your brother, but not embarrassing." When she didn't look up at him, he added, "Evony and I do that. In fact, we did just that last night. I wanted her to mi—"

"Okay, okay." She laughed as she pushed him away from her. "Stop it, Spar. What're you even doing here?"

"Figured I haven't embarrassed you in a while."

She didn't buy it, watching him for his true purpose.

He threw his arm over her shoulders. "I wanted to thank you."

Her brows furrowed. "For what?"

"Evony."

Her eyes widened, then her brows furrowed again. "I didn't give you Evony, Sparrow. And I had no hand to play in her being my twin."

He rolled his eyes. "When I sent word for her, you said you wanted a woman for me. Wanted someone I couldn't live without."

She looked like she was in a battle with herself before

settling on a smile. "And is she someone you cannot live without?"

"It hurts being away from her even these few hours."

Her smile turned warm as she leaned into his side. "I'm glad you have her, Spar, but I had nothing to do with that. She knew what she wanted when she saw you, and she went for it. It was entirely her doing."

He held her close. "Yes, she was quite determined to get me in her."

"Gross, Sparrow! I'm still your sister! Go tell the moron twins that!"

"Fuck no!" Sparrow laughed. "The moron twins want to hear it, which makes me definitely not want them to hear it."

"Ugh, Spar!"

He laughed harder and kissed her crown. "I love you, Ro."

"I love you too, brother."

"And I like to believe it was you, Ro. That you put it into the winds that I would find my one and so the winds carried her to me."

She gave an airy laugh and snuggled into him. "Well, then, you're welcome."

"And I think there is nothing better than to put it into the air for you too, Ro." Her head snapped up to look at him, but he continued, "You deserve this more than any of the rest of us. We've sheltered you too much. You deserve to find someone just as infuriating as Evony is for me. You deserve, more than anyone, to fall in love. And I know you'll find him, you'll make *me* an uncle with him."

Because he knew Miels was only a crush. She would find the man that filled her to completion. He knew it.

She gave that beautiful warm smile and fell back into his side. "Thank you, Sparrow."

CHAPTER 32
SPARROW

The weight of Evony's hand in his, the warmth that radiated from her, grounded Sparrow as they made their way across the greens to the dungeons.

Tristan was waiting along with two others at the top small room before they would make their way downstairs.

Sparrow eyed him suspiciously as the man leaned against the wall with his arms crossed and a too happy grin across his features. "Where's the other half of your moronic duo?"

"Bottom of the stairs. He went down to relieve the four that were down there with the prisoners."

Evony's free hand covered the one he had clenched in hers and Sparrow noticed the way Tristan's gaze shot there. "What's got you so smug?"

"I'm just thinking," he said languidly as he moved to stand up tall. "That it is no wonder you denied any shagging happening before. After hearing you two last night, there's no doubt in my mind that none of it was happening before." The grin was a sick mix of joy and wickedness. "You know how upset Miels is that he left the wing and didn't get to hear it?"

He was joking, Sparrow knew it. But like the times Miels joked, Sparrow couldn't control his urges to skewer the man. The only real thing that stopped him was Evony's hold, her body pressed into his side and her hand playing with his arm as she smiled into his bicep. "I'll kill you too Tristan, make James my second."

Evony's giggles grew and she kissed his bicep before looking up at him. "He's only teasing, my love."

Tristan's grin grew cocky, and though Sparrow had always known Tristan was as much an ass as his lookalike, in the past weeks while the man had controlled himself until he became accustomed to the newcomers, Sparrow had forgotten that much.

"Yeah." Tristan's eyes glimmered. "*My love.*"

The growl ripped through Sparrow's throat without his permission and he knew it was only Evony's magic around them that kept him from attacking his best friend. "She won't always be by my side, fucker," he grit out. "Then I'm going to kill you."

Tristan's lips tipped up. "Why do I have a feeling that's not true? The always at your side part?" He winked, then turned for the stairs, leaving the two men up top to guard as usual.

"He's teasing, Assassin," she attempted to reason with him.

He turned his chin down and whispered so only she could hear. "Logically, I know that. But biologically, you're mine, and I seem to be quite territorial."

She rose to the tips of her toes and placed a soft kiss to his lips. "I like you territorial."

Good. He didn't want to be chasing her off, scaring her into thinking he would take away her autonomy. He would never do such a thing, it was just a learning curve—getting used to this relationship, to the way he felt for her.

His lips tipped up and he nodded over to the stairs. "Let's go."

It was the last thing he wanted to do. Up in the top things he wanted to do though, every one happened to have Evony naked and that wouldn't exactly help with quelling this rebellion.

At the bottom of the stairs, Miels gave them a disgruntled hello—which made Evony giggle once more into his arm—then turned to lead them to whichever cells the men were being kept.

He didn't release her hand as they made their way over. He knew it would be ammunition to the prisoners, but he couldn't do it. Like touching her would both calm him against whatever they tried to throw his way—like when Miels and Tristan teased him—and relieve him in knowing she was by his side and safe.

It was an open cell system, where all the cells were held with doors that secluded them or opened them up to make one large space. It made it perfect for interrogating all at once, then one by one. It was also perfect for one prisoner to see the pain of another—though now the thought of such an act brought Gemma and Evony to mind and made him sick.

When they neared the area the prisoners were all being held, he stood up taller and brought a cocky grin to his lips. It always drove the men in here crazy and made them slip up without much threat.

"Well," he drawled as they stepped into the middle of the open cells. "Don't we all look cozy."

They grimaced at him but looked to perk up at Evony's presence. He didn't like that, but couldn't do anything about it. He needed Evony there, both to show her that he trusted her fully and to see if she picked up on any Southern behaviors that he or his men didn't get.

The rebels looked to brighten up a bit more when they noticed the grip Sparrow had on her hand, the way her thumb rubbed soothing circles onto the top of his hand. Their eyes sparkled with glee, and Sparrow knew sick comments were already settling into their heads. He did wonder though if they would risk a visit to Nuhmed or the Master Assassin's wrath at voicing said comments.

"Not as cozy as you, Assassin." The short, bulky one they'd picked out as the leader wiggled his eyebrows at their joined hands.

Miels obviously knew Sparrow would react poorly to any mention of Evony, so he began immediately. They normally didn't beat around their questions, preferring to not waste the time. It was only in moments where they knew fear wouldn't work that they resorted to time and confusion to get them their answers. "Why don't you tell us about your need for the Sacred Gardens?"

"Or how an upbringing in Azalea would lead you here? With the rebels?" Evony asked.

Sparrow was shocked to hear the question from her, even more so that only a moment down there told her at least one of these men was from Azalea.

Azalea was a small village in the middle of the Southern Lands, known most for their love of flower beds. It's where all men who found themselves hopelessly in love went for the most beautiful of flowers.

Sparrow would need to go when this rebellion was over. Take Evony and breed her in the middle of those fields.

The man with the twist to his lips smirked her way. "What makes you think any of us grew up in Azalea, pretty girl?"

She gave a smile that was both seductive and infuriating in the way it teased. "Wouldn't you like to know."

The bulky one turned to Sparrow. "You've found yourself a Southern girl, Assassin. Smart lass. They're more fun, no?"

Evony's hand in his soothed him from lashing out at the comment.

Then the man with the twist to his lips spoke. "Azalea had no ambitions. I wanted wealth. All they care for is family and love. This rebellion, the Sacred Gardens, it would give me so much more!"

"Azalea is wealthy with its flowers," Tristan argued.

"The Sacred Gardens hold ingredients only found there. Do you know how much they sell for in the Island Nation?" Greed filled the man's eyes.

"So you helped the rebellion for some money?" Miels concluded.

"And to hold power of the Sacred Gardens!" Another one answered though his accent wasn't the same. He sounded more Northern. "We would have all the nations at our mercy then!"

Sparrow had to fight his smirk. As if the North would allow this lot any control of the Sacred Gardens. He would've taken some of his men and killed them in the matter of moments had that happened.

"So you brought the South into this mess because of some greed?" Evony spit.

Another one smirked at her. "The South needs to have more fun. They are the softest of the lands."

"And if this greed had sent trouble to the South? Had women and children taken, played with." Evony's hand tightened in his.

Sparrow was thankful for it. As much as her words angered her, they made his vision blurry with fury.

"All power comes with some casualties, *princess*." He said

the word, not like he knew she was a Princess, but like he was trying to mock her.

Evony's lips twisted as she whispered under her breath just loud enough for all to hear, "Zuzveli yervoot."

The men on their knees all stiffened to their spots and stared at Evony with renowned interest. And one of them, a lanky one who had been quiet, stared at her in awe.

The others snapped out rather quickly and turned to Miels, Tristan, and Sparrow like they were waiting for something more exciting.

Sparrow wondered if the fascination with what she said was because they hadn't expected such old tongue to be known by anyone today. Though, most wouldn't even know that as an old tongue, and from the look on these men, they definitely wouldn't have known that much. Sparrow himself only knew a bit.

Zuzveli yervoot. Disgusting moron.

He'd never heard someone else speak the old tongue, and it turned him on to know Evony knew a bit of it.

"You men are trained," Miels continued. "Impressively so, from what I hear. How did Azalea lead to that?"

The bulky one snickered. "We are most of us from Haling." Then he smirked with pride. "We train our boys there."

Another that had been quiet looked to Evony, then glanced away quickly, his gaze constantly jumping back to her. "Then we had help. Our leader made sure we were trained properly. She is extraordinary."

Bulky stared at the man with wide eyes as if telling him to shut up.

"So that was your plan?" Sparrow asked, trying to control his unreasonable anger at anyone looking at Evony. "Train you to control the Sacred Gardens? She needed a hundred men at the Sacred Gardens?"

"No," Bulky spit. "She needed maybe twenty at the Sacred Gardens. More to transport to the ships. More on the ships. And more to force labor. But we all needed to help with acquiring the Gardens."

"So why give us all this information now?" Tristan asked.

Lanky still held that awe in his eyes. "She will laugh at your knowing this and still being two steps behind her. She will get us out. Protect us."

Sparrow didn't want to continue this any longer. He would be back to hurt them into more later, but for now, he nodded to his brothers to lock them up in their individual stations while he and Evony waited on the side, then they all left together.

When they were to the top, past the two standing guard, all three men turned to Evony as Sparrow asked, "How'd you know he was from Azalea?"

She shrugged. "He reminded me of someone from a neighboring village."

"Anything else?" Sparrow asked.

She shrugged again, looking sad. "Nothing you wouldn't pick up. What they said was all true. Haling has well trained men, and a few years ago, many left for more. We never heard much else. I guess none of us thought they'd join a group to better train and take over."

Tristan and Miels watched her closely and Sparrow nodded. He pulled her close and they left the dungeons.

They would need to question the men again, individually, and see what else could be learned. See if this was a planned explanation or if it was truly the whole truth.

Something in Sparrow told him it was the whole truth. That the leader used these men's greed to distract them. To cause so many problems, they were spread thin.

But it also told Sparrow that this leader was beginning to slip up. Because if this leader was going against him, she knew he'd be able to make his way through these men. She'd sent them in there poorly prepared, poorly numbered.

This leader was devolving.

CHAPTER 33
EVONY

King Edmund was standing by the opening to the gardens, as if he were expecting her, waiting for her. She'd told Gemma to meet her out there so they could go kidnap James away from the boys, and hadn't expected to meet with her father when she arrived a few minutes early.

She was still trying to get the thought of those prisoners from the day before—that one with the twist to his lips—from her mind, so she didn't realize until it was too late to turn around.

Since that night in Sparrow's room, she'd felt uncomfortable around him, but for Sparrow's sake, Evony tried. "Were you looking for me, King?"

He was an exceedingly handsome man, so the slight lift to a corner of his lips looked appealing rather than scary. Evony could see how that worked in his favor as the ruler of a nation.

He nodded back and turned so that they'd walk together into the maze of the gardens. "I thought I may find you out here. So unlike your sister, you gravitate toward the outdoors."

Evony wasn't entirely used to hearing Rosaelia referred to as her sister, even though she'd always known it. It took her a moment to realize Edmund was speaking of the Princess rather than Gemma.

"Has something happened?" She didn't know if she hoped so or not, at least so it would describe why he wanted to speak with her alone. A part of her knew she should ask him what it was about her that made him so suspicious, but something told her it would only push him further if she tried to deny it. So she remained quiet on the matter.

His hands were clasped behind his back as they walked into the garden maze. "No, nothing of consequence. We're in the ever-infuriating battle of finding out what the Islander sorcerers have plagued our peoples' minds with for this rebellion, so nothing new."

She nodded, but didn't say anything, waiting to see if he'd tell her what he wanted. Maybe he just wanted to spend time with her, she was his daughter after all. Maybe Sparrow had spoken to him about her hesitancies. But she doubted that. Sparrow would've told her if he'd done so.

He finally broke their silence. "Are you happy here, Evony?"

It was an odd question, but she answered honestly, "I am."

"Would you say you'd go back to a time when it were only you and Gemma and James?" He wasn't looking at her, his honey brown gaze staring blankly to the grass before them as they walked.

"I wouldn't leave Sparrow, if that's what you're asking."

A smirk quirked his lips, but he still didn't look at her. "Let's say Sparrow wasn't part of the equation, he's not part of either scenario, doesn't exist. You could remain here with your two friends or you could go off again, back to the life you had before."

Evony breathed out and looked over to her father. "I don't

know. I guess stay. James has become fast friends with Tristan and Miels, I wouldn't want to take him away."

And for herself too. She really loved Tristan and Miels, was truly beginning to see them as brothers the way Sparrow did. It'd be nice. Having three brothers.

There was a slight furrow to Edmund's brows as he raised his head, looking out to the gardens around them. "Do you understand the rebels?"

"What?" Not only was it a complete change in topic, she didn't understand the question. And it added to the pace of her heart beating, brought her fears that he didn't trust her to the forefront of her thoughts.

"Why they do what they do. Do you understand their reasoning, sympathize with them?"

She didn't know where this was going, but she wasn't sure she liked the sound of it. And still, she answered honestly, "I understand their anger based on what they've been told. If they think they're being played and cheated, yes, I understand why they're angry."

"But you don't believe their reasoning?" It was so interesting, the way he could ask questions without giving away any emotion.

"I think..." She thought about it a few seconds before answering, "whoever is trying to take over your throne has done well in making you the enemy. I think they took the vulnerability of your people and played with them. And it works so well because everything they're using to create these rebels is based on truth."

Surprisingly, his tone remained level as he defended himself. "The Master Assassin is only used in grave circumstances. The fact that people believe he will be sent to their doors if they don't follow every law, if they don't pay every tax, is preposterous."

"Agreed," she responded. "But still, he has been sent to homes, and the gossip mills have a way of twisting facts by the time they get to the other side of the country."

"The taxes have been used for the protection of the country, the preservation of the lands. I do not base how much each town gets by how much in taxes are received. It's all taken and split evenly to protect them all. The luxuries given to the wealthier villages are only the leftovers of the taxes that helped the poorer villages."

She didn't argue with him.

"My ban on sorcerers and magicians was only following my father before me, for the protection of the common folk. I have been trying to loosen it for years now, but it's slow going."

There was a hitch to her breath. So he wanted to talk about the fact that she had been sent away because he would have been more likely to kill her than not when he found out she was magically born.

But even she knew the Edmund of twenty years ago and the Edmund of today were very different people.

He finally turned to face her, stopped in the middle of the garden as they were. "I ask again, do you understand the anger of the rebels? Toward me?"

He searched her gaze and waited.

Did she understand them? In a sense, yes. But at the same time, no.

She knew everything he'd just said about how he runs his country was true, he truly was a good ruler. Though to the common folk, it could seem like he was taking more than he was giving. In actuality, Evony thought he gave far more than he received. But she understood why the rebels believed otherwise—Edmund lived in a palace, they didn't.

A palace that came with far too much stress for Evony's liking.

So no, she didn't understand them.

But...

But she and Gemma and James had been jumping from place to place for years, and every time they'd been in the Northern country, she'd had to be extra careful. She was always careful, even in the Southern Lands, since she didn't want anyone to know she was the Master Magician, but at least down there, she could practice basic magic without the turn of a head. In the Northern Lands, that would get her arrested. Well, as much arrested as they'd like to try. Her magic would've gotten her out of it.

But arrested, nonetheless.

So, yes, there was a bit of a bitter taste in her mouth for the Northern Lands. Especially since she'd always known that the King was her father.

"No." He never broke his stare. "I think it sucks that magicians, and even sorcerers, aren't allowed here, but you've done well to protect your lands. The slow change to allow magicians and possibly even sorcerers onto this land is going to cause more problems. It already has. I think every ruler has more on their plate than the common person understands, so no, I am not angry with you."

Maybe this confession would allow him to begin to trust her. But he almost looked like he didn't believe her. His expression never changed, but Evony could read the edge of disbelief in his gaze. Did he want her to be angry? She supposed that would make more sense and be easier to rationalize in his mind.

He gave a slight nod and turned back to the palace. "Shall we head back?"

She nodded without a word, feeling rigid beside her father.

By the time they were out of the gardens and back in the presence of those who worked throughout the palace, Evony's anxiety had bolstered and she just wanted to be with her friends.

Luckily, Gemma was sitting on a bench at the opening to the garden maze as they emerged. Her friend was by her side immediately.

Edmund gave them a close-lipped smile and bowed his head before heading inside.

"What was that?" Gemma asked as she rung her arm into Evony's.

"I'll tell you about it in the rooms. Let's get James."

†

She'd had to wrangle him away from training with the original trio by sending erotic images of her time with Sparrow into his mind, but eventually, James backed away.

Evony and Gemma stood off to the side of the training yard, watching the men when James stumbled with mock acts of vomiting and vile looks in Sparrow's direction. The Assassin had been confused, but when he'd caught Evony's wicked gaze, she was sure he guessed she'd done something to mess with her brother. But she didn't care, she wanted some time with her two closest friends.

Sparrow laughed it off as James walked away from him and toward the girls. Though Sparrow did follow close behind to give Evony a chaste kiss. For a Northerner, he was becoming more and more accustomed to their public displays. She loved it.

"All done so soon?" Gemma asked sweetly. The images had been her idea.

James flicked a glance between the two of them and grumbled, "I hate you both."

"Whyever so?" Evony's hand flew to her heart as Sparrow turned back for the mats, a chuckle deep in his throat.

James flicked her off as he dropped his training sword and walked with them out of the grounds. They were twenty yards out when James turned to Evony, his arm thrown over his wife's shoulders. "What exactly did you want, dear sister?"

"To hang out with my two favorite people. We haven't been the three of us in so long!"

"So which of us is it?" he asked.

Her brows furrowed. "Excuse me?"

"Which one of us is your second favorite person? Is it me? Must be me, otherwise there would've been no reason to send those horrific thoughts into my head and get me out of training," James answered.

Evony laughed, smacking him on the arm as Gemma lightly elbowed his side. "You're both it."

James scoffed. "Eve dear, we know Mr. Assassin dearest is your favorite person, so you only got one spot in that top two category."

She rolled her eyes and turned on Gemma. "This is what you plan on procreating with."

Gemma shrugged through a smirk. "I'm stuck now."

James pulled her into him, hugging tight and kissing the top of her head. "That's right, baby. No way out!" He turned back to Evony. "So which is it?"

She gave him a cheeky grin. "When you married, two became one. So Sparrow's number one and you"—she exaggerated her arms to include both of them—"are number two."

"Loopholes. I like it, sister," James praised her.

"Seriously, though, I miss being just us." They walked back to the outskirts of the maze garden. They'd likely remain out of the garden, walking laps before heading inside to enjoy a few hours holed up together.

"Me too." Gemma sobered a bit. "But I can't lie, I enjoy seeing the smile that comes for only one person, Mrs. Assassin."

James's free arm went around Evony's shoulder as he pulled her in so all three walked huddled together. "What do you think we would've done? If you weren't related to Rosaelia and Edmund?"

Evony didn't answer.

Gemma didn't answer.

It definitely was something to think about. The only reason she'd never considered another side to this deal was because of her familial relationship to the crown.

"I don't know. I like to think I'd choose this side, but honestly, I feel like I wouldn't," Evony answered.

"I don't think we would've chosen," James added.

"No?" Gemma asked.

He tsked. "No, I think we would let them handle their business and we would've continued on with the Master Magician, making our own way through life."

"I was thinking the same, but..." Evony started.

"But Sparrow," Gemma finished.

"But Sparrow."

She couldn't imagine a life without him in it any longer. Couldn't fathom a day where she had to wake up and not be huddled into his side. Or squished with his entire body weight. Couldn't imagine not taking his arm to their meals or not sharing breath with him every day. Couldn't imagine not getting reprimanded or not seeing the jealousy turn him stone cold with rage.

"You think you would've still fallen for him? You hadn't in

all the years prior." James had always known she was attracted to the Master Assassin, but he also knew it had meant nothing.

"I think when we got the missive to help them, I would've been intrigued enough to go, even without the family ties. And I think it definitely would be more work on their end to convince me, but I knew Sparrow was mine in that room when they saw us behind the masks for the first time."

Silence.

"Before or after dropping the masks?" Gemma asked.

"Before." She'd never put too much thought into it, but every part of her being knew a large part of agreeing to join the Northern Lands was due to the intrigue of getting to spend time with the Assassin, to learn him the way he had intended on learning her, to... have him. "He knew I was the Magician while you guys spoke. His gaze was on me like he was waiting for me to say something. I think watching him with that challenge in his eyes did it for me. So, I think if Sparrow hadn't been around, I would've heard them out, then went on our way. But with him... there was really never a question. Related or not."

"Oh? So we never would've joined the Islanders? Learned some sorcerer potions, recked a bit of havoc?" Gemma teased.

"I don't know," Evony teased along. "Maybe I'd play them both."

"Yes, we're working with the Islanders to learn their potions and with the Northerners so you're satisfied," James stated proudly.

Evony laughed. "Well, yes. Did you think I would be working with the Northerners just because we're related?"

"Oh, what are we to do with these fools." Gemma leaned in closer to her husband. "Cheat that King out of the throne so *our* heir can take her rightful place, that's what!"

Evony's grin grew wicked. "Finally. His distrust of us is becoming a nuisance."

In reality, it was a nuisance in more ways than one. Not only did it hinder her ability to build a relationship with the only blood relatives she had, but it also placed a wedge, small as it may be, between herself and Sparrow. He'd grown up with her father, looked to him as his own father, so the loyalties were split more for him than for her.

In a way, it was a good thing. At least now when they married, the family he'd be joining—biologically—would be the one he'd grown up with his entire life. It was twisted. They were her father and sister, but it felt more like they would become her in-laws rather than Sparrow's.

James hugged Evony in a little tighter before releasing. "Yes, yes, we will deal with him later. Now, how about you tell us about these prisoners and what we've learned."

Evony grimaced as they turned to make their way back to the palace and their suite. "Not exactly what I wanted this time for, but it is why we were called to the palace."

Now to tell them that the land that had been their main home their entire lives, the land that had raised them, the land whose customs they most valued, was also a part of this rebellion, small as the association may be.

Though Evony was proud to say, the Southern Lands weren't part of this war, just a few greedy Southerners. That is, if all those prisoners said was true.

She wasn't sure if it was her magic or intuition, but something told her it was—the South wouldn't be joining this rebellion.

CHAPTER 34

EVONY

That thought she'd had the day before, about not being able to ever wake up again without Sparrow beside her—and in turn go to bed—seemed to be like testing fates because Sparrow didn't show up to dinner.

When he didn't show the entire passing of the meal and the men insisted they didn't know where he was, she turned to the only reliable source of information—the staff.

"Gone? Gone where?"

"I am not sure," Atiana, the tailor's assistant—and only tailor who truly respected Evony's choice of trousers—responded. "I understand that he will not be returning until tomorrow."

Tomorrow? The bastard had left without her.

"Who's with him?" She tried to keep her tone level.

"He's gone alone, Mis—Evony." Atiana was still getting used to using Evony's name, a feat Evony had insisted she do. She gave Evony a small, teasing smile, her beauty unworldly in doing so. "I am sure, whatever the purpose, will be to keep you safe. Or surprise you."

Evony tried to plaster a sweet smile to the girl, but it was futile and Atiana knew it. "Thank you, Atiana. But he will still be a dead man."

Atiana kept her giggles in but couldn't fight her close-lipped smile as she nodded.

She was a beautiful girl, with long, dark hair and beautiful light brown eyes. Not quite hazel, but lighter than brown. She was definitely one of the beauties of the palace.

And only a couple of years older than Sparrow. It still surprised Evony that the Assassin hadn't been interested. And in turn, when she learned that Atiana, too, had never been interested.

She could tell the girl's heart was elsewhere even though the tailor would never admit to it.

Evony tried to keep that sweet smile plastered on her face as she made her way to her suite. The smile dropped immediately once she was inside and she could finally focus on being angry with him.

Did I just hear that you've left the palace alone? She knew there was a tinge of annoyance when she spoke to him through her mind, but it was exactly how she felt.

You were with Ro. It was my best opportunity. He responded through a laugh though she heard the slight anxiety of getting a random thought in his head. He still wasn't used to it.

Oh really? Trying to get away? She sent the thought as a tease, but a large part of her was afraid it was true.

Never. She could all but hear the smirk in his tone. *Just have a surprise for you.*

She could *hear* Atiana's 'I told you so.'

I don't want surprises, Sparrow. I want you by my side when I wake up, inside me moments before we fall asleep.

A knock came at her door as his thoughts reached her mind. *Watch what you say—or think. I cannot afford the distrac-*

tion, and an erection will only put me through pain as I ride fast so that I can make it back to you sooner, love.

Miels and Tristan were standing behind the threshold, small smiles on their faces. She couldn't help smiling back and moving to allow them entrance.

Fine. Have fun on your stupid surprise. In the meantime, Miels and Tristan are here, and I'm sure they can show me a good time before I head off to bed...

The growl shot through her mind as if he were standing right beside her. If it was that sharp in her mind, she could clearly imagine how primal it was vibrating from his chest.

I swear to the lords, Magician, I'll kill them when...

She cut off their connection because he didn't yet know how to reach out on his own and she knew it would drive him crazy. Good, maybe it'll speed up his coming home process.

She turned to the boys who had made themselves at home on the couch and crossed her arms. "How can I help you boys?"

Tristan's lips tipped up. "Thought we'd keep you company while Sparrow's disappeared. Believe he'd want that."

She smirked. "Believe you me, he's not happy about your appearance."

Miels's brow quirked. "And how would you know?"

You don't truly believe I'd be this calm if I had to go without talking to him in our separation, did you? Not knowing where he was? I'd go insane.

They jumped from their seats, the obvious race their hearts evident in their stares before they settled and sat back down.

"How"—Miels stared at her in awe—"did you do that?"

You can respond to me through our minds too.

Do you two do this often? Tristan attempted, and Miels jumped at hearing his companion's voice inside his head. *Talk when we don't realize it.*

No. But now I'm wondering why not. I should do this to him more, huh? We've only done it a couple times so far. He's still not used to it either.

This is freaky. Miels sent. "I like talking better."

She laughed. "Me too, but he's not exactly here for that."

"No." Miels threw his arm to the back of the couch and his feet up onto the small table. "Which means we can question you without his threats."

Her mouth tipped up. "I can still let him know what you're doing. Open it up so he can threaten you through your thoughts."

His grin dropped to a scowl. "You were more fun before you let him finish in you, Magician."

She laughed and moved for the small bit of space left between the two of them. "You know we did it right here last night."

Both seemed a little less comfortable in their positions, but neither moved as Tristan said, "So, sister, tell us, anything to signify what those men said was false and it isn't only them? That the South has truly joined?"

It was a good question. One she'd thought about endlessly. "No. But the South could still be involved, I guess. You lot know I've always stayed away from politics, so I never really paid attention to the South's problems. But they have with the North what the Islanders do—a wish to allow their magicians free rein the way Islanders wish to allow the same for sorcerers." Her voice dropped a little. "It's a reasonable wish."

Tristan leaned into her. "Did you worry a lot? When you crossed into the North before?"

She shrugged. "Not a lot. Definitely not as much as other magicians since I can protect us better than the others. But it was always there—would my being here cause us any problems? Whether or not we could get out, it was something we had to always consider that other Southerners don't. And I think the Southern people, like the Islander ones, see us simply as peers so it's like an attack on the entire peoples."

"So you think Edmund's wrong, for not having allowed sorcerers and magicians through?" Miels asked.

She shrugged. "I understand he was trying to protect his people. I'm not angry with him, but yeah, I think it's wrong. But he did what he had to, and now he's trying to take it away. I think it's just harder with the Islanders because their lives are so different and it's not as easy for you guys to check out what's going on."

Tristan's shoulder hit hers and stayed there. "I'm sorry, sister. For making your home the one place you felt the least comfortable coming to."

Miels's shoulder hit her other side. "We'll fix it, Eve. It may be slow, but we'll show the Northerners that magicians are their peers like the Southerners know."

Their heads tilted and rested against hers and she felt so safe cocooned between them. How she believed little sisters with a ton of older brothers felt.

After long moments of comfortable silence, Miels asked, "About being down in the dungeons, what was that thing you said?"

Evony had to think about it a moment, but then realized her old tongue wouldn't be recognized by most. "Zuzveli yervoot." She looked into the flames in the fireplace and fell a little deeper into the couch and their presence on either side. "It's something I've always muttered, an unconscious thing. Comes out when I'm truly disgusted. I don't know why, but that's the only real old tongue that comes out for me."

"Where'd you learn it?" Tristan asked.

She shrugged. "I don't remember. It's just always been there."

They didn't say anything more, just leaned into her and sat there, keeping her company in Sparrow's absence.

She was in love with Sparrow, but she loved these guys. The way she loved Gemma and James. Included them in the most important people in her life. And so in the silence of the room, she thanked the rebellion for bringing her to the palace and into the lives of these boys.

CHAPTER 35

SPARROW

The house was surprisingly clean, albeit slightly dust filled. It'd been a few months since Sparrow had come by, usually choosing to spend a weekend in his childhood home where he could clean the place and be by himself.

The dust had settled, though luckily for Sparrow, not much.

He didn't have time to clean it. He was only there for one purpose—to pick up the rings.

The journey to this end of the Northern Lands from the palace was about nine hours of straight riding, and it was dark by the time he reached it. He'd left the palace before Evony could see him and insist on coming along, though that reprimand through his thoughts when she'd found out still lingered at the front of his mind. And worse off, the nagging feeling that he had to get back to the palace and beat both his brothers to pulps, then fuck the shit out of his magician to remind her who she belonged to, was strong. Ludicrous, but strong.

Sparrow walked through the small cabin house, the living

area connected to the dining and separated by a half wall to the kitchen. It was comfortable and cozy and one of his favorite places.

He lit candles to light the area and took one with him as he headed for his destination.

Down the hall, he passed the staircase that led to the small rooms on the upper level. His father had always joked that he may have only had one child, but hopefully Sparrow would have a litter to fill the upper rooms. Sparrow had always insisted he would never marry, nor bear children.

But that magician of his was throwing everything around on its head because the grin that erupted on his features at the thought of Evony pregnant was too powerful to fight. Not to mention the thought of it happening time and again. He wanted to fill those upper rooms with a litter. And he wanted them all to be Evony's replica.

He laughed to himself as he pushed the door to the master bedroom that had been his fathers as the words echoed in his mind. *Their children.*

What was happening to him? He didn't know and was coming to find that he didn't care.

In his father's room, Sparrow pulled apart the board on the upper corner of the far wall and found the small crack of a safe his father had created. Inside was a tiny box with intricate detailing around the entirety of it. After creating the rings, his father had spent a long time making this box to hold them in.

Sparrow opened the tiny box and found them sitting beautifully within the small pillow his father had stuffed inside. It looked as if not a day had passed since they'd been made.

He grinned around the wild beat of his heart. He could officially make Evony his now. She'd gone from fake betrothed to real betrothed only three days prior, and by the end of the week, she would go from betrothed to wife. It was astounding how much he loved the idea, but his father had been right—she may live to drive him crazy, but he couldn't continue on without her.

Astounding indeed.

He closed the box and slipped it into the inside of his jacket pocket, then took the light as he walked out of the room. He snuffed the candles out before leaving the house and heading back to his horse.

It was late so the smartest course of action would be to remain at the house and head to bed, but he wanted to reach the palace as soon as possible. Even the few hours of being away from his magician's side was causing an ache he wasn't accustomed to.

Unfortunately for him, the straight ride back was halted when twice, he had to stop. Once, to find a different route when the one he was using was overtaken by a hoard of sleeping cows, and another when he heard a pack of wild night animals in the distance. It would be of no use attempting to go through them and get eaten before he could reach her. She would bring him back with her magic just to kill him herself.

It wasn't a straight ride.

What should have taken nine hours, took Sparrow ten. That hour didn't sound like much, but every second of it tortured him with the need to be by her side. But even as he arrived at the palace and left his horse with Gabriel at the stables, he knew it would be futile to go to her. It was just coming on dawn and she would still be sleeping. As tired as he was, he also felt restless with the need to present the rings.

But, he wanted to greet his future clean.

So the baths were the obvious first option. He'd taken the box out of his travel clothing, placing it off to the side with the spare clothes in the bathing rooms and gotten into the gloriously hot water.

He was cleaned and drying off in a matter of minutes, turning to the loose black trousers and pulling them on. He threw on a loose white shirt that opened at the pecs and lightly tucked it into his pants, then grabbed the box and placed it gently into his pocket. He didn't release it, instead tightening his hold as he looked to the doors that would lead him out of the bathing rooms and one step closer to her.

But again, he would take a detour.

Passing their suite, he headed to the end of the hall for the King's suite. Edmund was more than likely up by then, but even if he wasn't, Sparrow would wake the man. He didn't care if it made him grumpy, Sparrow needed to speak with him first.

He knocked on the door as a pretense only, slipping inside without waiting for a response.

And found himself shocked to see the moron twins seated with Edmund before the raging fireplace.

The possessive asshole in him narrowed in on the two, and he was moving before he could recognize his movements. He pulled both of them up by the tops of their shirts, turning them to face his sneer. "When I say, 'I'll kill you,' why is it that both my seconds are the ones not to take me seriously? Everyone else seems to take me seriously."

Miels rolled his eyes. "We're her brothers. You don't mind when James is alone with her."

"James is a married man." His fingers tightened around their collars. "You two are whores."

Tristan's lips tipped up. "Be nice, brother. We haven't whored in over a month." *Since they'd shown up.* "The one time we had a chance, buddy here *wasn't feeling up for it,* and I didn't want to go out alone."

Miels's eyes dropped at the comment. Not in the way that they would if he felt guilty for whoring without his brother, but in the way that almost said he wouldn't be doing so again. Ever.

Sparrow's brows furrowed, but now wasn't the time to question him about it. "In any case, the only thing truly keeping you two alive is that she'd be upset if I hurt you."

Miels's lips quirked into that cocky smile. "Yeah, yeah."

Sparrow shoved them away and took a seat on the chair across from the King. He watched the brothers look to the Edmund, as if they were having a silent conversation, before bidding them farewell to speak alone. Sparrow wanted to know what that look was about, but again, now was not the time. The only thing he was worried about at the moment was getting back to his suite.

Edmund leaned back in his spot at the end of the couch and analyzed him. As if figuring him out completely, the King asked, "Ready to talk about it?"

A smirk rose on Sparrow's lips. "Talk about what."

"The fact that you're in love with the daughter I never knew I had," he answered blatantly.

Sparrow blanched. "How..."

Edmund's brow quirked up as he smirked. "I knew you were in love with her the moment you refused to talk about your relationship."

Again, Sparrow was stupefied. "How..."

"You reacted to her in a way I've never known you capable. And every day since you refused to talk about it, I saw the way you slowly slipped deeper and deeper." He fidgeted with the cup of tea in his hand as he stared at Sparrow. "After I told you I'd drop it, even more so. You completely dropped your guard and anyone with eyes could see it."

Sparrow looked down to his hands as he rested over his knees. "I think I've known from the moment I saw her eyes through that mask the first meeting with the entire Posse.

She's infuriating and shameless and completely wrong for the palace." He lifted his gaze to the flames flickering away in the fireplace. Evony's fiery presence took root in his vision as it danced with the flames. "But she's also lovely and exhilarating and a shock of life. It's like she's brought life into me and all I can think about is how best to protect her and keep her happy."

"So why are you here, Sparrow, rather than at her side where I know you are dying to be?" He didn't all around look too happy about the question as he asked it.

"I'm in love with her, Ed. Ardently so." He almost felt breathless speaking the words into the air again. "I went back to my house."

Edmund sat up a little straighter from his lounge. He knew of the rings that Sparrow's father had made for him and would understand that a day's trip would have taken him to his child-hood home and back. He'd know it was to pick up said rings.

"I wanted your support. Before I present them to her." This would prove to Evony that he didn't distrust her.

"Why?" He sounded truly shocked. "She does not see me as a father any more than I see her a daughter. I am more likely to father you, Sparrow."

"Then do it for me." *Tell me you trust that this is my future.*

Edmund was silent for a long while. So long, Sparrow began to wonder if maybe Evony had been right and Edmund didn't want to give his support. Didn't want to include her as fully as she deserved to be included into the King's Posse.

"I trust that you know what is right for your heart, Spar-row. I trust that you would make the choice based off not only your heart, but your brain and soul too. And so I'll trust you this decision like I've trusted every other one you've made, son."

"I'd protect her with my life." He'd already said he didn't

see Evony as a daughter, but Sparrow couldn't help reassuring him.

Sparrow swore he heard *That's what I'm afraid of* from beneath the King's breath, but it was quickly covered by a "Then I suppose we have a wedding to prepare for."

Sparrow grinned up to the man that had raised him. "She must say yes first."

Edmund rolled his eyes. "Like anybody in this palace would doubt her answer."

The grin turned into a smirk. "She could very well tease me with rejections as punishment for leaving without her."

A low chuckle left him. "Yes. That does sound like her."

Sparrow stood and caught Edmund's stare. "I love her, Ed."

"I know," he said weakly. "And that is the only reason I am supporting this."

CHAPTER 36
SPARROW

She was a goddess sent from his father.

She had to be, laid out in between the sheets like that, hair splayed on the pillow begging to be touched. Cheeks flushed, begging to be caressed. Lips parted, begging to be kissed.

He kneeled at her bedside, lightly brushing the hair away from her face and just taking a moment to take this in. Her, in his—their—bed. The all too present beat of his heart. The future he could clearly see with Evony barefoot and pregnant along the yard of his home as the kids ran about. All of it seemed impossible, and up until a few weeks ago, they had been to Sparrow.

But not anymore.

She was it. What he'd been unconsciously waiting for.

He leaned in and kissed her lips. Pecked them like she had at that dinner a couple weeks prior. Again and again and again, incapable of stopping. He'd understood it weeks ago when she'd done it to him because he hadn't actually wanted her to stop, but being the one to initiate the kisses definitely felt more intoxicating than receiving them.

She moaned his name as her lashes fluttered, but she didn't wake.

Which gave him just enough time to adjust his body's apt response to his name off her lips. Especially done unconsciously. That territorial part of him loved that even in sleep, he was what she thought of. She *had* said always.

"Magician," his voice was raspier than he'd expected when he whispered into her ear.

She shuffled and called out his name once more but remained lost in her dreams.

He kissed her lips again, then muttered against her mouth. "Wake up, love." Another kiss. "C'mon, baby, I need to see those ocean blues." Another kiss.

She muttered against his lips, lashes fluttering even more now.

One more peck. "Wake up and I'll make sure to make your body tired enough to knock you right out again, love. Multiple times. My fingers, tongue, and cock all want a turn."

Her eyes popped open this time before closing back down again and fluttering as she rubbed them, fully coming to. Of course *that* had gotten her attention.

When she was able to focus, her eyes widened at the sight of him and she was out from under the sheets and flying into his arms before he could process her movements. "You're back!"

He was lucky not to fall from the sudden attack but latched on to her tightly and stood to both feet as her entire body clung to him. "I'm back, love, and you can rest assured I'll never be leaving your side again."

When she pulled back enough to look at him, her expression was stern. "Try that crap again, Assassin, and I'll keep my magic around you at all times. Like to see you try to leave without my knowledge then."

He laughed. "Now who's the overbearing one?"

She shrugged and kissed him. "You're rubbing off on me."

He wanted to continue kissing her, do it for the rest of his life, but his heart raced with the possibilities of the next moments, how much they would dictate the rest of his life.

"Would you like to know where I was all night?"

Her gaze narrowed but there was no accusation in them. "Do you want to tell me?"

"Oh, I'm going to tell you. I was just wondering if you'd like to know now or if I should play this out?"

She growled. "Behave, Assassin."

His cock stirred. "You were right. Telling me to behave makes me really not want to."

Her hips moved against his in the perfect motion to line her cunt up with his cock. "I told you."

He smirked, biting down on his lower lip as he took her in. He couldn't get sidetracked. "I went to my childhood home, the place my father raised me before he was killed."

She stilled in his arms, staring at him with some worry beginning to plague her features.

"I normally go to be alone, get away, but this time, I wanted to get back as soon as possible."

"So why go at all?" she whispered, all her fingers tangled at the back of his neck.

He swallowed. It was odd, how nervous he was considering he knew she would say yes. He softly dropped her to her feet and stepped back, taking in the worry beginning to edge into her features and wanting to wipe that look away. Instead, he reached for the box in his pocket and pulled it out.

Her gaze immediately dropped to it, a furrow edging between her brows before she glanced back up, waiting.

He breathed out again and dropped to a knee. It was a Southern custom, dropping to a knee to ask the woman to marry you. Northerners normally held one another's hands as the man asked. Formal. Intimate in its own ways.

There was an obvious hitch to her breath as he got to one knee, and she visibly tried to control her reaction. He assumed, because he was a Northerner, that she didn't want to jump to conclusions.

He couldn't help the small smile that began to pull at his lips. He opened the box and showcased the two rings—one smaller, one bigger—within. "When I was six years old, my father got a premonition of sorts, to make a set of rings with the rains of the day—the set that I would later use in my matrimony. It was the day Princess Rosaelia was born, the day you were born. We never put much emphasis on why he had felt it so important to do so that day, but now I know why. Because I would be presenting them to you, asking *you* to spend the rest of your life driving me insane."

She tried to stop a giggle as she bit her lip. Her eyes watered as she stared down at him, her gaze flickering to the rings, but ultimately settling on him.

"I told my father that day that I would never marry, and he laughed and told me I'd change my mind when a woman came around that I needed to have, to keep safe and content. I brushed it off. My entire life, I brushed it off. I'd always loved my father and trusted in everything he told me, but on this matter, I thought him insane. Up until a few weeks ago, there was never a woman I cared for and wished to keep safe other than Rosaelia, and I'd always looked to her as a sister and definitely never considered touching her. Never wanted to be around her at all times."

Evony swallowed and stepped up to him, lowering herself

onto his one raised thigh as her arms wrapped around his neck.

"I thought about you even when I was away from you. I think that's part of the reason I claimed you as my betrothed to Alexei, but it didn't feel like enough. I needed to be with you at all times." He felt the chuckle as he remembered all their moments from their short acquaintance. "I fought you every time, but I was secretly glad you forced your way into every trip I planned. I'd never even let myself think that, accept it, but I was so glad to have you around. It was like I knew you were more likely to get hurt with me than at the palace, but at least that way, I could protect you."

Her smile was wide, the water edging her eyes mixing beautifully with the sapphire of her irises.

"It's ludicrous, I know. Entirely so, but that's what father told me. That when I found the woman I would ask to be mine, it wouldn't make sense. It would drive me mad, but that I wouldn't want it any other way. I'd thought he'd lost his mind in some fairy tales, but he was right because I cannot spend another day not having you as mine, Evony. Be mine?"

She held his face in a gentle grasp between her hands as she stared at him. "Absolutely, certainly, entirely, unreservedly, fully, unconditionally, wholly, utterly, thoroughly, *yes*."

The laugh was loud as it escaped him, but there was no time for that, her lips were pressed to his and there was nowhere else he'd rather be.

†

"Whoa," Miels exclaimed. "Does it smell like sex in here!"

Sparrow rolled his eyes as he looked up from the table in the corner of his suite to find his two best friends came to visit him. But the grin was so wide on his features from his legitimate betrothal that he didn't even care about Miels's crass comment.

"What do you two morons want?"

Tristan turned a chair backward to sit on and smacked him on the shoulder. "Look at that smile, mate. I don't think I've ever seen a grin that wide on you. Is the Master Assassin meant to smile so much?"

"Where's the missus?" Miels turned another chair backward.

"Sleeping." The grin turned cocky.

"Ah ha." He clapped. "I know that scent when I smell it."

Sparrow rolled his eyes to his friend and sent a smirk of his own. "Of course you would. It's been coming from your room for a week now."

Miels blanched, that grin immediately dropping as he changed the topic before Tristan could comment more than an *I knew it* as his widened eyes jumped to his brother. "More importantly, Edmund told us the news!"

Sparrow's grin turned proud. "Oh?"

Both men laughed as they shook him by the shoulders. "You're getting married, brother!"

Sparrow laughed with them and fought their hands off. Finally, they all leaned into the table and Sparrow couldn't shake the happiness in him. "I'm getting married. She'll be mine."

"She already is, mate," Tristan grumbled.

"Has been since the beginning, brother," Miels added.

"I know. But officially. She'll be mine, and the world will know it and I'll sleep with her at my side every night and wake with her in the mornings. I'll be insufferable and overbearing and protective and possessive and somehow, she'll deal with it all. She'll act like it bothers her, even though I can see how much she enjoys it." Sparrow's joy was spilling from every inch of him. "It's already like that, but I don't know. I can't explain it. I need her to be mine. Officially."

"I would too if I had a woman, mate," Tristan said with his own wide grin. "I get it."

Sparrow met their gazes and realized how they were also beaming, their eyes shining with excitement. These were his brothers, and they were just as elated for his betrothal as he was. They may not have been blood, but they were closer brothers than most got.

Then Tristan smacked his shoulder, and Sparrow reciprocated, and Miels joined and they were laughing so hard, Sparrow couldn't remember the last time the three of them had been so carefree.

"Baby..." The door to their room opened, and Evony froze when she saw the guys. Sparrow pushed them away from him and met her beautiful gaze. "It's a good thing I chose to put on the shirt."

She moved her long, black locks to cover her chest, which was fairly noticeable through the white shirt, and closed the door behind her where most of the scent of their activities came from. She moved toward them at the table and stopped behind Sparrow, where she wrapped her arms around his chest and slid her hands into his shirt. She played with the hairs on his chest and he found contentment in the simple touch.

"You look happy there, sister." Miels's tone was teasing.

"Our brother give you a good enough time? You will be stuck with him for the rest of your life. Get out now if you didn't love it. I can always console you." Tristan winked.

Sparrow kicked him beneath the table. "The only reason you're not dead is because she's holding me."

Tristan's grin was wide. "I know."

Then Evony was giggling by his ear and everything that

wasn't her washed away. He leaned back into her and kissed her jaw. "He's given me the best of times. I stumbled when I tried to get out of bed, I'm so sore."

Miels's eyes twinkled with delight. "Ask your betrothed to kiss it better for you."

Evony's gaze matched his. "That *was* the plan."

Sparrow froze, then pushed the table against his brothers. "Get out." He turned to Evony. "Get on the table, Magician."

Evony moved with a wide grin. "You heard the man," she said to the boys. "Get out."

Tristan and Miels both shook their heads as they laughed and pushed out of their seats. They mumbled their congratulations for the betrothal and gave her quick kisses on the forehead before leaving the suite.

Sparrow licked his lips to the sight of her on his table. "Spread your legs, love."

CHAPTER 37

EVONY

The day she was old enough to understand the letter that told her of her past, Evony had resigned herself to the knowledge that she might never have her family. When she'd met Gemma then James, she'd known that wasn't true. She'd learned that day that blood did not dictate familial ties.

So it was in the bliss of their relationship that Evony realized the alternative—she would always have family, but she would never marry. By then, it had become clear to her that she could trust no one else, and so she'd lost all and any hope for the possibility.

Even when they'd arrived at the palace and she'd begun flirting with Sparrow, it'd been more for fun since she'd always found him attractive than because she truly hoped for anything to happen.

But life had a funny way of things.

Not only would she marry, she would also get the blood family she didn't think possible. Albeit with their own complications thrown in.

By the end of the week, the palace was abuzz with excitement for their matrimony. Evony and Sparrow both insisted it remain small, their little group being all that was needed.

And that it happen soon.

So soon, in fact, that they only gave the palace tailors just enough time to make their matrimonial attire.

They'd marry at the setting of the sun—a Northern custom.

She would walk down the aisle—a Southern custom.

The sun was about an hour away from setting when Gemma and James became her little annoying servants, doting on her every breath as she tried to get them to relax. Gemma helped her get dressed as Rosaelia volunteered to get her hair up. She lightly coated her lips with berry juice to make them shine, but that was it. She didn't want anything big, never had. And everyone was well aware that Sparrow would never want a big show. Honestly, she knew he'd be happy if she walked down in one of his shirts.

Rosaelia lightly curled her hair, loosely hanging pieces up with pins and giving Evony a careless look that made her look ethereal, especially in her ivory gown—another Northern custom.

Then everyone was gone from the room and she was alone with only James. He'd walk her down the aisle to Sparrow. In the South, it was the male the bride were closest to that would walk her down, unlike the Islanders who always used the father, the closest male only being used when a father wasn't around. In the North, no one walked down the aisle, they all simply met at the front, coming from opposite ends to meet as one.

James walked up to her and lightly brushed a lock of hair back. "You're so beautiful, Eve."

She smiled back, warmth filling her. "I feel beautiful."

His eyes watered, and her heart stopped at the sight as he brushed more locks back. "I know he loves you, Eve, but it's just so hard to imagine anyone good enough for you. Or Gem. I still know I'm not good enough for her. You two are too superior for anyone to stand the chance."

"What can I say, I felt bad for the Assassin." She gave a cocky grin.

He winked. "Keep feeling bad because we're delaying this wedding. I still haven't had the chance to threaten that betrothed of yours properly."

She laughed and fell into his chest, hugging him tight. "I love you, James."

"I love you too, sister." He kissed the crown of her head.

†

THE WEDDING WOULD TAKE place in the small church at the end of the palace grounds—a Southern custom, Northerners preferring a room more intimate to them or the outdoors.

Evony and James had just reached the open doors, Sparrow waiting at the altar with a priest and their small array of guests —Gemma, Rosaelia, Miels, Tristan, and King Edmund.

Evony clutched at James's bicep as the jitters began flying up her body, but damn, she'd never smiled so wide in all her life. Not even when James and Gemma were married, and until this point, that had been her most favorite day.

When they reached the front, James stopped her and turned her to face him as he took her face between his hands and kissed each of her cheeks. He stared down at her with such love, she read the brotherly affection there. The promise that although they weren't blood and it was because of the awful ways they'd been left to fend for themselves that they'd met, he loved her. She truly hoped he read the same thing in her look, because the thought of anyone but James walking her down this aisle was nonsensical. With a final wink, he placed Evony's hand in Sparrow's and backed up until he was by Gemma's side.

Sparrow took both of her hands in his, his gaze drinking her in as the priest began to speak. He'd open the matrimonial processions with a little speech of the meaning of the act—something used by all three countries—before moving onto the vows. Long vows were a Southern custom, in the North and Island counties, they merely said a phrase that made them one. And Evony had to admit, she preferred this particular custom. So much so that even Gemma and James had used the non-Southern custom.

The priest turned to Evony first—another more Northern custom, having the female go first. "Miss Evony, please recite your vow."

Evony's stare held on to her assassin's, her tone so light, she didn't even know if her family could hear, but she was so breathless with joy that it was all she could muster. "With this ring, I take your soul in exchange for mine."

She slipped the ring that the priest handed her onto Sparrow's left hand.

The priest turned to Sparrow. "Sir Sparrow, please recite your vow."

Sparrow almost looked to stand taller as he stared down at her, his grip tightened around her fingers and his voice grew like he wanted the whole world to hear it. "With this ring, I take your soul in exchange for mine."

He barely released her hand long enough to take the ring from the priest and slip it onto her left hand.

The final slip of the ring caused a rush to spiral through her body. As if the flames that she so loved to sit before, that they'd had their first real talks in front of, were spinning within her, looking for a place to call home. She wasn't sure if it was the excitement of officially being his or if it had something to do with the way the rings had been made—specially for them.

The priest looked between them and finally uttered the words she'd been waiting on. "I now pronounce you husband and wife. You may seal the exchange with a kiss."

The final vow of the priest was different in the North too, one that she found she liked equally to the Southern and Island ones.

Sparrow's hands moved immediately, one softly holding her face angled up to his lips while the other found its way to her ass and pulled her in closer. She wrapped her hands around his neck as their lips collided, sealing their forever.

When they turned back to the group, Evony didn't have a moment to think before they were huddled on all sides by the family, a huge hug. And surprisingly, even her father looked happy. It didn't look as genuine as everyone else's, and Evony didn't know if she was just imaging something that wasn't there or if he truly was a bit upset about the matrimony, but in her current state, she couldn't care less. This was all the celebration they'd get as they walked out of the chapel.

A custom both Northerners and Southerners shared—no celebration after the wedding, the couple was merely let out to go consummate the marriage. The Islanders, on the other hand, normally had a full night's celebration. Evony had always thought she'd liked the Islander's way of going about things, but she had to admit, she was glad they'd be allowed off to their beds.

Sparrow had even settled a small cottage by the end of the palace grounds for them, wanting to give them a semblance of privacy for at least this one night. Though realistically, they'd already been heard by anyone passing by their suite, but the thought was sweet, nonetheless.

When they were away from every prying eye—though Evony had no doubt there were servants hiding away and watching them from windows—Sparrow pulled on her hand and they began to run through the greens. The laughs bubbled out of them as they ran hand in hand and barefoot to the little cottage.

As they reached the door, Sparrow drew to an abrupt halt, turning and taking Evony into his arms to walk through the door—another Northern and Islander custom, Southerners sometimes following it too because of the corniness of it, but not because it was a cultural custom. Gemma and James most certainly had followed it. And not necessarily because of the corniness of it.

Sparrow slammed the door shut with his foot as their lips pressed together through their laughs. The fire was blazing in the hearth—servants no doubt having been around to light it and leave some food for them. It was beatifically cozy inside.

Sparrow let her to her feet, threw his matrimonial jacket aside, and cradled her face in his hands. She could feel the cold press of the ring on her skin and that just made her heart expand wider. She didn't know this much happiness was possible. "I've fallen madly in love with you, Magician."

Her heart stuttered, never able to come to terms with the reality of those words. "And I've fallen in love with you, my assassin."

His lips were on hers again.

What started off slow turned aggressive in a matter of minutes, his tongue lashing out and dominating hers as he pressed himself closer. He backed her up—fingers scraping into her scalp—until she hit the couch and fell back onto it.

He straddled her, his knees locking her in as he bent so the kiss wouldn't break. When breath was finally required, he pressed open-mouthed kisses down her jaw, biting down on her earlobe until her small moan turned into a desperate cry. Her hands raked his thighs, feeling the strength beneath the trousers as he hovered over her, his cock basically teasing her with its nearness to her mouth.

She licked his trouser clad erection. "If you're going to put it in front of me, at least let me have a taste, Assassin."

He grabbed her around the throat and tilted her head back so she could no longer play, hissing in her ear, "Don't worry, Magician, you'll get your turn."

He licked back up to her mouth and bit her bottom lip before pulling away only enough so they could both watch as his hands fisted into her beautiful gown and ripped it apart.

The part of her brain that mourned for the piece was quickly overshadowed by the desire that erupted at the animalistic show of brute strength and desire.

Her nipples peaked at the sudden rush of air as the dress fell apart to the waist, and his hands took no pause in reaching for her breasts, fingers tweaking and making her fidget beneath him. She arched her back off the couch, nails digging into his thighs, and all she knew was how wet she was beneath this dress.

"You know, you never did finish your feast." She watched him watch her and wasn't able to hold back the moan that escaped at seeing the hunger on his face.

He leaned into her, his tongue invading her mouth and tasting every warm corner before abruptly pulling away. He pushed off the couch, hands falling away from her breasts, and backed until he hit the opposite couch. Her body cried for his return.

He lounged back and spread his legs wide to accommodate his rock-hard cock. "Come here."

He said it softly and flicked his finger to show it was a demand, not a request. She had to bite down on her bottom lip and clench her thighs together to control her breathing before rising on unsteady legs.

Somehow, she still gracefully walked over to him, torn dress and all.

When she reached him, stopping between his spread legs, he looked like he was getting ready. "As you reminded me, love, I have a feast I never got to finish."

Because the King and his brothers had interrupted them.

There was no one to interrupt them now. Rebellion be damned, this was their night.

A smirk grew on her lips as she positioned herself onto his lap, straddling his hips and feeling his cock strain against his trousers for her wet folds.

His hands skimmed up her thighs and settled at her waist, so large his thumbs were grazing her breasts as he held her steady. His left thumb softly caressed the edge of her scar peaking past the dress at the end of her breast, but he only looked at her with desire. Some nights he was softer, loving to the scar. And others he treated her in the dirty manner she loved. Both were an equally perfect balance of everything she'd ever wanted.

With a final wicked stare that told her she was his to do with as he pleased, he refocused his attention on her breasts and began his feast.

His tongue was slow as it circled one nipple then made its way to the other. Over and over and over again, he drew a figure eight between her breasts, but never stopped to give her what she wanted. It was irritating how much he loved doing that.

She ground hard against him, the groan deep as it left him. "I swear to the lords, I hate you so much sometimes, Assassin."

Her hands fisted into his hair as he chuckled at her raspy comment, pulling until he was directly in front of one nipple. She forced him down until his mouth covered her whole. Her back arched as a moan escaped her without her control, and she felt him laugh under her.

Then he truly began his feast.

He didn't give her the chance to think properly as he suckled and bit one nipple before moving to the other, his opposite thumb and forefinger always playing with the nipple he wasn't tasting.

She was rubbing against him, feeling herself drip all over his trousers, already getting closer and closer to that release.

Then finally, though she'd barely been able to keep her eyes open, she looked down and found his gaze glued to her face, drinking in her response as he released his suckle and his teeth grazed her nipple before biting down for that sting of pain.

She came before she realized it was happening. Rode him and felt his tongue on her until she finally came back from the high. It was an intoxicating start to the night.

He leaned back, watching her breathing attempt to normalize with a too-cocky-to-be-worn-by-someone-already-too-attractive smirk. "Now *that* was a feast." He licked her breasts again, like he couldn't get enough.

Her lips ached to meet his again so she pulled on his hair and brought her lips down to his. Evony understood one thing as their tongues touched once more—why he'd ripped her dress in two. She didn't want to break and pull his shirt up, so her hands fisted into the fabric and pulled, ripping it entirely down the middle until it was hanging loose and his torso was open for her touch.

Her fingers raked him, feeling the touch of hair move through her fingers as her nails left pink marks. "My turn to feast."

She laid open-mouthed kisses down his neck, licking her way down to that spot below his ear and suckling. She didn't pull away until he groaned loud enough to scare wild animals, his fingers digging into her thighs, and his hips pumping up against her. She'd leave a mark for sure.

She licked back up to his lips as her fingers grasped at his hair and her chest pressed into his. The feel of her nipples rubbing against the hairs of his chest was another form of delicious torture as her hips began to rock against his again.

He growled, words slipping past the press of her lips. "Love, if you don't stop right now, I'm going to come."

She tsked three times. "We don't want that." The smirk grew on her lips, but she didn't stop. Her hips bucked against him, knowing the rhythm would drive him to an end as her nails scraped into his scalp and her tongue played with his.

"Then behave, wife," he grit out as his hips moved against hers, bucking up to rub himself through her folds.

That last word sent shivers down her entire body.

She kissed down his chest, moving off his lap as she reached the end of his trousers. "I believe I told you telling me to behave makes me really"—she began undoing the folds of his trousers—"*really* not behave."

He sprang free from the pants, raising his hips so she could pull the damned thing off. She did so quickly, needing, more than merely wanting, to touch him. Taste him.

She pumped his length twice, loving the way his hips twitched from her touch, then started at the base and licked the beautiful veins up to the tip. She did so again with every vein until he was an utter mess for her mouth.

She played with the tip a moment, knowing how he loved that initial swipe, and tasted the saltiness there, a flavor she reveled in—specially Sparrow.

Evony took his tip into her mouth, swirling her tongue

around to get a taste of every bit as his hips bucked up and he growled loud and primal. She had to clench her thighs together so tight, they were on the precipice of merging into one, both at his reaction and his taste.

"Fuck, Magician, I've missed that talented little mouth of yours."

She moaned against his cock as she took him in as far back as she could. His hips flew off the couch at the feeling of the vibrations and his hands fisted into her hair, almost choking her as he used her mouth to jack off.

She played with his balls and he damn near gagged her with the pressure of how far his cock moved down her throat. Somehow, that affected her as much as his touch on her clit as her hips bucked with the need to be touched.

She released his balls to touch herself, humping her hand as he settled, allowing her a bit of the control back. She popped him out of her mouth and licked to the very base, getting a taste of his sensitive balls as her gaze fluttered up to meet his.

"Maybe later I can use you as a bit of moisturizer." She stopped touching herself, her body aching at the loss, but she didn't care. Her hands pumped his cock and she elated in the pure astonished awe that filled his eyes at the comment. "But right now I want to swallow every last drop."

He hadn't let her get a taste last time. This time, she couldn't give it up. She needed this. Needed to feel the hot liquid fill her mouth.

She took him deep again and moaned to let the vibrations move through him as she slowly moved back to the tip. He roared her name as he came straight into her mouth, filling her exactly as she'd wanted.

When it ended, she swallowed down her new favorite flavor and watched the way his chest rose and fell as he watched her in awe. She licked the sides of her lips, drawing his attention. "Mm," she moaned. "You taste too good."

She waited a few moments, allowed his body the time to recover a bit before pushing to her feet and letting her fingers skim up her torso. She delighted in the way his stare followed her hands, taking in every movement. She played with her breasts, pinching her already sensitive nipples and whimpering at the bliss it brought. It was an altogether new form of erotica to touch herself as he watched.

Her gaze remained on him as her fingers finally moved to the dress lying around her hips and plucked her thumbs into the fabric to shimmy out. She let the dress hit the ground and stood before her assassin completely naked, loving the way he licked his lips in anticipation. She stepped out of the puddle of fabric on the ground and watched as his body already began preparing to be inside her.

"You're so beautiful, Evony," he whispered it like a prayer. "I cannot believe you're mine."

She'd known she'd loved him, but every time he did that—said those words—her heart expanded a little more. Her body grew wetter with need. But instead of moving to him, she turned and began to walk to the open door of the bedroom, knowing her hips were exaggerating her every step.

She heard his growl like a bear about to catch its prey only moments before she felt his grip around her waist and the feeling of getting thrown through the air.

She hit the bed on her stomach, the seductive laugh bubbling out of her as she felt the bed dip behind her. She barely saw him hovering on his knees behind her as she began to pick herself up, knowing being on all fours was giving him an entirely different angle.

His hand was in her hair before she could play too much, pulling her up so her back hit his chest and his mouth was at her ear, his cock pressing into her back hard and ready. Incredible. "Later, I'm going to take you like this. I'll press your face into the sheets as your ass begs for my attention." He spun her around and aggressively released her hair so she fell onto her back. "But right now, I want to watch my wife's face as I fuck her."

My wife.

Her heart erupted something new at the words.

They were married. They were one.

And she would never get tired of hearing the words uttered from his lips.

She knew her eyes were black with desire as her legs opened up for him. "Well then, my husband, take what's yours."

His fingers played with her folds, slipping through the wetness. "That's my girl."

He wasn't careful or soft or slow about it. He angled his cock to her opening and grabbed her hips, thrusting in with the vigor of a wild animal as he watched her mouth open in a cry. Her eyes fluttered as they fought to remain open and watch him in turn.

Her back arched as she watched him pound into her. Over and over and over, her hips rolling to meet his every time.

"You're hypnotizing, Evony."

Her heart stuttered at the crash of memory that came with that word. How he'd denied it the first time she'd asked, even though she'd partly known he'd been lying.

"So fucking hypnotizing." He fell over her, catching himself on his arms and locking her beneath him as he thrust harder and deeper still.

Her legs wrapped around his waist as her hands found their way to his back, bringing him in closer to her while her nails made their mark.

"Lords, Sparrow," she moaned. "Please don't stop. Don't ever..."

He kissed her, his tongue telling her how much he loved her in a way words would never be able to articulate.

And finally, she couldn't take it any longer.

He had to hold her jaw in place so she didn't thrash with her screams as she came, clenching around him with everything in her and feeling his climax hit. She loved the way he growled into her mouth as he spilled into her.

She felt him milk her insides, leaving his mark everywhere within her.

They breathed hard together, neither moving as their eyes met and they stared at one another.

"Wife," he whispered, the joy in his gaze all Evony needed to survive.

"Husband," she whispered back.

CHAPTER 38

EVONY

With all that was going on, it was easy for Evony to forget the rest of the world and bask in only her husband.

Husband.

She was already too used to the term.

But with the rebellion going on, they weren't given that glory to lie around and delight in one another. Plus, she had promised the Princess training, and although the others could handle it, she liked taking this bit off their plates.

But the biggest reason Evony insisted on training her twin was the time they'd get to spend together. It was really their only way since she had yet to find another way to connect with her womb mate. And part of her knew Edmund's distrust of her was probably seeping its way into Rosaelia.

Evony looked over the swords on the far weapons table, playing with a few to choose which one she wanted.

"I'm moving onto swords?" Rosaelia asked from behind her where she stood straight backed, knees bent, and hovering on her left foot. Balance was just as important as strength. Especially when using weapons.

"No." Evony turned around with a long bladed one with enough space on the grip for two hands. "I just want you to get an idea of the weight of them." Evony walked up to her sister. "You may break."

Rosaelia toppled, the sweat dripping from her brow, as she stared at the sword.

Evony handed it over, no use in playing this up, and watched Rosaelia's arm topple straight down. A small smile rose on Evony's lips.

Rosaelia lifted it, both hands gripping the weapon now. "Whoa. I definitely didn't expect that. Are they all this heavy?"

"No." Evony crossed her arms before her chest and watched the Princess's arms lightly shake and the sweat begin to bead down her face. "Most are heavier." It was quite the feat not to laugh at Rosaelia's bulged eyes. "I tried to get one with some weight, but it's definitely not the heaviest. There're lighter ones too, but I need you to understand that most won't be."

"Got it," Rosaelia said, dropping the sword blade down and breathing a bit harder than before. She was trying to keep herself composed. Evony liked that she tried to hide the weakness, tried to challenge for more.

Evony took the sword and walked it back to the weapons she had laid out on a table. "Now that you have an idea of what a sword feels like"—she picked up another weapon and turned back to her twin—"the actual weapon I think will do you best."

She held up a dagger. Not too long or short, perfect grip size for Rosaelia's hand, and the weight was just enough to be noticeable but not unbearable.

Evony handed the weapon to the Princess and watched as

she evaluated it. Rosaelia played with the handle, the edged tip, the entirety of it to get an idea of what the weapon had to offer.

"So we've practiced our punches. Our jabs and hooks and crosses and all. Now, we're going to practice them with the dagger in hand. These—especially if you perform the hook—will be more of a death blow than not, but I'd rather you learned those first for protection."

Rosaelia looked nervous, but she nodded and waited her instruction.

The time passed by quickly as Evony instructed her sister and Rosaelia followed, never once complaining. It was something Evony had come to appreciate from the girl, even growing up in all this privilege and power, she didn't try to turn on her instructors.

They were on their water break—a full body break for Rosaelia—when Evony caught the Princess staring at the ring on her left finger. She looked down to it too, her matrimonial ring that had been made for her the day she was born. She still couldn't believe it was only two days prior that they'd been married. They'd taken all of the day before to be holed in the cottage together, but they did have work to do.

Sparrow had a stack of missives to read about what his men from different parts of the country had found out about the rebellion, hopefully something that would tie together what the prisoners had said, and she wanted to do her part in training the Princess and looking into the books to help.

As Miels and Tristan tried more with the prisoners, and nothing new came out, Evony felt more antsy to be of aid. The prisoners weren't helpful, merely sitting in their cells and taking a visit to Nuhmed whenever they got too rowdy, waiting for when Sparrow felt like executing them. But at least the trips to Nuhmed meant they'd talk when asked a question. It was an experience even the vilest of them shivered at.

She was interrupted from her thoughts when Rosaelia spoke through her deep inhalations. "It's weird because you were already my sister, but ever since you married Sparrow, it's like I'm now considering you a sister."

Evony smiled. "It is weird, but also understandable. You've always seen him as a brother and you barely know me. It's probably easier for your brain to compartmentalize that I am a sister-in-law rather than a real sister."

"Are you not offended?" Rosaelia asked curiously.

"No. Plus, I've always known you were my sister, it wouldn't be fair to expect you to accept it immediately." Plus, Evony had Gemma and that was truly all the sister she needed.

"Right. Good." Rosaelia didn't seem too sure. "So how is it? Being married to Sparrow?"

Evony's grin was wide and wicked—always was when she thought of her assassin—as she glanced between the ring and her sister before settling on the latter. "That brother of yours has quite the stamina. I wouldn't be surprised if I wound up pregnant sooner rather than later."

It was obvious Rosaelia tried to hide her grimace at mention of her brother's sex life, but she puckered up at mention of a pregnancy. "Do you want children?"

"Mini Sparrows would be my preference, but I guess we could have a mini Evony too." The thought of having a family —and taking them back to Sparrow's childhood home—made her giddy inside.

"Have you two talked about it? Sparrow's always said he didn't want any. But then again, he also said he would never marry, so what do I know." Rosaelia took another large swig of water.

Evony shrugged. "He was talking to my belly like there was

already a child within last night. I think he thought me asleep, but... I think he wants them."

Rosaelia's smile was small and soft as she went to say something before getting interrupted. "Wants what?"

It was Miels.

Turning, they found everyone but the King and Assassin.

"Babies," Rosaelia answered as the group stopped beside the sisters.

"Babies?" Tristan looked to Evony, then to his brother, then back again. "You two trying for babies?"

"Well, I suppose any time you do it you're trying for babies," Evony responded nonchalantly, but the idea of everyone knowing she wanted Sparrow's children before she told Sparrow wasn't fun.

James laughed, throwing his arm around her as Gemma clapped her hands together. "We should try together. Our kids could be best friends. Or better, they could fall in love!"

James—with an arm around both of their shoulders—pulled them in close. "Calm down, both of you!" Then he turned his attention to Evony. "But you, a Master Magician and a Master Assassin's child? Why do I suspect all of your kids will come out Masters?"

"But that's not how it works," Rosaelia interrupted, her smile faltering a little.

Miels and Tristan, for their part, both wore their smiles, but Evony had come to know their grins and these weren't happy ones—they were trying-to-look-happy ones. Her brows furrowed. What did they have to be faking smiles for?

"We don't know that for sure. No two Masters have ever reproduced," James rebutted, then turned his attention back to Evony. "Think of it, you and Sparrow are some of the most powerful Masters. Both of you having kids together, I honestly have no doubt, we'd rule the world!"

Evony laughed because as much as she didn't like that the others didn't seem genuinely happy, she loved the excitement that radiated off of Gemma and James at the prospect of children. She also really loved the idea of being pregnant with Gemma.

"You mean *I'll* rule the world, they'd be my children." Evony snuggled into him.

He tsked. "I can control you, easy. It'll all be mine."

Gemma scoffed through a laugh. "Please, I'd have you on your knees in milliseconds. It'd be mine!"

James looked down to his wife. "She's right." He turned to Evony and nodded his head to Gemma. "It'd be hers."

Evony laughed, wrapping her arms around them. "If I ruled the world, I'd give it all to you."

"Told you." James sounded cocky and all Evony could think of was how happy she was with her life.

When they finally released from their hug, Evony found the others in a similar hold, with Rosaelia in the middle. It looked like they were mimicking them, but Evony had a suspicion it was so they could whisper to one another without getting caught. She tried to push it aside. She was being ridiculous. If nothing else, Miels and Tristan loved her.

"That's enough training for today." She forced the cheery nature to remain. "Let's get ready for dinner."

They all began to walk out as James's arm went around her again. "I do, of course, expect the first son to be named after me."

Evony tried to hide back her scoffed laugh as she nodded.

"And the first daughter after me of course," Gemma added.

"Anything else, my masters?" Evony asked.

James held her closer. "A variation of James for the second son wouldn't hurt. Wouldn't want the other boys upset because only one of them was named after greatness."

Evony couldn't hide it any longer, she burst out. This. This was true happiness.

†

It was unreasonable to hate the library as much as she did, but the entire place felt suffocating. Completely inexplicable considering she found no problems with her suite, so it wasn't a being indoors problem.

Maybe it was because of the memories the suite held.

Or the scent she constantly got to inhale while being there.

Either way, she'd be reading this book in her suite, preferably in the comfortability of the blankets with Sparrow sweat ingrained in every morsel of fabric.

It was a book of Masters, talking about the different kinds that have come up thus far, including two assassins a century ago and a magician around the same time. There was a healer too. Since hearing Sparrow's theory about Ashtyn, Evony had been more and more sure that the girl *was* a Master. It spoke of the different centuries and the Masters that each one had up until twenty years prior. They'd have to update this book now.

But more importantly, it gave backstories to each Master and their origin—Islander, Northerner, or Southerner. It was remarkable to see that they were always varied. Some generations, all the Masters were in one of the lands, and others, they were dispersed. Like now.

Sparrow in the North.

Evony in the South.

And Ashtyn, because Evony was telling herself the girl was a Master, in the North.

Although, had Evony not been hidden, they would be mostly Northern centered.

Mostly, because she also knew there was a Master Sorcerer in the Island Nation, but because of the lack of communication between them and those lands, she didn't know who it was.

There was also a Master Scholar in the southernmost tip of the Southern Lands. And a Master Grower in the Island Nation. He was a little more known since he tended to ask for ingredients from the Sacred Garden, but not as much as Evony would've liked. And if it bothered her, she could only imagine how much it bothered Sparrow not knowing everything about every Master. But the Master Grower was the main reason the Island Nation were still thriving in the freezing atmosphere they called home. He could make anything grow. Almost like magic.

Coupled with the Master Sorcerer, the Islanders had all they needed to prosper in the colder lands.

Evony moved for Sparrow's room, their room now that they were married, and huddled into the large pillows as she pulled the blankets to swallow her whole. She flipped the book to the first page and began reading the histories.

Truly, she didn't know what she hoped to find within it, but possibly a reason for Southerners interference other than the need for magicians to be allowed on the lands. Though Evony believed that was the reason the Southern people would join the rebellion—if they were part of it at all—but part of her knew it wasn't the entirety.

And though that was her main purpose for reading the book—because she wanted to help as much as she possibly could with this rebellion—the selfish part of her was simply curious. It was amazing how many little facts she could learn from the large book.

It was especially incredible to go through the tomb and not be able to find a single Master with Master parents. Not a single time when two Masters had gotten together. At least not the together—marriage or babies—that would be marked in history.

So she and Sparrow were an anomaly.

Had to be because never before her was there a Master whose identity wasn't known. Hiding a marriage or babies wouldn't be possible. And if she never revealed herself as the Master Magician, then even history wouldn't know of this union.

But she had to wonder what it *could* mean for her future.

She hadn't really put much thought into the fact that they were both Masters. Had honestly forgotten about it. She'd only seen Sparrow, not the Master Assassin. But now she had to wonder what that would mean for them as a family.

The book didn't end up helping her in the slightest with the Southern involvement problem, but that selfish part of her came back up and made her forget those problems. Told her to go back to the start of the book and go through the Masters again, if only out of curiosity to get a deeper reading of the Masters' past. Especially the magicians and assassins.

Especially the assassins.

She tried to answer all the facts within each Master's biography as if it were Sparrow's and surprised even herself at her ability to do so. She hadn't realized she learned him *that* well.

She snuggled deeper into the pillows and blankets, loving that it was mostly Sparrow's scent, and not hers, that embalmed her.

CHAPTER 39

SPARROW

The missives were both an important part of his day and a complete waste. There was something there, Sparrow knew that much, but he couldn't find anything to connect. Who was running this rebellion? And more importantly, why?

Was it just for power?

If they were smart, which Sparrow assumed they definitely were considering the handling of the rebellion, then they'd know that taking down the Northern crown wouldn't guarantee them power. At the very least, if they got greedy, the South had magicians they could use to protect. Then both the sorcerers and magicians would be vying for the power of the North. They could agree to split it so that the three countries were broken into two, and the two powers controlled the lands: Land of the Sorcerers and Land of the Magicians.

He'd heard tales of the two lands before.

Before they'd been split by territory and before there were Masters.

The North had always been a great barrier, but with them gone, things would get sticky very quickly.

And Sparrow still didn't understand how any of it was connected.

He was in Edmund's private study, knowing Evony wouldn't find him there—though he also knew if she really wanted to, she could use that Master Magician power of hers to track him down—but this gave him the semblance that she wouldn't walk in and offer herself as a feast. He couldn't take the distraction, especially when he was already victim to his constant wavering fantasies.

The door opened behind him.

"Knew I'd find you here," Edmund commented as their original little Posse of four walked into the room and shut the door behind them. "Is there a reason you're here?"

"Hiding from the missus." Sparrow's gaze flickered across each of their faces.

Edmund's brows rose. "Already?"

Sparrow tried to hide it since this *was* her father he was speaking to but couldn't help the quirk of one side of his lips. "She's insatiable, and I have business to attend."

"Ah." Edmund poured himself a cup of steaming tea and took a seat on the couch across from the armchair Sparrow resided in. "Newlywed bliss. A ravenous time in a man's life."

Sparrow tried to fight the smile as his gaze flickered over them again. "And I'm sure that's not what you lot came here to talk about." His gaze flickered to Rosaelia. "Especially you." And back to Edmund. "And you, for that matter. She's your daughter."

"We needed to talk to you." Rosaelia sat up straight from her spot on the ottoman farthest from the fireplace. "Without the... missus."

Sparrow's gaze narrowed. "Why?"

Tristan took the other end of the couch from Edmund, beside the arm Miels occupied, but no one spoke. Both Sparrow's seconds looked like they weren't exactly happy to be there.

"Why?" He really didn't want to ask again.

"Are you aware of Evony's attempts for children?" Miels finally broke the silence.

That was... what? He knew his brows were raised in shock, but he didn't know what this had to do with anything. "We hadn't spoken of it. Why?"

"Well the missus definitely wants children." Tristan sounded almost excited about the prospect. So why was he watching Sparrow carefully? And what was up with his pained expression?

They were questions flickering through Sparrow's mind, but all he could focus on was his definitive statement.

Evony wanted children. His children.

There was a sudden tightening around his heart before it all released and a litter of butterflies swarmed within him.

He wanted children too. A team of mini Evonys would make his life perfectly whole—and probably increase the amount of threats he sent to young boys, but hey, what else but a father's love.

"I don't see how that's any of your concern." He brought himself from his thoughts and tried to keep the utter excitement from his appearance. They were here for a more serious conversation, that much he knew without their telling him.

"You've always said you wouldn't have children," Rosaelia said evenly.

His gaze narrowed on her, but he tried to keep himself calm. "I also said I'd never marry. Things change."

"So you want them then?" Edmund asked, and the evenness in which he spoke made Sparrow sit up straighter.

He knew that tone. Knew it was the one Edmund used when he didn't want those around him to pick up on his intentions. Sparrow grew suspicious as his gaze jumped between the four people he trusted most in the world. Behind Evony.

Sparrow looked at the man that had raised him as a son—that technically was a father to him now—and answered with all the honesty he could. "The thought that I have to be responsible for a tiny thing, that it'll look up to me for guidance? It scares me. I don't want a child with Evony." They almost looked relieved. "I want a whole litter of them."

Edmund looked both happy and hesitant to hear it.

Sparrow pushed his missives aside and sat forward. "Why are you lot worried about our having children?"

No one looked in a hurry to speak.

Finally, Tristan answered, "We dropped by while Ro and Eve were training today. James and Gemma seemed happy to hear Evony wanted kids, possibly soon."

He called her Eve. Like Gemma and James called her Eve.

Sparrow's heart settled into the depths of peacefulness knowing his best friend loved her that much. Knew Miels did too. That as much as he liked to shit on the two of them for spending any time with her, he knew if anything happened to him, they would protect her with their lives.

"Okay?" Sparrow still didn't understand what this had to do with them.

Rosaelia looked to her father, then back to Sparrow. "It sounded like they'd talked about this before, Spar. Like they'd already thought about what would come out of the Master Magician and Master Assassin having children."

Sparrow was on his feet before he realized it. "What"—his fists turned white at his sides—"are you implying?"

"Why was Evony in such a desire to seduce you from the beginning? Maybe so it would go unnoticed by the rest of us if she used her magic to make you fall in love with her." Edmund remained seated and looked up to him with a calm countenance—the look he used as the King speaking to the angry groups that came to him with ludicrous requests.

"Are you insane?" Sparrow had never raised his voice at them before. He paced the room, then turned on his seconds. "You two as well?"

"No." They both stared at him with wide eyes before Tristan shrugged. "Well, yes. No." He sighed. "We don't want to. We love her, Spar. All of them. James is becoming as much a part of us as you are."

"But?" Sparrow grit.

"But," Miels picked up, "wanting an explanation isn't unreasonable."

Sparrow scoffed, falling back to the couch and resting over his knees. His blood was beginning to boil and he had to consciously keep himself in the present to stop himself from accidentally hurting them.

"Think about it, Sparrow!" Rosaelia was on her feet, and her tone told him how passionately she was trying to protect him. "They talked about it right in front of us. There has never been a child of two Masters, so it's not known whether you will have all Master children, but they seemed almost sure. Like they knew your kids would be powerful Masters. Like they'd *planned* it. And what better than the Master Assassin to breed with?"

Sparrow was inches from her before he realized he'd moved. Tristan and Miels at his sides, trying—poorly—to hold him back. "Do not speak of my wife like that."

Evony had been right. She'd feared they didn't trust her, and he let his loyalty to them blind him to it all. Not only did they not trust her—his *wife*—but they tried to reason with him?

"We have to think of this realistically, Sparrow. I understand you're in love with her, but what if it's all her magic at play?" Rosaelia's eyes pleaded with him. She herself didn't look happy about the statement she'd made as the one happiest for him to be in a relationship, but it was obvious her love for him trotted that.

Sparrow shrugged the men off of him and turned to the others. "That's what you all think? She's married me to breed my children? To make an army for herself?"

"I think she's trying to get revenge and saw the opportunity. Two birds," Edmund said calmly. Too calmly. It was the voice he used when he was hiding emotion, but Sparrow had learned to read him too well. He was more upset about this prospect than he was letting on.

"Revenge for what?" he growled.

"For the life she didn't get. For being cast away. For having to grow up in the forests. For having to scrounge for everything and live in constant change. For not having a family. Everything I did to her, Sparrow." Edmund's voice cracked, pained. He blamed himself for everything that happened to the second heir, and Sparrow knew he forever would.

But that was no reason to suspect his wife.

"Sparrow," Rosaelia called softly. "I've heard them speak of taking over. Father's heard them."

"If she were behind this, why send poison that could kill her?" He needed them to see reason.

"Just enough poison, Sparrow." Edmund rose to his feet. "And she said it herself, she wouldn't have died. She'd be tired. They knew what they were doing sending that much poison into the winds. She likely prepared herself before running off to tell us of the infiltrators. Calculated it so she'd fall just as you came into the library."

He couldn't look at the man any longer. Couldn't look at the Princess. The two people he'd thought would always be by his side. Two people he thought would protect his wife for him, especially since she was their family by blood.

"And you two are buying this?" Sparrow spit at his best friends.

"We weren't," Miels said.

"We don't," Tristan fixed.

"We argued with Ed for hours before," Miels defended.

"But then we were questioning the prisoners and they looked at her like..." Tristan explained. "Like they were waiting for her call, Sparrow. They straightened their backs to her with respect. It was that old tongue phrase she said, like it was telling them who she was."

Sparrow brought up a picture of Evony's laughs as she ran around the greens. As she jumped into his arms. As she kissed him. Her bright smile and those shining blue eyes. It was the only thing that would stop him from killing everyone in this room.

"And what," he said through a clenched jaw, "exactly do you believe she was telling them?"

"The amount of power having your children would bring..." Edmund reasoned from his spot by the couch. "Power like the type of control it takes to run a sophisticated rebellion."

He honestly couldn't believe what he was hearing.

Sparrow turned a blazing look on the man who had raised him, and he swore he felt hatred behind his eyes. "She's your *daughter*."

"By blood alone, Sparrow." Edmund's eyes didn't water, but there was a sheen there. Like he hated how much pain he was putting Sparrow through but would do it anyway to protect him.

"She's my *wife.*" *Why would you allow our marriage if you didn't trust in us? In her?*

"You know we don't throw the word around lightly, Sparrow." Miels's eyes pleaded. "She is our *sister.* But we have to know."

Sparrow scoffed and moved for the door, grabbing the latch and pausing with his back to the group. "She is my wife."

"And she is my daughter, Sparrow. I don't want to believe it," Edmund called to him, a final plea in his tone. "But she's said it as well—she is only my daughter in blood. She does not have a tie to us like you do, like she does Gemma and James. Rather, she has a lot of reasons to hate us. To hate *me.* I need to protect the throne, Sparrow. Protect Ro and Miels and Tristan and *you.*"

Sparrow scoffed, tired of hearing it all, and walked out.

✝

GIVEN they'd had their dinner before the groups little ambush, Sparrow had no other requirements for the night so he was bathed and in bed not long after storming out of Edmund's study.

He lay naked as he waited for Evony who had gone off to the library after dinner and had yet to return.

It was odd, how in such a short time, he'd gone from not trusting her to breath the same air as them to wanting only to breath her air. She'd become a vital part of his life, even before their trip to Brilfax Oak. He'd never admitted it, but she'd already gotten under his skin.

The way he'd wait for her to walk to dinner, knowing she would wrap her hand into the crook of his elbow.

The way his gaze would hover to wherever she was, no matter how discreetly, and watch her.

The way he'd take any excuse to touch her, knowing full well she would always make the move he desired and both loving and hating himself for it.

But she'd weaseled her way into his existence and there was no way to go on without her.

And now his family, the only four people he had ever trusted before Evony came about, were turning the tables on her. They made her out to be a rebel. And not only a rebel, but the rebellion's leader.

All for power.

It was preposterous.

Evony was graceful seduction and teasing lure, but all she truly cared about was being cared for. She'd play whatever card was dealt her way so that no one got close, but she wasn't the type to go after power. If she had been, she could have taken it long ago. And with no one's help. She was the Master Magician after all, power came easily to her.

So he still couldn't understand how the others didn't see that. Didn't see that Evony was a powerful empress on the outside, but inside, she was the sweetest of things. Didn't see that Gemma and James were just as sweet, more happy to stay at the palace and follow their instruction than take power. Didn't see that the three had gone without family for so long that all they wanted was for the group to accept them wholly.

Gemma and James and Evony were the absolute least of their worries. The three didn't care an ounce for control.

He was so lost in thought, he didn't hear her enter the suite until she was in the room, her gaze widening at seeing him lying naked above the sheets as her smile turned wicked.

"Well, hello, husband." She slipped off her bathing dress. "I quite like this. I propose we always greet one another this way."

Sparrow smirked as he watched her naked flesh draw closer to him with every tantalizing step. She crawled over the bed, toward him, like an animal on the hunt.

And he watched, perched up on his elbows, unmoving. He liked when she took control like this, when she teased him.

She crawled over his legs and straddled him but remained low so her chest fell in line with his face still perched up on his elbows as he was.

His eyes rolled up to look at her through his lashes as her fingertips began to run up his arms. "Have fun at the library?"

She grimaced. "I brought the books here. I don't like the library."

"Then why weren't you here when I got back?" *I could have ravaged you already.*

"I wanted a bath to clear my thoughts after finding nothing useful in those books."

His heart eased at her presence. "Have a nice bath?"

"Mhm." Her close-lipped smile looked mischievous as she watched her fingers move across his skin.

"I was with my friends." He knew his breath touched her breasts when he noticed the slight shiver of her skin.

"Oh." Her gaze never left her fingers. "Is that where you were hiding from me?"

"Mhm," he mimicked her nonchalance, then laid out on his back, hands beginning to skim her thighs. "They told me some interesting news."

Her eyes glimmered as she smirked at him. "Is that so?"

"Oh, yes." His fingers played at her hips. "Apparently, my wife is in the market for children."

Her eyes snapped to his, breath catching. "I wanted to tell you..."

His smirk widened when he saw just how worried she was that he'd be upset. He sat up, lips only an inch from hers, shutting her up abruptly. "Yes, it was quite the shock, especially when I've said all my life that I do not want children."

She swallowed, but Sparrow saw the hurt in her eyes. "That's okay."

He tsked, biting back on his smile. "No, you see it's a problem."

Her breathing hitched like she was truly nervous for his reaction. Ha. The group thought *she* was power hungry? "Sparrow, we don't need to ha..."

His hands skimmed down to her ass, resting over each cheek. "You see the problem there, Evony, is that we do *need* to."

"Sparrow, I won't force—"

He pecked her, just to the edge of her lips. "No, you won't." He kissed her lips for only a second. "But you see the problem is that now that I have you, I want more, Magician. I want a whole litter of you ruling my life."

Her breath hitched again, but this time Sparrow could see it was for hope rather than fear. She'd likely held on to hope so many times in her life that she was afraid to believe it now.

"I want them, love." He smoothed back some of her black locks and stared into her sapphire eyes. "I want to spend my days running after little rascals and my nights kissing down your swollen belly. I want as many as you'll give me."

Her fingers played with his face, tracing the outlines like she was trying to figure out if he were real. The water that was rising in her eyes told Sparrow that this, a family with him, was all she wanted.

"I love you, Assassin."

His grin quirked up one side of his face. "Then show me."

Her smirk was quick to follow as she leaned into him, her chest pressing against his as her hips rolled over his, their lips meeting. The kiss was feral, like she was taking what was hers and she had no plans of asking permission or moving slowly. He quite liked this side of her.

Her tongue slipped into his mouth, and he tried to allow her the control, but his tongue was fighting for dominance without his permission. She seemed to like that.

She pushed him back down onto the bed, her hips rolling over his as she looked down at him like the empress she was. He *loved* this side of her.

Her folds were wet as they ran up and down his length, dangling the ability to be inside her before him, then moving away so he lost the chance.

"You're a tease, Magician."

She threw her head back as a seductive chuckle left her lips, her hands moving to play with her breasts as she rocked over him.

He tried not to move, to be patient and enjoy this game she was playing, but it was far more difficult than he'd imagined. His fingers dug into her thighs seeking her attention.

She looked down at him with a wicked grin.

"Don't play with me, Magician."

Her chuckle was soft as she lifted herself from his hips and grabbed hold of his cock, leading it to her entrance and slowly sinking down. They both groaned as she moved him in, inch by inch. He tried to remain still as she created the pace.

Then she was moving.

Her pace was slow as she laid her hands onto his chest and closed her eyes, throwing her head back to enjoy herself.

This was the most erotic sighting of his life. He would be happy to remain lying beneath her, being used for her pleasure, for the rest of his existence. He was hypnotized by the way she moved over him.

Her pace picked up as she got more and more lost in the feeling, and his grip tightened on her thighs as he tried to control himself as he watched her, pumping into her from below. The longer he watched, the more he wanted to fill every bit of her with his seed, coat her in it, so there was no chance she wouldn't fall with child.

He knew she was close when her walls clenched around him, and he nearly spilled watching her and feeling her insides gripping his cock.

Then she was falling over the edge.

"I love you, baby. I love you, I love...fuck, baby, don't stop." Sparrow had no power in holding back. He came with her, filling her completely as the feelings rushed through him.

He watched the sweat glisten on her skin as her breath began to settle and she slowly picked herself off of his cock, settling back down on his hips as she leaned down and rested on his chest. His hands moved immediately to her hair, playing with the locks as they breathed together, her fingers playing at his ribs as her breath tickled his chest hairs.

"What are you thinking about, love?" His eyes wandered about the ceiling above them as his hands skimmed her hair.

He'd never felt so *good* before. So at ease, so relaxed. So sure that he had all he needed in life. Contentment. It was quite something.

"How scared I am of our relationship," she whispered into his chest.

He froze, looking down to the crown of her head and feeling the anxiety ricochet through him. "Why?"

"I never thought there would be anyone I'd be more loyal to than Gemma and James. That there'd be anyone else I would do anything for. You've completely turned my life around, Assassin."

He breathed freely, relaxing back down and pressing her tighter into him with both arms. "I feel exactly the same way, Magician. It's rather frightening."

"Mhm." She snuggled into him and all was silent.

He knew she'd fallen asleep when her breath evened out above him, but his hands never stopped caress her skin. He was intoxicated with the feeling of having her, like there was a chance it'd all be taken away.

CHAPTER 40
SPARROW

The palace bells only rang for emergencies.

These specific vibrations that knocked the dead out of sleep only rang when said emergency was an attack on the palace.

Sparrow sprang up and his gaze immediately latched on to Evony's confused state. "Get dressed, love. Looks like the rebellion's finally come to us."

Her eyes widened and sleep completely left her as she put on her trousers, vest, and boots, the feminine mirror to Sparrow's fit.

He knew he should leave, race to the forefront of this attack, but he couldn't leave her. She took his hand only moments after, and they raced out of the room, meeting with a disheveled Gemma and James coming out of their own suite.

Sparrow handed her one of his swords and saw the way both Gemma and James looked prepared with their own weapons. At least Sparrow knew that even if everyone else was suspicious of Evony, James would protect her with his life.

They raced past the servants in the halls. Protocol indicated that all staff race to their designated spots and wait. Most of them weren't trained. And those who were, not well enough.

Sparrow's men were already at the forefront, following the instructions Sparrow had given them weeks ago. *Take them alive, I want my dungeons filled with rebels. Need to hear from as many as possible.*

Because he needed to understand.

There were more rebels than Sparrow had believed. They came in from different angles—though none that Sparrow didn't have covered from trainings with his men—and filled the palace.

And though his men did a perfect job of controlling them, protocol also indicated half his men go to the servants and stay with them. If anything were to happen to the first line of defense, they'd be there to protect the weaker.

"For the Queen!" one rebel yelled as he raised his swords and led a group of seven toward them.

"For the Queen!" they, along with every other rebel in the corridors, yelled back.

"Don't you dare use your magic to protect me, Evony," Sparrow spit at his wife, but never took his eyes off the seven, now eight, nine, ten, coming for them.

Thankfully she didn't argue. "Okay."

The ten men were on them in seconds, and Sparrow's Mastery had them all knocked over in half as much time. He had a feeling the adrenaline helped with that, because even as a Master, it was quick. James helped keep them down by jamming the hilt of his sword into each one's pressure point to knock them out. Sparrow needed the time to try and control the urge to kill them for even the slightest threat to his wife.

It was only when he was able to turn his full attention on Evony that he realized not a single one had gone after her.

Tristan and Miels ran into the corridor, the former scream-ing, "Where's Ed?"

"Where's Ro?" Sparrow asked the more important question.

"With the Remedies Expert," Miels responded. "They won't be touched." His tone indicated no space for argument.

Good.

He turned just in time for the real masses to enter. There were so many of them, Sparrow had to wonder where this leader had found so many people to join her cause. How this leader had convinced *this* many people.

But he didn't have time to think about it. And he wouldn't be able to take them all alive, he knew that much. In order to get any, they'd have to kill the majority.

Thankfully, every single one of the people he cared most about in that corridor were perfectly trained. Gemma fought as well as Evony. James as well as Miels and Tristan. And all far above any of these rebels. And though a fraction of his atten-tions would remain on Evony, he was able to better whip his sword around knowing she could protect herself. He remem-bered her in Brilfax Oak perfectly.

His goddess.

Blood splattered around the corridor and matted itself onto his clothes, his hair, his skin.

On to Evony's clothes. Her hair. Her skin.

And still, her eyes shined that beautiful blue as she made her way through the masses trying to make it through this corridor—the one that would lead to the throne room.

Where was Edmund?

He was the King. He was the reason this was happening. Without him, the rebel leader would have the throne she wanted. Which just meant he needed to be kept safe at all costs.

It meant Rosaelia needed to be kept safe. As heir, if anything did happen to Edmund, the North needed her. And though Evony was also an heir, Sparrow knew she didn't want the throne. Knew she didn't even like the word Princess.

Like thinking of him conjured him up, Sparrow noticed the King run in from the opposite corridor, blood splattered and fighting his way through with two others by his sides.

Sparrow jammed his fist into the pressure point of two as his weaker hand whipped his sword around, slicing through two chests, but not deep enough to kill. *Keep as many alive as possible.* It was his rule.

All that mattered was that Rosaelia was kept safe, wherever she was, and the rest of their group was in this corridor. Where he could keep his eye on them. Where he could protect them. Where his Mastery was distracted *because* he needed to make sure they were all right, to protect them.

He'd trained Edmund. He'd trained his best friends, had been training James. He knew they could hold their own. Gemma and Evony too, who he hadn't trained, were amazing in battle. He'd already known that much about his wife, but was glad to find her best friend held the same qualities.

He was more glad when he saw body after body hit the ground around Evony because they weren't attacking her. She had the advantage to knock them out rather than kill them. Had he mentioned the no kill rule to her or was she able to guess based on what he was doing? He didn't remember mentioning it to James either, and his men never spoke about protocol outside meetings.

They worked better as a team than Sparrow could've imagined. And he'd imagined they'd work pretty fucking amazingly.

Until.

"Tristan, behind you!" Rosaelia's voice echoed in the corridor.

She wasn't supposed to be there.

Tristan was his second. He knew someone was behind him. He most definitely didn't need Rosaelia's help in figuring it out.

She was blood splattered too, and by the look of the dagger in her hand, she'd done well in protecting herself on her way over to them.

But no matter how she'd done it, she wasn't advanced enough. She'd only been training a few weeks.

Sparrow tried to make his way over to her, too much of his focus distracted with her presence—and the sprinkle that always remained with Evony—that he barely bent out of the way of two swords.

And there were too many bodies on the grounds to make it to her side before a sword was swiping through the air right for her chest, the man hardly paying attention to where he was swinging the weapon.

James pulled her out of the way, and the sword slashed into his chest just as Sparrow made it to their side and gutted the man who had tried to kill his sister.

He turned on the corridor and growled so loud, the grounds shook. "Kill the rest. I want this over with. Now!" He turned blazing eyes on Rosaelia. "Stop the bleeding."

He couldn't focus on James. He needed to take care of the rest.

Rosaelia stopped the bleeding with the pressure of her hands as Sparrow turned on the room and made full use of his Mastery, noticing both Evony and Gemma running toward them in order to get to James's side.

The blood really splattered this time.

Because he was taking no mercies.

Every single rebel still standing was a dead man, his men could figure out which the unconscious were when they began clearing the corridors. Sparrow only had to wonder how many more rebels were in the rest of the palace.

When he felt the need to kill slip past him, finally allowing his body to rest, he turned in his spot and took in the massacre around him. Bodies upon bodies littered the grounds, the corridors turned crimson.

Rosaelia stood by her father's side with blood-stained hands and watched him along with his two seconds and the King.

He turned for Evony who had helped Gemma raise James to standing. She slipped out from under James's arm, Gemma resting him against the wall, and ran into his arms.

"Are you all right?" She was fine, he knew it. But he needed to hear it. See it.

She shook her head. "Fine, my love. I'm fine."

He pulled her into his chest and hugged her so tight, the fear he hadn't realized had been so prominent finally escaping him. As he did so, he noticed all four of his closest family leaving the corridors, the guards already coming out to begin the hunt for any more conscious rebels.

She pulled away and glanced back at James before settling her eyes on him. "Are you okay, my love?"

"Perfectly." He kissed her. "Now go." Sparrow pushed her toward her two best friends. "Help Gemma. Take him to Ashtyn. I'll check on the others."

Evony looked to him with such gratefulness, his heart expanded to bear it all. "Thank you, Sparrow."

He cradled her face and dropped his forehead to hers so their breaths mixed. "Don't ever thank me for something like this. As if I would entertain the idea of not doing it."

She kissed him, soft and quick, then pushed away and moved for James's other side. She helped Gemma take him to the infirmary, and Sparrow knew instinctually that she was using her magic to help him as much as she could until they got to the incredible healer.

The original King's Posse were in the dining hall—the room only a few yards down from the throne room—when he walked in. The doors had been shut, and he closed them behind him as he entered.

His stare met Rosaelia. "Why do you insist on putting yourself in stupid situations?"

She looked sheepishly at him but didn't back down. "I needed to help you guys. I'm not a damsel."

He took a large breath to ease the anger. "Yeah, well, you almost got James killed."

"And I saved at least five of your men on the way over to you," she argued. When he quirked a brow, her form dropped ever so slightly. "Just because I got the rebels from behind and didn't kill them doesn't mean they didn't count."

"And we don't know if any of that was real," Edmund said before answering Sparrow's confused look with, "They could've 'tried to kill' James in order to make it more believable that they're on our side."

He scoffed under his breath. "Not this again." Then aloud. "What are you on about now?"

"Not a single one went after her, Sparrow," Edmund simply stated. "Is that incorrect? Tell me, did you see even one rebel try to go for her? They went for Ro. For everyone else. Why not her?"

"I don't care why they didn't go for her, Ed," Sparrow grit. "I'm just thankful for it."

And they hadn't gone for Ro.

Only one. And that was because he hadn't been paying attention. Neither Princess had been in trouble. Thankfully.

Edmund looked to him with sincerity. "Do you trust me?"

Sparrow didn't understand what that had to do with

anything but answered honestly and without hesitation. "Yes, of course I trust you."

"Then allow me to question her, Sparrow." His stare told Sparrow he wouldn't do it lest given permission. "Do not interrupt or defend. Believe that we at least deserve an explanation. That these pieces against her do make sense."

Sparrow hated that they needed this but couldn't argue that pieces *were* beginning to line up. He had no doubts that she wasn't the rebellion leader, but what was this connection?

His brows furrowed, and he looked down at his hands. At the ring on his finger. He loved her with every fiber within him, but he also needed all the answers. It would kill him not to defend her, but he would do this. For his family. For them to finally realize that Evony was the softest of creatures.

Sparrow sighed. "Okay."

CHAPTER 41
EVONY

Ashtyn had James mended in half an hour.

Three hours after that, he was cleared to leave the infirmary. Cleared to return to normal. The expediency of the healing only furthered Evony's belief of the girl's Masterhood.

Evony waited by the doors of the infirmary for the couple as Gemma helped James into a new set of clothes in Ashtyn's 'office.

"Are you okay, Sapphire?" Her sudden appearance made Evony jump.

"I thought you were helping with the other injured." She turned to her friend.

"I am," Ashtyn said. "But I also want to check in with you."

"I wasn't hurt," Evony answered.

"Physically." Ashtyn watched her like she'd cracked the code beneath Evony's mask. "Emotionally, though? James is like a brother, and he was almost killed. Your family was attacked. How are *you* doing?"

Evony looked down, feeling too exposed under the healer's

gaze. "Glad they're okay. Glad Gem and James are okay. Glad Sparrow's okay."

"And you?" Ashtyn wouldn't allow her to beat around the bush.

"I feel like no matter what I do, I'm not good enough. I saw the way my father looked at me before he left our presence." She hadn't told Ashtyn about the mistrust behind her father's eyes when he looked at her, but the way the medic watched her told her she knew.

"Sometimes there isn't much we can do about trust, Sapphire." Her gaze moved around the medics in the room, following Old Lady Arba a little longer than any of the others. "Sometimes, no matter how much we want it, it's not something that'll happen."

Evony wanted to turn the conversation around, learn about the look she gave the old medic.

But Ashtyn didn't allow it. "And other times, it's just about waiting. Sometimes, it just takes a little convincing. Maybe a little extra kick in the balls, but he'll get it. The King is a good man and eventually, he'll understand that he's got no reason not to trust you."

"Why do you think that?"

Ashtyn shrugged. "I see the way you talk about them. I've seen you lot around the palace. That's not something that can be faked." Her gaze met Evony's. "And I've seen the way you cherish the Assassin. The King will see that you would never do anything to hurt Sparrow. He's just a stubborn man who's always looking for betrayal."

"Why are you trying to comfort me right now?"

Ashtyn's smirk was snarky and loving all at once. "I like you, Sapphire. I don't want to, but I have a feeling you have that effect on people often."

Evony laughed. Truly laughed. And threw her arm around the healer. "Thank you, friend."

"Yeah, yeah," Ashtyn grumbled and pushed Evony off of her. "Now go back to sucking the Assassin's dick and get off mine."

Evony stood taller as her friends walked out of her makeshift office. "If that's what the medic prescribed, then I must!"

Ashtyn hid the laugh, but just barely. Evony still caught it, and her heart eased at the lightness of this new friendship.

✝

Sparrow's men worked quickly in clearing the corridors, both of the dead and the unconscious who would become prisoners. And, from what Evony heard, in doing rounds around and within the palace to check for any hiders.

They were still blood stained, though James's new clothes were clean, as they made their way to the dining hall where her magic told her Sparrow was. When they entered the room and immediately closed the door behind them, they met with the original King's Posse standing around in a serious discussion.

She was about to move to her husband when everyone's hard stares froze her to her spot.

"What happened?" James asked, ever the leader of their threesome.

Their gazes slipped to Gemma and James, analyzing them, before moving back to Evony. That unsettling feeling her heart hadn't felt in its entirety in weeks was back.

Her heart hammered as Edmund said, "What has happened? What was that out there?"

That sting of accusation, mixed with the level monotone,

stirred Evony's apprehension. She raked across them all, the way they all stood back. The way Sparrow stood with them, his brows furrowed like he was forcing himself to hold still.

"The rebels attacking?" Gemma asked slowly.

"Mhm," Edmund said with a harsh undertone. "Quite amazing, do you not think, that you came out unhurt?"

Evony looked to her friends, then back to the group. "James *was* hurt."

"Saving *your* daughter. Not that you lot didn't exactly get hurt either." James's tone was less friendly.

"I just find it interesting." The King's voice gave nothing away. "We were lucky to be unhurt. But I cannot fathom any of us lucky enough to not be the victim to the attack."

"What?" Gemma asked in a tone that indicated she thought the King had lost his mind.

Evony watched them. Miels and Tristan looked to her like they wanted to hug her, but there was a hint of mistrust behind their eyes that hadn't been there before. Or had she just never realized it?

And Sparrow's gaze was cold. Like he was trying to keep his feelings hidden. The room only held the closest people in his life, what would he need to hide from?

And why wasn't he moving for her?

"We were all there, daughter." Edmund regarded only Evony. "Not a single one moved against you."

"What are you talking about?" James fought. "She had just as many piled around her as the rest of us, excluding the Assassin, of course."

The Assassin.

Evony tried to meet his gaze, but he wouldn't meet hers.

She took a step forward, needing to be with him, but James's arm pushed out and held her from moving any farther.

"Why don't you just come right out and say what you want

to say, *King*," James spit the words out, putting special emphasis on the last one.

"Who is the rebellion's leader?" Edmund asked. "Who is this woman that has done a perfect job at leading the rebellion and keeping herself hidden?"

Why was Edmund the only one speaking?

"We were lucky to have the Master Magician around to help us, were we not?" Edmund's voice grew accusatory. "Or maybe that was the plan all along."

James turned to Miels with a harsh stare. "What the *hell* is he talking about?"

Miels looked hesitantly between the three of them before standing a little taller and sighing. "The rebels said all along they didn't know who was leading them, but that it was a woman. That the rebels would take over the palace so the woman—their leader—could infiltrate. That, if—when—successful, the King would be out of the way—and we all know the only way to do that is death—and she will have full reign."

They already knew all this.

James's jaw ticked as he broadened his shoulders to cover as much of Gemma and Evony as possible. "Okay?"

Evony's heart raced so fast, it was possible it'd rip through her chest before this ended. Because she knew exactly where it was leading. Knew James knew it as well and just needed to hear it.

She didn't allow her eyes to water as they settled on Sparrow who still refused to look her way.

Tristan picked up where his friend had ended. "What we didn't account for was that the woman could infiltrate at any time. We assumed she would wait until her rebels barged into the palace to come along. But what if she was already here? What if she'd been here all along and been made part of the investigation into what she was leading?"

Evony wouldn't allow herself to show any weakness. "You think I'm the rebellion's leader?"

"Are you?" Rosaelia's indifference was almost as good as her father's, no doubt a result of being raised as a royal in politics.

"Are you insane?" Gemma bit out at the same time she and James scoffed.

"It would be ingenious." Edmund had a cold look in his eyes that sent shivers down Evony's skin. This was worse than when he'd spoken to her in the bedroom with Sparrow asleep. "Infiltrate by making us trust you. Show yourself so it would be understood that the bloodline would fall to you if something were to happen. Marry in to create indestructible Master children. It is the ultimate power for the unwanted child."

The unwanted child.

And Sparrow still wouldn't meet her eyes. Still wouldn't move toward her. Still hadn't said a word. Merely allowed their accusations.

He looked rigid, like the first time she'd seen him in the meeting room when she'd presented her identity to the group. Except not meeting her gaze told her the feelings weren't the same as that day weeks ago.

"Sparrow," she said softly.

When his gaze finally met hers, fighting off the water that threatened to fill her eyes was far more difficult.

"You believe them." She was breathless as she said the words, but it wasn't a question.

He swallowed and there was a pained look in his eyes that Evony just wanted to kiss away. "Their doubts have merit."

Evony looked down to push the tears away. "Yes." When her eyes were dry, she looked back up to him. "They do make sense." There was no conviction in her tone, she felt too weak to argue.

That was on hoping. On allowing herself to fall victim to a 'what if.'

Evony clutched for James's arm still before her as Gemma moved to her other side and held her hand. She raised an invisible shield around them without processing that she'd done so. It was something she used to do when the three of them went anywhere together, but that she'd stopped doing at the palace. Around the Posse.

This was her fault. She'd allowed herself to believe in the hope and it had found a way to break her. It always did that.

Except she'd never cared as much as she did now.

Evony found Sparrow's gaze and didn't break as she spoke only to him. Because he was all she truly cared for. "I married you, Sparrow."

He took a minuscule step forward, his gaze softening, but Edmund interrupted. "Why continue to deflect? Why not merely prove you are not the leader?"

"How exactly do you expect her to do that?" James spit, the hatred audibly clawing up his throat.

But Evony didn't pay attention to any of it. Didn't—couldn't—break her gaze away from her husband. "I only felt love twice in my life; the first when I met Gemma and James, my sister and brother in life. And that was the only love I expected to feel. Ever. And I was okay with that, content." She felt the tears begin to prick her eyes, but she didn't look away. Wouldn't give him that mercy. "But I still fell in love with you. Gave you all my trust, my loyalty. I wouldn't have married you if even a pinprick's breath of me didn't feel it." Sparrow's mouth opened to speak, but Evony continued before he could interrupt, "I told you my loyalty was with you above all else. Above both Gemma and James." She wouldn't allow herself to cry, but she had no control of the wetness she felt in her eyes. "Apparently that wasn't enough."

"Evony." His raspy voice almost broke her. "I wouldn't have married you if I didn't feel the same way. I wouldn't have given you *that ring* if I didn't."

Evony's smile was sad. She was surprised she managed it. "Would you like it back?"

She desperately did not want to give it back.

He took a full step forward. "Absolutely not, Evony."

She swallowed back a sigh of relief.

He moved again, toward her, and banged into the shield that kept him ten feet away from them. He was startled before realizing what was before him. He slammed a fist into the shield as he looked at her. "Evony, drop the shield."

She swallowed and somehow found the strength to push the tears away and permit the anger to boil out of her. "Why? This protects *you* from *me*."

For some reason Evony couldn't imagine, anger settled into his gaze. "Don't be ridiculous, Evony. I don't need protection from you."

"But I'm the leader. I'm trying to take your *fucking* throne." She hated that throne.

"I don't have the same beliefs, Evony."

"No?" she grit out bitterly. "Just thought it'd be fun to watch them accuse me."

"You're not exactly making yourself look good," Rosaelia's soft voice interrupted. "It rather looks like you're trying to guilt him. Us."

Sparrow turned viscously on her. "Shut up, Ro."

Evony had never heard him yell at her before.

Sparrow turned back to her, a desperateness behind his eyes that almost broke her. "Evony, you are my wife, my whole life."

And still, she wasn't enough.

"I am a traitor, Sparrow," she bit out with all the pain that festered inside her. "I infiltrated to kill the lot of you." She scoffed. "Almost killed myself with that poison rather than let it do the harm to you and make my job easier. That was all just to make you trust me, right?"

There was a splint second of consideration in his eyes. Eyes that she'd learned to read with perfect accuracy.

That split second. That's when the pieces to her heart crumbled.

"You believe them." Her voice broke, and she was useless in attempting to stop the tear from traveling down her cheek.

Evony held James and Gemma's hands in hers, clung to them for strength. She wanted more than anything to drop the shield Sparrow held a fist against and run into his arms, but she couldn't be in a relationship like this. She needed to be with someone who had no doubts about what she'd do for him. And she only wanted Sparrow, so that left her with only one option. She would go back to living the life of her three-some, the third wheel to James and Gemma's marriage. It had been a happy life, and she was sure she could make it so again.

"I love you, Sparrow. And I will cherish our moments. Won't ever—couldn't even if I wanted to—regret marrying you. But I cannot be in a relationship with no trust." She gripped her friend's hands tighter, hoping the force of the grip would stay any more tears.

"Evony." He banged against the shield now. "Do not run away from this." The distress dripped from his voice as he banged more forcefully into the invisible shield.

Evony turned to her father and swallowed to rejuvenate her strength. "You will not have to worry about our betrayal. We will not be a bother to you any longer."

"Evony, do not fucking run away from me!" Sparrow spit into the air.

Evony turned with her friends, and her heart met the ground as it shattered.

"*Magician.*" The Master Assassin strength was somehow in his voice too. "Don't you dare fucking leave me."

She maintained the shield behind her as James wrapped his arm around her. The pieces to her heart crumbled beneath her feet as they walked out of the dining hall.

"Evony!" His tone begged. "Evony!" The silence rang behind the echo of his voice, and it killed every part of her not to turn around and run to him.

James led them to Gabriel by the stables and requested three horses saddled and ready. Gabriel worked quickly, likely seeing the distress in her eyes, and they were off in a matter of minutes. Without any belongings. She could always find them new belongings. She always had before.

Evony didn't allow the shield to drop until her magic could no longer hold it, miles out of reach from the palace grounds. Sparrow wouldn't be able to track them.

CHAPTER 42

SPARROW

He'd realized his mistake the moment he'd said the doubts had merit. *Made sense.*

Of course they made sense. Anything could've been turned around to make her look guilty. And he'd fallen for it, even if for the possibility of wanting to hear her side.

He'd broken what little faith she had in the world that allowed her to form relationships, that forming one with him had been a good idea. He'd given her everything she'd wanted, then nicely pulled it all right out from under her. He deserved the slow death James had threatened him with.

She'd been loyal.

From the moment their gazes met in that meeting room and he knew she was the Master Magician, she'd been loyal and she'd been his.

And he'd fucked it up.

Over situations *making sense.*

But he'd done it. For his family, the Posse.

The shield was still up, though she had to be far out by

then if she did as he suspected and went to the stables. And he knew she'd done so. Could instinctually feel that she wasn't there any longer. Could feel the way his heart ached to find her and hold her.

He wanted desperately to know how to speak to her through their minds, because he knew she was long gone and he needed to know where she'd gone. He needed to be with her. Needed to protect her.

He'd long since stopped banging on the shield and instead dropped his head between the arms he had against the magical wall.

"Sparrow," Rosaelia's soft voice entered the echo in his ears.

Edmund's, too, was soft, but matter-of-fact. "We still don't know it wasn't her."

He understood Edmund's need to be wary of everyone, as the King, he *needed* to be, but Sparrow couldn't take any more of this.

"It wasn't," he scoffed under his breath, then turned on the King and raged. "It wasn't her. It wasn't fucking her, Edmund! But whoever it was did an excellent *fucking* job at turning us against her."

This was their fault, all four of them, for even considering that Evony could be against them. This was entirely his fault for letting them entertain the idea.

"Sparrow," Miels called out with an apology already in his tone when the wall finally dropped.

Sparrow stepped past the shield and everything within him broke. His shoulders slumped, but he didn't move any further. He knew she was gone. Knew she would've used her magic to cover her tracks. And most importantly, knew she didn't have anything in this world apart from him, so he'd have no clues as to where to search for her.

And now she didn't have him either.

Except she'd always have him. But it pained Sparrow knowing she'd believe what they had was gone. That she'd believe what they had meant nothing to him.

What they have.

He wouldn't allow anything to tear that apart. If he had to, he'd spend the rest of his life looking for her.

SPARROW HADN'T BEEN able to look at the others.

He'd taken to his suite and locked himself within. But that was torture.

Her scent filled the space. The memory of her in every inch of the room. The memory of her echoed throughout every part of this palace. Of his life. She was his life.

The bath had wiped off the blood that still clung to his skin, and he hated the fresh feeling. Hated that Evony had still been covered when she'd left, and he had no idea if she'd stop to clean off. She didn't deserve to go on blood streaked as she was.

He pressed his back against the door to their suite and just stared at the common space. At the ground she'd giggled on as she spun like a child. At the table they'd shared a private dinner at. At the fireplace they'd sat before when he'd admitted —in not so many words—that he was hers.

The fireplace they'd lied before when he told her he had nothing to hide from her.

The flames they had stared into with only one another's company.

Every part of his life was hers now.

He needed her.

And she needed someone who wouldn't take her greatest fears and make them a reality. She needed someone who wouldn't even allow the split second's hesitation regarding her. She needed someone who would breathe only to make her happy.

Sparrow would be that person for her.

He would be what she needed.

He just needed to find her. Apologize. Beg for her to take him, flaws and all.

He pushed to his room—their room. It had long since stopped being his. It'd been theirs even before their time together at Brilfax Oak. Before she'd fallen from the poison. Before he'd admitted to being hypnotized by her.

It'd been theirs from the moment he'd laid eyes on her without that mask. Because he'd known he needed her when he'd realized that the blue eyes behind the mask were those of the Master Magician. He'd known she was his when those ocean blues met his and those beautiful lips tugged up at his reaction.

He'd refused to think it, but the excitement of knowing she would be around, that they would share a suite, had given him a renewed purpose for life. Everything he was, was hers.

That room was hers. Theirs.

He needed her.

The bed felt a hundred leagues larger than it had a month ago. How had he spent even a second within in without her before? How had he slept without the feel of her body pressed against his? How had his heart eased without her breath touching his skin?

How had life progressed without her in it? It felt impossible to remember a time without her.

The sheets smelled like her.

They enveloped him and strangled him, and he wanted to die wrapped in the fragrance.

The scent of their night together still clung to the sheets, and even bringing the fabric up to his nose wasn't enough. He needed to be inside her. To taste her. To have her.

He couldn't sleep without her. Would only know restlessness until she was by his side once more.

Every time he closed his eyes, that glistening tear he'd caused would torture him. Every time he opened his eyes, in need of the touch of his wife to calm his nerves, she wasn't there. Every time the memory of her leaving him flooded back to the forefront of his memory, the tears would build up.

But they wouldn't fall.

Not because he wasn't allowing them, but merely because they wouldn't. Maybe it was because he had no doubts he would hold her again. Even if he spent the rest of his life begging for forgiveness, he'd have her back.

He was out of the tortures of their bed the moment the birds chirping for morning came through the windows. He'd maybe gotten a collective eleven minutes of sleep through the night and hours of self-hatred.

It was undoubtedly the worst night of his life.

Worse than watching his father murdered right before him.

Because this was Evony. And as much as he'd loved his father, no one compared to Evony. *His magician.*

The walk to the dining hall was even worse, like that final stab twisting in his heart. Because she wasn't holding his arm. She wouldn't be scooting her chair closer to him and making inappropriate innuendos. She wouldn't look to him with those shining blue eyes and remind him all was right in the world.

The corridors were still bloodied, but it was obvious the servants had done a magnificent job cleaning the day before since it was nowhere near the massacre scene it had been.

Sparrow scoffed. He still had prisoners to deal with.

The Posse were all in their unassigned assigned seats when he entered and again, his heart sank at the emptiness at the opposite head to the King. At the emptiness beside Miels.

At least the others looked as restless as he felt when he took his seat in the silence of the room. The servants didn't question the whereabouts of the missing three, but something in the way they moved told him it was the least of their worries. They were likely too busy with the mess in the palace.

The silence echoed in the room.

So loud it rang in Sparrow's ears.

He'd never minded silence. But now, he hated every second of it.

Edmund finally cleared his throat. "It's been a rough couple of days. It was a rough night. But today, we need—"

"I'm going to get Evony," Sparrow interrupted.

"We still have the prisoners, Sparrow," Edmund reasoned, looking almost displeased with his words. "This rebellion is priority. We need to deal with them—"

Sparrow slammed his fist over the table. "This isn't up for debate. I *will* find my wife. *She* is my only priority."

No one tried to argue again, but their stares burned Sparrow's skin. Miels and Tristan, at least, looked guilty. Out of the lot, Sparrow knew they were hurting the most with the loss of their friends. Knew they trusted that Evony hadn't been involved, even if the evidence made her look good for it.

They barely ate, all of them obviously preoccupied with their own thoughts. And Sparrow had a feeling Edmund's didn't have to do with getting his daughter back. How could he still imagine her the leader of this? Believe her involved in any matter?

How had he been okay with this marriage if he felt truly settled that Evony was the enemy?

Sparrow knew the answer to that last question—Edmund had seen Sparrow's happiness and hadn't wanted to take it away. Wanted to give him this small semblance.

Even though it'd now been ripped away.

Sparrow was about to let his frustration out when the doors to the hall banged open and little Etel barged in with heavy breath. Miels was on his feet and stepping to her in a blink of an eye, but she stayed him with a hand, and he froze in his spot.

So this was the girl.

She bent at the waist to catch her breath, then met Miels's eyes, the trust within her own brown ones everlasting. "Rebel. In the hall. Tried attacking." She said each sentence with a huff.

Sparrow sprang to his feet. They all did. And moved for her.

But all for a different reason than why Miels moved for her. But she stayed him again, with a look this time. As if telling him not to touch her, like she was trying to hide this relationship. If Sparrow weren't in such heartache at the moment, he would find it adorable that she thought she could hide anything from him. The only reason they'd lasted this long was because Sparrow had given his best friend the benefit of the doubt.

But it wasn't time to think about that.

They followed Etel out of the dining hall and up to the depths of the second floor. Sparrow grumbled at two guards on the way over to have the entire palace grounds rechecked. Twice.

Sparrow's brows flew up when they turned the corner. Because there he was, the rebel. Unconscious and tied to a pillar.

Little Etel had done this? Impressive. No wonder Miels had fallen for her.

And it was obvious he had fallen for the girl. Sparrow had never seen his brother look at anyone in the manner he currently was. Had never seen him give so much undivided attention to someone as they merely stood there. Is this how Sparrow had looked to his brothers when Evony had come around? It was almost embarrassingly corny.

Sparrow moved to the man's side and kicked him. He had no time for games. This would be the first prisoner he spoke to, and he would get a confession that Evony wasn't a part of their little charade.

The man jumped conscious and scurried back when he realized the group standing above him. His gaze glued to Etel's for a moment and narrowed. "How did *you*—"

Miels half blocked Etel and sneered at the man. "I believe in cases like these, we are the ones asking questions."

The rebel sneered back, then looked around. "Would you like me to wait then? Until the entire *Posse* is here?"

Sparrow quirked a brow but refused to put words into his mouth.

"The wife and cousins?" The rebel's eyes met Sparrow's in a seductive manner. "Or would you wish to tell her while you're buried deep?"

Sparrow's heart ached at the loss of her presence, but he smirked anyway, forcing a glimmer to enter his eyes—made possible by the memory of Evony writhing above him. "I'd prefer to tell her while she's coming, *friend*."

He sneered. "That girl is the biggest bane of our existence."

Edmund stood taller to Sparrow's side. "Is that so?"

"One week after her appearance!" he spoke softly, then his anger grew and spit flew from his mouth. "One fucking week after her appearance! We were going to come then!" He pulled on the fabric that tied him to his spot. "The Queen saw her and stopped it all! We could've had it all, but everything was pushed and changed and fucked because of that fucking wife of yours. We would've been victorious before!"

Sparrow's foot flew through the air without his permission, but that's what happened when someone spoke of *his wife* in that manner. The man's nose had to be broken with the speed and strength Sparrow put into the hit.

He bent at the knees and got in the man's face. "I suggest you learn to speak with respect for *my wife*."

There was pure hatred in his eyes, but he gave a singular nod.

"This Queen of yours stopped because of Evony?" Tristan reiterated.

Sparrow backed from the man so he'd feel freer to speak.

The man swallowed. "She looked frantic when the girl came. We couldn't figure out why. Still don't fucking get it. But after that, she started employing different tactics. *That girl* didn't do a thing, yet the Queen was adamant we get rid of her first." His eyes sparked with intrigue. "What is it about her? What's so special that the Queen feared her?"

She's the Master Magician. And Sparrow had a feeling this Queen knew that.

"She stole my heart," Sparrow answered.

The man grimaced, unhappy with the answer.

CHAPTER 43

SPARROW

They had two guards peel the rebel away from the pillar as Sparrow raced to the stables, the rest of the group quick on his heels.

"Sparrow, where are you going?" Rosaelia called.

"I'm not waiting any longer." He controlled his breathing. "Was that enough proof that she wasn't part of your little game?"

"Sparrow." Her hand landed on his arm and stalled him. "I'm sorry."

"I don't need your apologies. I just need her by my side again." He wouldn't hold a grudge against his family. It would take too much out of him and it wasn't worth the energy. He just needed to right their wrong. Right his own wrong.

Ashtyn was in the stables when they reached it, looking to be arguing with Gabriel about something completely unimportant to Sparrow at the moment.

"Did you see which way Evony rode off?" he asked Gabriel in hopes it would give him some idea of where to begin looking.

"Why wouldn't you know where your wife has gone?" The accusation was harsh on Ashtyn's tongue.

Sparrow ignored her and turned to begin preparing a horse. Rosaelia answered instead, "We messed up, accused her, all three of them, of being part of the rebellion."

It was only in hindsight that Sparrow wondered why Rosaelia would've trusted Ashtyn enough to tell her as much. But the reminder that Ashtyn wasn't a gossip, and was known to be friends with his wife, was probably the answer.

"Are you insane?" It seemed Ashtyn truly didn't care for the way she spoke to them that day. "All she's been worried about is fitting in with your lives and being good enough for you, and you turn on her like that! How pretentious could you be?"

Rosaelia recoiled but took the insult with a high head. Rosaelia wouldn't argue the truth. None of them would.

Gabriel began preparing two more horses. "I didn't pay attention to their direction. After I got their horses ready, one of the horses became uneasy. I needed to deal with it."

She would've made sure Gabriel was too busy to see them leave. She would've covered her tracks. If it weren't keeping him away, he'd be ridiculously proud of her.

Edmund was at another horse when Sparrow turned on him. "What do you think you're doing?"

"This is my fault." Edmund met his eyes and the regret was plain behind the honey brown orbs. "I need to come. Help find her."

Sparrow understood where the King came from. He hadn't let anyone into his life in almost two decades, so he'd pushed when Evony had come. And now, he had to figure out how to take all of that back.

"No," Sparrow barked. "You are the King, you have a land to run. You are needed here. Especially after such an attack on the palace."

Edmund looked like he was going to argue.

"This isn't a discussion, Ed." Sparrow finished preparing his horse and turned to fully face the man who had raised him. "You'll apologize and make amends when I bring her back. Until then, you have politics to play."

Edmund didn't look happy about it—he quite literally looked frighteningly unhappy—but he muttered, "Okay."

Tristan and Miels had their own horses ready.

"You're staying too, Miels." Sparrow didn't leave any room for argument. "Ed needs someone with him."

"There're a fuckton of guards. He'll be fine." Miels tried moving back to his horse.

Sparrow grabbed his arm tight. "Stay." When Miels tried to fight against his hold, Sparrow leaned into his ear. "I know you would prefer to—need to—remain by *her* side." Etel hadn't followed them to the stables, rather waiting at the edge of the palace doors with her arms crossed before her chest. Sparrow's lips quirked up as Miels froze and followed Sparrow's line of sight to the Remedies Expert. "Be happy, brother. I believe Etel's claim on your heart may calm any storm I feel about your being around Evony."

Miels quirked an amused brow.

"I said may." Sparrow winked and turned to his horse.

He was shocked to find not only Tristan aboard a horse, but Gabriel, Ashtyn, and Rosaelia. Rosaelia too? She'd taken Miels's horse.

"This is as much my fault as Father's," she argued before Sparrow could speak. "He cannot leave, but I can."

Her green eyes were so unlike her twin's blue that it completely changed their appearances to Sparrow. They looked identical. But to him, they couldn't be farther apart. Rosaelia was his sister. Evony was his wife.

And it was obvious by the look in his sister's eyes that she needed this—to come with them. "Okay."

They rode off to the edge of the palace grounds, away from any other prying ears, when Ashtyn turned on him. "Where are we going?"

"I don't know," Sparrow bit out, staring out at the trees and trying to think of a place Evony had spoken more fondly of. A place she would run to.

He had nothing.

Evony didn't have a home.

"We cannot chase blind, Sparrow," Ashtyn fought.

Sparrow turned his horse, not dining this moment with any more time when Gabriel cut him off by stopping his horse before Sparrow's.

"Listen to her, sir." He was a shy, quiet kid, so Sparrow was impressed he stepped before him. But now was definitely not the time.

"Gabriel, out of my way."

Gabriel stared him down, and Sparrow felt an ounce more respect grow for the man, but he had no time for that at the moment.

"You're being rash, Sparrow!" Ashtyn called from behind him.

Sparrow sat frozen on his horse, his back to Ashtyn as she continued.

"You're not thinking straight. If you were, you'd be going into this with a plan."

He turned on her, his voice harsher than any he'd ever used toward her, toward an innocent. "What plan, healer?" Gabriel's horse was in front of the medic before Sparrow could process it, but his gaze never wavered from Ashtyn's. "She had nothing before she came to us. What evidence do we have to point to her direction? They had no stopping grounds. They could've gone anywhere!"

He doubted Evony had told Ashtyn about her past since he figured she would've notified him of that, but Ashtyn was very intuitive. Even without a backstory, she'd figure most things out. She probably knew that much about the Magician.

Ashtyn was calm when she spoke. "You're right, they had nothing when they came here. But now she has you."

He scoffed. With the ass he'd made of himself, he'd be lucky if she'd still have him.

"She does. She loves you. She couldn't give that up as much as she'd like to. The way James and Gemma would never give one another up."

Yet he'd given her up. Not truly but letting even the slightest bit of doubt settle into his thoughts had shown her enough. He was no man for her.

But he had to make it right. Tell her how much he loved her. How he couldn't live without her around to drive him crazy. He had to show her that he would trust her fully for the rest of his life, if only she chose that moment to come back to him and never leave him again.

"I thought you didn't believe in love." He sneered.

"I'm not naive, Assassin," Ashtyn said softly. "I see the way you two look at each other. The way you two react to one another. And if she has you, then she has all that you have."

She has all that you have.

"Sparrow lives at the palace. We know they're not here," Rosaelia said.

Except Rosaelia didn't know that Evony knew all about his childhood home. A home that was never protected and would be completely open to her as his wife. Something Rosaelia wouldn't know about because she'd only ever heard of the place twice: once when she was told the story of how he came to be with them and a second time a few years prior when Edmund had to explain to her where he'd gone for the week.

But Evony knew far more about the old home. She'd heard stories of times he and his father had played in the yards. She knew of the day his father had made the rings. She knew of the day he'd been killed and the week following before Edmund had found him. She knew about every visit he'd taken there throughout the years. And every quirk and memory he had of the place.

And the best routes to get there.

He'd told her everything about himself, and this house at the southwest of the Northern Lands was a large part of him. One of the most important, before Evony had come along.

His breath left him as certainty settled in.

"You know where she is?" Gabriel sat up taller.

Sparrow gave a single nod and turned to stare in the direction that would lead home. "She's home. My home."

Rosaelia's breath dropped. "Your childhood home? She knows where it is?"

No one but Edmund knew of the location. The five guards who had been there to take him with the King had all grown elderly or gone away by then.

"She knows everything about me," he whispered into the air.

Ashtyn rode her horse beside his. "Then let's go home."

Home.

Ten hours and he'd be with her again. He'd be home.

CHAPTER 44
EVONY

It was a quaint house.

Large enough for a family, but not so big that every child could have their own room. At least not the litter she and Sparrow had spoken of.

The fields surrounding it were expansive enough for the kids to run and chase and live but were protected on all sides by the trees. Trees they could climb and swing from the way Evony had. The small river passing by the east side of the house was just big enough for the kids to learn to swim.

She would have loved to raise her children here.

When they'd entered the day before, the remnants of her heart had flown into the winds as she'd stepped into the house. Into the life she would never have.

They'd hardly spoken during their entire ride the day before. With the directions clear in her mind from the stories Sparrow had told her, Evony had led them without a hitch.

She'd gone a little slower than she would've liked because of James's recent injury—even cleared by Ashtyn, the man would need to take it a little easier—but they'd made it undisturbed. When they'd arrived, Evony had merely washed off the blood that still stained her—impressively, even this home had a standing faucet; her father hadn't skimped out on any of the Northern homes—and gone to bed.

In his father's bed.

His bed.

Sparrow had told her how he'd been sleeping in it every time he'd visit the home. And once Evony's magic cleared the home of the light dust that had settled, she even smelled the faint scent of him on the sheets.

But it was light.

So light, she wasn't entirely convinced she hadn't imagined it.

She'd spent some time walking the house in the middle of the night when the scent became too much for her heart to take. If this was just her imagination, she didn't know how she would survive not ever having him again.

She'd stopped at the door beside the one she'd slept in.

There was a small bed in this room and it was obvious not much had changed in the room since Sparrow had lived in it. Not much had changed in the entire home, but this one especially.

Evony could picture it—a little Sparrow running about the space and going to bed in the small bed not quite in the middle of the room. It was a little farther to the opposite side: farthest from the door, back to the wall. Sparrow had always had it in him.

Evony felt the water begin to fill her eyes but pushed it aside.

She moved back to the master suite and found her spot in a rocking chair that looked out to the greens from the windowed double doors.

She'd been a fool to think that the fivesome would so easily trust her and allow her into the folds of their dynamic. To think that she and Gemma and James were accepted and a valuable part of the dynamic of the group. She'd been a fool to think that Sparrow would trust her above all else the way she had him, above the family he'd known his entire life.

Her heart had always made her a fool.

She'd thought herself past this.

But she wasn't. Sparrow had broken her walls and invited himself to rule her heart.

Part of her tried to understand his side. If Gemma or James had come to her with a problem regarding the Assassin, would she believe them? Would she at least want to hear an explanation?

The logical side of her said yes, of course.

But there was nothing logical about the way her relationship with Sparrow had progressed.

She would have listened to her friends. Of course she would have. Evony trusted them above all else, the way Sparrow did his Posse. The difference, she knew, would have been the way it was presented.

Accusations were thrown at Evony without any communication, without the possibility that they could be wrong. She'd been caught and they were merely waiting for the excuse that would get her out of the predicament. They'd ruled her guilty before she'd walked into the room.

She would never—could never—do that to him.

If her friends came to her with a problem, she knew that doubt could, and would, be a funny thing. And she knew she would feel it make its way through her every thought. But that was when she'd turn to him and ask about the predicament. Evony wasn't afraid of communication, no matter the outcome. A lifetime of rejection had taught her to handle any and all of it.

So she would handle this rejection. The worst one she'd ever had to endure.

What hurt the most was that a part of him, no matter how small it may be, believed that she had somehow used magic to get into the family. To get into his heart and make her way to the top.

The tears edged back to her eyes.

She sighed and turned from the darkened greens to the mirror that stood across from the chair. In it, Evony saw the beautiful face of the Princess of the Northern Lands.

Except this Princess had blue eyes.

Down by the crook of her neck and shoulder, she had the light indentations of a bite mark still healing that was barely visible under the moonlight. Soon, she would have no more evidence on her body of their time together. Only memories of being with him, of the month of pure bliss she could never have imagined, that would carry her through life.

She looked back out to the night and fell asleep in that chair with a million pictures of Sparrow running through her mind.

She'd woken later than she had in a long while. The dreams of Sparrow, smiling at her, kissing her, being hers, had been too good to let go of.

She'd passed Sparrow's old room again, then passed the stairs that would lead to the upper rooms that had never been used when Sparrow and his father lived in the house, and into the dining hall that connected to the living space and was just barely closed off from the kitchen.

Gemma and James were huddled in whispers when she walked out in the same trousers she'd used her magic to clean the day before.

"What're you two whispering about?"

"We're betting how long before he finds you," Gemma answered softly.

Evony closed her eyes to the flutter in her stomach as she took the chair opposite them the table. "Gem, please."

"It's what James would do for me and I for him. It's what you would do for Sparrow and he for you, Eve. He loves you."

Evony closed her eyes to the hope that still found a way to blossom in her chest, then stared back at her best friend. Gemma's hazel eyes were warm and kind as they watched her. "We'll go into town and grab a meal. We should be good to head out later tonight. Or tomorrow if you'd like another night's sleep here."

"I bet today. Thought he needed the time to figure out you'd choose to come to his home," Gemma said with a sweet smile.

"I don't think he's that bright." James's smile was far more snarky. "I said end of the week."

Evony sighed. "You guys aren't funny."

"We're not trying to be," James said. "I want to beat him to a fucking pulp for hurting you, but he *is* in love with you, Eve. He trusts you, I know he does. He'll be here."

"But we won't." She made sure her tone was definitive rather than pained.

He smirked. "I'll tie you down if I have to, Eve."

"I think you two forget that *I'm* the Magician here."

"No," Gemma teased. "We just don't care." Her smile dropped and she reached for Evony's hand. "I suspect he's obsessed with you, Eve. I'm adding to my bet that he's going to be insufferable with the amount of times he checks you over for injury and apologizes." Her hand squeezed Evony's. "And we know you want to be here when he arrives."

Evony rolled her eyes. "I hate you guys."

James reached for her other hand. "We know. That's what makes the relationship fun."

Evony sighed. "How about you go make your relationship fun somewhere else?"

"Fine." James pulled on Gemma's hand. "I'll go fuck my wife in that steaming bath. You—eat an apple, they're amazing." He nodded to a few apples sitting on the table that he'd no doubt picked from the trees earlier that morning.

Evony grabbed one and showed it to him. "Yes, sir."

She watched her best friends walk off to the washroom, then turned to the double doors that led to the back of the house.

The greens were lush, like they knew she would be walking out and they wanted to look their best. She ate as she took her boots off and let her feet fall into the dewy grass. She walked a lap around the greens, imagining a little Sparrow running about the yard. He would have been alone with no siblings to chase after him. It was both a lovely picture and a painful one. There was the positive of the awful experience he'd gone through at only eight years old—he'd gained a sister and two brothers.

She then imagined another little Sparrow, one with her blue eyes. Then another little Sparrow that would look just like original chasing after him.

Brothers.

Running after each other in the game only they understood.

She breathed out as she looked up at the house. Gemma was right, she didn't want to leave. She wanted to stay right in that house until Sparrow found her. She wanted to believe that he loved her, that he wanted this life.

But she also knew she could not allow herself to continue to fall victim to the desire to live up to the picture of the 'good' girl who happened to be a magician, because that wasn't the case. She *was* a magician and she would not fall back any longer in the fear that they would not like that part of her. It wasn't just a part of her, it was all she was. And it was the reason they doubted her. That everyone doubted her.

✝

"Babes." Gemma's voice broke through her daydreams as she sat out on the greens, staring at the small river off to the side and imagining a family enjoying a hot day in it. "Babes, time for food."

Evony turned to find Gemma and James standing at the double doors in the early afternoon breeze.

"We need a real meal, Eve," James called.

Evony pushed herself out of the dreams that brought water to her eyes and moved to her best friends. They left the horses and chose instead to walk to town. It was only half a mile out, and Evony's magic allowed her to know exactly which direction to lead them.

Her magic also allowed them to have their meal—steaming lamb and vegetable stew with chunks of bread—for free, a fact she always felt poorly for. She hated that they stole from families who would need the money. When she came across a stack of coin, she would send it over here.

It was only after full stomachs that they walked about town.

James led them with an arm thrown over his wife's shoulders as he held Gemma close. Sparrow had spoken of his little town and as much as it hurt to miss him, she loved that she got to experience it, if only for a short period of time.

Evony got the feeling of a sickly-sweet scent as they

walked, a scent that seemed to grow stronger as they moved. She assumed it was her magic picking up on a scent that she wasn't too fond of, considering neither Gemma nor James seemed bothered by it. But it tickled her nose and she really wanted to turn away from it.

It was when they turned the corner onto a cobbled walkway that Evony realized why her body was so averse to the scent. It was something she'd learned long ago: a potion that could wipe out a magician's power—albeit for a short period of time. In her distraction, Evony had forgotten about the potion and thought it a scent associated with the town.

She saw the powder thrown in the air before she could process to lift a shield to protect them. That wasn't supposed to happen. She should've been able to lift the shield. She was a Master.

And if this was what she was thinking of, powder wasn't required. So it was something else that fell over them. Something that made Evony's eyes shutter closed and her thoughts black out.

CHAPTER 45

SPARROW

S he was there.

She'd found solace in his house.

Sparrow jumped off his horse without coming to a full stop when he saw the three horses tied to a tree by the house, and ran to the door to burst in.

To find it empty.

"Evony," he called out as he began to storm through the house.

Not a soul filled the living area, the kitchen, the rooms, the upper floors. Empty.

"Evony," he called again as he stepped out to the backyard.

"Sparrow." Rosaelia's soft voice brought him back.

He turned to the four who had followed him into the house, and he knew there was a pain and desperation in his eyes that they'd never seen before, that he didn't even know he possessed before *her*.

"We'll find her, Sparrow." Tristan's tone was commanding, one he'd never used on Sparrow. "She's still around. We'll get her back."

Ashtyn stepped up to him and took his hands softly into hers like she was trying to ground him. It was moments like these that Sparrow truly believed she was a Master Healer. Because she didn't only heal physical injuries, but helped with mental and emotional ones too.

"The horses are here, which means they were here," she spoke evenly. "I'd bet they got hungry. Is there a place to get food around here?"

He swallowed back the relief of almost having Evony back. "There's a town a half mile north."

"The horses are tired." Gabriel nodded back to the lot they'd left in the yard. "We can run there just as quickly."

No, they couldn't. But Sparrow understood the man's concern, and he was right. Sparrow tried to shove the adrenaline pumping in him at the thought of being around her again and nodded as he turned in the direction of the town.

He walked—quickly—but it gave them the breath of air that he hadn't allowed the entire trip. Rosaelia especially would need it. She'd been quiet in the pursuit, never once complaining, but she was out of breath and he still loved her as a sister. He couldn't continue to push her like that.

His mind ran through every feeling in the book at the possibility of being around his magician again, and before he knew it, the time it took to walk to town had passed and they were standing at the edge.

"The real problem," he said, "will be finding them in the town."

It was still light out, the sun about an hour from setting.

Sparrow walked them into town and the first tavern off to the right—his favorite—to ask what, he wasn't sure.

They'd only been in a moment when an elderly woman off to the side smiled at Rosaelia. "Ah, sweetheart, you've brought more friends."

More friends?

Evony had been there.

Of course she'd come to his tavern. He'd told her it was his favorite.

"Yes." He smiled back. "You wouldn't happen to have seen which direction the others went?"

The old woman smiled. "Sure. They were headed to Old Soar's, asked about a spot to buy cloaks. Though why they wanted cloaks when the weather is beginning to loosen, I wouldn't understand."

To hide behind. To leave him. He needed to get to her.

Sparrow's smile was generous. "Thank you."

They were out the door, and Sparrow tried to calm his walk as he headed in the direction of Old Soars, the town's best tailor.

They were about halfway toward the shop, which was on the other side of town, when Ashtyn's hand struck out. "Wait!"

Sparrow didn't want to stop.

"Do you smell that?" she asked, and her pace began to pass his.

"What?" Gabriel asked, his attention focused on her.

"Gwendolyn Powder."

Sparrow froze, his full attention moving to the medic. "What did you just say?"

"What is Gwendolyn Powder?" Rosaelia asked.

"A potion dried into a powder so light it can disappear into the winds, the one and only way to cast a magician powerless. It only works for a period of time, but without the power, magicians are regular people and it becomes a lot harder to defend themselves. Especially against a sorcerer," Gabriel explained.

Sparrow knew of the powder, had read about it countless times. But he'd never realized that he would recognize that scent. It had been in the air at the village explosion where Evony had used her power to move the vial and protect him.

They'd tried casting her powerless even then.

"Why would they need to protect against a sorcerer?" Rosaelia asked, worry beginning to creep into her voice.

"Only sorcerers can make potions, so they would be the only viable fight to a magician," Ashtyn finished.

The only reason Gwendolyn Powder would be in the air would be to stop a magician. As they rounded the corner and Sparrow felt the itch of sweetness coat his throat, he knew the only reason to have this much Gwendolyn Powder was to cast the Master Magician powerless.

His heart fell to his stomach.

"The powder is fresh." Gabriel's voice was calm. "It normally vanishes within an hour. This fresh means it was just thrown which means they're not too far."

Ashtyn shook her head. "Let's find Sapphire. Then we can look for this magician." She didn't look happy about leaving someone defenseless to the powder, but she looked determined to find Evony.

Gabriel grabbed her arm and rounded her to him. "We need to find the magician, Ash."

"No," she fought. "We need Evony and Gemma and James. Then we'll have more help for the magician."

Gabriel merely stared at her, and Sparrow knew that the stablehand knew his wife was the magician. That would be a line of questioning for another time.

"They're one and the same, healer," Tristan said.

Ashtyn's brows furrowed, then widened as she turned on everyone. "Evony's the magician."

"Master," Sparrow answered, the antsy need to move and find her building within him.

Ashtyn's breath caught, then she turned on Gabriel. "You knew too."

"Guessed." He shrugged in that sweet manner of his.

"You can excite about this later." Sparrow closed his eyes and let his mind draw up a picture of the town he had frequented a million times before. In this part of town, there lay many buildings, most of which were businesses that created a Main Street for the townsfolk to stop by when getting their shopping done. "I need to get to my wife." *Before she's hurt by whatever plan this sorcerer had for her.*

Whoever took his magician would need a more remote location, and the best spot for that would be a building behind him, a large chapel that was no longer in use. It had been the room where the King would see his people before Edmund's father came to power and the people of the Northern Lands stopped following the chapels.

His eyes popped opened and he turned to stare in the direction he knew his wife waited for him. Then he was running, no longer able to wait for the others.

✝

THE HALLS LEADING to the main room of the chapel were empty but for the candles lighting the way. The large double doors to the main room lay open.

He ran into the large empty room to find Gemma and James on their knees to his right and Evony on her knees to his left. Standing before them on the dais were three women.

He froze abruptly in the middle of the room when a sword whipped out and stopped just before Evony's throat as the women stared at him expectantly. They knew he'd be here for her.

Evony looked a little whiter than usual, and Sparrow hoped that merely had to do with the Gwendolyn Powder and not anything else they may have done to her.

All three women's lips tipped up, and the one holding the sword grinned, a crazed look in her eyes. "Truly? I thought the marriage a hoax, but it seems our assassin has found his weakness."

Other than the lighter edge to Evony's skin, all three looked unhurt. But he couldn't be completely sure of that. Now, more than ever, he was glad he hadn't come alone. If anyone got injured, they would need Ashtyn's help.

Sparrow's gaze narrowed on the one holding the sword, then moved to the one in the middle. She looked familiar but he couldn't put his finger on where from.

"Who're you?" Only years of training kept his voice calm when Evony was less than an inch from a sword's tip.

The woman laughed, cruel and barely there, as she glanced at the others standing behind him, then settled her gaze. "Do you not recognize me, Master?"

Sparrow ignored the mock in her voice at calling him a Master. "I do, but I can't place you."

"Honest. I like that."

"So why don't you join me? Who are you?"

She smiled like she'd enjoy the way the answer would affect them. "My name is Rowena."

Rosaelia's breath hitched from behind him.

Evony's breath hitched from her spot on her knees.

Tristan's breath.

And that's when the name clicked in his mind. The painting of the two girls sitting on either one of her knees. This was the long dead Queen of the Northern Lands.

Except she was no longer dead.

And she was holding his wife—her own daughter —hostage.

He tried to remain calm, unaffected. "If you are Queen Rowena, then you know that *that* is your daughter your lackey is holding a sword to."

"And the Master Magician too, Assassin, do not forget that." She was toying with him. "Your Northern blood does not take away from her magician's blood. She is a *magician* through and through, whether you wish for it or not."

"I'm aware, *Your Highness*. And she is my magician." He knew the bitter taste was beginning to drip through, but he couldn't help himself. Threats against his wife made him unhinged.

But that little comment was worth it because he noticed the ever slight delight in Evony's eyes when he said it. When he accepted her as the Magician. As his.

"You will take a magician?" Rowena asked unbelievingly.

"She *is* my wife."

"And beautiful, too. I see you couldn't have one, so you went for her twin. Cheap shot, Assassin. But we both know you do not like magicians. That you do not trust them."

Sparrow's jaw grit at the way Evony's eyes fluttered. She believed the words coming out of her mother's mouth. She believed he didn't like magicians. That he didn't trust magi- cians. That he didn't trust her.

And it was all his fault.

He needed to beg for her forgiveness.

But first, he'd take her out of this dangerous situation.

When Sparrow didn't speak, Rowena asked, "What if I told you I could wipe the magician out of her? She'd be normal for you."

Sparrow had to relax his jaw, force his body to remain still when all he wanted to do was attack her like a wild beast hunting prey. He could not let her see exactly how much her comments disgusted him. "You will not touch her."

"So you like her with magic?" Rowena genuinely sounded surprised by his answer though her tone still edged on a sardonic tease.

"Wouldn't have her any other way. Magic is who she is."

And again, the slight relaxation in Evony's chest at hearing him accept her was all Sparrow could focus his periphery on.

Rowena opened her mouth to speak, but Rosaelia beat her to it. "Mother? You're...you're alive?"

Her voice almost broke Sparrow. He couldn't imagine the amount of pain she was in. Evony had grown up knowing she was unwanted by both parents. Rosaelia had always believed both her parents loved her. That had her mother been around, she would've loved Rosaelia as much as Edmund did.

Sparrow had believed the same.

"Bright child, aren't you?" The one standing before Gemma and James asked. The two by Rowena's sides were mere lackeys, like all the other rebels. Rowena was pulling the strings here.

"But... why?" Rosaelia stayed behind him, but Sparrow knew the hurt was evident in her features. She was such a sweet girl, she wouldn't know to hide her weakness.

Rowena's laugh held no conviction. "I was only your father's bride and the Princess's mother when I was Queen. I wanted *power,* and I wasn't given any. Now, I will take it. All that was mine. I will take it and rule this nation the way I was meant to decades ago."

"So you lead a rebellion? You hold a sword to your daughter?" Rosaelia asked the questions Sparrow knew they were all thinking. "You'd kill her?"

"I'd get rid of you too if you weren't so useless. I don't have to worry about you rising above me, *little child.*"

Sparrow could hardly peel his gaze from the sword that was only an inch from marring Evony's skin. He listened to the conversation, allowed his periphery to focus on the others, but all his attention was on her. His beautiful wife.

And she was watching him.

She couldn't turn her head, but her eyes were shot to the side so she could take him in. As if she was trying to make sure *he* was okay.

"You cannot be serious! You mean to kill her?" Rosaelia was growing hysteric. Sparrow knew only an entire life as the Princess kept her sane at the moment.

"Blame yourselves." Rowena smirked. "Had you not brought her along, I would've continued to believe her dead. Now, I know I shouldn't have trusted a bunch of men to do the work."

Sparrow's heart dropped as his eyes flew to the late Queen. "You ordered Evony's execution?"

"But of course." The woman looked proud.

"She was two years old!" Sparrow spit and forced himself not to move when he noticed the blade's tip move closer to Evony's skin.

"She was already showing signs of how powerful she would be, my *zuzveli yerevoot*," she spit those last words like that was her name rather than 'Evony.' "I had to get rid of her. Find my shock when nine years later, I hear there's a Master Magician. I knew immediately it was her. But if she continued to hide herself, continued to be dead, I wouldn't bother myself with it." Rowena moved to Evony and tilted her chin to meet those blue eyes. "Shame they asked for your help, isn't it, *zuzveli?*"

Sparrow's jaw ground at her use of that word. Calling his wife that word. Realizing how Evony had known that word to begin. Because her old tongue vocabulary was smaller than his, though zuzveli had always held strongly to her memory.

To have a mother who referred to her as a zuzveli yervoot. Sparrow had to wonder when Evony had learned what it truly meant, if she even remembered that. Wondered if she remembered at all that her mother had apparently called her that.

"It was the best thing that ever happened to me." There wasn't a shred of fear in Evony's voice. Not an ounce of care for being referred to as a disgusting moron.

And Sparrow's heart fluttered at the sound of her voice. At her strength.

Rowena grimaced and dropped her touch. "Oh, you foolish, romantic girl. How I bred both of you is beyond me." She stepped back onto the dais. "Don't you see that he doesn't love you? If he did, if any of them did, it wouldn't have been so easy to settle the doubt into their minds."

"How did you do it?" Tristan asked from behind him.

Rowena shrugged, proud. "I was married to the man. I knew it wouldn't be too difficult to settle the doubt in him. Knew he would already be wary because of her past, so really, I only had to allow some rebels to make her sound like she was on our side. Tell them not to attack the Princess—because they wouldn't know how to tell the two apart—so that it would seem that they were protecting their leader. Edmund has always been a simple man. He turned on his daughter twenty years ago and he turned on her again now."

"But twenty years ago, he didn't know about that daughter," Rosaelia fought.

Rowena's smile was pitiful. "He would've killed her, Princess. I say this to you as a woman and not someone vying for the crown, he would've killed her."

"How'd you know she'd be here?" Sparrow asked because

he needed to know. "How'd you know we'd be coming? You were waiting."

Rowena's smirk was cocky now. "Call it a lucky guess. I had a lackey follow her as much as they could before the magic got too much to fight. I merely *hoped* she would come into the town." She eyed Sparrow like she would enjoy the pain Evony's loss would inflict on him. "As for you? Look at the way you watch her. I knew you'd come for her. Had to change plans again, figured I could rid of the Master Magician *and* the Master Assassin in one go." She smiled again. "It is amazing, objectively speaking, that you two found each other. It's a shame I'd have to be rid of you before you could give me asset-worthy grandchildren."

"And what're your plans now?" Ashtyn asked as if they didn't already know.

"Your little trick in bringing that magician into your ranks only delayed my ambitions, it did not stop me. I just had to switch tactics. Find the Master Sorcerer to help me get rid of *her*."

"What exactly is the Master Sorcerer meant to do?" Gabriel's voice came from behind Sparrow.

"She is the only one able to take the magic of the Master Magician. You did not think I would kill her without taking her power, did you?" Rowena looked very pleased with herself.

"So where is she? Your Master Sorcerer?" Ashtyn growled.

"Be patient, child. I have been. For eighteen years." Rowena did not move. She just stood in the middle of the dais and watched them, knowing they wouldn't make a move lest Evony were hurt.

The second lackey didn't even try to pull a weapon on Gemma or James, Rowena was smart enough to know they wouldn't risk Evony either. She truly had crafted this perfectly.

Minutes ticked by and Sparrow felt the adrenaline rush

through him at the need to be by Evony's side, to touch her and hold her close and never let her go again.

Then smoke appeared behind Rowena, and he knew the Master Sorcerer was there. And annoyingly making a grand entrance too.

Rowena stepped to the side, allowing for the woman to step out for them to see. She looked about Rowena's age. Beautiful. And she too, looked familiar to Sparrow for reasons he didn't know.

Again, if Evony weren't in danger, he'd be loving the opportunity to learn more about another Master. He'd known a bit about her past, but nothing substantive. At least, he'd known her name, unlike Evony's.

Her gaze raked over everyone in the room before meeting his eyes. Her brown orbs racked over him and widened as they stopped near his hand before going back up to his gaze and narrowing on him. She almost looked like she was assessing how she recognized him. Did he know this woman?

Her gaze moved to Evony, stopped on her hand, then moved back again, eyes narrowed as she assessed him. "What is your name?"

He didn't wish to have another conversation. He just wanted to hold Evony. So only half his attention was on her when he answered, "Sparrow."

The sorcerer stepped down from the dais, the silence of the room ringing in the air as she took the two steps down and walked up to him. She stopped only a couple of feet away. "You should know as an assassin, Sparrow, that you should always have your eye on the threat."

All his attention was on that sword to Evony's throat. He didn't care how powerful this woman thought she was, he wasn't scared of anything but that. "That's what I'm doing."

He saw her smile from his periphery. Not a cruel one, but

something sweet, like she was happy with his answer. Like she approved of it. Her attention on him was almost fond, as if she didn't only approve of his answer, but of his entire manner at the moment.

Her features were back to stoic when she next spoke, "Release her, Lany."

"But..." the one holding the sword began.

"Now," the sorcerer demanded, then the sword was gone from Evony's throat.

Relief flooded Sparrow as he heard Gemma and James stand and back away from the other lackey. He watched Evony slowly rise to her feet. She was still weak from the Gwendolyn Powder. Maybe they'd given her something else too, because he didn't remember Gwendolyn Powder doing anything else but deeming a magician magicless. If they hurt her, he'd rip them limb from limb.

The sorcerer turned her back on him—a bold move—and walked back to the dais. She stopped in her original spot and turned to watch them. Neither he nor Evony had moved. He wasn't sure what game this was.

Rowena looked confused too, but Sparrow had a feeling she wouldn't say a word against the Master Sorcerer. At least, not until she had what she wanted.

The sorcerer looked between them, a quirk lifting the edges of her lips upward before her gaze settled on Evony. "Well? Don't be shy. Greet your husband."

Sparrow didn't move for fear of this being a trick but watched as Evony made a single stumbled step back like she was testing the sorceresses' word. With another step and no movement on the dais, she turned and ran to him.

Her arms and legs wrapped around him, and Sparrow knew he had to be careful not to crush her lungs with the amount of pressure he put into the embrace. Not only was he getting her back after being an ass and accusing her of being the rebel leader, but she was no longer in harm's way, a fact his body didn't seem to realize as it held her closer still.

It was like coming home again.

He wanted to shut his eyes and get lost in her presence, but instead, he kept his gaze on the dais.

He felt Evony's lips on his neck, reminding him that that mind of hers was always in the Rivorbant Waters. "All I wanted was to see you one last time, then I didn't care what happened to me."

"Don't say that, baby." He kissed her neck. "Don't ever fucking think it. If something happened to you, I'd come with you. I'd end my life to continue with you."

Rowena looked like she was about to make a comment when the sorceress's hand shot up and stayed her. She watched them with a spark of joy in her eyes.

And reluctantly, Sparrow let Evony go so she'd drop to her feet.

She didn't step away. Instead, she glued herself against his arm, but allowed him to push her behind him. The tight hold she had on his arm reminded him of every walk they'd made to the dining hall at the palace and again, he couldn't breathe from the happiness of having her back.

Sparrow was about to question what had just happened when the Master Sorcerer turned to the three women who stood beside her on the dais and threw a powder.

The shock filled him the same moment he saw it settle on Rowena and her lackeys. But before the powder settled, the three were gone.

What the hell had just happened?

"What. The. Hell. Was that?" James muttered, holding Gemma behind him the way Sparrow held Evony.

"That"—the sorcerer turned back to them—"is a powder

that will make them very weak. They're lucky they ran out from under it before it could all settle, but rest assured, they're not going to be the same power-hungry vixens. They won't have the energy."

"Was this your plan all along?" Tristan sounded in awe.

Her smile was sad. "No. But rest assured, neither Master before us will ever have to worry about harm from me."

"Why?" Rosaelia's shock left no room for emotion.

Smoke began to fill around her—and that's when Sparrow realized she'd dropped a potion—as she looked to Evony, a fondness settling into her gaze before her eyes moved to him, and he swore he saw happiness. "Take care of her, son."

And she was gone.

CHAPTER 46
EVONY

"Son?" Evony turned into Sparrow's arms, her hands playing with the edges of his hair at the base of his neck as she stared up at him.

His eyes were slightly wider than normal. "I... I don't know."

"Maybe both of our mothers are still around," she whispered so only he could hear and watched his small nods like he was still processing everything that had just happened.

The fact that his mother may be the Master Sorcerer and she may have just helped them out of this situation.

But if she were his mother, then it meant there was one case of a Master having a Master child. The first recording—even though they may never officially record it—ever.

Then his face was in the crook of her shoulder and he was breathing in her scent, and she knew that he didn't care to think of the sorcerer at the moment. His arms were so tight around her, it was almost difficult to breathe.

Before she could hug him back, he dropped to one knee, and his hands touched every inch of her. "Are you hurt? What did they do to you, Evony? And don't even think about lying to me, Magician."

She giggled. "Nothing."

His tone was harsh. "What part of 'don't lie to me' didn't you understand?"

Her giggles grew. "Aren't you meant to be groveling for forgiveness?"

"After I know you're unhurt, trust me, I will." His hands touched her everywhere again. Peeled her shirt to look at the scar—kissed it tenderly—before moving on.

Evony rolled her eyes as she met Tristan's knowing, twinkling ones, and her smile grew. Then she met Gemma's eyes and rolled her own as the girl mouthed, "I win."

When he was finally satisfied with his checks—at least for the time being—his forehead dropped to the bottom of her chest as his hands wrapped around her hips. "I am so sorry, Evony. I swear I trust you. I'm sorry I even let the doubt enter. Magician, I am so s..."

She pulled on his hair to get his attention, and looked down at his beautiful eyes. "I know. And I'm sorry for overreacting."

He jumped to both feet. "You didn't overreact. As a matter of fact, you're under-reacting at the moment."

She tried to hold back her laugh, but a small one escaped. "Sorry. Being powerless and held at sword point kind of washed away everything else." She pushed his hair behind his ear and stared up at him. "And I truly do understand why you considered it. I just wish you would've talked to me about your doubts."

"Me too," he whispered, his forehead falling into hers.

"But next time, when there's a threat before you, you pay attention to it!" Evony smacked him. "Do not do anything so reckless, you insufferable, incredible man."

He smiled down at her and cradled her face as he leaned in to kiss her. "I love you, Evony. I'm sorry that I made your biggest fears come true. But I love you, and I swear I'm going to spend the rest of my life proving it. Just please. Please, come home with me."

"You know I'm dramatic. I would never have survived not being around you, Assassin." Lightening the mood was working.

He smirked, eyes closed like he was taking it all in. "I would've burned down the world to find you, Magician."

She giggled. "I know."

And she did know it. She'd known it every second she'd refused it with Gemma and James. She'd known it when she'd slept in his house. She'd known it the moment she'd taken the horses. She'd been hurt, but she'd never doubted for a moment that he'd come for her.

It was part of the reason she'd wanted to leave. Make him suffer a little longer than merely a few hours.

Then his lips were on hers and it'd only been a day and a half since they'd last touched, but her entire being lit up like it'd been ten years. Yeah, she definitely never would've stayed away from him.

She kissed him back fervently, wanting to fight past the need for air to keep tasting him when a throat clearing came from beside them. Evony pulled away and looked over Sparrow's shoulder to find it had been Gabriel who had cleared his throat, reminding them—and Gemma and James who were equally pressed together in a passionate embrace—that they were not alone.

Evony bit back her laugh and turned to the friends. Tristan was before her in seconds and she was off her feet and in another tight embrace.

"Don't test me, Tristan," Sparrow barked which only made Evony laugh.

"I'm sorry, too, Eve," Tristan whispered to her. "I swear, you are our sister. Miels would be here too, but..."

"It's okay, Tristan. You're my brother. Miels is my brother. I would've missed you two almost as much as Sparrow."

"No," Sparrow's bitter tone interrupted. "You wouldn't."

Tristan and Evony stared at one another and laughed before he dropped her back to her feet. Sparrow wrapped his arms around her waist and held her back against his chest as Tristan moved for Gemma and carried her in a similar embrace. When he dropped Gemma, he gave James a more manly hug, but it was obvious he hadn't wanted to hurt the man. A new brother.

Rosaelia was still frozen in her spot at the realization of the Queen's survival. She looked so hurt, Evony felt a sisterly bond to protect her.

"Are you hurt, *Magician*?" Ashtyn's voice was teasing and accusatory, but Evony could see the concern in her eyes.

Evony smiled. "You know my secret."

She shrugged. "Whatever."

Evony laughed, and her gaze flickered to the man standing behind Ashtyn, just too close to go unnoticed. "You seem to be taking it well, Gabriel."

He shrugged and genuinely looked unconcerned. "I've always known."

Sparrow's arms tightened around her waist, but he didn't speak. His breath tickled her hair as he dropped kisses to the back of her head, her neck, her shoulder.

James, his arm wrapped around Gemma's shoulders and holding her tight, interrupted, "Well, how about we go back to that little house of our assassin's, get cleaned up—again—and figure out what the fuck just happened."

He was walking away with Gemma before anyone could agree with his statement. Ashtyn turned close on their heels, Gabriel right behind them.

Tristan met Evony's eyes and made a dramatic eye roll before he stopped at the doors and waited for Rosaelia.

Evony's gaze turned back to her twin, who looked to just be coming out of her reverie. Rosaelia's glazed-over eyes washed over Evony, the arms wrapped around her, Sparrow behind her, then her face like she was taking it all in.

"Ro," Sparrow called to her. "Ro, are you all right?"

Rosaelia blinked fast a few times, then she was with them again. "Fine."

She most definitely was not fine, and they all knew it, but they could discuss that at another time.

Rosaelia's stare met Evony's. "I'm sorry. For causing doubt in the minds of everyone. For almost ruining your happiness."

Evony leaned back into Sparrow. "You wouldn't have ruined anything. I would've made you lot feel sorry for about a week then given in and come back. If for nothing else, then just to have Sparrow in me again."

Sparrow's bark of almost suppressed laughter hit her neck as he shook his head. "Always in the Rivorbant Waters."

She tilted her head back to kiss his jaw. "Right. So let's go home and you can give my body what it wants."

He pulled out from behind her and took her hand in his. They waited beside Tristan at the doors and turned to Rosaelia who was back to staring at the dais.

There was a lot to discuss, but now was not the time for it.

Rosaelia finally turned to them and took Tristan's elbow.

✝

THEY SLEPT the night in Sparrow's home. Her home.

Evony woke before everyone else and turned in Sparrow's embrace to watch his chest rise and fall. His black stubble enveloped that mouth so beautifully, she could stare at him all day and not grow tired of the view.

His body beside hers, naked and flush with hers, only made her want to get closer. To wake him with her mouth. Or push him to his back and ride him until he awoke, coming inside her. She wanted to do it all, even after the number of times he'd satisfied her the night before to "show her how sorry he was."

She kissed his chin and basked in this moment before pushing away from him and using her magic to force his arm off of her waist so she could get away. She pulled on his shirt—not having one of his shirts would've been her breaking point for sure by week's end to get back to him—and moved for the glass door that led to the greens.

She stepped just outside the door and looked out to the breeze in the trees, the flow of the small river, the birds flying in the early morning air. She breathed in the reality that this was all hers. That she would have those children, the blue-eyed Sparrow and the original's clone, running after one another and learning how to fly from trees. She would be able to fill the upper rooms like Sparrow's father had wanted and bring new life to this home. She'd give the castle she'd been offered to Gemma and James, and they'd only live a mile away from one another. And they'd always go back to the palace.

But she would have it all. A family.

Her own family.

Hers.

Arms wrapped around her waist, and a naked chest touched her back. He pushed her hair to one side and kissed the hollow between her neck and shoulder. "Don't use your magic on me, Magician."

She fought her lips to remain still. "Whatever could you mean?"

He kissed the side of her neck, and she tilted her head to give him more space. "I mean, the only way you could've gotten out from under my hold was with your magic. Don't try it next time."

"You use your Mastery to keep me down. Why shouldn't I use mine to get out of it?" she teased.

His lips quirked against her neck. "That's my normal strength, Magician. It's not my fault you're weak beneath it."

Her head fell on his shoulder, and she stared out at the trees. "I think I'll go find Gem and James. We could leave again. Apparently, you haven't learned your lesson."

His hold tightened around her waist. So much so that there genuinely stood no space between their bodies. "I'm never letting go of you, Evony."

She shook her head. "Everyone seems to keep forgetting. *I'm* the Magician."

He smirked and kissed her behind her ear. "I don't forget, love. I just don't care."

Her heart fluttered. He'd said it before, but it still sent her on a little chase every time she heard it. Being the Master Magician had been the reason she couldn't form relationships her entire life and now to know that it didn't matter. That he'd have all of her? It was overwhelming.

She used her magic to peel his arms off her and didn't need to see the tension rise in him to know it had.

He growled and there was a hand around her throat before she could turn around. He slammed her against the glass door. "What part of don't use your magic against me didn't you understand?"

Her eyes twinkled with mischief. "All of it, I think. I believe you should teach me a lesson, Assassin."

His thumb brushed her bottom lip as he wet his own. "Keep it up and the lesson will be withholding your orgasms, *Magician.*"

She gasped and clung to his waist.

"How many times do you think I'd take you to the edge and not allow the release?" Now his eyes were twinkling with mischief. "I believe I could keep it up all night."

She pulled him closer still so his cock lined up with her cunt. "So cruel."

"I'm an assassin, love." His thumb caressed her throat as he held her against the door. "I'm meant to be cruel."

"Not to your wife."

His gaze softened and that thumb was back to brushing her bottom lip. "No." The amount of love in his eyes was unmatchable. "Not to my wife."

CHAPTER 47

EVONY

The most intriguing part of the long ride back to the palace was when Sparrow told her about Miels and Etel. He'd pulled her ahead and told her to cast a shield around them so the others wouldn't hear. That he wasn't sure what it was and didn't want to spread the news.

But Evony couldn't wait to get back to the palace and tease the man.

They'd left Sparrow's home early so they'd make it back to the palace by late afternoon. And surprisingly, they'd made it almost perfect timing.

Before they reached palace grounds, Evony reached out to Miels, *Please tell me I'm not interrupting while you're balls deep in Etel.*

The mild fear of a voice in his head was obvious to Evony before he responded with his usual cocky demeanor. *I'm going to kill that husband of yours.*

Hey, be careful what you say. I'll kill you for threatening him.

You have to be here to kill me, sister.

She smiled as they reached the edge of the palace grounds. *Come out to the stables.*

Before they made it halfway to the stables toward the left of the grounds, Miels and Edmund were out of the palace. Miels ran for her, and Evony jumped off her horse to meet him halfway.

"I'm sorry, Eve," he muttered into her hair. "I swear I trust you. I love you, sister."

"I love you too, Miels." She smiled up at him.

He put her down as the others got off their horses in the middle of the greens, and Miels turned to James. "Now for the real person I missed."

Evony gasped in offense, and Gemma giggled as the two hugged.

Tristan joined them, and Evony's heart expanded at the sight of them. Her brothers.

Gabriel grabbed for as many reins as he could take. "I'm going to take the horses in. Feed them. Clean them up."

Ashtyn took the other reins. "I'll help."

"Course you will." Gemma winked at the healer and got a scowl in return.

"Thank you, Gabriel," Evony sang out to him as Sparrow's arms came around her.

"You're welcome." He was a quiet, almost shy man, but there was a spark in his eyes as he said, "Magician."

She laughed as they walked off and Edmund joined their group.

Evony felt awkward before the man who had created her and raised her husband. Before the man who was the reason behind all the mistrust against her.

His hands were clasped behind his back as he approached her. Them. Sparrow was keeping to his word and not leaving her.

Edmund looked like he didn't know what to say. He stood handsomely before them, at forty-four, his training making him look amazing enough for all the servants to gossip about. His usual confidence was gone as he watched them, unable to come up with something to say.

So Evony took pity on him. Because as much as it hurt to not be trusted by him, she understood his need to keep his family safe. "Wait until you find out who was behind all this. Then your doubts against me may make a bit more sense." Edmund's brows furrowed, and Sparrow held her closer. "Mother knows best, right?"

Edmund still looked confused, but he stood up tall and met her eyes. "I don't care who's behind it. I've done this to you time and again. You were hidden at birth because of me, and you were shunned from the palace because of me. I have a lifetime of apologizing to do, daughter. But I'll start with today. I am terribly sorry for my actions."

Evony's hands landed on the arms Sparrow had wrapped around her. "I know."

Edmund's eyes landed on her hands over Sparrow's and there was a warmth there Evony didn't think she'd ever seen directed toward her. He met Sparrow's gaze. "I'm sorry to you too, son."

Evony felt Sparrow's smile on the back of her head as he kissed her. "I know."

Edmund gave a small smirk. "I suppose you two will be quite loud tonight? Shall we give you the small cottage again?"

Tristan grumbled. "Should've given it to them last night."

Miels pushed Sparrow. "I missed it again. I'm camping outside your door tonight. I'm not missing it anymore."

Sparrow growled at his best friend. "I'm going to kill you."

"Plus, they live across from us." James smirked at his friend. "You'll be hearing it from both sides."

Miels winked as a smirk grew. "Kinky."

"That's enough, the lot of you," Edmund reprimanded. "I am still her father."

They laughed as they moved toward the palace. Then Evony's smile dropped, and she froze when her gaze landed on the stables. On the couple stopped before the wooden building talking to Papa Ignatius.

"Papa Iskan," she called. Then louder. "Mama Beni."

She pulled away from Sparrow's embrace and moved for them with a grin that only continued to grow.

Papa Iskan turned and that smile of his warmed Evony back to those short days of their acquaintance in the South. She hugged him and Mama Beni, and it was like embracing a grandparent. Or what she assumed embracing a grandparent would be like.

"Ah, little bird." Papa Iskan's eyes shined on her. "I knew we'd find you here."

She smirked. "Is that so?"

He gave a cocky nod of his head. "Of course. Once I heard the Master Assassin was betrothed, I knew it."

Sparrow stopped at her back. "Is *that* so?"

"I knew you'd find your way to him, *little bird*." Papa Iskan winked at her.

"Would've been nice of you to let me know, old man."

He tsked. "Where's the fun in that?" He looked between the two of them fondly. "Tell me, does he run your blood?"

"Incredibly so."

Papa Iskan and Mama Beni both laughed at her response.

"Should I be proud of that?" Sparrow whispered into her ear.

Evony tilted her head back and whispered, "Incredibly so."

Edmund allowed another moment for them, then interrupted. "Why don't we go inside? Evony can introduce us and then they can go off, as I presume our assassin is barely containing himself from dragging his wife to their suite."

"Incredibly so," Sparrow growled, and they all laughed.

✝

GEMMA AND JAMES pulled her into their suite before Sparrow could come out of the baths. She told him through their thoughts, but James jammed the door with furniture so Sparrow wouldn't be able to barge in.

"I don't think my husband's going to be too happy that you kidnapped me." Evony grinned as she situated herself at the end of their couch.

James sat pressed right up against her as his arm flew around Evony's shoulders, then he pulled Gemma into his lap. "Your husband can kiss my ass."

"Hey." Gemma played with his bottom lip. "That's my job."

James's eyes twinkled, and he leaned up to kiss his wife while his hips thrust ever so slightly into Gemma.

"Whoa." Evony pushed at them. "I'm still right next to you!"

They didn't budge, James being damn near double her size, but he did break the kiss and plant one to Evony's temple. "Sorry, sister."

"We just wanted to see how you were doing," Gemma explained. "Without that assassin of yours glued to your back."

Evony smirked. "He wanted to join me in the baths too. I was about to let him when Rosaelia decided she'd be coming in too. Then I saw Miels and Tristan go into the men's baths so I'm guessing they're goading him now."

James gave her an unimpressed look. "Insatiable, the both of you."

Evony shoved him again. "You're one to speak. I had to suffer the two of you for three years!"

"That's because Gemma's insatiable. I'm a victim here."

Gemma gasped and elbowed her husband in the gut. "Asshole." James kissed her neck as she turned to Evony again. "Back to you. How're we doing?"

Evony couldn't work around the wide grin. It would become a permanent part of her features. "We are... incredible. I still cannot believe we were lucky enough to fall into this life."

Gemma rested her head on James's shoulder and took Evony's hand in hers. "It is remarkable. To think we went from unwanted orphans in the forests to being the air our husbands breathe."

Evony giggled and met James's gaze as he shrugged. "It's true."

Evony snuggled into his arm. "Thanks for being with me. Every step."

James kissed her crown. "Thanks for having us. Every step."

Her thoughts flooded with every moment she'd had with her brother and sister. The times they'd been in the forests or lied about their relationships in order to share James's cottages. The times they'd held each other when they were upset and the times they celebrated a victory. The highs and lows and everything in between.

A banging came from the door and knocked her out of those beautiful memories.

"Go away," James called out.

Sparrow banged again. "I have no problems breaking down this door."

Gemma met Evony's mini eye roll with a smirk. "I told you. Insufferable."

"Quite." Evony laughed as she moved for the door, her

magic pushing the furniture jamming it aside. She opened it to come face-to-face with the Master Assassin in only sleeping trousers. Her insides tightened at the knowledge that he'd be buried deep inside her again. "Husband."

His smirk looked too wicked. "Wife. Time for bed."

"You're quite insufferable. Did you know that?" Evony leaned into the door.

His gaze raked down her form like he was already eating her up and settled between her thighs. "Drown me, and you won't have to worry about it any longer."

Evony felt the wetness between her thighs begin to soak through her trousers and called out to her friends. "We'll have a day, just us. Later." She would say tomorrow, but she had a feeling her husband wouldn't quite be done with her yet.

"Good girl," Sparrow purred and pulled her into him and backward to their suite.

CHAPTER 48

SPARROW

Miels gave him a teasing, excited smile as he sang, "I heard you two."

"And I'm going to kill you," Sparrow sang back with his own teasing smile.

Miels dropped the bucket of daggers in the middle of the forest clearing as they waited for Tristan who had been kept back in order to help Gemma and Evony with something.

"How did you have time to listen anyway?" Sparrow felt light. "Didn't you have your own lady to please?"

Miels grabbed a dagger and turned with a scowl. "Not exactly."

Sparrow's grin fell. "Problems with the missus?"

"You came out of your problem. I'm still in mine." Miels moved to stand beside Sparrow as they both looked out in the direction of the palace. They'd chosen a clearing near enough so they'd be close to their women. "This emotional business isn't any fun."

Sparrow chuckled. "No. But it is rewarding."

Miels knocked Sparrow's arm. "Yeah, yeah. I heard how

rewarding it was. Tris had been right—you two are fucking loud. I barely even had to stand out in the hall, I heard you in my room."

Sparrow's grin grew. He loved how loud they were. He loved how loud Evony was. That he could hear exactly how pleased she was every time he touched her, kissed her, fucked her.

And he loved that everyone else could hear it too. That everyone else could hear exactly who she belonged to. Who he himself belonged to.

Miels interrupted his train of thought. "If you've known all along, why threaten me around Evony?"

Sparrow turned to analyze his brother and saw the confusion and desperation in Miels's eyes. Whatever was going on with him and Etel, it was hurting him, and Sparrow hated that the man would have to endure it to come out the other end. "I haven't known all along. I figured it out when Tristan said you turned down an opportunity to go whoring. Knew I wasn't crazy, and that was what I'd smelled from your suite a couple weeks prior. Knew you wouldn't break the 'no palace women' rule if you didn't absolutely need to. Knew with your secrecy that she was *very* important."

Miels's gaze dropped to the dagger in his hands. "She is. I hate it. I hate how much I want her. How much I need to be around her. I hate that she has this effect on me. I hate that I've fallen for her and she couldn't be bothered with me. I hate her, Sparrow."

Sparrow's heart went out for the man. He understood every single one of those emotions. "No, you don't."

When Miels looked back up, Tristan was walking toward them. "No," he whispered. "I don't. I could never. She's my whole world."

"From the way she looked at you, I'd say the feelings are

reciprocated, brother." Sparrow wasn't one for comfort, but he tried anyway.

"She does," Miels said with surety. "But it's not enough."

Tristan was about to be with them when Sparrow clasped his brother's shoulder. "It will be."

Miels gave him a thankful grin, then turned the cocky one on as Tristan joined the group. "What did the beautiful ladies want?"

Tristan's gaze jumped to Sparrow, and he winked. "My attention."

Miels jumped for Sparrow before he could get his hands around Tristan's throat. "Calm down, brother. We don't need any more bruises."

"Your luck has run out," Sparrow growled at the both of them. "I have James now. I don't need you two as my seconds any longer. Watch what you say about *my wife*."

Tristan's chuckle was cocky. "She said you've been extra possessive lately. Said she likes it when you pull her hair and tell her whose she is. What she is to you."

Sparrow's cock twitched, and he had the overwhelming desire to turn back to the palace and find his wife. Fuck her against the wall of whatever room or corridor he found her in.

Tristan grabbed for a dagger and threw it into the trees. It struck high and he turned a proud smirk on the two of them before stopping his gaze on Miels. "Now, I think you have some explaining to do, brother."

Miels's brows furrowed. "About what?"

"The Remedies Expert." Tristan quirked a brow. "You didn't actually think you could stare at her the entire time we were speaking to that rebel and we wouldn't notice."

Miels's cheeks pinked for the first time ever, and he rolled his eyes with a slight quirk to his lips. "I'm beginning to understand Sparrow's urge to kill you."

"He has the same urge to kill you." Tristan laughed.

Miels threw his dagger next. "Not anymore. I'm no longer a threat."

Tristan's eyes shined and his grin grew wicked. "So you're as spoken for as Sparrow? And James was always spoken for. Am I the only single one left?"

Sparrow picked up a dagger. "Yes." He winked at the dirty blonde. "You whore." He threw his dagger farther than the ones they'd thrown.

┼

HE WAS in James and Gemma's suite because Evony had insisted on finishing whatever she was playing at with Gemma, and Sparrow wanted to be anywhere she was.

He sat on the couch with James, and both men threw their feet up on the small table and watched their wives.

"I still intend to beat you to a bloody pulp, Assassin," James said casually.

Sparrow's lips twitched upward. "Oh?"

"You hurt her. I don't care that I knew you would run back and beg her forgiveness. She still cried herself to sleep that night."

Sparrow's heart hollowed out and shattered to his stomach. She hadn't told him that. He watched that wide smile on her face as she and Gemma put the final touches on the little piece they were making. "I deserve it."

"I know," James said matter-of-factly. "I just have to wait until Eve's not around. She'd beat *me* to a pulp if she heard I touched you."

Sparrow laughed. "That's my girl."

James's lips quirked up as he watched the women. "I

wanted to beat you, but I never considered even for a second that you weren't hers, Assassin. She may be too good for you, but you are worthy enough to make every dream of hers come true."

Sparrow's heart fluttered in a million directions and he wanted to jump with the elation. With the knowledge that he would have her every day for the rest of his life. With the fact that she'd drive him crazy always and yet he'd run back for more. Because she was his and he would prove every second that she'd made the right decision falling in love with him.

Sparrow whispered, "Thank you."

Not a moment later, Gemma jumped into her husband's lap the same moment Evony jumped into Sparrow's. He caught her around the waist and brought her in close. Even just the few hours away from her touch had made him miss it painfully. He knew the feeling would always be there, as it always had been, but that it would settle in time. When his heart finally accepted that she was with him and would never leave his side again.

But he suspected it would take a few weeks minimum before his heart accepted it.

They held up a small piece of clothing.

"One of the servants is pregnant." Gemma smiled. "She's expected to pop in one month. Isn't this the loveliest piece for the babe?"

"The loveliest." James kissed her jaw.

Evony's shining eyes met Sparrow's. "You like it?"

"I love it." He kissed her jaw. "In fact, I think you should make another."

Her brows furrowed. "Who else is pregnant?"

He smirked and brought her in closer by the hip as his free hand landed on her stomach. "You will be. Soon."

Her eyes widened and her grin grew. "Assassin." Her finger grazed his jaw. "Behave."

He growled low enough for only her to hear. "Tell your friends it's time to go, love."

†

THEY GOT in one round before dinner.

He'd get in another two, maybe four, before he allowed her sleep that night. He was insatiable for the taste of her.

They sat around the dining hall, their new King's Posse which included the Master Magician and her two friends. The eight of them. This King's Posse felt full. Right.

"I'll be questioning the prisoners come tomorrow. We shouldn't have to worry about Rowena for at least the foreseeable future." Sparrow leaned back into his chair at the King's left.

Edmund had been made aware that his late wife was actually alive and the one leading this rebellion. His entire composure had fallen and he'd asked for some time alone, not because he had loved her, but because of how much he had respected her, cared for her in his own way.

Sparrow couldn't imagine the pain. It wasn't the same, but the thought of having Evony ripped from his side and mourning the loss just to have her show up again two decades later on a mission to kill him was unbearable. It wasn't possible to imagine it in their circumstance though. Because if something ever happened to Evony, Sparrow would end his own life. If Evony turned around on a mission to kill him, he'd drop to his knees and allow her the pleasure.

"No," Edmund declared. "Come tomorrow, you'll be on your way back to your home."

Sparrow's brows knitted together. "Why?"

Edmund's gaze softened as it jumped between Sparrow and his daughter. "You two never got to enjoy a honeymoon. I suspect a week in your home, undisturbed, should be sufficient enough. At least for now."

Evony leaned into Sparrow's arm and wrapped herself around it. "Mm," she moaned against his cheek. "A week of tasting you and nothing else in my mouth. It's too much. I think it may spoil me away from food altogether."

His cock jumped, and a growl left him. "Magician." When he turned to meet her gaze, their mouths almost touching, he had to refrain from throwing her over his shoulder and finding an empty room because he would not make it to their suite. "Behave."

She pecked his lips, and it was like being transported back to that dinner with Alexei. He leaned into her kiss and loved that the entire group saw it and knew he was in love with her.

When he pulled away, Evony remained cuddled into his side as he met Rosaelia's green orbs. She looked lovingly at the two of them.

Then she surprised Sparrow altogether. "I think we need to look into the Island Nation. Get Rowena before she starts trouble again. Protect the Islanders and us."

Both peoples. Because Rowena had shown them that this wasn't a war with the Islanders, but simply with her.

The determination in Rosaelia's eyes told Sparrow she already had a plan, and she did not intend on being swayed from it.

"Yes." Edmund sighed. "But first, we must get the prisoners speaking."

Tristan leaned back in his chair with a small smile. "And we will."

James had the same cocky lounge. "Faster than the Assassin could."

Sparrow scoffed as Miels laughed. "We'll put you out of a job while you're getting your dick sucked, Spar."

Sparrow smirked. "Evony's an heir. My job is secure."

"I don't know," Evony moaned into his ear. "You may need to allow me to suck it twice a day if you'd like me to secure your position."

He growled, kicked out of his seat, and had Evony over his shoulder in one motion. Her trouser preference worked in his favor in moments like these when he didn't have to worry about the skirts.

He slapped her ass as he walked out of the dining hall. "Deal."

CHAPTER 49
EVONY

EVONY

The most intriguing part of the long ride back to the palace was when Sparrow told her about Miels and Etel. He'd pulled her ahead and told her to cast a shield around them so the others wouldn't hear. That he wasn't sure what it was and didn't want to spread the news.

But Evony couldn't wait to get back to the palace and tease the man.

They'd left Sparrow's home early so they'd make it back to the palace by late afternoon. And surprisingly, they'd made it almost perfect timing.

Before they reached palace grounds, Evony reached out to Miels, *Please tell me I'm not interrupting while you're balls deep in Etel.*

The mild fear of a voice in his head was obvious to Evony before he responded with his usual cocky demeanor. *I'm gonna kill that husband of yours.*

Hey, be careful what you say. I'll kill you for threatening him.

You have to be here to kill me, sister.

She smiled as they reached the edge of the palace grounds. *Come out to the stables.*

Before they made it halfway to the stables to the left, Miels and Edmund were out of the palace. Miels ran for her and Evony jumped off her horse to meet him halfway.

"I'm sorry, Eve," he muttered into her hair. "I swear I trust you. I love you, sister."

"I love you too, Miels." She smiled up at him.

He put her down as the others got off their horses in the middle of the greens and Miels turned to James. "Now for the real person I missed."

Evony gasped in offense, and Gemma giggled as the two hugged.

Tristan joined them and Evony's heart expanded at the sight of them. Her brothers.

Gabriel grabbed for as many reins as he could take. "I'm going to take the horses in. Feed them. Clean them up."

Ashtyn took the other reins. "I'll help."

"Course you will." Gemma winked at the healer and got a scowl in return.

"Thank you, Gabriel," Evony sang out to him as Sparrow's arms came around her.

"You're welcome." He was a quiet, almost shy man, but there was a spark in his eyes as he said, "Magician."

She laughed as they walked off and Edmund joined their group.

Evony felt awkward before the man who had created her and raised her husband. Before the man who was the reason behind all the mistrust against her.

His hands were clasped behind his back as he approached her. Them. Sparrow was keeping to his word and not leaving her.

Edmund looked like he didn't know what to say. He stood

handsomely before them, at forty-four, his training making him look amazing enough for all the servants to gossip about. His usual confidence gone as he watched them, unable to come up with something to say.

So Evony took pity on him. Because as much as it hurt to not be trusted by him, she understood his need to keep his family safe. "Wait until you find out who was behind all this. Then your doubts against me may make a bit more sense." Edmund's brows furrowed and Sparrow held her closer. "Mother knows best, right?"

Edmund still looked confused, but he stood up tall and met her eyes. "I don't care who's behind it. I've done this to you time and again. You were hidden at birth because of me, and you were shunned from the palace because of me. I have a lifetime of apologizing to do, daughter. But I'll start with today. I am terribly sorry for my actions."

Evony's hands landed on the arms Sparrow had wrapped around her. "I know."

Edmund's eyes landed on her hands over Sparrow's and there was a warmth there Evony didn't think she'd ever seen directed at her. He met Sparrow's gaze. "I'm sorry to you too, son."

Evony felt Sparrow's smile on the back of her head as he kissed her. "I know."

Edmund gave a small smirk. "I suppose you two will be quite loud tonight? Shall we give you the small cottage again?"

Tristan grumbled. "Should've given it to them last night."

Miels pushed Sparrow. "I missed it again. I'm camping out at your door tonight. I'm not missing it again."

Sparrow growled at his best friend. "I'm going to kill you."

"Plus, they live across from us." James smirked at his friend. "You'll be hearing it from both sides."

Miels winked as a smirk grew. "Kinky."

"That's enough, the lot of you," Edmund reprimanded. "I am still her father."

They laughed as they moved toward the palace. Then Evony's smile dropped, and she froze when her gaze landed on the stables. On the couple stopped before the wooden building talking to Papa Ignatius.

"Papa Iskan," she called. Then louder. "Mama Beni."

She pulled away from Sparrow's embrace and moved for them with a grin that only continued to grow.

Papa Iskan turned and that smile of his warmed Evony back to those short days of their acquaintance in the South. She hugged him and Mama Beni and it was like embracing a grandparent. Or what she assumed embracing a grandparent would be like.

"Ah, little bird." Papa Iskan's eyes shined on her. "I knew we'd find you here."

She smirked. "Is that so?"

He gave a cocky nod of his head. "Of course. Once I heard the Master Assassin was betrothed, I knew it."

Sparrow stopped at her back. "Is *that* so?"

"I knew you'd find your way to him, *little bird*." Papa Iskan winked at her.

"Would've been nice of you to let me know, old man."

He tsked. "Where's the fun in that?" He looked between the two of them fondly. "Tell me, does he run your blood?"

"Incredibly so."

Papa Iskan and Mama Beni both laughed at her response.

"Should I be proud of that?" Sparrow whispered into her ear.

Evony tilted her head back and whispered, "Incredibly so."

Edmund allowed another moment for them, then interrupted. "Why don't we go inside? Evony can introduce us and then they can go off as I presume our assassin is barely containing himself from dragging his wife to their suite."

"Incredibly so," Sparrow growled and they all laughed.

✝

GEMMA AND JAMES pulled her into their suite before Sparrow could come out of the baths. She told him through their thoughts, but James jammed the door with furniture so Sparrow wouldn't be able to barge in.

"I don't think my husband's going to be too happy that you kidnapped me." Evony grinned as she situated herself at the end of their couch.

James sat pressed right up against her as his arm flew around Evony's shoulders and pulled Gemma into his lap. "Your husband can kiss my ass."

"Hey." Gemma played with his bottom lip. "That's my job."

James's eyes twinkled, and he leaned up to kiss his wife while his hips thrust ever so slightly into Gemma.

"Whoa." Evony pushed at them. "I'm still right next to you!"

They didn't budge, James being damn near double her size, but he did break the kiss and plant one to Evony's temple. "Sorry, sister."

"We just wanted to see how you were doing," Gemma explained. "Without that assassin of yours glued to your back."

Evony smirked. "He wanted to join me in the baths too. I was about to let him when Rosaelia decided she'd be coming in too. Then I saw Miels and Tristan go into the men's baths so I'm guessing they're goading him now."

James gave her an unimpressed look. "Insatiable, the both of you."

Evony shoved him again. "You're one to speak. I had to suffer the two of you for three years!"

"That's because Gemma's insatiable. I'm a victim here."

Gemma gasped and elbowed her husband in the gut. "Asshole." James kissed her neck as she turned to Evony again. "Back to you. How're we doing?"

Evony couldn't work around the wide grin. It would become a permanent part of her features. "We are...incredible. I still cannot believe we were lucky enough to fall into this life."

Gemma rested her head on James's shoulder and took Evony's hand in hers. "It is remarkable. To think we went from unwanted orphans in the forests to being the air our husband's breathe."

Evony giggled and met James's gaze as he shrugged. "It's true."

Evony snuggled into his arm. "Thanks for being with me. Every step."

James kissed her crown. "Thanks for having us. Every step."

Her thoughts flooded with every moment she'd had with her brother and sister. The times they'd been in the forests or lied about their relationships in order to share James's cottages. The times they'd held each other when they were upset and the times they celebrated a victory. The highs and lows and everything in between.

A banging came from the door and knocked her out of those beautiful memories.

"Go away," James called out.

Sparrow banged again. "I have no problems breaking down this door."

Gemma met Evony's mini eye roll with a smirk. "I told you. Insufferable."

"Quite." Evony laughed as she moved for the door, her

magic pushing the furniture jamming it aside. She opened it to come face-to-face with the Master Assassin in only sleeping trousers. Her insides tightened at the knowledge that he'd be buried deep inside her again. "Husband."

His smirk looked too wicked. "Wife. Time for bed."

"You're quite insufferable. Did you know that?" Evony leaned into the door.

His gaze raked down her form like he was already eating her up and settled between her thighs. "Drown me, and you won't have to worry about it any longer."

Evony felt the wetness between her thighs begin to soak through her trousers and called out to her friends. "We'll have a day, just us. Later." She would say tomorrow, but she had a feeling her husband wouldn't quite be done with her yet.

"Good girl," Sparrow purred and pulled her into him and backward to their suite.

EPILOGUE

EVONY

She'd thank her father tenfold for offering them this honeymoon.

You taste like you need more of my cum in you. Sparrow watched her as he licked between her folds.

She moaned at the sound of his voice in her head. He'd insisted they only speak through their minds that morning so that he could learn to communicate with her like that. So he could learn to initiate calls.

She both loved the plan and hated that Sparrow stopped any time she said anything aloud rather than sending it through their thoughts.

Her legs closed around his face, holding him in place. *Please lick me, Sparrow. Make me come on your tongue first.*

Mm, I don't know. My cock wants in you.

Evony's thighs squeezed tighter and she delighted in the sound of his chuckle against her sex. *Please. Then I can taste myself on your tongue while you fuck me.*

He growled. *You know how to convince me, Magician. You taste divine, love.*

"Sparrow," she cried out, clinging to the sheets around her.

He stopped licking, his mouth closing as she tried to push her cunt into him. He just stared up at her, waiting.

Please. Please, Sparrow. I'm sorry. Just suck me. Please. She cried as she yelled through her thoughts.

His chuckle was cruel as his tongue shot out to her clit. *That's my good girl.*

Then he was unforgiving with the attention he gave her clit, licking and sucking until her back arched so deep she was sure to have broken it altogether. She screamed, unable to keep the sound from coming from her mouth as she screamed to him through their minds too. *Sparrow, Sparrow, Spar, Spar, SPARROW!*

Her legs shook over his shoulders with the aftermath of yet another orgasm. He'd given her so many in the past week, Evony wasn't sure how her body continued to handle more.

Aftershocks still lingered through her body as Sparrow licked her from cunt to lips, dipping his tongue into her mouth as he growled to her. *Taste yourself, love. So fucking ripe. My cock is dripping for you.*

He didn't wait for her to respond as his cock impaled her and hit her in that spot that made her claw at his back. They still kissed as he began moving in her, loving her and torturing her all at once.

Sparrow. She breathlessly called his name as she thought it to him.

He kissed, licked, sucked his way from her jaw to her ear, down her throat, over her chest. All of the skin he could get to. Bites and love bruises and kisses galore. *I need everyone to see these marks from a mile away.*

Evony clawed at his back as he put special attention to that spot beneath her ear, suckling it as he fucked her, his hands dancing over her skin from nipples to her clit and back.

And all too soon, the pleasure was too much for her body to handle and she screamed his name so loud with her climax, she knew those in the small village heard her.

He grunted, growled, and bit at her. And all the while he called for her. *Evony, Evony, Ev, Ev, Evony, E...* "Evony, fuck!"

She was dripping slick between her legs by the time their aftershocks stopped and they merely stared at one another. Sparrow's deep browns taking her in with all the love in the world.

"Husband," she rasped as her finger traced his nose.

He bit at her finger. "Wife."

She smiled up at him. "I can finally speak to you again?"

He kissed her finger softly, then allowed it to continue tracing his face. "I missed the sound of your voice. We can practice speaking through our minds again another time."

"I love you," she said as she stared into those eyes that she favored above all else. "I love this home. I love the greens outside and the trees for the kids to fly from and the river for them to learn to swim in. I love everything about you and this house."

A lightness filled his eyes. "Why don't I get you cleaned up, then we can walk the greens."

She gave him an enthusiastic nod and laughed as he picked her up bridal style and moved them to the private bathing chamber and straight into the bath.

She kissed him as they sat in the bath and waited for the tap to fill it with hot water. Then she let him wash her because he enjoyed doing so, and she enjoyed pleasing him.

When they finished with the bath, Evony allowed Sparrow to carry her to the hearth on the far end of the master suite and start the fire to dry off in front of as he towel dried her hair.

He kissed her shoulders from behind as they dried and

Evony closed her eyes to soak in the feeling of being taken care of.

By her husband.

Only two months ago, she'd first been sitting in the inn with Gemma and James, watching as Sparrow and Rosaelia arrived for the meeting a day early. Only two months ago, she'd been convinced that she would forever be the third to Gemma and James's relationship. Only two months ago, Evony had believed she would never find a love for herself.

And now she had Sparrow.

Sparrow, who worshipped her and wanted to take care of every part of her. Sparrow, who infuriated her and turned her on to no avail. Sparrow, who was the perfect brother and friend. Sparrow, her assassin.

When they were both dry, she turned in his arms and gave him another soft kiss before allowing him to dress her in a light frock so they could go for a walk in the greens.

He dressed in a breezy pair of trousers and one of those large white shirts she loved to steal.

They were barefoot as they stepped out of the double doors from their bedroom to the greens and moved for the edges, where the trees lined the yard, where the sound of the river could be heard.

At the edge, Evony turned for Sparrow and hugged him close as she stared up into those eyes again. "I hope our first son has your eyes."

He gave her a warm smile. "Do you?"

She nodded slowly. "They make me feel at home, no matter what. I hope at least one of our children has your eyes, but I especially hope our first son has them."

"Why's that, love?"

"He will have your father's name. I would like him to look like the original as well."

Sparrow's eyes widened. "He will have my father's name? You've decided that, have you, Magician?"

Her lips twisted into a snarky grin. "Yes."

He held her face gently in his hands. "Are you sure, Evony?"

"Your father loved you as dearly as I know you will love our children. He deserves to be remembered. I wish I knew him."

"I wish you did too." He kissed her forehead and remained there. "I love you, Evony."

Evony hugged him closer. "I love you too."

with the
Rains
catching
Dawn
catchers novella 1
NELLY ALIKYAN

WITH THE RAINS CATCHING DAWN

ETEL

Rumor already had it that the servants despised her. Actually, not entirely a rumor. Etel knew they despised her. Not all of them, but the ones who had deigned to give her the time of day when she first arrived at the palace. The others were as kind to her as they would be to a stranger.

But the ones she had been friends with? They hated her.

They blamed her for her natural gift of understanding the remedies that came from herbs, the lands, and the rains that befall their world.

They blamed her for moving up to a suite where she held her workstations in the front room and her bedroom behind a door. The suite was a modest living space in the world of palaces, but for a servant, it was a high luxury.

And Etel loved her little home.

But everyone else despised her for it. Even the servants she had no problems with. She could see they were jealous. Though it pained Etel to see it, she understood it.

She'd only ever been happy for the servants who had been promoted before she'd become Remedies Expert, but Etel knew most didn't see it that way. For most servants, the promotion of one of them was a smack in the face to the rest of them. What Etel didn't think they understood was that she and every other one of the promoted servants had earned their way up. She knew she deserved it, yet felt guilty about enjoying the small luxuries the promotion came with.

She knew those old friends of hers would never understand, so she did not bother attempting to reason with them. They hated her.

It was for that reason specifically that Etel found herself enjoying her walks along the greens from time to time, even late at night. She made sure to carry a pouch of herbs on her person lest she need it for her own protection—a mix of spices that would burn an attacker's eyes completely—but in all the months she'd been on these walks, she'd yet to need it.

Or yet to be noticed.

The guards around the palace greeted her with a nod of the head in passing, but that was the extent of recognition Etel normally got from anyone at the palace.

And she was glad for it. The last thing she needed was the servants hating her even more because a guard fancied her or gave her any sort of attention, even if completely platonic. She knew that would only make their assaults worse.

The night was reaching the late midnight hour when Etel began heading back to the palace, knowing she'd steal away an apple from the tree harboring the kitchens and run off to her rooms on the second floor.

Another great part of her suite—it was on the second floor. Two above the lower levels of the other servants. Because she was no longer considered a servant, and that ticked off just about all her old peers.

"Etel!"

She stopped dead in her tracks, her heart picking up. Not

out of fear, but rather of shock. No one ever called to her. Or used her name. Even the servants who knew it called her other names.

But worse of all was hearing the name from Tristan, the Master Assassin's left-hand man.

"Etel," he called again as she pushed herself to turn to him.

He was jogging to her from the dungeons building. Etel had heard they had someone down there, that the Master Assassin had dealt a visit to Nuhmed for the man, and she could only wonder what he'd done to deserve it.

"I'm glad I caught you." Tristan smiled down at her in what was more a formal rather than friendly manner. "Would you mind running this to Sparrow?" He handed her a letter.

Etel barely felt it as her hand reached out to grab for it. Her brows furrowed. "It isn't sealed."

His lip twitched up on one side. "I'll trust you not to peek."

Etel was still caught on the fact that he'd known her name.

He nodded down to her like all the other guards on the palace grounds and turned back for the dungeons before she could give a response.

She stared off after him until he was no longer in sight, then forced herself to turn around and head for the opposite side of the palace. The King's wing. The Master Assassin's suite.

The trip was short and Etel did a perfect job of blending into the walls so as not to bring to attention that she was headed for the King's wing. She knew she shouldn't care what the others thought of her since it'd always be negative, but she couldn't help it. It was a lonely world.

She was about five steps from the Master Assassin's suite's door when she heard a crash, along with a banging.

Another step brought her closer to the door where she heard the giggles of the woman the Master Assassin had surprisingly taken to his suite, the Princess's cousin. The Princess's perfect likeness of a cousin.

Another step and another little crash, the Master's growl this time. Deep and guttural and filled with the name of the woman within the suite. *Evony.*

Etel's cheeks lit up before she could control the reaction because though she may not have any personal experience in these matters, she had a feeling she knew exactly what was happening in there.

Etel rushed to the door then, knocking before anything else could be heard. She didn't want to interrupt the Master's *time* with his suite mate, but Sir Tristan had asked her to deliver this missive and she would do just that. Enough people hated her already. She wouldn't add the Master's left-hand man to the list.

It took a moment, but the door opened to a beautiful, giggling Evony.

A beautiful, giggling Evony who wore only the Master's shirt, whose hair was mussed, and who shined with a light sheen of sweat.

Behind her, a mess of papers on the ground was all Etel could see. Her cheeks burned as the image of their time presented itself into Etel's mind and didn't release. Because though she didn't have much to go off of personally, Etel had quite the imagination. She'd seen a couple of the married help enough times to know what the Master and Princess's cousin were doing in that suite.

Etel forced herself out of her thoughts dand stuttered, "Is the Master here, miss?"

As if she hadn't just heard them. Her cheeks burned brighter yet.

Evony leaned against the door without a single ounce of

shame for what they'd been caught doing. Oh, to be so confident as her.

Sparrow moved for the door only a moment later, stopping just behind his missus in only a pair of trousers. Sweat also lightly tinted his skin, and hair mussed even more so than Evony's.

Etel couldn't help when her gaze latched on to the Master's chest—that chiseled body that came from hours of training and that speckling of hair—then jumped to Evony's shirt. Evony's bare legs to the Master's trousers. She couldn't help jumping back and forth and knowing they'd thrown on a single article of clothing so they could go back into their activities after her interruption.

Etel wondered if she'd explode from embarrassment. She knew her cheeks were just about ready to as they blazed against her skin.

She forced her hand up to present the missive. "From Sir Tristan, Master."

The Master smiled at her lightly. "Thank you, Etel."

Etel made a small bow, then hurried on her way, ready to be far away from their room and her interruptions.

It was only when she was halfway down the palace that she realized he'd called her by her name. The Master Assassin knew her name. Though it shouldn't be shocking coming from him. He knew everything. It was part of his job.

And he *had* been the one to promote her.

The reminder that she so rarely heard her name uttered by another a stab to the chest.

Etel paused for a deep breath, then hurried along on her way once more. She hadn't been able to stop at the apple trees but knew there would be some for her to take in the kitchens. If she said she needed the apples for her remedies, the servants wouldn't be able to attempt to refuse her. Though they hardly ever did. Merely ignored her presence or mocked it.

Even worse was the fact that Etel was still burning from what she'd heard in the King's wing. Because even though she had an imagination, she was a Northerner and unused to this outward show of intimacy, the uncaring nature in which they opened the door—most of the servants would be. She quite liked their boldness though, if she thought about it.

"No need to harvest the tomatoes, Jauc." Betti, the older of the servants who hated Etel, someone who had seemed almost grandmotherly to Etel before, laughed. "There's a bright, big one there."

Etel realized a moment too late that she'd stepped into the kitchen with the main group of six servants who hated her. The six with whom she'd used to laugh and cry with. Whom she used to be a friend to.

Then she was promoted as the Remedies Expert and they hadn't been pleased. It's when Etel had realized she'd never truly had friends, merely people who were good enough to her because they were all in the same station. True friends, she knew, would've been happy for her opportunities.

"I'm merely grabbing some apples," Etel responded meekly. She hated how weak she sounded around them but couldn't help it.

Etel had her hands on three apples when Stell's fingers brushed her hair back the way she used to when Etel was upset, and for a moment, Etel was transported back to the time they had been friends.

"Aw, come, friend. What's got you so flushed?" Her tone mocked as her fingers dangled by Etel's hair, almost seductively. It was another one of the ways Stell teased her—she was the most *experienced* of this lot and loved flirting with Etel to make her uncomfortable.

Etel knew she was only mocking, yet answered for the slight chance she may be accepted, not as a friend, for she knew she could never find true friendship with these six, but as a peer. "I was sent to the King's wing to deliver a missive to the Assassin." She placed the three apples into a little sack, then looked up to the others. "I heard him and the Princess's cousin in his suite...enjoying one another. They were...hardly dressed."

There was no widening of eyes or shock or confusion or anything that would compare their reactions to Etel's. Rather, they seemed bored with the information and, at the same time, amused that Etel was so innocent that it had affected her so. Still, she knew the rumors would spread, if only to give them something to speak of.

Etel knew she was more innocent than the average servant. Knew that many of them found companionship with one another. But she also knew most of the servants held on to that Northern upbringing and were more reserved in their show of affections.

What she hadn't realized was that the information she'd given wouldn't shock this group in the slightest. She shouldn't have been surprised—Stell was one of the most experienced of all the servants, most of the others within this group not too far behind her. It had been something she's learned when they'd ridiculed her promotion—that she never truly knew them anyway. *They* were definitely the anomaly to the Northern born servants.

"*That* is it?" Betti snickered. "Child, everyone in the palace knows those two have been fucking each other's brains out since the moment she moved in. What? Did you think they were merely sharing a suite? That the Assassin would share his suite for any other reason?"

Etel could feel her skin heat up with more shamed embarrassment now.

Jauc, the only male of the group, threw his arm around Betti, but he was no closer to being friendly than the others had been. "Be kind, Bet. No one tries touching Little Expert. How is she to know?"

Stell picked an apple out of Etel's sack. "Not to mention, those two aren't shy about showing their relationship. The way that girl holds him in public, I can vividly picture the way she fucks him. Kind of erotic. I touch myself some nights thinking of it."

Etel's eyes widened even though she knew she shouldn't be showing them any reaction. She couldn't help it. They were Northern and she'd been naively sheltered from speech like this her entire life.

"Aw, Stell." Shawna laughed. "The girl will just erupt if you speak to her so. Don't you know she's more naive than a child about the pleasures of the body?" She quirked a brow in Etel's direction. "I guess to become an expert, you need to throw out the rest of your brain."

"C'mon, the lot of you." Again, Jauc made it sound like he'd defend Etel, but merely had his own ways of mocking her. "Give the girl a break. Some people just don't have the equipment. Or working knowledge of said equipment."

Etel cleared her throat, failing to recognize the way everyone stiffened before her. She reached for another apple from the bowl in the middle of the large kitchen island and threw it into her sack. "I must return to my rooms. You lot have a good night."

She turned and stumbled straight into a large chest.

Great, another one to ridicule me was all she could think before looking up to meet the eyes of the Master Assassin's right-hand man. Miels.

Those perfect dark green eyes, that hair that looked too soft to touch, and those delicious-looking lips.

Her heart jumped up to her throat, then plummeted to the ground. "Sir—"

"You lot aren't tired?" Miels interrupted her, not even acknowledging her presence but staring at the others behind her.

Etel didn't see them, but heard them stumble around and throw out their apologies to the man before her. Then the kitchen was empty. Eerily silent.

Etel took that as her cue to leave as well. She realized, again a moment too late, that though he'd been ignoring her presence, the question had been directed at her too. After all, he was still her superior.

Etel gave the slightest of curtsies, her head bent slightly, then moved around him.

She was stopped with a hand on her forearm, and again, her heart raced up and plummeted back down. Then raced with the excitement of being touched by *Miels*.

She met his gaze, worried she'd done something to add him to the list of people who despised her.

His eyes shined. Mischief and delight lining the edges.

At least that's what Etel thought. Those feelings had never before been directed toward her.

"Where do you think you're going, little one?"

Continue the story in
With the Rains Catching Dawn...

DON'T FORGET TO REVIEW!

†

Thank you so much for finishing your read! Don't forget to leave a review or rating on all platforms as it helps me as an author more than you can ever imagine!

†

Amazon and Goodreads ratings help the most but feel free to talk about it everywhere else too—including social medias, blogs, Youtube reviews, and most importantly—word of mouth, and more.

FOLLOW NELLY'S SOCIAL MEDIA

Follow Nelly's social media to get the scoop as it's happening!

- tiktok.com/authornellyalikyan
- instagram.com/authornellyalikyan
- youtube.com/NellyAlikyan
- amazon.com/author/nellyalikyan
- goodreads.com/nellyalikyan
- facebook.com/authornellyalikyan
- pinterest.com/insinpublishing

JOIN NELLY'S NEWSLETTER

†

Sign up for Nelly Alikyan's newsletter to be the first to know about new releases and cover reveals, receive exclusive content —like a special scene or two—and be up to date about any other exciting news, i.e. events, signed copies, etc.

www.nellyalikyan.com

ACKNOWLEDGMENTS

First of all, I think it's imperative that I thank Maria V. Snyder because it was while reading her Poison Study series that this book came to mind. While the books are really nothing alike, it was while I binged that trilogy in February 2021 that the story of Evony, twin sister to the Princess and love interest to the Assassin, came to mind. This story is literally my favorite—this series with all six books a superior one in my charts—so I need to thank Ms. Snyder.

To my first language—even though I'm definitely far more fluent in English now—for giving me inspiration for the 'old tongue.' If you didn't know any Armenian before, you learned something from reading this now!

To my copyeditor for helping me clean this baby up, thank you Ellie! To my proofreader for catching all my imperfections, thank you K.I Ziggler!

To Khadija for all those comments you gave while reading the earlier copy. It still makes me smile to read those!

To my family who help me along the way, picking out covers to going along when I get excited about this series. For always supporting me.

To all the readers out there who take in these stories and fall as in love with these characters as I am. I'm so thankful to be able to tell their stories and it makes me so happy to know that you guys love them as much as I do.

MEET THE AUTHOR

Nelly Alikyan is a girl from the Los Angeles Valley who's constantly on the move—from Boston to London to wherever she chooses next. She's the only reader in her family—not her only cause as the black sheep—and has dreamt of being a writer for as long as she can remember.

For more books and updates:
www.nellyalikyan.com